SIDNEY'S COMET

'We can only speculate concerning the party these beings were having when the first load of catapulted Earth garbage came through their realm. They were known to revel in the pleasures of non-flesh, and this particular party must have been no exception. Gentle, lilting music and delicate fragrances carried by the sweet solar breezes that moved between the stars and flower planets near their realm probably wafted across their non-human tympanic and olfactory sensors. It is not difficult to imagine the outrage felt by these bodiless beings when they smelled the reek of earth garbage! The ''fleshcarriers'' could not have selected a worse place to hurl their poorly constructed, dripping containers!'

'It's a garbage comet, Mister President,' Munoz said. 'Our own damned trash is coming back! . . .'

SIDNEY'S COMET

Brian Herbert

A STAR BOOK

published by
the Paperback Division of
W. H. ALLEN & Co. PLC

A Star Book
Published in 1984
by the Paperback Division of
W. H. Allen & Co. PLC
44 Hill Street, London W1X 8LB

First published in the United States of America by
Berkley Books, 1983

Printed in Great Britain by
Hunt Barnard Printing Ltd, Aylesbury, Bucks.

ISBN 0 352 31521 0

SIDNEY'S COMET

PROLOGUE

Humming the Hymn of Freeness, Sayer Superior Lin-Ti moto-shoed over the top of the hill as he had done each morning for centuries on the domed asteroid of Pleasant Reef. This was in a distant, private corner of the galaxy, the breeding and training ground for the young men of Uncle Rosy's Sayerhood.

Now, in the verdant valley below, Lin-Ti could see the silver-tipped spires of the Great Temple punching through a low fog that lay across the valley floor. From their cave habitats in the hills, white-robed youngsayermen hummed softly as they rolled down along winding motopaths toward the temple. The horizon was close on this little asteroid, and a hazy red outline along the limit of Lin-Ti's vision marked the approach of the new day's sun.

With a new vinyl-bound history primer under his arm, Lin-Ti felt excitement at the prospect of the lesson he would begin teaching today. *This garbage comet matter has been a mystery for too many years,* he thought, *and now, thanks to the Sayerhood history writing team...*

As he reached a fork in the motopath, a ground squirrel darted across the path and disappeared into a clump of Scotch broom. Lin-Ti slowed to roll over an arched bridge to the left, then mento-commanded his shoes to resume speed.

Twenty minutes later, the Sayer Superior stood somberly at a podium with the history primer in front of him. An odor of newness from the book touched his nostrils, and he smiled. *My Rosenbloom, but I love the smell of new things!* he thought.

Lin-Ti glanced around the sunny ordinance room at a seated assemblage of youngsayermen in their hoodless white smocks of purity. Each held an open edition of the primer, and waited to read along with the instructor. One youngsayerman in the first row reminded Lin-Ti momentarily of Onesayer Edward, with the same long body and fat features. Lin-Ti recalled nearly four centuries earlier, when a then Youngsayer Edward had stood with him at the tutelage console... such a bright youngsayerman, with so much promise...

A wave of sadness passed over Lin-Ti as he thought of Onesayer Edward's tragic fate. But as he gazed around the cheerful room and saw attentive young faces looking back, Lin-Ti began to feel better. It was still in the room, and Lin-Ti heard his own muslaba robe rustle as he shifted on his motoshoes. He leaned one arm on the podium for a moment, then pulled it back and stood erect.

The Sayer Superior was a large man with the shaven head of the Sayerhood, made to look larger by the platform on which he stood. His face had the lineless clarity and serene countenance of one who had never deviated from the Master's path. In fact, you had to look upon the man for only a short time to know why Uncle Rosy had selected him. Lin-Ti cleared his throat, then read from a looseleaf introduction sheet. Words flowed quickly and smoothly across his lips, like a brook racing over stones to the sea:

"There are special places in the universe, places which even Uncle Rosy never imagined. Of this there is little argument today. Some say God dispersed varying life forms for the purpose of determining the most perfect state of life other than His own. Others are not so certain about the reason for the creation of such special places.

"Imagine one of these places... a magical realm having no

land or water mass occupied by beings without bodies or flesh, but possessing the most highly developed senses imaginable. Senses without flesh? A realm without land or water? We did say the realm was magical, did we not?

"We can only speculate concerning the party these beings were having when the first load of catapulted Earth garbage came through their realm. We know they were partying, for that was all they had ever done. They were known to revel in the pleasures of non-flesh, and this particular party must have been no exception. Gentle, lilting music and delicate fragrances carried by the sweet solar breezes that moved between the stars and flower planets near their realm probably wafted across their non-human tympanic and olfactory sensors.

"At their party, they undoubtedly had non-physical things which tasted or sounded good, looked attractive or smelled divine. They even had things which felt good to them. It was like any human party in these respects, except all sensual pleasure experiences were accomplished without flesh. For as these beings knew, 'Flesh clings to senses. Senses do not cling to flesh.' In their experience, senses were pure and magical. On the other hand, flesh was believed to inhibit sensual enjoyment, and was associated with dirty and distasteful things. As they often said, 'Flesh stinks when it gets old or when it perspires. Dirt clings to flesh.'"

Lin-Ti looked up, catching the gaze of the youngsayerman who reminded him of Onesayer Edward. Lin-Ti looked back at the looseleaf sheet, flipped it to the other side. The swift-flowing words began anew:

"Students of such phenomena understand that there is a point at which flesh, aided by technology, approaches a more perfect state. But flesh never quite measures up. This is the problem of infinity and of geometrical lines that cannot intersect, of time warps that do not overlap and of lives that never meet. An entity can be there but not there at the same moment, making it impossible to capture from outside its dimension.

"We have reliable reports indicating that the beings of which we speak spent thousands of years enjoying one party. It took them that long to reach a crescendo of pleasure, the point at which all sensual receivers were fully open. It was somewhat akin to a citizen of the American Federation of Freeness on 'full automatic' with respect to consumption, and was a very high state of existence for that particular realm.

"With their olfactory sensors fully open to pick up delicate solar fragrances, it is not difficult to imagine the outrage felt by these bodiless beings when they smelled the reek of Earth garbage! The 'fleshcarriers' could not have selected a worse place to hurl their poorly constructed, dripping containers!

"After accumulating Earth's waste for nine years, these beings implemented an appropriate method of returning all of it to the senders. For life forms having their durations measured in thousands of human years, this was quite an immediate response."

Lin-Ti slipped the looseleaf sheet to a shelf in the podium, and looked up. "In examining the new primer," he said, "you will note marvelous detail, down to precise conversations . . . even emotions and thoughts. You all understand how this information was developed?"

"Yes, Sayer Superior," a youngsayerman in the center of the room said, "from the lifelog tapes we have on each government employee—from cell memory readings taken when they touch security monitor identity plates. We have the minutest details on their lives!"

The youngsayerman who resembled Onesayer Edward was not paying attention. He flipped ahead in the text, read a conversation in the middle of the first chapter:

"'. . . It's a garbage comet, Mister President,' Munoz said. 'Our own damned trash is coming back! . . .'"

The youngsayerman looked up, catching the full impact of Sayer Superior Lin-Ti's disapproving stare. The offender blushed, then turned back to the title page. . . .

Sayers' History Primer

August 24, 2605–September 1, 2605

*Dedicated to the memory
of our Beloved Master,
Willard R. Rosenbloom*

PLEASANT REEF PUBLISHERS
New Series   **2698**

ONE

**BACKGROUND MATERIAL, FOR
FURTHER READING AND DISCUSSION**

¹ mento / 'mentō / vb: activation of a mechanical device through
thought transmission.

² mento / 'mentō / adj: used as modifier, as in "mento thought
transmitter" or "mento brain implant."

From the *New AmFed Dictionary*
(Seventy-First Edition)

Thursday, August 24, 2605

At shortly past noon on Garbage Day minus eight, General
Arturo Munoz slapped on his gold-brimmed military cap angrily as he and a larger man moto-shoed toward the door of

7

Munoz's private lunchroom. The windowless little room was chrome and white plastic, illuminated by rows of overhead fluorescent cubes. Some said the room was too austere, particularly for a council minister. "Council ministers should be models of consumption," they said. But the General did not listen to such talk. A plate of aromatic syntho-steaklets lay untouched on the table behind him. Despite hunger pangs, he felt too upset to eat. The President had called an emergency council meeting, and General Munoz did not know why.

"I don't have time to discuss the Black Box of Democracy with you now!" Munoz snapped as he mentoed the hall door. He felt a click-thud in the back of his brain, waited impatiently for the door to open. "The Black Box is bluffery, I tell you! The most monstrous bluffery imaginable!"

Munoz slammed a clenched fist against the stubbornly immobile door, heard the other man mumble something. Then Munoz snarled, "Dammit, Dick. This brain implant you gave me is acting up again!"

The much taller and consumptively heavy Dr. Richard Hudson was in his usual place at the heels of his superior. Hudson held two typed sheets. His gaze flitted away nervously under Munoz's ferocious glare. "The implant is not standard consumer issue, as you know, Arturo," Hudson said. "That's why you and I can read one another's thoughts...and those of anyone else."

"I know, I know...."

Hudson wore a hoodless white, gold-sashed ministerial robe with a gold cross and chain about the neck. General Munoz's robe was identical, except his garment had multi-colored battle ribbons across one side of the chest. Both men were in their early forties.

"There were bound to be bugs," Hudson said.

"Yes, but why me? You installed twelve of these 'special' devices...in our brains and in the brains of my most trusted people.... But my implant is the only one to act up! I'M THE LEADER, DAMMIT, AND I CAN'T EVEN MENTO DOORS LIKE THE LOWLIEST CONSUMER!"

"I'll laser-set the frequency for you again, Arturo." Hudson fumbled in a robe pocket with his free hand. "Now where did I put that laser pen?...Must be in the other pocket...."

Munoz glared at the still-closed door.

"Just listen to this Bu-Med report for a minute," Hudson

said. "It is most unusual." He smelled heavily spiced steaklets.

General Munoz shook his head slowly in exasperation. To Hudson, the cap worn by the orange-mustachioed General appeared laughably large on such a small man, but he suppressed the thought.

"Make it fast," Munoz said, glaring sidelong at Hudson. "We're due at an emergency meeting."

Hudson was a nervous, bespectacled man with a bald pate and a fringe of black hair. His influential position as Minister of Bu-Tech had been arranged by Bu-Mil's powerful minister, General Munoz. Hudson shifted uneasily on his mento-locked moto-shoes as he glanced down at the report.

"There is great power in the Black Box of Democracy," Hudson read. "Uncle Rosy may still be alive and living inside the structure."

"We've heard this nonsense before," Munoz scoffed. "The Black Box is our 'guardian of democracy.' It will respond to any threat, 'internal or external.' It's all conjecture, Dick. Wild conjecture."

"Maybe not. Bu-Med says they brought in an unusual client two weeks ago . . . a fellow who said he had once been a Sayerman inside the Black Box. He wrote an article on the subject, was trying to get it published."

"A Sayerman?"

"According to the report, Sayermen are those brown-robed fellows who never speak . . . the ones who come out of the Black Box to perform mysterious rites at the electronic security monitors. As you know, Uncle Rosy mandated the placement of these monitors at the entrances to all government buildings."

"More fakery," Munoz said with a sneer. "Those 'legendary and impenetrable' security units they assemble inside the Black Box . . . I say it's all for show."

"Listen to this," Hudson said, looking down at the report as he flipped to the second sheet. "Their client's exact words: 'Uncle Rosy has a great chair in the central chamber of the Black Box of Democracy. Adjacent to this chair are three chrome handles. If actuated, the first handle is capable of blowing Earth apart. . . .'"

"Oh, come now!"

"'. . . The second can alter the planet's orbital trajectory and speed. The third would release an army of ten thousand armadillo killer meckies to do Uncle Rosy's sacred bidding.'"

General Munoz tilted his head back and laughed squeakily. Holding his oversized cap to keep it from falling off, he said, "Sounds like they've got a real live one over there, Dick. We'll visit the Bu-Med psycho ward to consult with him, of course."

"According to the report, this man does not appear to be deranged. They've done brain-chem tests for schizophrenia and other disorders. Additionally, a complete memory scan was performed. He has full and coherent recollections of all the events described."

"There must be a logical explanation for this." General Munoz caressed his mustache as he thought.

Hudson met Munoz's gaze, said: "The fellow claimed a 'selective memory erasure' procedure was performed on him when Uncle Rosy released him from the Sayerhood for relocation in mainstream society. But unknown to Uncle Rosy, something apparently went wrong with the erasing equipment and the memories remained intact."

Munoz's dark eyes brightened. "Couldn't this have been a dream that was very real to the man? So real that he thought it actually occurred?"

Hudson's brow furrowed. "I don't think so."

"My intuition tells me you aren't so certain." Munoz smiled as he read Hudson's thoughts.

Flustered, Hudson said, "In large part, the human brain remains a mystery to us. We're always learning new—"

"I thought as much!" General Munoz snatched the report. He rolled it up and hurled it across the lunchroom. "NOW RESET MY TRANSMITTER!" Munoz removed his cap.

Hurriedly, Hudson folded the report and slipped it into a robe pocket. Then he brought forth a white, pen-shaped device, placing the tiny silver tip of it against the back of Munoz's head.

"Wonder what that fool President wants now," Munoz said.

"Don't talk for a minute." Hudson mentoed the device, saw a tiny lance of red light flash against Munoz's head.

Munoz jerked.

"All right," Hudson said, replacing the unit in his robe pocket. "You can open the door now."

Sidney Malloy's galaxy blue autosedan accelerated up the onramp to the Campobello Expressway, pressing him against the back of his bucket seat as the car picked up speed. Following the magnetic lure of buried wire, the car fell silently and smoothly into place in midday traffic. Sidney glanced over his shoulder, watched the grey-glass tower of his condominium building disappear behind other similar structures.

The sameness of his lifestyle with that of most other people depressed him momentarily. Sidney knew this was a bad thought, a selfish thought. He turned forward, trying to think of something else.

As Sidney turned his head, a yellow autosport darted past on the left and cut in front of him. This activated the collision sensor on Sidney's vehicle, and his car braked suddenly, slamming him against his shoulder harness.

"Damned hot dog," Sidney cursed softly. "His manual override ought to be jammed down his throat!" Sidney mentoed his rooftop signboard, flashing an angry message to the offending driver:

"SLOW DOWN, YOU FOOL!"

The reply came quickly, in bright green letters half a meter high:

"EAT MY DUST!"

The yellow autosport darted to the right, taking an exit into New City's central shopping district.

Sidney's pre-programmed car took the next exit, negotiating a spiral offramp onto American Boulevard, a broad avenue dotted with pink, lavender and yellow synthetic flowers and plastic maple trees. On each side of the boulevard, miniature expressways for moto-shoeing people carried four lanes in each direction. Sidney saw moto-shoers entering and leaving the skating thoroughfares via ramps. They traveled in lanes of varying speeds, from a slow right-hand lane to faster lanes at the left. Many wore multiphonic headphones over their ears, and Sidney saw their pudgy bodies undulate to the music he could not hear.

They shouldn't move like that, Sidney thought. *The Conservation of Motion Doctrine....I'm not the only one with shortcomings!*

At a stoplight, Sidney watched a maple tree shed plastic leaves and sprout new ones. Workcrews in bright orange windbreakers carried plastic bags emblazoned with the Bu-Maintenance crest, which they filled with leaves and litter. The air was still.

The car accelerated, gliding on its air cushion past the Black

Box of Democracy, an opaque doorless and windowless meg-
alith surrounded by rolling green plastic lawn. There were
people reading an inscription plaque on the structure, and others
taking pictures. Children played on the lawn.

In the next block, the Uncle Rosy Tower fronted a curving
section of the boulevard. Sidney looked up through the glassplex top of his autocar as it rolled by the tower; he could barely
make out the ring of the revolving Sky Ballroom on top of the
structure.

It's Thursday, he thought. *Only two more days until my
reunion. Just think . . . twenty years. . . .*

Now Technology Square was directly ahead, and Sidney
saw the sun peeking through a swirling cloud over New City's
skyline, reflecting off tinted glass windows on the government
office towers that ringed the square. A Bu-Cops car sped by,
its purple lights flashing and siren wailing. Other sirens screamed
in the distance. Throngs of people stood in the square, and
more streamed in from all directions.

Something big's going on, Sidney thought.

His car stopped as programmed several hundred meters from
the square, and he short-stepped out onto a platform. As his
car disappeared into an underground parking tube, Sidney mentoed his moto-shoes. They flipped out of their plastic ankle
cases and lifted him gently onto their wheels, and he began to
roll down a ramp to the skatewalk. A warm breeze blew across
his face as he picked up speed. Changing lanes expertly on the
crowded skatewalk, he moved to the slow lane and took an
exit designated "TECHNOLOGY SQUARE."

The square was dotted with planter boxes, white plastic
benches and modernistic government-commissioned sculp-
tures. A large fountain at the center adjacent to Uncle Rosy's
towering mechanical likeness sprayed the air with a thin, metallic moisture. The air was alive with people noises. *Angry
noises*, Sidney realized.

Recognizing his regular datemate in the crowd of jeering
onlookers watching a demonstration, Sidney rolled up beside
her. As he came to a stop, Sidney focused upon Carla Weaver's
high cheekbones with a red painted beauty mark on one side.
Her nose was distinctly Roman and classically perfect. Curly,
golden brown hair swirled about the shoulders of her carmine
red pantsuit.

"What's going on, Carla?" he asked.

"Doomies," Carla said with a glance in Sidney's direction. "Real freakos. They say a comet is coming!" She laughed, looked full at Sidney with heavy-lidded lavender eyes. "It's supposed to destroy us all!"

Carla studied Sidney, noted fat pouches and chubby cheeks beneath large round hazel eyes which stared back innocently. Dark, curly lashes framed the eyes, overhung by thick, dark eyebrows, a high forehead and curly black hair that was thinning at the temples. *He's not very good-looking*, she thought, concentrating upon Sidney's pug nose and ears which protruded like wings. *And he couldn't be as good in bed as my new pleasie-meckie*.

"We've all heard rumors the past few days," Sidney said, wondering why Carla continued to stare at him.

"Lies," she shot back without a shade of doubt in her tone. "You saw the President speak last night, of course."

"Yeah. I saw." Sidney shook his head negatively as a young girl with straw-blond hair attempted to hand him a pamphlet. On the cover he saw a picture of a terrifying fireball streaking toward New City while people panicked in the streets below. Large red and yellow letters on the pamphlet proclaimed: "ARRIVAL OF THE GREAT COMET!"

"Go on, get out of here," Carla said to the girl. Then Carla touched a button on her belt to activate a synchronized autoclapper recording and joined in as a group of onlookers jeered, "Chicken Little! Chicken Little! The sky is falling!"

Uncomfortable in the crowd of jeerers, Sidney considered an excuse that would permit him to leave. But a sudden numbness hit his brain. With it he heard the echoes of distant, murmuring voices. It was an angry cacophony of sound, and Sidney thought he heard the words "filth" and "unfit." As he rubbed his forehead, the murmuring receded, and he peered through the crowd at the focus of their attention.

A tall man with pale skin and high cheekbones stood at the base of Uncle Rosy's mechanical likeness, speaking through a bullhorn. Thick clusters of standing supporters protected him on all sides, their arms locked in defense against a contingent of electro-stick-wielding Bu-Cops. As each supporter fell to the onslaught, others rushed to close the hole. Sidney saw them bear their pain heroically, silently. Other doomies attempted unsuccessfully to distribute literature through the crowd.

In an emotion-laden voice, with his Adam's apple bobbing,

the tall man implored, "FLEE WHILE YOU CAN! A TER-
RIBLE BLOOD-COLORED FIREBALL WILL DESCEND
UPON US! AS THE GREAT COMET NEARS, THERE WILL
BE PANIC, LOOTING AND MURDER! THE SEAS WILL
RUSH ACROSS THE LAND! SEEK HIGH GROUND! FLEE
WHILE YOU CAN!"

Although the man was fervent, Sidney detected an inner
serenity about him . . . a deep strength that showed when he
stopped speaking, lowered his bullhorn and looked from face
to face across the crowd. Sidney felt a sudden urging to catch
the man's gaze, to be recognized as someone different in a sea
of sameness.

But as the speaker's gaze moved toward Sidney, a woman
with dark, ringletted hair interrupted his concentration to call
out, "HOW ABOUT A BOAT, NOAH? SHALL WE BUILD
A BIG BOAT?"

The crowd roared with laughter.

"I KNOW WHAT!" the woman exclaimed, moto-shoeing
forward and turning to face the crowd. She removed a vial
from her purse, held her hands high and poured white pills into
one hand. "COMET PILLS!" she screeched. "THE VERY
LATEST ITEM, LADIES AND GENTS, GUARANTEED TO
WARD OFF ANY EVIL INFLUENCES THE DREADED
STAR MAY IMPORT! ONLY THREE FOR A DOLLAR!
STEP RIGHT UP!"

Catcalls and the staccato thunder of auto-clappers drowned
out the man with the bullhorn.

Sidney looked past him and up to the giant mechanical
likeness of Uncle Rosy. A rotund, friendly-looking fellow,
Uncle Rosy sat in a great armchair with his hands outstretched,
palms turned to the heavens. In his left hand he held a cross,
and in the right a machine gear, symbolizing the unity between
religion and technology. Sidney looked beyond this to the new
Bu-Industry Tower under construction on the southwest side
of the square, and then over the building tops to scan a cerulean
blue, nearly cloudless sky. *Could it be?* he thought.

"Do you notice anything strange about his appearance?"
Carla asked.

"Eh?" Sidney dropped his gaze, met the eyes of his ques-
tioner. "Sorry, Carla. What did you say?"

Carla glared disapprovingly, as if to say that only non-
patriots dared look for fireballs in the sky. "I SAID," she

repeated angrily, "do you notice anything strange about his appearance?" And she cast her gaze toward the man with the bullhorn.

Sidney studied the demonstration leader again, noted wrinkled, worn clothing, milky white skin and a mane of disheveled black hair. "Yes." Sidney spoke carefully: "His skin is unusually pale. He doesn't glow like the rest of us."

"Right! Obviously, he's had his mento thought transmitter disconnected. Some of those other freaks are the same way. It's positively un-AmFed and unconsumptive!"

"Yes," Sidney said. Then he intoned: "Truly we are blessed."

The police reached their prey now, pouncing upon the man with the bullhorn in a great phalanx of blue uniforms, gold buttons and flashing electro-sticks. The bullhorn was ripped away, and Sidney grimaced as he saw a club smash against the man's face. With the blow, Sidney felt a surge of intense pain on his own cheek and nose.

The reality of this sensation was more shocking to Sidney than the pain. *How can I feel what is happening to him?* he wondered, lifting a hand to his face.

"Oh my . . . oh!" Sidney exclaimed.

"What's the matter with you?" Carla asked.

"I'm okay," Sidney lied, closing his eyes while trying to overcome the pain. He dropped his hand, opened his eyes and saw Carla staring at him with a perplexed expression. "I shouldn't feel this way," he said, "but the violence is so sickening. . . ." Sidney watched in horror as the demonstration leader clutched at his face. Blood oozed through the man's fingers, trickling down his arm.

"That doomie deserves it," Carla said.

Now the murmuring, angry voices returned to Sidney's awareness, and they grew louder quickly until he was able to make out complete sentences:

"You suffer, eh, fleshcarrier?" a tenor voice said. *"Think of our plight then, mired in the decaying rot of Earth garbage!"*

"What a stinking, terrible thing to do!" shouted another, deeper voice.

The voices faded as quickly as they had come, leaving Sidney stunned. He glanced around nervously, caught Carla's inquisitive gaze.

"Are you all right?" she asked.

"Yes, yes," Sidney snapped.

"You're behaving so strangely...."

"Don't worry. I'm fine." Sidney cleared his throat, looked away.

They watched three policemen kick the demonstration leader along the ground with steel-toed boots. The man curled into a ball in a pitiful attempt to protect himself. Strangely, Sidney felt sharp pains on his head, arms and torso, as if he too were being kicked and beaten, and he heard cruel, cackling laughter in a distant cavern of his brain. Sidney chewed at his lower lip, struggling not to show discomfort. The crowd clapped and called out derisively as the man's unconscious and bleeding form was dragged to a waiting van.

When the van doors slammed shut and it began to roll away, Sidney's pain subsided. *That was the damndest thing,* he thought, turning to leave. "See you at coffee," he said, feeling his moto-shoes click into gear.

Carla nodded, but she continued to stare at him curiously.

Now the comet pill woman called out again: "THESE DOOMIES ARE DOING US A GREAT SERVICE! MORE NUTS FOR OUR THERAPY ORBITERS MEANS MORE EMPLOYMENT IN BU-MED!"

Saddened at the spectacle, Sidney moto-shoed across smooth concrete toward a massive white-glass office tower which bordered the square. Pausing at an electronic security monitor just outside the main entrance, he pressed his palm against an identity plate and mentoed: *G.W. seven-five-oh, Malloy, Sidney...Central Forms.*

A vacuum surge pulled against his hand, then released him as a red light on the monitor turned to green. Glass doors slid open, and he rolled into the lobby.

Sidney paused at the elevator bank marked "SUB 501— SUB 700," gazing above the hypnotic dance of blue floor indicator lights to one of many pictures of Uncle Rosy that ringed the lobby. The soft background notes of Harmak played a "Melody For Progress," causing visions of home furnishings, autocars and bright clothing to float across his brain. Uncle Rosy seemed to look directly at him with concerned, benign eyes, and Sidney felt a force compelling him to reach for his back pocket. Dutifully, he brought forth a tiny red, yellow and blue volume. Gold leaf lettering on the cover announced its title: *Quotations From Uncle Rosy.*

Touching a button on the book cover, Sidney auto-leafed

through the pages, only half-conscious of people around him doing the same thing.

"I can't believe our Uncle Rosy wrote this more than three centuries ago," a woman said. Then, in the precise and emotionless tone of a Freeness Studies Instructor, she commanded, "Turn to page one-three-four."

She paused momentarily as pages auto-flipped.

"There will always be non-believers," the woman read reverently, "dangerously insane people who will stop at nothing in their attempts to disrupt our holy order. They will predict all manner of plague and catastrophe, insisting that God disapproves of the manner in which we live." She closed the volume, and Sidney looked up to see her smile softly. She had flaxen hair, and with a glance toward the square she said, "They are wrong, citizens. This is God's land."

The group closed their volumes, murmured, "Truly we are blessed."

Sidney waited as people destined for lower floors took places in the back of a large elevator, then he rolled on and stood at the front. Mentoing *sub-five-oh-three*, Sidney felt a click in the back of his brain as the car's computer accepted his command. The doors closed.

*   *   *

Sayer Superior Lin-Ti looked up, and his words slowed as he stopped reading from the text. "Those voices," he said, "you understand who they were?"

A short youngsayerman rose and responded: "Yes, Sayer Superior. They were the beings whose realm was invaded by Earth's garbage. The ones who turned the garbage into a fiery boomerang comet."

"And why did they speak to Malloy?"

"We have heard stories, Sayer Superior. I believe Malloy was a . . . well . . . a dolt of some sort. And they wanted him to botch up Earth's plan to stop the comet."

"That is correct. To put it bluntly, Sidney Malloy was a no-talent jerk . . . working in the lowest level of the most useless department in the government. . . ."

*   *   *

It was shortly after noonhour, the beginning of Carla's daily shift. Her rotatyper platform stood to one side of the sprawling Presidential Secretaries Pool, and beyond the tap-tap-whir of mento-activated machinery she heard the faint, gelatinous purr of Harmak.

She thought of Sidney as she adjusted her earphones, of the strange way he had behaved at the demonstration and of his attempts to be more than a datemate with her. Lately, Sidney had been most persistent.

Carla watched the letter "e" appear on her rotatyper screen, then called out, "Lower case 'r,' period, return, tab, upper case 'j.'"

She paused to make an entry on a Time and Motion form, then watched the typists encircling her platform as they mento-activated the keyboards in front of their chairs. One did upper case, another lower case, yet another was responsible for numbers, and so on. Six typists sat around each rotatyper caller, although Carla had heard of a new machine developed by the Sharing For Prosperity people that would accommodate ninety-five typists, each having only one key to operate.

All across the floor Carla could see great mounds of paper. There were stacks of paper on desks, on sidechairs, on window-sills, on the floor, spewing out of computers and in autocarts which rolled back and forth down each aisle delivering and removing. Brown and gold pamphlet meckies rolled along the aisles as well, full to bursting on all four sides with red, green, yellow and blue government pamphlets. A round, four-faced head on a stick neck rose from the center of each meckie's rack, above which was a square tophat that proclaimed "TAKE SEVERAL" in flashing purple lights on all sides. Department of Quality Control personnel wearing black uniforms and shiny yellow half-lemon helmets rolled from machine to machine, checking to be certain that all equipment malfunctioned according to standard.

Carla focused upon a sign on the back of one Quality Control Technician which read, "EACH BREAK IS A NEW TASK." Then she noticed a typist glaring at her and removed her earphones to ask, "What is it now, Margaret? Don't you like the way I'm calling out punctuation again?"

Margaret shook her puff-curled silver hair before replying haughtily, "I don't like the way you call out anything. You think you're better than we are." She glared at Carla, then added in a sing-song tone: "We've all seen you making goo-goo eyes at Chief of Staff Birdbright!"

"I don't think I'm better than any of you," Carla huffed, looking back with hostility in her lavender eyes.

"You don't even go to coffee with us now that you're a G.W. two-five-four. Well lah-dee-dah!" Margaret rolled her eyes upward. "That's still only one two-hundred-fifty-fourth of a job! My brother is a G.W. fifteen!"

"You're just bitter because you didn't receive a higher calling, Margaret. I got the assignment you wanted."

Margaret whirled around angrily on her swivel chair, rose and then sat back down abruptly. A hush fell across the floor as ten white-robed men carrying grey urns emblazoned with the Presidential Seal rolled single file into the department. Margaret recognized General Munoz at the head of the procession.

"The Council of Ten!" Carla whispered excitedly. "But they were just here yesterday for their regular—"

"Shuttup!" Margaret commanded, her voice a hostile whisper. "We can see who it is!"

Everyone rose silently, bowing their heads.

"Bless this mess," the council ministers called out, reaching into their urns and scattering confetti as they rolled through the department. "Bless this mess. . . ."

From his oval office on the two hundred eighty-fifth floor of the White House Office Tower, President Euripides Ogg heard the distant whine of police sirens. The President was a massive black man in a satin gold leisure suit—in his early fifties but with a lineless face. The eyebrows were dark and bushy, contrasting with a wave of golden hair that was combed straight back from a widow's peak.

Ogg stared intently at a desk-mounted video screen as the Technology Square demonstration broke up, squinting his blue-green eyes as sunlight from a solar relay panel outside the window glinted off the screen. He took a deep puff on a tintette, and exhaled blue smoke thoughtfully. Ogg snapped a glance at a sign above the doorway, mouthed the familiar words: "Faith, Consumption, Freeness." A half-read Sharing For Prosperity report lay on the desk in front of him, and he tried to get back into it. Forty-two additional tasks that could be shared. . . . Uncle Rosy's Thousand Year Plan. . . .

He sighed.

The President looked up, and through drifting blue smoke saw Chief of Staff Billie Birdbright standing in the doorway. A handsome, tanned man of middle years with bright yellow hair and a small dimple in the center of his chin, Birdbright was in constant demand as a bedmate with the ladies of the office.

"The Council is here, sir," Birdbright said. "Shall I send them in?"

Ogg nodded.

As the council ministers moto-filed in, Ogg tapped impatiently on his desk with one finger. General Munoz led, followed by Dr. Hudson, who moved along behind the tiny Mexican-American general like an oversized shadow.

Can't trust those two, Ogg thought. *Something disturbing about their alliance ... and Hudson made moves on my sister ... until I appointed her mayor of that therapy orbiter.*

Munoz and Hudson were followed by all the ministers of the various governmental super-bureaus. Each wore a hoodless white ministerial robe with a gold braid sash and a gold cross and chain which dangled from the neck. Munoz carried his military cap in one hand.

Cassius Murphy, the jovial Minister of Bu-Bu, followed, then Bu-Free's tall and angular Jack Ramsey. *Both are neutral,* Ogg thought. He glanced at Bu-Health's Salim Bumbry and at the reddish-skinned American Indian Jim McConnel of Bu-Med, who entered eighth and tenth. *So are they.*

As the ministers took seats silently in comfortable red nauga suspensor chairs which formed a half circle in front of Ogg's desk, Ogg singled out Kevin Osaka, the small oriental minister of Bu-Construct. *Still not sure of him,* Ogg thought. Osaka noticed the President staring at him and looked away nervously.

"Good afternoon, gentlemen," President Ogg said, scanning the faces in what he hoped was a somber manner. He nodded to Ezrah Sims of Bu-Cops and to Bu-Industry's Marc Trudeau, men he considered loyal, then looked at his lifelong friend, Pete Dimmitt of Bu-Labor and said, "Nice to see you, Pete. Feeling better?"

"Yes, Mr. President. The leg's doing fine." Dimmitt touched a star-shaped Purple Badge on his left lapel proudly. This was the nation's highest mark of valor, evidence for all to see of

Dimmitt's "conspicuous bravery" in the face of a disintegrating product: his moto-shoes.

General Munoz placed his cap on the lap of his robe as he sat down crisply. *Why in the hell has he called us in?* Munoz wondered. *Probably another foolish Job-Support idea to waste my time. . . .*

Munoz studied President Ogg closely, noted anger as the big black man crushed out his tintette in an ashtray. Ogg's penetrating, blue-green eyes flashed at Munoz for a second. Then Ogg looked away and mentoed a "coffee" button on his desk panel. "Gentlemen," he said, "in a few minutes you will see something extremely important."

That procession of coffee secretaries again, Munoz thought, reading the President's thoughts with the brain-implanted transceiver given him secretly by Dr. Hudson. Munoz flicked a piece of confetti off his robe angrily. *How many times is he going to show that to us?*

As Ogg watched, Dr. Hudson cleared his throat and squirmed into a chair next to the thin and mysterious General Munoz. The pupils of Munoz's eyes were almost pure black, and he stared back at the President in cool disdain.

Something about his eyes, Ogg thought. *He almost seems to be laughing at me.*

I am laughing at you, Munoz thought, reading the President's mind again.

Ogg saw Munoz sneak a glance and a smile in Hudson's direction.

Only Munoz, Hudson and ten trusted conspirators had received the mind-reading units. Munoz recalled his doubts when Hudson installed the transceiver. . . .

". . . Will I really be able to read minds with this?"

"You'll see for yourself in a few minutes," Hudson had said.

Munoz remembered his response: "Now I will see who is loyal to me and who is not!"

"This transceiver will operate electronic gadgets like any consumer-issued unit," Hudson had explained as he worked, "but it has a nice additional feature. . . ."

Munoz returned to the present, watched President Ogg clasp his hands on the cluttered desktop and glare around the room. Unaware of Munoz's prying, Ogg said, "I have called this emergency session because the Alafin of Afrikari is due to arrive in my office at seven-thirty tomorrow morning."

Munoz read the President's thoughts and cursed under his breath.

Ogg rubbed a finger on the edge of his desk as the ministers whispered in surprise. "I should say a projecto-image of him will be here," Ogg explained. "The old fool is still afraid to fly."

"He has demanded an audience?" Bu-Cops' craggy-faced Minister Sims asked.

"Yes. By telephone just an hour ago." Ogg chewed his lower lip. "The Alafin says his astronomers have seen a comet which appears to be on a collision course with Earth."

"I thought that was just a rumor," Sims said.

The council ministers whispered to one another again.

President Ogg fixed an icy gaze on Hudson. "What I want to know is this, Dr. Hudson. You *have* told me everything about this alleged comet? It is a bunch of garbage, isn't it?"

Hudson wiped his brow with a white kerchief, glanced at Munoz.

Tell him, Munoz mentoed. *Better to hear it from us.*

"Uh, no sir," Hudson replied nervously. "I mean, yes sir. It *is* garbage."

"Dammit to Hooverville, Hudson!" President Ogg thundered. "IS IT GARBAGE OR ISN'T IT?" A bulky mechanical arm popped out of the desktop, smashed a clenched fist down with tremendous force on the desk. WHAM! Papers scattered in all directions. CRASH! A brass lamp rocked and fell to the floor. The arm flexed back into its compartment.

Hudson shivered with fear, smoothed the fine muslaba robe he wore across his lap with one hand. He glanced at Munoz for support, then stammered, "S-sir, it's d-difficult to ex—"

"It's a garbage comet, Mr. President," Munoz said. "Our own damned trash is coming back!"

President Ogg sat back in stunned disbelief, slack-jawed and mute.

"The th-thing is huge, sir," Hudson said, "and Earth is directly in its path!"

Hardly able to speak, Ogg said, "I can't believe. . . ." His voice trailed off, and a pained silence fell over the room.

Bu-Bu's Cassius Murphy broke the silence. Looking at Hudson, he said, "You mean it stinks?"

"Why yes," Hudson replied. "I suppose it does."

"That's interesting," Murphy said with a wry smile. "If it kills every last one of us, will it still stink?"

Hudson shook his head, rolled his eyes upward.

"Those deep space shots we've been making for the past nine years," Munoz explained, looking at Ogg. "A Bu-Tech computer miscalculated their trajectory."

"Now w-wait just a minute," Dr. Hudson protested, staring through sweat-fogged glasses at the battle ribbons on General Munoz's chest. "The electro-magnetic catapults are operated by Bu-Mil people. Your staff should have checked the figures before making the shots!" Hudson took a deep breath, realizing he was treading on dangerous ground in speaking to the General this way.

"I don't know about that, Dick," Munoz said calmly. "There's nothing in the procedures manual to that effect."

"It was only a tiny miscalculation," Hudson said plaintively, looking at President Ogg. "Just one-nineteenth of a percentile!"

"A tiny miscalculation!" Ogg half rose out of his chair. "It doesn't seem so tiny to me!" He sat back, lit a tintette and blew an angry cloud of yellow smoke in Hudson's direction.

"Tiny in galactic terms," Hudson insisted. He removed his horn-rimmed glasses with shaking hands, wiped the glasses on his robe and put them back. "And besides, my bureau didn't manufacture the Comp six-oh-one computer. Bu-Industry did that, and they didn't follow Bu-Tech's specifications. The circuit board that failed and caused a one-nineteenth of one percent trajectory error was constructed to consumer quality instead of industrial quality."

"Hold it right there!" All eyes turned to Marc Trudeau, the Minister of Bu-Industry. Seated at the end of the semi-circle on the President's right, Trudeau's heavy brown face sported a bright pink mustache that had been dyed to match a new line of kitchen appliances. With his features contorted in indignation, he gripped the chair arms and said, "All circuit boards are manufactured in space . . . on therapy orbiters. How can we be expected to monitor quality with crips and retardos doing all the work?"

The President's gaze was bone-chilling as he asked: "Why did you entrust such a critical part to the therapy orbiters?"

"It wasn't our fault," Trudeau said. "Some therapists from Bu-Med came into my office one day and asked to be given tours of our manufacturing and assembly lines. I didn't see anything wrong with that, and a couple of days later they came back with a list of tasks they felt could be better performed by handicapped personnel. One of those tasks was the assembly of circuit boards."

Jim McConnel, the portly Indian minister of Bu-Med, rose angrily and snapped: "I'm not going to let this mess land in my lap! No one told us we were manufacturing critical components! And don't forget that Bu-Construct pressured us to build more orbiters!"

Immediately, all the other ministers leaped to their feet, clamoring for attention. They argued heatedly for several minutes, with the ones who had not yet been blamed choosing sides. Ogg let the melee continue awhile to see if he could make sense out of the alignments among those ministers of doubtful loyalty. But no clear patterns emerged, and as the alliances shifted back and forth, Ogg finally demanded: "STOP THIS FOOLISHNESS! TAKE YOUR SEATS IMMEDIATELY!"

The ministers fell silent and resumed their seats.

"Now I will show you what the President's office can do," Ogg said.

Munoz knew what was coming.

The office door swung open, admitting a procession of coffee secretaries. They rolled in single file, dressed in dark brown mini-dresses bearing the gold encircled lapel crest of a steaming cup of coffee. The first in line was a consumptively rotund redhead carrying a trivet. With a curt smile, she placed the trivet on the President's desk, did a one hundred eighty degree spin on her moto-shoes and rolled out the door. The second girl carried a large coffee pot, which she placed on the trivet with equal fanfare. Next came eleven pudgy saucer bearers, and a saucer was placed in front of the President and on the little tables next to the ministers' chairs. They were followed by eleven cup bearers and then by a pneumatic brunette who poured the coffee and returned the pot to the trivet.

"Very impressive, Mr. President," several ministers said as they watched buxom blond twins remove the coffee pot and trivet. "Very impressive, indeed."

I call that showing off, Munoz thought as he watched the women leave. *Twenty-seven girls to serve coffee to eleven of us!*

"Thank you," the President said as he mentoed the door closure. "Now let's get back to the matter at hand." Addressing Dr. Hudson, he said, "Just forty-eight hours ago you assured me that no comet was heading toward Earth."

"That's true, sir. I replied so at the time because I did not believe it to be a comet."

"Why not?"

"Many bodies of matter move through the heavens, sir, not all of which are comets. This particular object is of unique origin . . . and unlike any comet I have observed, it has an extremely dense mass. Most comets are a 'bag of nothing,' in that they consist of gas particles surrounding an ice nucleus. While their tails may stretch for millions of kilometers across space, they typically don't have much mass."

"Tell him about the spectral analysis, Dick," Munoz said.

"It's burning common garbage, meteorite chunks, nuclear matter and the like," Hudson said. "I suppose it's a comet, Mr. President. It's closer to that than to any other phenomenon. But this baby's unlike any other comet in the universe!" *It's also burning human bodies from our burial shots,* Hudson thought. *Such a nasty detail.*

Ogg took a sip of coffee, asked angrily, "Why didn't you level with me in the first place? You knew something was heading toward us."

"You don't like to be bothered with technical details, Mr. President. Besides, until now, we didn't have enough photographs to plot the course."

"It'll hit us? For sure?"

"It is on a definite collision course with Earth. We were trying to save you a lot of trouble. . . ." Hudson's voice trailed off.

President Ogg spun his chair around to stare out the window. He focused on an imposing grey General Oxygen factory in the distance, with seven tall stacks rising out of a domed base. *Maybe we should turn this over to a committee,* he thought. *A lot of people could be kept busy. . . .*

After several minutes of pained silence, Salim Bumbry, Minister of Bu-Health, said, "Shouldn't we make an evacuation plan, sir . . . to help people reach higher ground?"

President Ogg did not turn around. He could imagine Bumbry sitting there—the youngest minister, precisely-trimmed brown hair, a neat beard and pale green eyes. Definite presidential stock. "No, Bumbry. We can't do that now, don't you see? I've told the world it isn't coming."

"Announce new evidence."

"No. Too embarrassing . . . and I'm up for re-election Tuesday."

Munoz, monitoring the thoughts of the speakers, noted that the President was worried about losing votes. Bumbry was genuinely concerned about human life. *Always knew Bumbry was poor political stock,* Munoz thought.

"How much damage will it do?" Ogg asked, turning around to face Hudson. "And where will it hit?"

"It isn't a question of damage, sir. Nor does it particularly matter *where* on Earth it hits." Hudson squirmed in his chair. His eyes flitted around nervously behind the glasses. "This comet is very large, and grows as it accumulates space debris. If that baby hits us, the entire planet is going to be garbage!"

Ogg felt numb. He could not think of anything to say.

Hudson tried to take a sip of coffee, but his hands shook so badly that he sloshed liquid on his white robe. He placed the cup on the sidetable, coughed. "Laser penetration readings and gamma ray cameras show this to be the heaviest mass ever to approach our system. We think our garbage shots ended up in the Fourth Columbarian Quadrant . . . near a black hole."

Hudson paused as he noticed President Ogg shaking his head from side to side in disbelief. Angry words seemed on the tip of Ogg's tongue, but were not uttered.

"Our garbage shots probably reactivated a dead sun," Hudson said. His gaze darted away under the President's intense scrutiny.

"My Rosenbloom!" one of the ministers exclaimed.

We can't admit the truth, Hudson thought, feeling uncomfortable. *No one has any idea why that stuff is coming back!* "If put on the periodic scale," Hudson said, "where the highest present density is one hundred eighty-six, this fused mass would have a reading of five thousand, three hundred eighteen. It would crack our planet like a wrecking ball hitting glass."

"We plugged the problem into Comp six-oh-two," Munoz said. "That's the computer which replaced the six-oh-one."

I'd like to get rid of all computers, Ogg thought. *The tasks they steal from people. . . .*

Munoz read this thought, then said, "We can deflect the damned comet, Mr. President."

Ogg brightened. "Ah!" He turned to Hudson. "For sure?"

Hudson nodded. "The best plan has us changing the comet's course by using an E-Cell powered mass driver. We'd push the comet as it passes the Leviathan planet of Kinshoto in the Bardo-Heather Group. Lots of nitrogen in that planet's atmosphere."

"We're reviewing military dossier files now," Munoz said, "searching for the best man to head up the mission." Munoz felt a numbness in his brain, heard echoing, far-off voices. *"Forget the dossier files,"* a voice said. *"Choose Sidney Malloy. He's the only one. . . ."* Munoz shook his head, tapped at the rear of his skull above his implanted mento transceiver. *Dammit*, he thought. *It's acting up again.*

When Munoz's head cleared, he heard Hudson speaking: "Kinshoto's atmosphere is nearly seventy thousand kilometers deep and supports no known life forms. If we can lock onto the comet with fire probes and guide it through that nitrogenous region, it may burn up."

"That planet is BI-I-IG!" Munoz said.

"What's the likelihood of this comet hitting Earth?" Bu-Med's Minister McConnel asked.

General Munoz reviewed the speaker's thoughts, noted something new. An escape plan . . . bribe money paid to a shuttle commander . . . intended refuge on one of the orbiting solar power stations. *How did he find out?* Munoz wondered.

Hudson, responding to McConnel, said: "Ninety-eight point nine-one percentile. We've been monitoring it from deep space tracking stations. It's coming back along the identical course of our garbage . . . and burial . . . shots. We've since corrected the error, of course."

"Wonderful," President Ogg said, his voice dripping sarcasm. Mumbling something about bodies coming back, he spun his chair again and watched a distant transport shuttle land at Robespierre Magne-Launch Base. "How much time do we have?" he asked.

"Fourteen days," Hudson said, trying not to betray uncertainty in his tone.

As the ministers left the oval office single file, President Ogg singled out Hudson: "Dr. Hudson, I would have a word with you in private."

Surprised, Hudson turned back and resumed his seat. "What

is it, Mr. President?" he asked, timidly.

Ogg scanned the papers which had fallen to the floor, leaned down and retrieved a long, narrow piece of electronic billing paper. Looking at Hudson, he said stiffly, "This is the monthly microwave radio call log for the therapy orbiter of Saint Elba."

Hudson gulped.

"It states that you called my sister six times this month, all on scramble code." Ogg glared ferociously. "What did you discuss with her?"

"N-nothing important, Mr. President."

"Then why was it necessary to use a scramble code?"

"P-personal matters, sir."

"Personal matters?" Ogg sat back, a sneer on his face. "How can you have personal matters with someone tens of thousands of kilometers away?"

"L-look, Mr. President. I know you don't like me. That's why you made Nancy mayor of Saint Elba three months ago . . . to get her away from me." Hudson read Ogg's thoughts to confirm this statement.

A faint smile touched the edges of Ogg's mouth.

"I love her, Mr. President. And . . . she loves me!" Hudson took a deep breath. He stared at the broken lamp on the floor.

"Love? You're right about one thing, Hudson. I *don't* like you. You're a weak, sniveling—"

"I'm not good enough for your sister, right, Mr. President?" Hudson said, feeling his face flush hot with anger. He adjusted his glasses, focused upon the massive black man seated on the other side of the desk.

"That's exactly right, Hudson. If not for Munoz's influence, you'd still be a lab technician." Hudson had read this thought previously and was not surprised to hear it spoken.

I'll ruin you, Hudson thought. *I'm going to show General Munoz an invention this afternoon that will knock you out of the oval office!* "I do have certain . . . talents, shall we say?" Hudson said, beginning to taste the pleasure of prospective revenge.

Noticing a twinkle in Hudson's eyes, Ogg was thrown off balance momentarily. Ogg fumbled with the call log sheet, glanced down at it and said, "I notice you called her almost daily in the early part of the month . . . but in the past week and a half there have been no calls. Why is that?"

"A minor disagreement, Mr. President."

"Over what?"

Hudson felt the advantage swinging to Ogg again. "She wants me to s-stand up to you, sir."

Ogg laughed cruelly. "And tell me what you think of me, eh, Hudson? You don't have the guts!"

"M-maybe I do, sir."

"Eh? What's that?"

"May I speak candidly, sir?"

"Yes." Ogg set the call sheet down, clasped his hands on the desktop and glared ferociously at Hudson.

"YOU'RE A BIGOT, MR. PRESIDENT!" Hudson said, blurting it out. Hudson's eyeglasses slipped to the end of his nose. He pushed them back.

"A bigot!" Ogg rose out of his chair, hulked forward over the desk. "A bigot, you say?"

"That's the real reason you don't want me to be permies with Nancy, isn't it? I'M WHITE AND SHE'S BLACK!" Hudson felt relief at getting the long-suppressed statement out, but was fearful of the consequences.

"Look at my council of ministers, Hudson! An American Indian, an oriental, six whites, a Mexican, a black. Does that sound like the council of a bigot?"

"You didn't select them, sir. They were chosen by council votes when vacancies arose."

"I could have vetoed any one of them, including you." Ogg sat back down, glared at a wall.

"True enough, Mr. President. But even so, this represents your public self. I'm speaking of your real self."

A shocked President Ogg felt Hudson's words slash into an area of consciousness he had not considered. *Can this be so?* Ogg thought. His gaze snapped toward Hudson as he asked, "Who put those words into your mouth?"

"They are my own, sir. I have discussed the matter with Nancy, but the words are my own."

"She agrees?"

"I believe she does."

"You surprise me, Hudson." Ogg lit a tintette nervously, blew a wisp of lavender smoke across the desktop.

Hudson saw near admiration in the President's dark brown eyes, that and confusion. Deciding not to press his advantage,

Hudson said, "I have to call Nancy right away, sir. An official call."

"Concerning what?"

"Saint Elba is on the route of the comet intercept crew. It is the first recharging station . . . and the place where the two mass drivers will be constructed."

"Mass drivers?" Ogg tapped his tintette on an ashtray.

"Remember we discussed that during the meeting, sir? They will connect fire probes to the comet's nucleus, and guide it . . . ."

"Yes, of course. Do what you must, Hudson. Do what you must."

Hudson rose. "Unless you have something further, sir, I should leave now."

Ogg nodded, stared at his tintette despondently. *I should control everything,* he thought. *I AM PRESIDENT! But even the tiniest matters elude me . . . . My own sister opposes me?*

As Hudson left the oval office, he realized he had seen a heretofore unexposed side of the President . . . unrevealed even to one able to read the thoughts of others. Maybe Ogg was not so bad after all. Still, forces had already been set in motion, and within days Hudson was confident that a new government would take power.

Mayor Nancy Ogg held a red towel in one hand as she turned sideways to admire herself in a poolside mirror. Her skin was sleek, wet and light brown, the swimsuited figure trim and regal. Three red clasps secured the wet, black hair in a Mohanna Dancer's tail. A triangular Bu-Med crest graced the waist of her suit, and superimposed over that was the tiny silver cross denoting her mayoral rank.

In an adjoining area of her suite on the L_5 therapy orbiter of Saint Elba, the pool constituted a private place for her, and was, as she often liked to mention sarcastically, "one of the perks of power." Overhead, a reflected midday sun flooded the room with light, and as she looked up she saw one edge of the orbiter's night shield.

Five more hours, she thought dejectedly, *and that shield will block the sun again. My Rosenbloom, but I hate this place!*

She dropped the towel and stepped quickly onto the diving board. Springing twice at the tip of the board, she leaped into the air, bent gracefully and touched her toes before cutting neatly through the water. The pool was pleasantly warm.

When Mayor Nancy Ogg came to the surface, Security Sergeant Rountree stood at the pool edge, looking down at her. Trim, tall and muscular, he cut a dashing figure in his gleaming black and gold Security Brigade uniform. She was attracted to him, but had done nothing to fulfill her desires. A person of her status could not mingle with inferiors. A telephone cord at Rountree's side had a cordless tele-cube which danced in the air above the phone cradle.

"Telephone call, Honorable Mayor," the sergeant said, delivering the crisp rotating wrist salute of the Brigade.

"I am not to be disturbed in here!" Mayor Nancy Ogg snapped, treading water at the center of the pool. Her eyes stung, and she blinked, thinking, *Too much chlorine in the pool again. . . . Doesn't anyone ever listen to me?*

"But it's a radio call . . . by microwave from Earth."

The Mayor scowled, then muttered something and swam smoothly to where the sergeant stood. As she grasped the plasticized pool edge, the tele-cube dropped to meet her, hovering in midair before her mouth.

"This is Mayor Nancy Ogg."

"Nancy?" Hudson's voice crackled over the distance and immediately there came a scramble-code beep.

She motioned the sergeant away. Her eyes followed Rountree's buttocks, then moved up his muscular back to the broad shoulders and wide neck.

Rountree flicked a glance at her as he pushed through a double exit door. She saw him smile.

"Yes, darling," Mayor Nancy Ogg said to Hudson.

"I've just come from a meeting with the President," Hudson said, breathlessly. He sat on the edge of his desk, spoke into an intercom.

"And how is my dear brother?"

"He is well."

"Do you love me, Richard sweets?"

"You know I do."

Mayor Nancy Ogg detected irritation in the tone, then asked: "And that is why you called? To tell me you love me?"

Hudson scowled. "No. There are problems here on Earth."

"You haven't called me for almost two weeks. Why not?"

"I've been busy, Nancy. You know of the comet?"

"Rumors," she said, kicking the water playfully. "Tell me you love me."

"Nancy, I don't have—"

"Say it."

The line beeped.

"All right. I love you. Now will you listen to me?" In his New City office, he could hear water splashing at Nancy's end and realized she was in her pool. Hudson shook his head slowly in exasperation while staring out the window at an autocopter as it landed in a cloud of dust on a nearby rooftop. Sunlight flashed off the windows of the autocopter.

Mayor Nancy Ogg swam on her back to the center of the pool. The tele-cube followed her, remaining in midair several centimeters above her mouth. "I'm listening," she said.

"The comet is not a rumor, Nancy."

"Oh come now, Dick. Our therapy cells are overflowing with doomies. But you're not going to tell me that—"

"I don't have time to explain, but the danger is very real."

Mayor Nancy Ogg swam to the opposite side of the pool. The tele-cube followed her, and she spoke as she climbed out of the water. "Can it be stopped?"

"Saint Elba is the closest orbiter to the flightpath of a ship we're sending . . . and you have the manufacturing facility we need. . . ."

"I get the feeling I'm not going to like what you have to say next," she said, throwing a towel over her shoulders.

"Pay close attention to this. You must construct two E-Cell powered mass drivers, type J-sixteen with twin R-eleven fire probes on each. Scale everything up twenty-eight times."

"Twenty-eight times? Are you kidding?"

"Our calculations show it will scale up with no problem."

"No problem? We'll have to hand-make a lot of this, with no molds, no standard parts that big. That will take time!"

"Put everyone to work on it. This is a Priority One."

"We don't have an assembly area that large."

Hudson hesitated as he heard a scramble code beep, said, "Knock out the partition walls in Hub Sections A and B."

"But we have work in progress in those areas, government contracts to fill . . . deadlines to meet."

"Stop everything else, and I do mean EVERYTHING. Move it all out. Catapult it. Whatever, but get it to hell out of there."

Mayor Nancy Ogg dried her legs angrily with the towel, said, "And even if we get the damned things built, how are we going to get them out? The space doors are too small! I know, I know . . . put a crew to work on that too. . . ."

"Finish the mass drivers by Friday of next week. At noon."

"A week from tomorrow? All I can say is we'll try. . . ."

"Not good enough. No excuses on this one, Nancy."

"I'm an administrator, not a technician!"

"Delegate it!"

"Will that be all, Dr. Hudson?" she asked, coolly.

"Nancy, please believe me when I say that I WILL get you off that orbiter." *I can't tell her how we're going to beat her brother in Tuesday's election,* he thought. *The ties of blood. . . .*

"Why did my brother have to send me here?" she wailed. "I've been on this Godforsaken orbiter for three months!"

"Be patient. We can't let personal problems interfere with a world crisis."

"Such a convenient excuse. If not for that one, you'd have another."

"One more thing, Nancy."

"Personal or official? I'm ready to hang up on you!"

"Official. Have a charging bay available for the ship when it gets there. Use Number One Argonium Gas. Check the charger now for malfunctions. There won't be time for that later. . . ."

Hudson heard a click.

"Nancy?" he said. "Are you there?"

The line beeped, went dead.

* * *

At a study carrel in the Pleasant Reef Library, a youngsayerman read the first question of his homework assignment:

1. State two reasons why Uncle Rosy led the AmFed people to believe he had died and then went secretly to the Black Box of Democracy.

In ornate script, the youngsayerman penned the answer on a separate sheet of ruled paper: "a.) Our Master felt strongly that the AmFed system eventually had to survive on its own. He chose to monitor electronically all aspects of AmFed life in secrecy, adopting a policy whereby his control would be withdrawn gradually. In essence, it was a weening. b.)..."

The youngsayerman scratched his shaven head, trying to come up with the second part of his answer. Glancing at the adjacent carrel, he read another student's answer and then copied it onto his own paper: "b.) Uncle Rosy discovered the secret of long life, which he dispensed only to himself and to his sayermen. He did not feel an economic system could survive if such knowledge was released to the entire populace...."

TWO

BACKGROUND MATERIAL, FOR
FURTHER READING AND DISCUSSION

Javik, Thomas Patrick—D.O.B. 10/20/68—Atlantic City, N.J.—
Skill Quotient: 1000 (perfect)
Attitude Quotient: 135 (poor)

2585: Graduate of P.S. 502, New City, Md. . . . aptitude in math
and physics . . . disciplinary problems.

2588: Graduate of Space Academy . . . Mass Driver Mechanics . . . 3.93 G.P.A. . . . 5-day suspension for fighting.

2588–2593: 2nd Lt., Space Patrol, light cruiser duty in the Ross
Asteroids . . . Promoted to 1st Lt. . . .

2593–2602: Resource Protection Patrol, Dune Region, Moon . . . one
A.W.O.L. reprimand . . . promoted to Captain and given
command of a Baltimore class cruiser at the outbreak
of the Atheist hostilities.

2603: Distinguished service in the LaGrange Four region . . . saved
2 AmFed base ships and destroyed an entire enemy fighter
squadron . . . dishonorably discharged for striking a superior
officer . . . no court-martial due to exemplary war record. . . .

2603–present: Garbage shuttle pilot, New City, Md.

> Excerpts from one of 300 military dossier files
> known to have been in the possession of
> General Munoz

Thursday, August 24, 2605

On the afternoon of Garbage day minus eight, Tom Javik found
himself looking forward to the class reunion. He thought of
Sidney as he switched off the autopilot and pushed the control
stick forward with an effort that made the muscles on his arm
stand out.

Good old Sid, he thought. *Hard to believe it's been twenty
years. . . .*

The heavy lift garbage shuttle Icarus rumbled and shook
like a great awakening beast, then banked right slowly and
made its way around New City's field of solar power microwave dishes. Now Javik could see Robespierre Magne-Launch
Base beneath the sun to the west, with its grey E-Cell silos,
compactor buildings and mass driver tracks.

"Robie clears us for landing," a gravelly voice to his left
said. "Pad four."

Javik glanced at his wiry-thin co-pilot, Brent Stafford, nodded. Stafford's face was creased beyond its years and made
him look more like forty-eight than thirty-eight. The hair was
blue-black, tousled. He sat hunched over a computer screen,
perspiring in the mid-afternoon heat. This summer had been a
scorcher.

Javik verified the clearance on his own screen, cracked:
"Tell 'em to evacuate the area. This heap handles like a flying
sack of potatoes. No power, controls shot to hell. . . ." He wiped
his brow, scowled. "And no air conditioning. Jeez that load
stinks today!"

"Cattle carcasses," Stafford said, nodding in the direction
of the underdeck cargo hold. "They didn't seal up those drums

worth a damn. Saw 'em load on a bunch of cobalt and zirconium waste too. The packages were dripping radioactive...."

"Don't worry about it," Javik said. "You knew what you were getting into when you signed on for garbage duty."

"Aw, what the hell. Guess it beats pushing paper at some desk." Stafford smashed a fly against the side of his keyboard with one fist, wiped the insect off on his pantleg.

"Not like the old days, is it?" Javik said, glancing down at his stained grey and blue garbageworkers uniform. "Remember those Space Patrol outfits? White and gold with ribbons across our chests?"

"Yeah. The ladies sure went for 'em."

Javik grinned, wiped a hand through his shock of amber hair. "Uh huh! Hey, remember that Polynesian girl I met in the astro port?"

Stafford smiled, glanced out his starboard window as he heard the sonic thump of a catapulted load. "Port Saint Clemente," Stafford said. "Greatest little spot in the asteroid belt. You met her at the hot springs...love at first sight."

"Thought I was gonna go A.W.O.L. and become permies with that lady," Javik said. "But the war..." His voice trailed off. "Well, you know...."

The Icarus hovered over its landing pad now, and Javik watched grey-uniformed men below scurry to get clear.

"Never saw you any closer, pal," Stafford said. He studied his friend, noted that Javik's long legs had to be turned to one side to fit under the instrument panel. Lines were beginning to appear around deeply set blue eyes. The aquiline nose had a scar at the bridge from one of many barroom scuffles. A little pouch of fat had begun to adhere beneath Javik's chin, evidence that he no longer sustained a rigid conditioning program. In the old days, Stafford could hardly keep up with this man. Of late, it had been the other way around.

Javik hit the retro rockets button, flipped a switch to activate the para-flaps. "C'mon, c'mon," he husked impatiently. He was cursing when the rockets finally ignited, but Stafford could not hear the words in the roar. The Icarus settled onto a concrete landing pad. "Okay!" Javik yelled, hitting switches and pushing buttons. "Shut her down!"

Javik was first to the door. He waited as one of the base crewmen drove an escalator unit into position. Javik mento-locked his moto-boots and was bounding down the steps before the mechanism had clicked into place against the Icarus. Stafford followed.

"Hey you guys!" a pig-faced base sergeant called out. "Remember the Conservation of Motion Doctrine! No exercise outside a Bu-Health gym!"

"Stuff that full-employment hype, Peterson!" Javik barked. "We're doin' our bit hauling garbage to the catapults!" Javik reached the ground, short-stepped to the sergeant and pushed him in the chest. "You wanna ride in that ship full of stink, buddy?"

The sergeant rolled back against the escalator, nearly falling over. "You're not in the Space Patrol anymore, hot-shot!" he screamed. "I'm gonna teach you a lesson!" The sergeant locked his moto-boots and grabbed a wrench from the escalator cab.

Javik hit him before he could swing the wrench. Two clean belly punches and a forearm across the face put the big man down, writhing in pain.

"One of these days, hot-shot!" the sergeant moaned. "I'll get you!"

"Yeah, yeah," Javik sneered. "Can't you see I'm scared to death?" Javik activated his moto-boots, rolled toward a waiting autocar at the edge of the landing pad. "C'mon, Staf," he said. "Let's hit the baths."

General Munoz closed a manila file folder, added it to a large stack on the left side of his desk. He squirmed in his chair from sitting too long, rubbed the corner of one eye. *Which one?* he thought. *Which one do I choose?*

He felt stiff, and stretched his arms straight out in front. There was a buzz in his left ear, and he picked at it, squinting one eye as he did so.

"Over here, fleshcarrier!" a voice said. It seemed to come from the corner to Munoz's left.

"Huh?" Munoz said. He lowered both hands to the desktop, and slowly . . . ever so slowly . . . his jaw dropped, leaving his mouth agape. For as General Munoz looked at a small round trash can in the corner near a disconnected disposa-tube, he saw a banana peel fly out and hover in the air. A candy bar wrapper followed, then a paper cup and half a cheese sandwich—all remains of the General's lunch. The items hovered for a moment, then began to spin rapidly in a ball.

"What the hell?" Munoz cursed.

Suddenly, the ball of garbage became a ball of fire. *"Die, fleshcarrier, die!"* a voice screeched. The fireball flew toward Munoz's face at blinding speed, and it was all the frightened little general could do to duck out of the way. As he ducked under his desk, the fireball whizzed overhead, striking the wall behind his credenza.

When Munoz looked back, terrified, he saw the ball of burning garbage drop to the credenza top and spark. The fire smoldered, and Munoz wrinkled his nose at the odor.

"Not very pleasant, is it, fleshcarrier?" the voice said. This time, the voice came from the smoldering fireball. *"I'm a sample of my big brother! You won't be able to dodge him when he comes!"*

"Who are you?" Munoz asked, still cowering under his desk. "And why are you doing this?"

"Listen, fleshcarrier, and listen carefully. For you don't have much time. Sidney Malloy is the pilot you need." The voice gave Sidney's consumer identification number, then faded away.

Munoz inched out from under the desk. He fell into the chair, fumbled for a pen and a sheet of paper. With shaky handwriting, Munoz scribbled Sidney's name and I.D. number.

Who is this guy? Munoz wondered, staring at the note. He reached for an unread stack of dossier files. *Maybe we have something on him here. . . .*

About ten minutes before the afternoon envelope stuffing session, Sidney sat at his desk on the Job Station Beasley Floor, thinking about the violence he had seen on his way to work. It troubled him deeply, although he was sure he should not feel this way.

Sidney stared at the five meter high metronome mounted on a high octagonal platform at the center of the department. Light from an overhead fluorescent fixture glinted off the metronome's shiny brass surfaces. A simple plaque on each face of the platform bore this inscription:

SHARING FOR PROSPERITY.
Another way to share as
we build a better future.

Sidney had seen the plaque in other places, the axiom having been taken out of *Quotations From Uncle Rosy*. Both his motorboat and vacation condominium were owned on a time-share basis, with Sidney holding a one-fifty-second ownership in each. This gave him the use of each for one week out of the year.

He mentoed a desk-mounted automatic thumb. It flipped through a thick stack of mail in front of him. A letter bearing the seal of the Presidential Bureau caught his eye. Stopping the thumb, he read the letter to himself in a low tone: "Mister Malloy: . . . We are making the following recommendations after reviewing the activity at your work station. As you know, energy management is a top priority of this administration, since energy expended outside a Bu-Health facility is not Job-Supportive. Our recommendations cover hazards which, if not remedied . . ."

Two packing meckies appeared at a recently vacated desk in the next aisle, carrying cardboard cartons. Short and squat, they had blinking red and yellow lights and tin can heads. One eye was centrally positioned. No mouth, ears or nose. The meckies emptied the contents of the drawers on top of the desk, then lifted one end of the desk, causing the items to slide neatly into waiting boxes. They worked quickly and efficiently, and soon rolled away with their loads in the direction of the elevator bank.

Sidney heard a familiar voice, turned his head to the left and glanced at Malcolm Penny, the owlish Second Assistant to the Assistant Administrator. Penny was conducting a departmental tour, and a group of G.W. eight hundred trainees rolled along behind him, hanging on every word.

"The Presidential Bureau has seventy-nine departments," Penny explained in his high-pitched voice, "one of which is Central Forms. Job Station Beasley is one of the authorized jobs in Central Forms." He waved an expansive arm, added, "This station takes up an entire floor." The group rolled slowly by Sidney's desk, made a right turn onto the main aisle.

Someone sneezed at a nearby desk.

"May Rosenbloom bless you," a woman said.

"Beasley Station has twenty-six sections," Penny continued. "Each section has five item counters, two projection-graph operators, three trash can auditors, one manual sergeant and one attendance monitor. All draw up reports, in exquisite detail,

of course. Comprehensive reports are the life blood of th
government."

The trainees nodded in agreement.

Sidney looked back at his letter from the President, read·it
first recommendation: "On numerous occasions, you were ob
served balling up pieces of paper and hurling them into th
waste receptacle. Papers should not be balled up, and shoul
be slipped into the waste receptacle with a minimum expen
diture of energy...." Sidney yawned and looked around th
room.

From his desk near the metronome, he could barely mak
out a row of red, yellow and blue alpha-numeric charts along
a distant wall directly ahead of him. That was the file depart·
ment. A double swinging door in the wall led to the depart·
mental archives. Along an equally distant side wall were the
committee rooms, and along the other side were the managerial
offices and supervisorial cubicles. The tiny figure of Admin·
istrator Nelson could be seen approaching from his office. The
KWAK! KWAK! of automatic name-date stampers rang from
all around, accompanied by the sounds of auto-staplers and
collators and the punctuating squeaks of autocarts as they stopped
at each worktable to pick up paper. It was warm in the room,
and the ever-present, gelatinous purr of Harmak forced Sidney
to fight drowsiness.

Sidney shook his head to clear it, turned around to face
Melinda Brown, a yellow-haired G.W. seven-five-oh at the
desk behind his. As she slipped a green plastic paper clip onto
a file, the paper clip broke. Smiling winsomely, she reached
into a dispenser for a replacement.

"Plastic is fantastic!" Sidney intoned.

"Yes," she agreed. Still smiling, she placed a new, orange
paper clip on the file. "Every break is a new task."

The noise of machinery and buzz of conversation gradually
slowed and stopped. Sidney turned to watch Administrator
Nelson ride a lift to the top of the metronome base. It was
nearly time for the afternoon envelope stuffing session, and
every employee had a stack of form-change announcement
cards and a stack of white envelopes in an automatic stuffing
tray. Sidney glanced at the large red button on his desktop near
the base of the stuffing tray. He placed the forefinger of his
right hand over the button.

Administrator Nelson was a small man with a friendly, elf-like face. Tiny eyes peered from under a translucent green visor that nearly covered the upper part of his face. He cleared his throat, amplified his melodic voice with a tiny silver microphone clipped to his tie: "Good afternoon, employees of Job Station Beasley! Before getting on with the important task at hand, I would like to take this opportunity to give thanks to our gracious benefactor, Willard R. Rosenbloom."

Murmuring their lines on cue, the employees intoned: "Thank Uncle Rosy. We are all employed."

Administrator Nelson continued: "Uncle Rosy is proud of each of you. Every person in this room holds a share of the Sacred Job that was created for our benefit."

And the employees murmured: "Praise be to Uncle Rosy. He loves us all."

Nelson touched a heat switch on the metronome, setting the device into operation. Click . . . click . . . click . . . click. The pendulum swung back and forth, a passage every fifteen seconds. Sidney pressed his red button with each metronome click, activating his envelope stuffer at the rate of four per minute.

After several minutes, the metronome automatically slowed, making a click every twenty seconds. Then it slowed again, to a thirty-second click. Sidney's eyelids grew increasingly heavy. He dozed off. Then, half awake, he tried to catch up by pushing the button several times in rapid succession.

"No, no Malloy!" a voice said. "You're going too fast!"

Startled, Sidney looked up to see the scowling face of Malcolm Penny staring down at him through round spectacles perched on the end of a disapproving nose.

"Oh!" Sidney said, sitting up straight. "I'm terribly sorry!"

Penny shook his head disapprovingly, set his jaw. "And your desk, Malloy . . . it's not organized according to standard!"

"But I thought it—"

"Your day calendar and auto-staple remover, man! Don't you ever look at the manual?"

Sidney heard a metronome click, pushed the stuffing tray button. "I'm sorry, Mr. Penny," he said. "I'll correct it right away."

The Second Assistant to the Assistant Manager straightened, still shaking his head. "See that you do," he snipped. Then he rolled down the aisle to look for other violators.

• • •

Still angry over his encounter with the base sergeant an hour before, Javik stepped out of a Bu-Health surge-pool. Smelling the back of his hand, he shook his head and thought: *Still a trace odor of that god-damned garbage. The shit permeates every pore in my body....*

Javik shivered as he walked dripping wet across the blue Italian tile of the main bathhouse toward a line of naked men and women waiting to get into Tanning Room Five. His leg and arm muscles ached from the weight exercises he had completed fifteen minutes earlier.

"This old body can't take it anymore," he muttered.

Finding a place in line, Javik looked around and motioned to a towel monitor standing nearby. A dark-haired young man wearing the silver and gold leotard of Bu-Health moto-shoed over, draped a long white towel over Javik's shoulders.

"Sign here," the young man instructed, thrusting a Tele-Charge board under Javik's nose. Javik unsnapped a transmitting pen from the board, squiggled his name across the tiny screen. A green imprint of Javik's signature appeared on the screen as he wrote, and as he finished, his consumer identification number and the amount of purchase appeared. All this faded quickly, being replaced by a flashing orange "Thank You." The young man retrieved his Tele-Charge board and rolled back to his post.

Javik pulled the towel around his shivering body and felt its warmth take hold. The line moved quickly. Soon he had signed another Tele-Charge board and was in the warm, brightly lit tanning room. It was a high-ceilinged room, with eighty-eight levels of tanning slabs stretching upward, connected by steel ramps and clanking conveyor lifts. Harmak played "Dreamer's Lullaby," one of the new restful background tunes. The smell of perspiring bodies wafted across his nostrils.

"Hey Tom!" The voice came from above. Javik looked up, saw the goggled, ruddy face of Brent Stafford smiling down over the edge of a third-level tanning slab. "I saved you a place!" Stafford motioned for Javik to come up.

Javik stepped onto the clanking conveyor lift, rode it to a third level ramp. From there it was only a few short steps to the tanning slab beside Stafford. Javik removed his towel, donned a pair of goggles and dropped face down onto the warm, clear glass of the slab. Heat lamps all around warmed his body, soaking into every aching muscle. "Ah!" Javik sighed. "That feels good!"

Stafford turned to face Javik, peering through his goggles as he asked, "When's the big reunion?"

"Saturday night." Javik focused upon body smells carried by a downdraft.

"Twentieth, isn't it?"

"Uh huh. Old P.S. five-oh-two. Be nice to see the bunch again . . . Charlie, Bob, Sidney. . . . Hey, I wonder if Sidney ever permied up with Carla. . . ."

Stafford sat up, sprayed water over his body with a passing porta-shower. "You know, Tom," he said, measuring his words carefully, "You'd do well to watch that temper. With good behavior, I've heard it said you can get another commission."

"Yeah, yeah. I know." Javik shifted on his belly, turned his face away from Stafford.

"Could have been worse, buddy. You might have been court-martialed and shot for that . . . but they took your war record into account."

"Am I supposed to thank them for that? Hell, they should thank *me* . . . and you too . . . for what we did."

"You've got to see their point of view."

"*Their* point of view?" Javik felt rage rising inside. "I belted that wet-behind-the-ears gay major after you and I were almost shot down by an Atheist fighter squadron!"

"They don't see any justification for hitting an officer, Tom. You know that."

"We saved two base ships with a little initiative, and that armchair fairy read us out for not getting the proper authorizations!"

"I know, I know." Stafford sounded sleepy.

"Now it's happening again, Staf. That damned garbage shuttle's driving me crazy."

Stafford turned to his back. "You're right. I can't argue with a word. But we've got to use our brains . . . you know, play their silly games a little."

"We bust our asses and what do we get? Some creep spouting off about rules and procedures! Well for Christ's sake! I'm a Star Class Captain, not a stinking garbage shuttle pilot!" Javik paused, breathing hard, turned to face Stafford. "Get the hell off my case, will ya, Staf?"

"Damn you!" Stafford said. His creased face stiffened. "I'm

trying to help you, you hothead! Can't you see that?"

"I don't need your help!"

"Yeah? Then get the hell away from me!"

Javik rose with his towel. "You're a little old lady, Staf. Always telling me the safest things to do, aren't you? Well, I've had enough! DO YOU HEAR ME? ENOUGH!"

"Everybody in the place hears you," Stafford sneered.

Javik turned without another word and stalked off. *Pleasure domes*, he thought. *Maybe a forest maiden will calm me. . . .*

Sidney did not have to look at his watch to know it was time for the second afternoon coffee break. He was already nearing the elevator bank when the bell rang. Carla waited in the elevator as usual, holding the door open. Sidney rolled on without a word.

"Perfect timing again," Carla said as the doors whooshed shut. She placed both hands in the pockets of her carmine red pantsuit and mentoed: *Sub-nine-sixty-six, Presidential override. Code twenty-four.*

"That Presidential override is nice," Sidney said, knowing what she had done. "Our car used to stop at every floor before you got it."

"Just don't tell anyone about it," she said focusing on Sidney's receding hairline and high forehead. "I had to pull strings to get it."

"How did you manage it?"

Carla smiled. "Leave a girl some secrets, Sidney." She thought of Chief of Staff Billie Birdbright. *Billie likes me enough to give me an override. But when will he get around to asking me out?*

The car dropped quickly and silently, depositing them at the entrance to the Cave Coffee Shop. It was an immense, dimly lit restaurant, dotted with hundreds of tiny tables. Each of the four perimeter glassite walls looked out upon one of the irridescent bat caves that honeycombed the ground beneath New City.

"You're quiet today," Carla said as they took a seat at their usual window booth overlooking an underground waterfall. She looked at his soft-featured face, with its familiar pug nose and wing-like ears at the sides. "You aren't worried about a comet coming, are you?" She laughed.

"No. The doomies are crazy. I was just thinking about my

job again . . . and wishing to Uncle Rosy I'd taken a physical for the Space Patrol twenty years ago."

"But your . . ."—Carla looked around, whispered—". . . disability. It would have shown up." She touched a tiny dice cage mounted on the table, looked at him intently with understanding in her eyes.

"Maybe not." Sidney watched people beginning to stream into the coffee shop. "The incorto dispenser my father implanted . . . in place of my appendix . . . has an x-ray scrambler. It takes special equipment to detect it."

"Your father was a great surgeon," she said, looking at him tenderly. "You seem so unhappy in Central Forms. Could it be that you would prefer life on a therapy orbiter?"

"With the exception of missing you, it might be more interesting." He laughed nervously. "Look at me, Carla. I want so desperately to be a gallant captain at the controls of a space cruiser, on a great mission to the outer reaches of the galaxy. And here I am . . . hundreds of floors underground!" He fell silent, gazed out into the cave as a flurry of large butterfly bats passed in front of the waterfall, then disappeared behind a blue and white stalagmite formation.

"I'm sorry," she said. "Really I am." She reached across the table, took his pudgy hand in hers. "You always had that romantic dream of running away to the sky . . . even when we were kids."

Sidney fought back a tear, turned to study her classically featured face, with its straight Roman nose and high cheekbones. A red painted beauty mark dotted the left cheek, and long curls of golden brown hair cascaded onto her shoulders. People thought Carla of average build, and the muscle tone of her body provided evidence of time spent in Bu-Health gyms. Sidney tried to smile, said, "I remember we used to play condominium together. And we promised to become permies someday. . . ." He cleared his throat.

"The grown-up world isn't simple," Carla said.

"Can't we find some way to work it out?"

"No!" She spoke firmly. "We've been through that before . . . the probability of cappy offspring and all. It wouldn't be fair to them."

"But that's only a fifty-fifty chance. And even if there was a handicap, maybe we could find a doctor who would—"

Her voice grew cool. "No," she said. "Absolutely not." She

pulled her hand away, noticed Chief of Staff Birdbright slide into a booth two tables behind Sidney. Birdbright smiled at Carla. She looked away, said to Sidney: "Let's order now. Everyone's arriving."

They mentoed orders into a tabletop receiver. Then they fell silent while waiting for the order to arrive, glancing at one another for several agonizing moments without speaking.

The coffee shop was full now, and Sidney listened to a talkative silver-haired girl at the next table. "I don't know what happened to Abercrombie," the girl said. "One day I came to work and he wasn't there. Then packing meckies cleared his desk. Judy asked her supervisor, but he just said, 'Abercrombie is no longer with us.' It's all kinda weird, if you ask me."

A tray holding two Styrofoam cups of coffee and a plate of mini-donuts popped out of the table between Sidney and Carla. Carla signed a Tele-Charge board mounted next to the dice cage, then mento-spun the dice. Her results appeared on the Tele-Charge screen.

"Five sixes!" she exclaimed. "That puts me in the Trip to Glitterland Sweepstakes! Now you try it!"

Sidney signed the board, mento-spun the dice cage.

"Aw," she said, her voice reflecting disappointment. "Only a pair of fives."

"Oh well," Sidney said, reaching for his coffee cup. "Guess I wasn't meant to do anything exciting."

"I can't believe it!" she said. "Just think! I could be a winner!"

"Uh huh."

"Isn't Freeness wonderful?"

"Yeah." Then his voice grew more cheerful as he said, "I'm happy for you."

Carla knocked over her coffee cup in her excitement, spilling liquid on her dress. "Darn!" she said, quivering as she reached for a napkin. "I'm so excited I can't stop shaking."

Sidney used his napkin to wipe the table.

"Thank you," she said, dabbing at the dress with her napkin. "I'll change as we leave. There's a venda-dress machine in the lobby."

"That reminds me," Sidney said. "What are you wearing to the reunion?"

"I don't know." She lifted her gaze to the attentive eyes of Billie Birdbright. "I'll shop for it tomorrow."

• • •

General Munoz did not like to be kept waiting. Slapping his gold-braided military cap rhythmically against his thigh, he moto-paced the length of Dr. Hudson's office. Passing from sunlight to shadow, he mentoed the digital cuckoo clock on the wall, noting the readout beneath the closed cuckoo bird doors: P.M. 3:39:26. He spun angrily as he reached an end wall, then saw Hudson standing in the doorway, holding a red velvet box.

"Sorry I'm late," Hudson said nervously. He entered and set the box on his desk. Adjusting his horn-rimmed glasses, he said, "You're going to like this."

Munoz's dark eyes flashed. "Hrrumph! Nearly ten minutes wasted! My time is valuable, you know!"

Hudson kept his gaze on the box, smiled proudly at the corners of his mouth. "Open it."

Munoz rolled to the box with his orange mustache curled into a scowl, but there was a glint in his eyes. Setting his cap on the desk, he opened the box, then stared at a burnished gold cross and chain which lay on red velvet. "A cross? But I alrea..." He stopped, noting Hudson's bemused expression. Munoz lifted the cross out, studied it intently.

"It looks like the cross you've always worn, General. But it's more. Much more. The wearer of this baby commands all AmFed weather control machinery. Simply touch the cross with either hand and mento-transmit."

Munoz looked at the cross with distinterest.

"This is a nicer, more compact system, General. We can dismantle the weather console now.... All that bulky equipment has been replaced by one little device. You can play God with this little unit, changing the weather as you please, wherever you are."

Still no response from General Munoz.

"To monitor the results, you simply close your eyes and there it will be, dancing on the insides of your eyelids."

"Uh huh."

"Try it."

Munoz took a deep breath, touched the cross with one hand and thought of a tidal wave hitting an unpopulated stretch of Kamchatka coastline. He dropped his eyelids and saw a great

wall of blue green ocean thundering toward shore. There was
no sound in his vision, and the tidal wave hit land with un-
harnessed fury, destroying trees and land shapes in its path.

"Interesting," Munoz said. He opened his eyes, looked at
Hudson with the expression of a spoiled child who wanted a
better present. "Nice gadget, Dick," he said.

Hudson gathered his robe and sank into his big chair. Slipping into their unspoken conversation mode, he mentoed: *It's
a subliminal transmitter, too, Arturo.*

Munoz brightened. *Yeah? It'll change votes in Tuesday's
election?*

*You bet. As you know, every consumer-issued brain implant
has a subliminal receiver, originally for the purpose of picking
up advertising suggestions from Harmak and from National
Home Video.* Hudson noticed Munoz looking out the window,
added: *Now we don't have to worry about retaliation from the
Black Box to a military attack. You can take power peacefully.*

Uncle Rosy was a crafty bastard, Munoz mentoed. *I still
think he spread that retaliation story as a bluff.*

"What time shall I arrive for dinner Sunday?" Hudson asked,
making harmless conversation for the benefit of anyone who
might be eavesdropping.

"Six or six-thirty. We'll play a little Knave Table afterward."

Hudson took the old cross and chain to a wall-mounted
disposa-tube, dropped it on a shelf door which opened as he
approached. *I thought you would be pleased with the new cross,*
he mentoed. *But you don't seem to appreciate it.*

The shelf door snapped back into place. Machinery inside
the wall whirred.

It pleases me, Munoz mentoed. *But wait until you hear what
popped out of the trash can in my office this afternoon. You
know how you're always telling me I should reconnect my
disposa-tube? Well, listen to this. . . .*

That night, Sidney mentoed his bedside dream machine,
instructing it to take him on an ego pleasure space fantasy. He
fell asleep within minutes, imagining a wonderful, magical
adventure. . . .

"Fsssing! Fsssing! Fsssing!" Death rays from his one-man
gunship, the Galilee, cut through space, making sounds that

were only possible in fantasies. Three exploding balls of orange and purple ahead marked the dream-precise hits: three Slavian warships!

"Half-human monsters!" Captain Malloy cursed under his breath. He mento-banked the gunship, headed back to astroport.

"Captain Malloy!" the speakercom blared. "The President wishes to speak with you!"

In his dream, Sidney listened as President Ogg explained: "The Slavians have diverted a great comet, Captain! It's on a collision course with Earth!"

"How diabolical, Mr. President!"

"The reason they are masters of the Humboldt Star System, Captain. There is strength in being evil!"

"What are my orders, sir?"

"The comet will pass near you in sixteen minutes," Ogg's dream voice said. "Stop it, Malloy. You're the only force between us and destruction!"

"I'll do my best, sir."

"If you succeed, there's nothing you can't have . . . riches, beautiful women . . . even the AmFed Presidency!"

"I don't want any of those things," Sidney's imagined self told the President. "I'll do it because . . . because . . . duty calls!"

Sidney saw his dream ship now from a detached vantage point, watched it bank gracefully and slide through frigid black space toward a huge rainbow-colored fireball that was bearing down on Earth. Then he saw himself lying in bed with a determined but contented expression as he experienced the dream.

"Awaken, fool!" a voice from afar said. Then another voice, equally distant and echoing, said, *"We refuse to tolerate the stench and degradation of AmFed garbage! Take it back and die, fleshcarriers!"*

Sidney turned in his sleep, flailing and kicking as he struggled desperately to awaken. After what seemed an interminable period, he opened his eyes. Sticky and hot with perspiration, he stared into the blackness of his room.

Those voices again, he thought. *Am I losing my mind?*

Unable to return to sleep, Sidney mentoed for his pleasiemeckie. He heard the closet doors open, and the smooth whir of machinery as the meckie approached. *It's not Carla,* he thought, feeling the bed shake as the meckie got in and climbed under the covers. *But at least I'm not alone. . . .*

*   *   *

In the privacy of his rock-walled cave room, Sayer Superior Lin-Ti popped a minicam cartridge into the video machine. The machine was bright red plastic, with a wide oval screen. As the film began, black gothic letters announced its title:

Pleasant Reef
August 14, 2605

Two days before anyone knew of the comet, he thought. He watched his own image appear on the screen, standing at a tutelage console with a hooded youngsayerman. . . .

Sayer Superior Lin-Ti: "Following the questioning period today, I will make an announcement concerning your future."

Youngsayer Steven: "My primer tells me that Uncle Rosy granted non-revocable trade status to the Afrikari nation. It does not say why this was done."

Sayer Superior Lin-Ti: "Uncle Rosy developed a special friendship with the first Alafin of the present line, Alafin Inaya, more than three centuries ago. The Master does not reveal such details to the history writers, of course, but he and the Alafin struck up their friendship during a game of Swahili Croquet in the Alafin's capital city. After that, they often vacationed together during Uncle Rosy's last years in public life."

Youngsayer Steven: "I have no other questions today. What is the announcement?"

Sayer Superior Lin-Ti: "An opening is available in the Black Box of Democracy. It is the Sixty-Six Sayer position. If you accept, you will be known as 'Lastsayer.' Do you accept the calling?"

Youngsayer Steven (without hesitation): "I do."

Sayer Superior Lin-Ti: "You are to replace Twelvesayer Robert, with everyone below that level moving up a notch. Twelvesayer suffered from Box Fever and had to be removed."

Youngsayer Steven: "I am not familiar with that malady."

Sayer Superior Lin-Ti: "Alas, he went mad from the regimentation and confinement to the Black Box. The poor man wanted to be like any consumer, even spoke with apostrophes."

Youngsayer Steven: "How unfortunate! What became of him?"

Sayer Superior Lin-Ti: "Uncle Rosy personally administered selective memory erasure and gave him AmFed identity papers. I understand he is going to work in the travel division of Bu-Free."

Youngsayer Steven: "That should make him happy."

Sayer Superior Lin-Ti: "Uncle Rosy is most compassionate!"

Youngsayer Steven: "Peace be upon you, Sayer Superior...."

Lin-Ti flipped off the video machine and rolled to a brown nauga chair next to his bed. There he re-read the following day's history lesson....

THREE

"I feel complete. This is my legacy to the nation."

> Remarks made by Uncle Rosy to his personal secretary,
> Emmanuel Dade, concerning the recently completed
> Black Box of Democracy. Uncle Rosy disappeared three
> days later (on May 16, 2318) after personally supervis-
> ing selective memory erasures on everyone involved
> with the project. (From E. Dade's unpublished notes.)

Friday, August 25, 2605

"What the hell happened?" General Munoz demanded. His
orange mustache bristled as he glared at Dr. Hudson. "Another
miscalculation?" Munoz stood in the center of his living room

module with his hands thrust deeply into the pockets of a dark brown robe. His new gold cross hung about his neck, outside the robe. It was well past midnight, the first hours of Garbage Day minus seven, and his hair was sleep-tousled. A brass table lamp near the window cast yellow light against the General's side, leaving half his face in shadow.

A fair-haired, taller man of perhaps thirty-five stood in a gold robe at the General's side. Hudson recognized Colonel Allen Peebles, the General's adjutant and lover. The younger man had pale blue eyes which to Hudson seemed to look at some indeterminate point in an unfocused distance, as if Hudson was not there. Hudson had long since learned to control his thoughts of revulsion in the presence of these two, since they, like Hudson, were fitted with mento transceivers.

"We have problems," Dr. Hudson said, a bit out of breath. He removed his overcoat, slung it over the back of a white nauga chair and slumped into the chair. "As I told you on the phone, our biggest concern is that the comet's speed has increased dramatically. We now estimate its arrival in seven days rather than thirteen."

"Oh damn!" Colonel Peebles said, speaking in an exaggerated lilt. He took a seat in an adjacent chair, crossing his legs gracefully.

"I hate surprises," Munoz said. Continuing to glare at Hudson, he popped a sleep-sub pill and washed it down with a water capsule.

"And I've just discovered a second computer error," Hudson said.

"The new Comp six-oh-two?" Munoz asked.

"No. This time it was the Willys twelve-forty that calculated the comet's E.T.A. . . . off by six hours."

"In the wrong direction, I presume?" Munoz said.

"Naturally."

Munoz shook his head, stared glumly at the floor.

"The comet is not behaving according to known laws of physics," Hudson said, rubbing the fringe of black hair on one side of his head. "Just one hour ago, it made a ninety-four degree turn, veering off into space for a time. Then it made another sharp turn, back to a collision course with Earth."

"How odd!" Peebles said. "What are we to do?" He sat sideways in the chair to look at Hudson, an arm draped across the chair back.

"Silence!" Munoz commanded, shooting a fiery glance at his adjutant. "I have to think!" Munoz moto-slippered to the couch, sat down with his hands grasping his thighs. "How could the comet change like that?" he asked, staring at the floor.

Hudson shrugged. "I don't know. This thing's a complete mystery to all of..." He stopped as Munoz looked up and glared at him. Such words had been spoken before.

"Get out new orders, Allen," Munoz said. "Have the crew ship ready three days earlier...by Tuesday afternoon at fourteen hundred hours." He turned to Hudson.

Hudson spoke as Munoz was formulating a new thought. "I'll call Saint Elba and have the mass drivers moved up too."

"Right," Munoz said. "And tell 'em to double-check the E-Cell charging bays. We don't want any last minute problems."

"I'll reiterate that."

"Anything else?" Munoz asked.

"We'll have to set up new recharging stations along the route in deep space," Hudson said. "The others are placed incorrectly for the new course and time. I'll refigure it right away."

"Good," Munoz said. "We still have the matter of the pilot. There's no time left...."

"Have any more garbage balls spoken to you?"

"What do you mean by that?" Munoz snapped.

"Maybe you were tired. The mind and eyes can play tricks...."

"It was in flames, and came right at my face! I was there! And listen to the clincher: there is a Sidney Malloy!"

"Yeah?"

"He's a nobody in the Presidential Bureau—Central Forms."

"You're not actually thinking of using him?" Hudson asked.

"I have a strong feeling—call it intuition, I don't know. Something tells me...."

"We need to go on more than intuition," Hudson said. "Everything rides on this mission, Arturo. This calls for the best, only the very best."

"I know."

"Did it occur to you that your trash can magic trick might have been performed by the Black Box?"

"No," Munoz said. "I'm sure they had nothing to do with it."

"On what evidence? You puzzle me, Arturo—relying so heavily on intuition for critical decisions."

The General's black pupils became steely hard. "And you are a man of facts, Dr. Hudson. Precise scientific facts." Munoz fingered the burnished gold cross which hung from his neck.

"I am—and there is a concise scientific answer for every question."

"Don't be so sure of that. I'll tell you one thing. Anyone that can make a ball of burning trash speak to me has my undivided attention. The voice told me to use Malloy, and I'm damn sure not going against its wishes. Hell, Dick—maybe that was God himself. Speaking to ME!"

"Okay, okay. This Malloy—can he be trained?"

"Anyone can be trained," Munoz said. "You know that. And Malloy knows a pilot—one of the three-hundred on whom we have files."

"Oh?"

"Javik," Colonel Peebles said. "He's a ruffian."

"Funny thing though," Munoz said. "This Javik is sharp, maybe the best we can find. He knows the Akron class space cruiser and has exceptional reaction times." Munoz lifted a manila folder from the coffee table, handed it to Hudson.

Hudson thumbed through Javik's dossier file. "He's had mass driver mechanics training, too. . . . Odd that he'd know Malloy. . . . They went to high school together. . . ."

"Javik is bull-headed and quick-tempered!" Peebles said.

Hudson nodded. "Poor attitude quotient," he said, reading from the report. "Gets in fights all the time."

Munoz shook his head in exasperation, spoke tersely to Peebles: "His bull-headedness . . . as you call it . . . was actually independent decision-making. He took out an entire enemy fighter squadron with one star class cruiser. . . ."

"And a Major's jaw with one punch," Peebles said. "I saw him knock Neil Smalley down. In fact, it was my testimony that got Javik tossed out of the service."

"The decisions he made were absolutely correct," Munoz insisted. "His only error was in striking an officer. Major Smalley shouldn't have pressed him about procedures."

"It won't matter anyway," Peebles said, raising his blond eyebrows. "He's on a six-day pass and is nowhere to be found . . . I'll bet he's shacked up."

"You're going to send Javik and Malloy on this mission

together?" Hudson asked, looking at Munoz.

Munoz nodded, then glanced at Peebles. "You'll find Javik, Allen," Munoz said, smiling knowingly, ". . . when you hear what I have in store for him."

Peebles did not reply, stared at the General impertinently.

"The ejection pods on his ship will be disconnected, and the rocket engines will have a certain . . ." Munoz paused, glanced at Hudson with a mischievous smile.

Hudson returned the smile. "I believe planned obsolescence is the term for which you were searching, General," he said. "The radio has been prepared similarly."

Peebles brightened. "That sounds pretty good. . . ."

"And no rescue craft anywhere in the vicinity," Munoz said. "The world will never know that a comet really threatened us, or that he stopped it."

"What about an enforcer?" Peebles asked.

The General raised an eyebrow. "An enforcer?"

"Yessss," Peebles said, his voice a cruel purr. "Conceivably, Javik could repair anything you disconnect. And we don't want any chance of him getting off a distress call."

"True."

"Let's send along Madame Bernet." An evil, purse-lipped smile danced along Peebles's mouth.

"Ahh!" Munoz caressed his mustache. "The Montreal Slasher!" He turned to Hudson. "The meckie is available?"

"Yes," Hudson said. "Just back from a mission. Madame Bernet silenced eight guys on that one . . . permanently."

"This will be delicious," Peebles said, smiling like a death's head. "But alas," he added sadly, "it will be the last mission for our finest killer meckie."

Munoz rubbed his temple. "Bring Malloy and Javik to me," he said.

Four hours later, inside the Black Box of Democracy . . .

With his ankles crossed beneath his body, the tall fat man known as Onesayer Edward sat naked on a blue and gold prayer rug with one hand resting on each knee. Soft morning rays of sunlight warmed from an overhead skylight warmed his bare shoulders and the back of his shaved head. Flicking a downward glance at his pendulous stomach and at the great folds of flesh which cascaded to the rug from every part of his body, he imagined that he must resemble a wallowing hippopotamus. Onesayer grimaced at a surge of pain from one ankle, tried to think the things he was supposed to think.

The prayer rug was on a loft of Onesayer's private Black Box of Democracy penthouse, and in the background he heard the soft, lilting notes of the Hymn of Freeness. Uncle Rosy had written that tune. It was the theme song of the Sayerhood.

Gazing at a burnished bust of Uncle Rosy which rested on the leading edge of the rug in a pool of sunlight, he noted the floating red arrow at the sculpture's base pointed straight ahead and sharply down. This indicated the precise location of Uncle Rosy's immense chair on the main level of the building. An inscription on all four sides of the bust's pedestal carried the admonition: "Keep The Faith."

I cannot get into this, Onesayer thought. *And it used to be so easy!* He sighed twice, causing his flabby chest to rise and fall like an undulating wave, then stared at the sculptured, cherubic face of Uncle Rosy.

He thought back to his boyhood on the asteroidal sayer's retreat of Pleasant Reef, and upon the two hundred eighty-seven years he had spent in the Black Box. Remembering the first day he had seen Uncle Rosy sitting upon the great chair, he recalled being in awe of the Master's presence. To Onesayer, Uncle Rosy seemed godlike, always sitting in the shadows and never revealing his face.

Flicking a fly off his leg, he thought, *I was one of the original sixty-six....the Master brought me from Three-Sevensayer to Onesayer in ninety-three years, skipping me ahead of others, putting me in slots that became available....*

Onesayer glanced at his onyx class ring angrily, recalling Uncle Rosy's exact words to him, spoken nearly two centuries before: "I will step down within fifty years, Onesayer Edward. You will become Master. Be patient, and all will come to you."

Be patient! Onesayer thought bitterly, looking up at the ceiling in dismay. *How long do I have to wait? I know all about Freeness and Sharing For Prosperity....I have served on twenty-seven bureau monitoring teams....*

Uncle Rosy's words came back once again: "You will be the Protector...the Chosen One...." Onesayer lowered his gaze. *Ha!* he thought, glaring at the bust of Uncle Rosy. *He is always coming up with new excuses for not stepping down, saying I have much to learn....*

His thoughts were interrupted by an intercom buzzer whose

rapid-fire tones told him the Master was calling. Onesayer mentoed the circuit to open it, replied aloud, "Yes, Master?"

"The new Bu-Industry Tower, Onesayer. You are prepared for our ten A.M. dedication?"

"Yes, Master. There is plenty of time."

"See that you are prompt."

"I have never been otherwise, Master."

There was a long silence at the other end of the line, followed by, "Our new Lastsayer will meet you at the helipad."

"I am aware of this, Master. He will be trained properly."

"Very well, Onesayer. And do not forget to show him the Bureau Monitoring Room afterward."

Onesayer Edward rose wearily after the conversation ended and short-stepped across a hardwood floor. He rode the escalator downstairs, then made his way across the cool blue slate of his dining room module to the bedroom module. There he looked at a row of identical friar brown robes in the closet and said to himself mockingly, "Let me see now. . . . Whatever shall I wear today?"

Mayor Nancy Ogg stood at the Hub Control Room viewing window, watching as two space tugs pulled containers of raw materials to a loading dock near the newly enlarged double doors leading to Hub Sections A and B. It was midmorning Friday, and she had supervised all night as meckie and human workcrews enlarged the doors, tore out partition walls and removed work in progress to make room for assembly of the mass drivers.

It's going well so far, she thought, yawning as she stared at a box of sleep-sub pills on the console. A hunger pang shot across her midsection.

Mayor Nancy Ogg glanced to her left at a tap-tap-whirring sound, watched a floor-mounted electronic mail terminal spew out a letter. One of three electronic mail terminals, this unit was reserved for classified correspondence. A flashing blue light on the machine indicated it was a Priority One transmittal.

Gliding gracefully to the terminal, she tore the letter off and examined it.

From Dick, she thought angrily, reading the heading. *Well, I don't care to hear from him!* She rolled the letter into a ball and hurled it across the room.

Mayor Nancy Ogg returned to the viewing window, watched

through tear-glazed eyes as the space tugs released their containers on the loading platform and then left via the docking tunnel to retrieve additional containers.

She turned to stare at the ball of paper as it lay on the floor near the Control Room's bank of C.R.T. screens. *I'd better look at it. Duty before personal matters.*

She knew this was a rationalization. Actually, the personal aspect interested her more than any professional message the letter might contain.

Mayor Nancy Ogg unrolled the ball of paper and pulled at the sides to flatten crinkles. This is what she saw:

CONFIDENTIAL—FOR EYES ONLY
TO: HON. N. OGG, ST. ELBA MAYOR, L$_5$, EARTH QUADRANT
FROM: DR. R. HUDSON, BU-TECH MINISTER, NEW CITY, EARTH

HAVE M.D. SHELLS READY TUES NOON STED FOLL FRI—ASSIGN DISPENSABLE CAPPY CREWS TO FIN INT WORK IN FLIGHT.
PERSONAL—DO NOT REPEAT—EXTREME DANGER—KILLER MECKIE ON SH V. WILL SILENCE CREW AFTER MISSION.
KEEP PATIENCE. CHANGES SOON. TOLD YOUR BRO HE IS BIGOT.
LOVE YOU.—DICK

Mayor Nancy Ogg wiped tears from her cheeks, mentoed this response via the same terminal:

CONFIDENTIAL—EYES ONLY
TO: DR. R. HUDSON, BU-TECH MINISTER, NEW CITY, EARTH
FROM: HON. N. OGG, ST. ELBA MAYOR, L$_5$, EARTH QUADRANT

WILL DO BEST. AVOID CHANCES—WELCOME HERE IF MISSION ABORT.
BRING BIGOT WITH YOU. I FEEL SAME!—NANCY

*　　*　　*

Ninety-three years later, these electronic letters would be reprinted in a Sayers' history primer. . . .

Sayer Superior Lin-Ti held the volume after reading from it and gazed around the Great Temple ordinance room at young-sayermen who eagerly awaited the continuance of his reading.

It was late fall on the domed asteroid of Pleasant Reef, and through a tiny northeast window Lin-Ti could see golden brown leaves dropping one at a time from a gnarled old oak. Already, he had read the new history primer twice—so he knew what came next.

"I will skip the following section," Lin-Ti said, touching a button on the book to flip several pages. "Nothing of note occurred at the meeting demanded by the Alafin of Afrikari. He sent a projecto-image of himself to the oval office on the morning of Garbage Day minus seven. You can read details of the meeting if you wish on your own time. Suffice to say that President Ogg and the council ministers denied the projected Alafin's charge of a comet heading toward Earth along the same path as the AmFed deep space garbage shots. A malfunction of the Alafin's telescope was suggested."

Lin-Ti glanced up at the ceiling as he recalled the story: "A confrontation occurred during the meeting when a projecto-image of the Atheist Premier demanded inclusion in the meeting, fearful that the other two nations of Earth were plotting against him. His projection was permitted to enter. After learning of the alleged comet, the Premier made his customary complaints, alleging that the AmFeds had overcharged the Union of Atheist States for E-Cells. As usual, the Premier felt the AmFeds were sabotaging his nation's energy development programs for the purpose of keeping them economically captive. We will discuss the 'Economics of Freeness' next week. For the present, we will pick up our studies immediately after the meeting. . . ."

*   *   *

Hudson and Munoz moto-shoed across Technology Square after the meeting with the Alafin of Afrikari. Deep in thought, Hudson scarcely noticed bits of paper from the prior day's doomie demonstration which swirled in a gentle breeze at his feet. "Have you spoken with that officeworker yet?" Hudson asked. "What's his name?"

"Malloy. No. We're waiting for them to find Javik. The guy's a real carouser—we lost his trail at the pleasure domes."

Hudson focused upon the giant Uncle Rosy meckie perhaps twenty-five meters to his left, saw it rise and stand with its hands clasped in front. "It's time for the hourly address," Hudson said, slowing his shoes. He glanced right at the much smaller Munoz.

"Keep rolling," Munoz said irritably. "Another minute of horse—"

"Arturo!" Hudson rasped in a low tone, catching Munoz by the arm. "Remember appearances!"

General Munoz scowled, stopped reluctantly with Hudson to watch the meckie. The meckie spoke loudly in the kindly voice of Uncle Rosy, recorded three centuries earlier:

"Right living means consumption, citizens. It means buying and using the fruits of another person's labor. As you use what another man has wrought, keep in mind that he also uses what you have wrought. This is a wonderfully balanced system, but it depends upon YOU."

With these words, the meckie pointed a bulky forefinger down at the people who stood in the square. It closed with an appeal for all to report shirkers to the Anti-Cheapness League, then resumed its seat.

"I'm skeptical about the comet intercept plan," Hudson said, glancing down at Munoz. "Two mass drivers with fire probes on each side of the nucleus, attempting to shift a comet's direction. . . ."

"We've done it before," Munoz replied, staring at the Uncle Rosy meckie. He resumed moto-shoeing. Hudson fell in at his side.

"Sure," Hudson said, "In the lab and on seventeen small comets that followed predictable courses. But this thing's huge and jumps all over the place. I wouldn't bet on it being co-operative."

Munoz shook his head. "You're a chronic worrier, Dick. Comp six-oh-two worked it all out."

"A computer. We know why the six-oh-one was scrapped."

"Uh huh," Munoz said, rolling around a pebble. "The trajectory error on our garbage shots. But we don't know for sure that this error caused a pile of junk to come back at us. We used it as an excuse."

"And don't forget the E.T.A. miscalculation by the Willys computer," Hudson said ominously.

"Freaky errors that will never happen again. The odds have to be in our favor now."

"You're an expert on odds, Arturo . . . at the Knave Table. But this is no card game."

"I have a feeling," Munoz said. "Call it the intuition of a winner."

Hudson rubbed an itchy eyelid and fixed his gaze with the other eye on a woman in a red taffeta dress who stood in the motopath ahead feeding pigeons from a package of vendo-crumbs. "I wish to hell we had more time to figure this out," Hudson said. "Everything's too damned rushed."

"I agree with you there."

"Consider this, Arturo. We know a great deal . . . can control voting patterns, even the world's weather and economy. But stop to think. What *don't* we know?"

"I don't see what you're driving at."

"Start with the comet—and those strange voices that give you commands."

"Commands?" Munoz said, haughtily.

"Suggestions, then."

"It's true we don't know the comet's origin," Munoz said, slowing to roll around the woman in the red dress.

Hudson followed, again falling in at the General's side. "Or why it follows an erratic path," Hudson said.

They looked up at the sound of thumping rotors, watched an auto-heliwagon as it landed in front of the new Bu-Industry Tower several hundred meters ahead of them. "More security monitors from the Black Box of Democracy," Munoz said.

"How do they work?" Hudson asked. All we know is that they come from the Black Box and are required at the entrances to all buildings."

"You're the scientific whiz," Munoz said, scornfully. Penetrate the Black Box . . . or get one of those monitors into your lab."

"One doesn't go about tearing into Uncle Rosy's creations indiscriminately. They're sacred, you know."

Munoz spit on a plastic petunia garden beside the motopath. That's what I think of Uncle Rosy," he said.

Dr. Hudson glanced around nervously. "You shouldn't do that," he said in a low tone.

"You told me they use indoor surveillance units the size of a pin tip," Munoz said. "If that's true, I can say anything I please outside!"

"I said I *thought* they were doing it that way. I have no proof! A beam might be trained on us right now, picking up every word. We don't know how it's being done."

"Or IF it's being done. This whole Black Box thing smacks of bluffery to me."

The card game expert again . . ."

"Well, find out, dammit! You can check anyplace for bugging equipment . . . on the premise that an enemy of the state might have put it there."

"We shouldn't talk this way," Dr. Hudson said. He rolled along silently, and as he watched, four security monitor units slid off the rear of the heliwagon and rolled to positions at the building entrances. Dr. Hudson glanced at Munoz and mentoed: *We've taken hundreds of specks to the lab. All have turned out to be paint or dirt. They could color the micro-units to match any paint color . . . and with today's signal camouflage technology. . . .*

"Jesus!" Munoz said.

Hudson glared down at him, mentoed: *And add Uncle Rosy's disappearance to the list.*

"Suicide," Munoz said. He picked up Hudson's glare, mentoed reluctantly to finish his statement: *He didn't want to grow old; he arranged for someone to hide the body.*

Maybe, Hudson mentoed. *And maybe not.*

They took a narrow side motopath toward the Bu-Mil and Bu-Tech towers, watched through widely spaced plastic poplar trees as two men in brown friar robes touched a security monitor unit and then raised their hands heavenward.

Hudson shook his head, looked away. He had seen the ceremony many times and had no idea what it meant.

"They don't speak," Munoz said, feeling his words were safe. "Rumor has it they're mute."

"Impossible," Hudson said. "Uncle Rosy would never permit cappies to remain on Earth."

Munoz picked at a front tooth with his forefinger. He nodded without saying anything.

They watched as the robed men rolled up a ramp to enter the heliwagon. When the men were inside, the heliwagon rose swiftly into the air, banked and flew off in the direction of the Black Box of Democracy.

Moments later, Dr. Hudson rolled alone up an entrance ramp to the Bu-Tech Tower. He pressed his palm against the electronic security monitor's black glass identity plate, mentoed: *G.W. one, Dr. Richard Hudson, Bu-Tech Minister.*

He felt a strong vacuum against his hand. Then it released, and a red light on the monitor turned to green.

As Dr. Hudson stood at the security monitor, two sayermen wearing brown-hooded robes rose above Technology Square in a pilotless heliwagon. Onesayer Edward squinted in sunlight from the east, extended his left hand to Lastsayer Steven, who sat to his right. "Peace be upon you," Onesayer said, raising his voice over the thump of rotors.

Lastsayer touched his brown-and-gold onyx ring to a like ring worn by the other man, coughed and replied, "Peace be upon you, Onesayer. Thank you for instructing me in the Holy Order." Again, he coughed.

"Nasty cough," Onesayer observed.

"Felt it coming on yesterday," Lastsayer sniffed, looking at Onesayer's wide, puffy-fat face. "I have been tired since arrival."

"Rocket lag. I see it all the time." Onesayer reached into his robe pocket, removed a chrome pillbox. He selected two yellow pills and handed them to Lastsayer. "Take a Happy Pill and a water capsule," Onesayer instructed. "You'll . . . uh . . . you will feel better." *My speech,* Onesayer thought. *It slips into apostrophes . . . another sign of my break with the Master. . . .*

Onesayer watched the younger man hesitate and then accept the pills. Lastsayer had clear, wrinkle-free skin, like that of all sayermen. Moderately plump, he had an upturned nose and light green eyes that darted nervous glances around the edge of his hood. *He looks so innocent,* Onesayer thought, recalling a time nearly three centuries earlier when he had been t..e same way.

Lastsayer held the pills in an open palm, looked at them inquisitively. "These are allowed?" he asked. "I have heard—"

"They are not *allowed,*" Onesayer said, "but take them anyway." He smiled, adding, "We do not take many of them, you understand . . . maybe seven or eight a day. You never had one?"

Lastsayer smiled nervously, coughed again. "No, but I see no harm . . . if you approve." He popped the pills in his mouth and swallowed them.

"How are things on Pleasant Reef?" Onesayer asked.

"In turmoil. Our women have demonstrated the past two weeks. Can you imagine? They demand positions in the Sayerhood!"

"They share the Sayerhood now!" Onesayer said angrily. "Is it not enough for them to raise the youngsayermen of our order?"

"Apparently not." Lastsayer gazed out the window, saw a white Product Failure van speeding along the expressway below, red lights flashing. He was unable to hear the sirens over the thump of rotors.

"And Sayer Superior Lin-Ti . . . He is well?"

"Yes. He spent countless hours tutoring me."

"Your tutelage is far from complete. Uncle Rosy even reminds *me* that I have much to learn."

Lastsayer nodded. Presently he said, "I saw the Uncle Rosy meckie on its feet as we landed."

"A message on right living."

"The history primer told me of this, Onesayer. The meckie holds a cross and a machine gear, and I was taught the significance of these symbols."

Onesayer looked out the window, saw the Black Box of Democracy two blocks to the right. Feeling a need to say the correct things, he said, "You studied the near civil war between the Christian Church and the technologists, I presume?"

"Yes," Lastsayer said. "Two armed camps . . . bitter feelings. . . ."

"Over petty matters, as the Master pointed out at the time. He brought the adversaries together."

"By protecting the economic base of each side," Lastsayer said, demonstrating his knowledge. "In the end, it all boiled down to economics, with each side wanting more followers and more property."

"It is good that you paid attention to your lessons. That is why you were selected for Earth duty." Onesayer watched another heliwagon prepare to take off from the roof of the Black Box while their craft circled half a block away, waiting for clearance.

"Thank you, Onesayer. But it is more than the text which interests me now."

"How so?"

"A story was told to me on Pleasant Reef . . . by one of the child-bearing women . . . that Uncle Rosy met with the Christian cardinals privately after the truce."

"What did you hear about that?" Onesayer snapped, realizing the emotion of his response was more automatic than real.

"That Uncle Rosy attempted to convince the cardinals to give up the cross symbol . . . in favor of a human brain design. According to the story, Uncle Rosy felt the brain—as a miraculous and basically mysterious entity—was a more proper symbol of the universal God."

Onesayer scowled, glared out the window. Presently he said, "Uncle Rosy is a complex man, at once a great economist and a man of the cloth. What you heard is true, but this was not supposed to be mentioned on Pleasant Reef."

"I will give you the name of the woman."

"Good. The Master prefers to tell that story himself." *I don't really care about this*, Onesayer thought. *Let Uncle Rosy's whole damned system fall into disarray.*

"I did not know," Lastsayer said.

"Act as if you are not familiar with the story when the Master relates it to you."

"Yes, Onesayer."

"The cardinals were a stubborn lot, Lastsayer, and became extremely upset at Uncle Rosy's suggestion. Our Master decided to back down upon seeing their reaction, fearful that he might upset the delicate truce."

"Thank you for telling me this."

"You have an alert mind, Lastsayer. I like that."

Lastsayer Steven did not respond. He watched the other heliwagon take off. Their craft began to descend.

"Symbolism is very important, Lastsayer. Tragically, the cross Uncle Rosy's meckie holds may have led to the Holy War of twenty-three-twenty-six." *Another of the Master's errors*, Onesayer thought.

Lastsayer's green eyes flashed intently. "How is that?" he asked.

"As you know, the first Council of Ten was formed in the negotiations between Uncle Rosy, the scientists and the cardinals."

"I know: equal input from the cardinals and the scientists. But that was formed seven years before Uncle Rosy withdrew to the Black Box."

"Correct. After Uncle Rosy's withdrawal in twenty-three eighteen, a popular movement fanned by Cardinal John of

Atlantic City and other Christian zealots demanded a holy war against all other religions. They said the cross held by Uncle Rosy was a sign of approval from the Master."

"I was not aware of that," Lastsayer said, watching the glassite roof the Black Box grow closer while their craft descended. "Did Uncle Rosy approve, considering his feelings about a universal, rather than a Christian, God?"

"Uncle Rosy has always been torn between religious and economic issues. He likes to say economic considerations are more important...."

"But you are not so certain?"

"I too have much to learn."

Lastsayer thought he heard bitterness in the other man's tone. He thought for a moment, then said: "Should Uncle Rosy have stepped in *before* the holy war started? I mean no disrespect."

"He wanted to give the AmFeds free reign, except in the case of a government overthrow attempt. He did not wish to meddle too much, but when he saw the destruction being caused by AmFed bombs..." Onesayer fell silent. Dust swirled on the rooftop from the wind of the helirotors.

"He saw the economic futility of destroying foreign markets," Lastsayer said. "That would have put millions of AmFeds out of work!"

Onesayer sighed. "The AmFeds became so emotional over their holy war that they forgot about economics entirely."

"So the Master intervened, with you as emissary. Sayer Superior told me of your important role."

The heliwagon jolted as it landed.

A smile moved across Onesayer's large mouth. "I merely delivered a written bull to the Council of Ten reminding them of their economic responsibilities," he said. "I did not speak a word to them, of course. We are not permitted to address common people."

"The bull spoke of the Principle of Economic Captivity, I presume," Lastsayer said. He heard the heliwagon's engines begin to whine down.

"Yes," Onesayer said. Their safety harnesses snapped off automatically. He placed a hand on the front of each armrest. "The bull also specified that three nations would be established on Earth... the American Federation of Freeness, Afrikari and the Union of Atheist States. In its public version, this became known as the Treaty of Rabat. It survives to this day."

"Christian, pagan and atheist." Lastsayer pursed his lips thoughtfully. He rose when Onesayer did, added, "What a great man the Master is! I look forward to my first session with him!"

Onesayer led the way down the aisle, said with a turn of his hooded head to throw words over one shoulder: "You will never see his face, of course. No one has, since he entered the Black Box."

"Oh, but just to be near him. The thrill of it!"

Onesayer nodded as he rolled onto an exit ramp, recalling a time long before when he had felt the same way.

Sidney turned sleepily in bed, throwing one arm over a rubber-skinned pleasie-meckie that lay beside him. "Carla," he whispered in an awakening haze, "I love you, Carla."

His eyes popped open, and when he became aware of reality, Sidney cursed at his misfortune. He pushed the meckie away.

The naked pleasie-meckie had fine-toned muscles like Carla's, with an aquiline nose and shoulder-length, golden-brown hair.

Sidney mentoed it to life. *Away*, he commanded tersely. *Return to your station.*

Obediently, the pleasie-meckie rose and dressed quickly in undergarments which lay in disarray on the floor. Then, as Sidney watched, it rolled into the closet and took a standing position to one side. He turned away, stared at the spray-textured ceiling. Sidney heard rustling in the closet for several moments. Then the meckie closed the closet door and Sidney was left alone.

He stretched and yawned. As usual, it was late morning when he awakened, and Sidney could see synthetic sunlight through the open doorway of the bathroom module. Moments later, he stood naked from the waist up at a grooming machine in the bathroom.

The tiny modular room was warm and cheerful, with a planterbox of plastic marigolds along one wall beneath a sun-lite panel. White synthetic light from the panel warmed his left side.

Thinking about his strange space dream of the night before and of the haunting, recurring voices, Sidney waited while an electric shaver at the end of a right-handed meckie-arm trimmed the stubble off his face. The U-shaped grooming machine,

Sidney's height overall, peered back at him with its mirror face between seeing-eye meckie-arms on each side. An array of brightly colored buttons above the machine's sink could be mento- or hand-activated. Gold lettering across the top of the mirror proclaimed: "UNCLE ROSY LOVES US."

Sidney turned his face to one side when the shave was finished, trying to find a better angle in the mirror. This made his ears seem to protrude less, but the pug nose looked worse. He sighed, wondered sadly, *Why can't I be better looking? I'm not even average!*

The meckie-arms took Lemon Delight Shaving Lotion from a dispenser next to the mirror and patted Sidney's face. The lotion stung; his eyes watered. Sidney always resented mechanical grooming, but held up his arms cooperatively while deodorant spray was pumped all over his pear-shaped torso.

In the next grooming maneuver, Sidney knew he had to be careful. He watched with trepidation as the left meckie-arm grasped a toothbrush and took on a load of Shiny Bright Toothpaste from a wall dispenser. A smiling picture of President Ogg looked back at Sidney from the dispenser with a message printed across perfectly even, sparkling white teeth: "VOTE FOR OGG."

The toothbrush darted into Sidney's open mouth and surge-scrubbed every tooth. Several times recently, not paying sufficient attention, Sidney had failed to open his mouth. The disastrous result: sticky white paste rubbed all over his nose and chin. *Not this time*, he told himself. The meckie finished with an automatic rinse, gargle, face wash and set of Sidney's curly black hair, all accomplished without strangling, drenching or costing him the loss of any hair.

After breakfast, Sidney moto-shoed across his small condominium unit to the living room module. This too was a cheerful room, despite the location of Sidney's unit at the building core where it could not receive natural light. Bright splashes of gold and orange washed furnishings and walls with color. An orange, plastic-encased videodome dominated the room's center, directly beneath a ceiling-mounted sun-lite panel.

He rolled past the videodome, pausing in front of a wall decorated with a gold and black checkerboard design. Concentrating upon one of the squares, he mentoed an unseen combination dial and heard the click of tumblers as he projected each number. The square slid away, revealing a lighted wallsafe filled with leatherbound scrapbooks and an assortment of personal treasures. He selected two volumes and an old-style pen, went with them to the couch.

Sidney sat down pensively, stacked both volumes on the coffee table and opened the cover of the top one slowly. A handwritten title had been scrawled across the yellowing first page in large, childish script:

MY PILOT LOG, VOLUME ONE

Property of Captain Sidney Malloy
American Federation Space Patrol

He turned the page, read his fantasy: "I joined the Space Patrol as a lad of ten, assuming the duties of cabin boy on the Star Class Destroyer AFSP Nathan Rogers. Within six months, my leadership abilities became so apparent that I was promoted to Captain and given command of the ship."

He looked away, smiling as he thought, *Did I really write this?*

Sidney continued reading: "My first assignment: seek and recapture the escaped arch-criminal Jed Laredo. Laredo is wanted for detonating a powerful ice bomb following his escape from the asteroid colony at LaGrange Six. Twelve-thousand inhabitants perished in the explosion. He is believed to be hiding near an abandoned mining base at Agarratown on the Celtian planet of Redondo. . . ."

He flipped the ensuing pilot log pages, read the successful and heroic conclusion of his fantasy mission. Other fantasies followed, entered meticulously beside blueprints and specifications on a variety of spacecraft.

In one sense, the space scrapbooks seemed childish to him now, but still he felt the longings he had experienced as a youth. The exploits were not real . . . he had always known this . . . but the adventures contained a spirit of hope . . . a certain innocence and naiveté concerning his future. This morning, as he prepared to write about his confused ego pleasure dream of the prior evening, Sidney still had hope . . . but it was not so bright and untarnished as it once had been.

He sighed, placed Volume One to one side and opened the next scrapbook, his fourteenth. Flipping to a blank page, he began writing: "While patrolling the Signus XX-4 Quadrant in the Summer of 2605, I received urgent word...."

How can I get this down? he wondered, rubbing the pen thoughtfully against his lower lip. *Those strange, maddening voices....*

Interrupted by the doorchime, Sidney mentoed his new singing wrist digital. A sultry female voice sang to him cheerfully in a sing-song tone: "A.M., ten-forty-one-point-three-four."

Wonder who's there? he thought, welcoming the interruption. He replaced the volumes in the wallsafe and resealed the panel.

As Sidney opened the hall door, Bob Hodges, his tall and thickly-muscled downstairs neighbor, rolled in without an invitation. "Hi Sid," he said cheerily. "How ya doin'?" Hodges was puppy-friendly, thoughtless but well-meaning.

Sidney regrouped his thoughts and returned the greeting. Then he led the way down a woodgrain linoleum hallway to the living room module.

"How about a little video?" Hodges asked, seeing the videodome as they entered the room.

Sidney grunted in affirmation, rolled directly into the videodome without another thought and sat in his favorite bucket seat, one of four inside. He sank into the videodome chair, consumed by the billowing softness of authentic Corinthian vinyl. Mentoing a channel selector to the left of his seat, Sidney watched a green button on the selector depress.

"Have to make sure you watch enough home video," Hodges said, laughing. "Hear you had a recent visit from those folks at the Anti-Cheapness League."

Sidney heard the videodome door slide shut. An overhead light dimmed. "It was nothing," he answered matter-of-factly. "They were investigating a faulty videodome report. Someone did a line test seconds after one of my dome circuits blew. With no repair order in on my set, they were concerned that it might have been down for several days."

"Oh," Hodges said. "No big deal."

"Naw. I gave them details on the video programs I'd been watching before the blowout, signed their form and they left." Sidney mentoed channel forty-seven on the selector.

Sidney watched three-dimensional screens all around light up, giving viewers the illusion of being seated in a crowded auditorium. People chattered at nearby seats, and Sidney made out details of their conversations.

"Jimmy Earl is next," a young man in the crowd said, "with the latest from Rok-More. Then the Mister Sugar Follies."

"How exciting!" a woman in a fur coat said.

Spotlighted at center stage, a man in a white sequin Western outfit spoke excitedly into a handheld microphone. "The latest from Rok-More Records!" he said, waving an arm to his rear toward a mini-stage containing a spotlighted record cube display. "Donna Butler's in the Happy Shopping Ground, folks, but her songs will never die! Supplies are limited, so order 'Donna's Greatest Hits' now! As a bonus for those of you in our home video audience, I'll throw in this delightful little 'Heart of Gold' pendant." He held the pendant up, added in a voice grown suddenly tender, "Donna's signature is on the back, folks. Won't you pledge your undying love for Donna? Order now!"

The audience auto-clapped and cheered as a product number appeared on a sign above the record cube display. Sidney felt a chill in his spine from the patriotism of the moment, and mentoed the number into a Tele-Charge board that was connected to an arm of his chair. He signed the board with a transmitting pen, noting that Hodges was doing the same.

With glazed eyes, Sidney watched the Mister Sugar Follies now, a group of twelve men clad in blue-and-white soft drink cans. After an explanation by one that they were permitted to expend energy since it was Job-Supportive, the men danced stiffly in a row like tin dolls to a twangy tune. As they kicked their feet in near unison, Sidney noticed his throat gone dry. The subliminal receiver in his brain had been activated.

"You thirsty?" he asked, glancing at Hodges.

"And how!" came the reply. "Feel like I'm out in the desert!"

Sidney mentoed for drinks, and presently two frosty cans of Mr. Sugar popped out of a table compartment between their chairs.

As Sidney drank the icy cola, an unbearable itching sensation took over his body.

"Quickly!" Hodges said, feeling the same thing. "Mento for your Itcho-Spray! The commercial's on!"

Sidney had barely noticed the Itcho-Spray Man on stage, and he quickly mentoed for the product.

"You DO have some on hand?" Hodges asked, near panic.

"Certainly. But I think . . . I'm going to have to scratch—"

"Don't do it! You have to use the product! Hang tough, man! Hang tough!"

"Aaaagh!" Sidney grunted, fighting an overwhelming urge to claw his back, chest and legs.

A white ball of Itcho-Spray popped out of the table compartment and floated in the air above their heads. It exploded in a little "pop," showering them with clear liquid droplets.

They sighed in unison as the itching crisis subsided.

"Relief is just an Itcho-Spray away!" the Itcho-Spray Man said.

The spotlight shifted to a smiling President Ogg now, who stood at a podium bearing the Great Seal of the President of the American Federation of Freeness. Sidney felt the videodome vibrate as the crowd auto-clapped and roared its approval.

"Employment and consumption are at record levels under my administration!" the President boomed. "A vote for me is a vote for prosperity!" He delivered a short speech concerning his past accomplishments and promises for the future, then short-stepped to one side of the podium and bowed. He blew kisses and waved as the curtain closed.

"Who you gonna vote for?" Hodges asked, leaning toward Sidney to be heard over the crowd noise.

"I don't know," Sidney replied. "Probably Ogg again. Ben Morgan may be all right, but we don't know much about him."

"Better the evil that we do know?"

Sidney laughed.

"Think I'll go with a punch-in this time," Hodges said. "I like General Munoz."

Hodges's last words seemed exceedingly loud to Sidney, as the crowd noises had subsided quickly. Another commercial was onstage now, a chorus line of dancing soap bubbles selling laundry detergent. "But I've heard he isn't interested," Sidney said.

"Maybe not," Hodges concurred, shrugging his shoulders. "But I have to vote my conscience. It came to me last night like an inspiration. I'm convinced he's the only man for the job."

Sidney glanced at his wrist digital, mentoed it to activate the sexy-voiced time singer. She reported that it was eleven twenty-nine. "Time to get ready for work," Sidney said.

* * *

Another holy water break approached. Before dismissing the class, Sayer Superior Lin-Ti explained the mechanics of the subliminal transmitting device:

"Following Dr. Hudson's instructions, General Munoz established the vote percentile he desired. One-hundred percent would be too obvious, of course, so he chose something more reasonable—around fifty-seven percent. Then he touched the cross with both hands instead of the one-hand method used for weather control. While touching the cross, Munoz transmitted his auto-suggestion.

"This caused a powerful beam to enter the brains of millions of AmFed consumers, tapping their subliminal receivers and forcing them to vote as the General wished. To reinforce the auto-suggestion, he re-broadcast several times a day in the days preceding the election. . . .

* * *

"This is much more than a room," Onesayer Edward said as he and Lastsayer Steven rolled into the Bureau Monitoring Room at a little past one o'clock Friday afternoon. "Actually, it takes up the entire second floor of the Black Box."

"Most impressive," Lastsayer said. He looked around the room curiously, watched sayermen scurrying about with microcomputer printouts. Other sayermen sat on high stools at consoles along each wall, operating C.R.T. screens, minicam receivers and computerized memory terminals. A background hum of pink sound muffled most of the noises, making the room seem relatively quiet.

"You are versed in Rosetran, I presume?" Onesayer asked.

"I know fifteen computer languages," Lastsayer said, gazing up with light green eyes at a large "Keep the Faith" sign on one wall beneath a sun-lite panel.

"You will begin at Station Five," Onesayer said, nodding toward a workstation along the wall to their left. A large red Arabic numeral "5" on the wall marked the station. He looked down at the smaller Lastsayer, saw him nod.

"This is a highly efficient operation," Onesayer said as he led the way to Station Five. "We accomplish a great deal with very few sayermen. Sophisticated machines do most of the work. Sayermen scrutinize problem areas flagged by the machines."

Lastsayer noticed it was a bit warm in the room, and said, "I believe I am familiar with everything here. We had a mockup on Pleasant Reef."

One of two stools at Station Five was occupied by a hooded sayerman who sat with his back to them mentoing entries on a console keyboard. The keys moved up and down without being touched. Onesayer and Lastsayer stopped a meter behind the occupied stool, continuing their conversation.

"Every citizen of the American Federation works for the government," Onesayer said. "So they regularly pass through our electronic security monitors. There, cell readers pick up every memory in their lifetimes. . . ." He paused at Lastsayer and smiled broadly. "I am sorry. You did mention being familiar with everything."

Lastsayer smiled in return, nodded confidently.

"You understand the drawback of the electronic monitors, do you not?" Onesayer asked.

"The delay factor. Citizens who do not pass through the cell reader for a time have a gap in their lifelog files."

"Right. This gap can range from a few hours to several days. Even today, people stay home sick with common colds."

Lastsayer looked at Onesayer closely, noted a red streak in the corner of one eye. "Odd is it not, Onesayer Edward? All the terrible diseases modern medicine can cure, but the common cold remains a mystery."

The sayerman on the stool turned abruptly at the mention of Onesayer's name, looked startled. "Oh!" he exclaimed, nearly falling off his stool in an effort to stand up. "I did not see you there, sir!"

"Quite all right, Ninesayer," Onesayer said.

Ninesayer stood up straight to face Onesayer and extended his left hand. Onesayer and Lastsayer extended their hands as well, and the three men touched class rings, murmuring in unison, "Peace be upon you."

Ninesayer had large, loose cheeks and tiny blue eyes which peered back at Lastsayer from beneath an oversized hood. He seemed a friendly sort, and smiled pleasantly while Onesayer introduced them.

"Lastsayer will be working with you," Onesayer said.

"I could use some assistance," Ninesayer said, glancing at his battery of electronic equipment. "We have two rather large problems at the moment."

"I had not heard," Lastsayer said, wrinkling his brow in concern. "Life on Pleasant Reef is rather sheltered."

Onesayer explained about the garbage comet and told of the plot to overthrow the AmFed government. Then he turned to Ninesayer and said, "Show us General Munoz. He worries me."

Ninesayer nodded, mentoed Munoz's consumer identification number. A darkened minicam screen on the wall flickered on, revealing General Munoz seated alone at his desk. Munoz rubbed the cross which dangled from his neck with both hands, smiled craftily.

"Run the tape back five minutes," Onesayer instructed. "Let us see what he has been up to."

Ninesayer mentoed the machine, causing the tape to roll back.

"All right," Onesayer said. "Hold it right there!"

The sayerman watched as General Munoz closed his eyes and held both hands to the cross. An intense expression came over the General's mustachioed face, and he sat motionless for perhaps a minute.

"He is using the subliminal transmitter again!" Onesayer said excitedly, "making voters punch in his name for President!"

"We obtained details on its operation from C.M. . . .uh, from cell memory readings on his co-conspirator, Dr. Richard Hudson," Ninesayer explained, glancing at Lastsayer. "Munoz's first broadcast occurred last night."

"You can use the term 'C.M.R.' around me," Lastsayer said.

"Munoz is power-mad," Onesayer said, "and has access to dangerous technology. According to his C.M.R., he intends to destroy Afrikari and the Union of Atheist States with earthquakes and other . . . 'natural' . . . disasters the minute he feels he can get away with it."

"Without regard for the economic havoc it will cause to the AmFeds?" Lastsayer exclaimed. "Hoovervilles will spring up all over the landscape!"

"The man is extremely dangerous," Onesayer said, closing his olive eyes momentarily in abhorrence. "Eighth generation radical Christian."

"A direct descendent of Cardinal John of Atlantic City," Ninesayer said.

"And the last in his line," Onesayer said. His words were measured and angry.

"Homosexual," Ninesayer explained, glancing at Lastsayer.

"Oh," Lastsayer said.

"And . . . he will be dead within seventy-two hours," Onesayer said. "Uncle Rosy has placed a contract on him. It will be a nasty accident."

"Product failure?" Lastsayer asked.

"Of course!" Onesayer said, smiling. "Uncle Rosy never misses an opportunity to help the economy!"

*   *   *

It was early morning on Pleasant Reef, following the daily prayer to Uncle Rosy, and Sayer Superior Lin-Ti stood considering the lesson. A youngsayerman entered the ordinance room late, taking his seat sheepishly under the glare of Lin-Ti. It was the tall, fat one whose appearance was so reminiscent of Onesayer Edward. Lin-Ti scowled at the offender, then opened his history primer, removing a bookmark ribbon. . . .

FOUR

BACKGROUND MATERIAL, FOR
FURTHER READING AND DISCUSSION

Dr. Hudson: "I started where Uncle Rosy left off, so the mento transmitter is as much a credit to him as it is to me. Uncle Rosy was a brilliant man of science, you know. He made many pioneering discoveries in the area of thought-transmission for the purpose of operating consumer products."

Student: "Uncle Rosy was motivated by economics, was he not, Doctor Hudson?"

Dr. Hudson: "Mentoing and increased consumption go hand in hand. But in reviewing copies of his lab diaries, I detected a reverence for the mysteries of the brain. Listen to this excerpt: [after pause] 'Our technology cannot begin to approach the beauty, the precision, the wonderful balance of the human brain.'"

Minicam transcript from Dr. Hudson's Boston College class-

room, October 8, 2587 (six months
prior to Hudson's appointment as
Bu-Tech Minister).

Saturday, August 26, 2605

Garbage day minus six arrived without Sidney's knowledge.
Understandably, this information was kept on a "need-to-know"
basis.

Sidney awoke early in the morning to a jangling telephone
next to his bed. When he opened his eyes sleepily, a cordless
tele-cube floated in the air above his face. Carla was on the
line, announcing she could not make it to the reunion. Her
doctor had diagnosed a virus.

"Why don't you take two Happy Pills?" Sidney suggested
as he stared up at the cube. He brushed a lock of hair out of
his eyes. "Maybe you'll feel well enough to—"

"I don't want any more pills for awhile," Carla's tele-cube
voice said firmly. "I need rest."

"There are sleep-sub—"

"Real rest," she interjected.

This sounded strange to Sidney. He could not recall a day
when she did not take a pill. But he decided not to argue.

"Goodbye," Carla said.

Sidney watched the tele-cube float back to its cradle on the
phone, thought, *Our relationship stinks!*

He and Carla had known each other nearly all their lives.
Their parents had been close friends, and he had been her
datemate since high school. But Carla always seemed to treat
him more like a brother than a boyfriend . . . and there had never
been any physical intimacy. Sidney had been counting on the
reunion to put their relationship on a new track. He had planned
it all out. *I was going to be so suave and sophisticated*, Sidney
thought.

He felt his entire body shaking. *I mustn't become upset*, he
thought. Sidney closed his eyes and lay back on the bed, recalling his father's exact words, spoken so many years earlier. . . .

". . . It is absolutely imperative that you remain calm. The
incorto injector I have surgically implanted in your body is not
available to the public."

"I have the only one?" the nine-year-old Sidney had asked.

His father had nodded. "Its development was ordered stopped many years ago as a Bu-Med Job-Support measure. The device has not been perfected."

"Why not?"

"The injector has a major deficiency. Its operation can be blocked if your adrenalin level rises too much. This would result in a massive breakdown of your nervous system. . . ."

Sidney sat up on one elbow and as he recalled the conversation he gazed at a picture of his father on the dresser. A glint of synthetic sunlight touched the shiny gold electroplate frame and reflected off the polished plastic surface of the dresser top. He saw the same eyes and nose as his own, but the features were not so soft as Sidney's. His father smiled faintly in the picture, but there was deep concern in the eyes . . . possibly a fear of what the world had in store for Sidney.

I don't want a massive breakdown, Sidney thought.

Unable to return to sleep, he lay back and watched artificial dawn sunlight filter into his bedroom module through a single overhead sun-lite panel. He longed for the mercy of slumber. How attractive to remain there and not face the world! Like a whirligig, this thought rotated in his mind. But then he recalled the strange voices which had interrupted his ego pleasure dream two nights before. *When will they come again?* he wondered.

Old thoughts mixed with new ones. *I wish I had a dashing career in the Space Patrol,* he thought. *Carla would be my permie then.* This brought on a disturbing realization, as it occurred to him that his latent disability was the key to all his problems. If not for the affliction, life could have been so perfect!

In his despondency and anger, Sidney mentoed for his pleasie-meckie. The closet door popped open, and the scantily-clad meckie began to roll forward. But Sidney felt an inexplicable surge of guilt and resolved to overcome his sexual cravings.

Get back! he mentoed angrily.

After the pleasie-meckie returned to its closet station, Sidney lay in bed thinking and wishing for the rest of the morning. During several moments, he even found himself questioning the AmFed Way . . . for the first time in his life. Maybe his disability was not to blame after all. Maybe it was the system.

I can function in society! he thought, tormented. *But the system won't allow it, won't give me the opportunity!*

Eventually he discarded such thoughts, trying to see the

good side of things. For deep inside, Sidney Malloy believed in the AmFed Way. And in the Doctrine of Greatest Good.

When Sidney finally arose, he felt numb and more down than up. Thinking of the voices and of his depressed state, he considered going to a drive-in psychiatrist's window. But he discarded the idea in favor of a Happy Pill. There had been rumors that the psychiatric windows actually were fronts for therapy recruitment, that the resident analyst could declare anyone incompetent and have him sent to a therapy orbiter.

People had been known to disappear.

He felt better after the pill, and kept himself busy that afternoon inside the videodome. The dome was a room-within-a-room, a place where reality could be forgotten. Sidney Tele-Charged several products that were advertised on the screen. He felt better with each purchase.

Early in the evening of the same day, Sidney rolled off the elevator at Parking Level One wearing a black paper tuxedo with no hat. He unlocked the autosedan door with its plastikey and slid into a bucket seat which swiveled invitingly to meet him. The seat clicked into place as the door closed. A shoulder harness snapped shut across his body. Dashboard dials lit up . . . green, red and blue.

Sidney mentoed a destination into the car's computer, felt cool vinyl against his paper clothing as he sat back in the soft seat. The vehicle's sexless computer voice blared, its tone high-pitched and irritating to him: "Destination . . . Sky Ballroom . . . thirty-nine twelve American Boulevard. . . . Confirm please. . . ."

Sidney did not hear the instruction, was thinking about the reunion and about Carla.

"Confirm please. . . ." the computer insisted. "Confirm please. . . ."

"Yes, yes," Sidney said irritably, sitting forward and focusing his eyes on a red "CONFIRM" light that blinked rapidly on the dashboard. "Confirmed."

The autosedan began to move, and Sidney again sat back. It darted up a ramp to street level and surged unhesitatingly through automatic doors, its collision sensors probing the darkness ahead.

Minutes later, he moto-shoed off an elevator at the entrance to the Sky Ballroom. A gold and blue wall banner above a long reception table carried this announcement:

WELCOME NEW CITY HIGH GRADS! CLASS OF '85.

Sidney paused at the reception table, and in a moment was watching himself in the magik-mirror while a woman fastened a plastic nametag to his lapel. It was a full-length mirror, showing a reflection of the side of his body that was away from the glass. Sidney concealed his right hand from the mirror, held it behind his protruding stomach and wiggled the fingers. The image wiggled its fingers. When the woman finished fastening his nametag, Sidney faced the mirror and stuck out his tongue. It reflected only the back of his head and body, as if he were standing behind himself.

Sidney became aware of a fair-haired man in a Space Patrol uniform who stood along a side wall. The man seemed to be watching Sidney with pale, unfocused eyes, and Sidney recognized the eagle pin of a full colonel on his lapel. A nametag below that read: "PEEBLES."

Is he really looking at me? Sidney wondered. *Or at something else?* Sidney turned his head the other way, saw only a bare wall.

Sidney put the man out of his mind and rolled through double swinging doors into the main ballroom. There were happy crowd sounds in this room, and a band tuning its instruments. He searched for familiar faces.

It was a crystal clear night, with twinkling stars and a crescent sliver of moon which shone through an overhead glassplex dome. People played talking video games, electronic dice and galactic pool along one wall. Sidney paused to watch as a man he did not recognize auto-shot a ball into one of the side pockets of the galactic pool table. A wallscreen above the table lit up with brilliant flashes and sparks of orange and blue as the ball disappeared into the pocket.

"The synthetic black hole pockets are clever, don't you agree?" a man to Sidney's left asked. "They consume matter almost as voraciously as real ones."

Sidney turned toward the voice, nodded to a tall, amber-haired man in a white, long-sleeved Greco tunic. Trimmed in gold braid, the tunic had military epaulets and a Space Patrol crest on each sleeve. "Tried to bring back a real black hole one time," the man said, studying Sidney's round face closely. "Damn near killed me!"

"Is that right?" Sidney said, interested.

"Say," the man said, looking down at Sidney with an eyelid flicker of recognition, "aren't you Sidney Malloy?"

"Yeah. I am." Sidney noted the man had deeply-set blue eyes and a straight, sharp nose. The features were distantly familiar. Suddenly the identity jumped out at him. "Tom!" he said, half yelling with excitement. "You're Tom Javik!"

"How ya been, buddy?" Javik asked, embracing his old friend.

"All right," Sidney said as they pulled apart. "Who else is here tonight?"

"Just got in. Let's find a table."

They selected a window table. From his chair there, Sidney could see why this was called the Sky Ballroom. It "kissed the very boundary of the heavens," just as the advertisements had promised. New City stretched out below in all directions, "a sea of lights beneath a universe of stars."

A dance floor and slightly elevated stage occupied the center of the room. Above the floor a delicate aquamarine crystal chandelier seemed sky-suspended. Fifty-one musicians onstage tuned their guitars and practiced the hip gyrations they were allowed to perform.

"Whatcha been up to?" Javik asked. He rubbed an ingrown hair sore on the side of his neck.

"Not much. I'm a G.W. seven-five-oh in the Presidential Bureau. Central Forms. You're still in the Space Patrol, I see."

"Naw. I borrowed this tunic from a friend. I got in big trouble—had to take garbage shuttle duty in the Transport Corps." Javik wrinkled his nose angrily.

"At least you're flying," Sidney said, furrowing his dark eyebrows thoughtfully. "I'd trade places with you in a minute." Sidney studied a swiveling song request panel mounted at the table center. "They've got old tunes here," he said. "Remember the Space Boogie?"

"Hey hey!" Sidney detected sadness in Javik's tone. "How about the Gimme Gumbo Rock Waltz?" Javik asked.

Sidney searched the list, pointed. "Yeah. It's here."

Javik laughed and looked around. He squinted to look across the room, then pointed and said: "Near the wall. That guy in the blue tux is Jerry Sims!"

"Oh yeah," Sidney said, unenthused. "I didn't know him as well as you did." Sidney looked back at the song request panel, mentoed it to see another reader-card.

"Excuse me a minute, Sid," Javik said, rising to his feet. "I just want to say 'hello.'" He moto-shoed to the table and spoke with his friend for several minutes.

When Javik returned, he asked about Carla. Sidney thought of his pleasie-meckie which resembled Carla, and he smiled with some difficulty. "We're still datemates," he said. "She was supposed to be here tonight, but called and said she wasn't feeling well. Had a new dress picked out, too."

"Too bad." Javik's deeply-set blue eyes flashed mischievously. "Hey, we should have bought renta-dates for the night!"

"Naw," Sidney said, laughing. "Those girls giggle too much."

"Know what you mean."

Just then, a waitress in a striped black and yellow tigress outfit rolled over, flopping her pointed mechanical ears joyfully. "Good evening, gentlemen," she purred. "What would you like to have?"

Javik glanced at Sidney and winked, then replied, "Raspberry fizzle."

"Make it two," Sidney said. He studied her figure when she was not looking, then glanced at Javik and saw him wink back. They watched the waitress' long slinky tail drag behind her as she left.

"Know what I wanted to say to ask her for," Javik said, smiling as he locked gazes with Sidney.

Sidney smiled uneasily in return, watched Colonel Peebles slide into a seat several tables away. Peebles stared at Sidney with unfocused, glazed eyes.

"That guy over there," Sidney said, nodding his head to one side. "He seems to be staring at me."

Javik turned in the direction Sidney had designated, then quickly snapped back to look at Sidney. "Peebles," he hissed. "What's that bastard doing here? He wasn't in our class!"

Sidney shrugged, stared at the song request panel. "Where do you know him from?" he asked.

"The a-hole testified at my discharge proceedings. Made the Space Patrol toss me out on my butt. He's a fairy, you know, like the pretty-boy Major I punched out." Javik glanced around nervously.

Sidney did not ask for further details. The two men fell silent, then looked up at the stage where a man in a white tuxedo spoke into a microphone: "We are about to begin your program, grads! Make your song requests now. Keep in mind that musical performance is a Job-Support profession, and as such is exempt from the Conservation of Motion Doctrine. . . ."

As Sidney and Javik watched the program, Carla stood at her vanity mirror, thinking of Billie Birdbright.

Birdbright would arrive in a few minutes, and she pictured his handsome, bronzed face in her mind . . . the strong, dimpled chin and wavy, bright yellow hair . . . those playful, smoke-grey eyes. She used a small brush to paint a tiny black beauty mark on her left cheek, turned her face slightly to admire it from a different angle.

I have a right to be happy, Carla thought, thinking for a fleeting moment of Sidney as she placed the brush on her makeup table. *I couldn't be expected to pass this chance up.*

She sprayed perfume on her neck and practiced smiling in the vanity mirror. Carla saw moist lavender lips that matched the color of her eyes, bun-swirled golden-brown hair with a godiva fall and a black ruby clasp to one side. The evening dress was lavender mache, with the bodice cut in a long narrow vee, exposing portions of her bust and midriff. She pulled some of the fall hairs forward over each shoulder, and they cascaded over her breasts.

Carla moto-spun approvingly before the mirror. She knew she would be Birdbright's bedmate that evening just as the other girls had been. With this in mind, she selected every article of clothing and toiletry with care. A quiet time in the videodome watching a roller rock concert along with vi-do dinners and wine capsules would start the evening off well. . . .

The doorchime rang.

Oh! Carla thought with a start. *I'd better start dinner!*

She moto-hurried into the kitchen module and took two ceramic vi-do trays of porkchops with applesauce and synthetic baby peas from the freezer. She popped them into the micro-wave oven.

Sidney mentoed nine song request buttons, with instructions to run a tab in his name. The bandmembers began to perform, gyrating their hips wildly as they did a hard-driving rock song with an oboe lead.

"It's Space Boogie time!" Sidney exclaimed, thinking of Peebles but forcing himself not to look in that direction.

"Wouldja look at that!" Javik said excitedly, pointing at a man with short-cropped saffron yellow hair who was moto-shoeing down a nearby aisle. "Hey Bob!" Javik called out, waving his hands. "Over here!"

Javik turned to Sidney. "It's Bob Maxwell!"

Maxwell smiled as he saw them and rolled to their table. "Well!" he said in the old familiar husky voice. "You fellows are a welcome sight!" He pulled a chair from an adjacent unoccupied table and sat down.

They stack-clasped hands like schoolchums. It came naturally, as if there had not been twenty intervening years.

Sidney looked at Maxwell, noted a big man with tiny metallic blue eyes, a small mouth and a weak chin. A few lines around the mouth, but otherwise he had not changed much. "You look to be in pretty fair shape, Bob," Sidney said. "Been working out?"

"Some. Maybe a couple of kilos heavier than in high school." Maxwell paused and touched a belt button to auto-clap with the crowd as they did a New City High yell. Sidney and Javik joined in too.

"We are tops. . . . Class of eighty-five!" the partyers chanted. "We are tops. . . ."

"Remember the pranks we used to pull?" Maxwell asked as the chanting died down. He looked across the table at Javik. "Like the time I dropped a dehydrated sponge in your glass of milk?"

Javik sat back and belly-laughed. "Scared the hell out of me when it puffed up! I was madder'n hell!"

Sidney laughed too, adding, "And the time we went to Liberty High with buckets of Markesian slime. . . ." He nudged the table in his mirth, causing it to rock.

"The funniest damn thing!" Javik said, beginning to gasp as he laughed. "We greased . . . the hallways while they were in class, then . . . ha! . . . watched as they fell all over the place!" He broke down laughing.

"No way for 'em to catch us," Maxwell recalled, revealing small, even teeth as he smiled. "The harder those Liberty High punks tried, the more they fell! Your idea, wasn't it, Sid?"

"Guess it was," Sidney said.

"Sid always had the imagination," Javik recalled. "How about those stories he made up to scare the girls when we parked at Lookout Rim?"

Presently, the waitress arrived with a tray containing two red drinks in tall glasses. She placed the drinks in front of Sidney and Javik, then turned to Maxwell.

"Nothing for me," Maxwell said. He waved a hand to send her away.

They listened to wailing band music for several minutes while Javik and Sidney sipped their drinks. After a while, Sidney tapped his foot to the music unconsciously.

"What's that tapping noise?" Maxwell asked.

Sidney stopped tapping, felt hot in the face.

Maxwell leaned over to look under the table, then straightened and glared at Sidney with unfriendly little blue eyes. "Was that you?" he asked.

"Yeah," Sidney admitted sheepishly. "Guess it was."

"Energy conservation," Maxwell said officiously. "Do it in the gym, man, not here!"

Javik swallowed a sip of his drink, wrinkled his nose in anger. "Criminy," he said. "Ease up, Bob. We can relax the rules a little tonight!"

Maxwell flashed a cool look at Javik, then turned to watch the band as it began to play a rock waltz. The lights dimmed for the number, and couples took to the dance floor, where they short-stepped onto disco spinners. Each couple grabbed an invisible force field pole at the center of their spinner, causing the device to start slowly into motion . . . whirling one way and then the other in time to the music. Some dancers wore lighted disco shoes in various colors, and soon the floor became a blur of lights.

Javik asked a woman at another table to dance. Sidney watched Javik roll by Peebles's table, saw Peebles's expression turn to hatred as Javik passed. Then Peebles's cool, emotionless eyes took over once more as Javik and his partner reached the dance floor.

Sidney heard Maxwell say something, turned to face him. "What?"

"Tom's the same old operator," Maxwell said.

Sidney sipped his drink through a straw, tasted the sharp bite of iced raspberry liqueur. "Yeah," he said. "Say, what line of work you in?"

Maxwell stiffened. "Spent some time as a shredding machine operator in Bu-Cops. Then I volunteered for another assignment . . . in cooperation with Bu-Med."

"Oh yeah?" Sidney said casually, watching the disco dancers perform. "What's that?"

"Can't say, really. It's classified." Sidney noticed that Maxwell's facial muscles were tight.

"Sounds interesting, Bob."

Moments later, Javik returned to the table. It was break time for the band, and the ballroom lights brightened. "Nikki Johnson," Javik said. "Says she's been permied and divorced four times."

Sidney swallowed a sip of liqueur, looked over the top of his drink at Javik. "You got her life story in five minutes," he said, laughing. "See what you can get out of Bob here. Says his job is classified."

"Is that right?" Javik asked, his curiosity peaked. He reached across the table, patted Maxwell on the shoulder and said, "You can confide in us, Bob. We're old pals, remember?"

"Well," Maxwell said, wriggling uncomfortably. He chewed at his upper lip, looked around. "It's the reason I don't drink anymore." Maxwell thought for a moment, then removed a tiny brass-plated computer from his jacket pocket. "Carry this everywhere," he said nervously, leaning forward and dropping his voice to a whisper.

"What is it?" Javik asked, reaching out in an attempt to touch the unit.

Maxwell pulled it away, said flatly: "A bio-medical surveillance monitor."

Javik rested his hand for a moment on top of the song request panel at the center of the table, then pulled it back as he asked, "What the hell is that?"

"In fisherman's English, it's a cappy-finder."

Sidney swallowed hard, listened as Javik said, "A cappy-finder?"

"Yeah. I could turn it on right here and walk around until the yellow light starts blinking. That would indicate we have a shirker on our hands, someone with a medical problem he isn't revealing . . . or a person with a problem he doesn't know about himself."

Sidney's blood ran cold with fear. He coughed, felt a shiver run down the center of his back.

"You okay, Sid?" Javik asked.

"Yeah." Sidney coughed again. "Got a little swizzle down the wrong pipe."

"Turn it on," Javik urged, looking back at the little brass computer.

Sidney stood up hurriedly, felt himself becoming unglued. "Excuse me," he said, his voice faltering. "I'll be right back." He scurried away, consumed with the necessity to flee.

But Maxwell flipped the device on before Sidney got away. A yellow light on the unit blinked rapidly, then stopped as Sidney escaped down the aisle. Maxwell's gaze followed Sidney.

"What does it mean?" Javik asked.

"Our friend has a problem," Maxwell said, rising to his feet. "And he acts like he knows about it."

"Sid looks healthy enough to me. Maybe your monitor needs adjustment."

"Just calibrated it," Maxwell said, replacing the unit in his jacket pocket. "Can't let this rest, you know. The man needs therapy." He watched Sidney slip into the restroom.

Javik jumped to his feet, said in a low, angry tone: "Why? He's not hurting anyone!"

Maxwell rolled away from the table in the direction Sidney had taken. Javik was close behind. "He's hurting employment," Maxwell said, glancing over his shoulder. "Each therapy client supports seven point-three-two-five Bu-Med employees. I've seen the figures."

"Hang the figures!" Javik rasped in Maxwell's ear. "We're talking about Sid Malloy. He's a friend, not a god-damned statistic!"

"Friendship has nothing to do with it," Maxwell said coldly, turning a corner and rolling to a stop outside the restroom. "It's my sworn duty to take him in. Look, Tom, I had no idea this was going to happen."

"Then forget it."

"Can't. Rules are rules."

Presently, Sidney rolled out of the restroom. When he saw Maxwell waiting for him with an all-knowing expression, Sidney thought, *Now I've had it*. His legs began to shake. Quickly, the knees seemed ready to give way.

An attack, Sidney thought. *I'm having a breakdown!*

"Malloy," Maxwell said in an authoritative tone. "I'm going to have to . . ."

But Sidney grew woozy and did not hear the ensuing words.

His knees folded, and he leaned against the wall for support.

Javik rolled to Sidney's side and held him up by the right arm. "You'll be all right," Javik said. He pulled at Sidney's arm. "C'mon, buddy. Let's get out—"

Maxwell pushed Javik in the shoulder. "Can't let you do that," he said.

Javik shook him off angrily, shoved past and went toward the elevator bank with Sidney.

Sidney felt his left arm shaking uncontrollably now, only half saw Javik and Maxwell through seizure-glazed, unfocused eyes. The Space Patrol crest on Javik's sleeve came into focus, then blurred.

Sidney saw the outlines of people as they turned their heads to watch, felt the prying press of eyes he could not actually see. Then Sidney's vision cleared momentarily, and he saw an angry Maxwell blocking the path, his arms folded across his chest and his face contorted in angry determination. Maxwell's lips moved, but Sidney swooned and the words sounded garbled to him, as if spoken underwater: "Hold...it...Tom... you're...not...go...ing...a...ny...far...ther!"

Upon hearing this, Javik's mind went blank with rage. He pushed Sidney to a sidechair. "Rules be damned!" Javik yelled, grabbing Maxwell by the collar. "I'll kill you, you rotten son-of-an-atheist!" He hit Maxwell in the face with a roundhouse right and fell to the floor pummeling his opponent with unanswered punches.

Sidney saw the unfocused images of people all around, pointing at him and turning their faces to the side in revulsion. "A cappy," one man said, his tone lilting and cruel. Sidney rolled his eyes in that direction, saw the lapel tag and shoulder epaulets of Colonel Peebles.

Sidney tried to control his left arm, but it flailed wildly. He glanced down at it, saw that it was contorted at the elbow and wrist joints, bent in a horrible manner like pictures he had seen of clients on therapy orbiters.

"Isn't it disgusting!" Peebles exclaimed.

"Let Bu-Cops through!" a woman said. "Make room!"

"How interesting," Peebles said. "Look at his face....It's twisted on the same side as the arm!"

"We shouldn't have to look at this!" a woman said indignantly.

In his pain, the voices Sidney heard became increasingly distant, increasingly muddled. *"Don't fight it, fleshcarrier,"* he thought one said. *"This could save you!"*

When the police stormed in, Colonel Peebles rolled forward to guide them. "Over there," he said, motioning to Javik, who was rising to his feet, apparently tired of hitting the prone form of Maxwell. Bloody and bruised, Maxwell dragged himself along the floor to get away. Then he tried to stand, but slipped back to the floor.

Two policemen grabbed Javik, but he broke free, knocking both of them down. Three more cops rushed over now with electro-sticks, and they shock-pummeled Javik to semi-consciousness.

"Kill him!" Maxwell yelled from his position on the floor. "Kill the bastard!"

"This man is my prisoner," Peebles announced as Javik was subdued. Peebles flashed a red Bu-Mil priority card. "Take him to Compound Five at the Bu-Tech Space Center."

"Yes sir," a police corporal said.

"And put the cappy in Therapy Detention," Peebles ordered. "Don't lose track of him, corporal. General Munoz wants to be kept advised of his whereabouts at all times. . . ."

Later that evening, Carla stood in the bathroom doorway of her condominium in a lavender bathrobe with a white-and-gold rope sash. Fluttering false eyelashes at a bare-chested man who sat on her waterbed with covers drawn across his lap, she asked, "May I offer you a tintette?"

"Yes," Billie Birdbright said. He smiled. "Thank you."

Carla removed a packet from her robe pocket, lit a lime tintette and puffed on it for a moment. Then she moto-slippered to the bed, trailing pale green smoke behind her. Carla sat on the edge of the waterbed, placed the tintette in his mouth.

Only moments before, she had been consumed by animal passion, had known Birdbright's strong and tender embrace. *A fantastic bedmate,* she thought, kissing him on the cheek. She studied Birdbright's profile as he smoked. The high cheekbones, tan skin and firm jaw gave him a virile appearance. Birdbright was the handsomest man she had bedmated.

In her thoughts, she compared Birdbright with the male pleasie-meckie she kept in the closet. Birdbright was the first man she had known whose sexual abilities approached those of the machine. *Billie may even be a little better*, she thought.

The words of a girlfriend spoken ten years before came back to Carla as she recalled being self-conscious at first about the ownership of a pleasie-meckie: "Even permies have them," the friend had said. "It isn't discussed much, of course, and the meckies do arrive in plain unmarked boxes. . . ."

Carla smiled at the recollection. Since that time, she had traded in her pleasie-meckies twice a year, always Tele-Charging the finest, strongest model available. *I owe it to myself*, she thought.

Birdbright tapped the tintette on a nightstand ashtray, looked at Carla inquisitively. "Whatcha thinkin' about?"

"That wouldn't interest you," Carla said with a smile. "Tell me what a Chief of Staff does. You're a G.W. three, aren't you?"

"Two." He set the tintette on the ashtray. "I assist the President in all areas. He likes me to delegate as much as possible, of course."

"Job-Support," she said.

"Precisely. But some matters are . . . rather delicate in nature." He beamed.

"How exciting!"

"I can give you one example, I suppose, without revealing exact figures. . . . Recently, I reviewed the forms budget for the year twenty-seven-sixty-two."

Carla did a quick mental calculation, then exclaimed, "A hundred fifty-seven years from now? But there must be a million variables between now and then! How can you account for every one of them?"

Birdbright smiled confidently as he explained: "Through charts and projections on the activity in every governmental office, we know exactly how many people will be employed in each bureau that year, what they will be doing, where they will live. . . ."

"And their names as well?" she remarked with a teasing smile and a toss of her golden-brown hair over one shoulder.

His smoke-grey eyes flashed, but he smiled quickly. "All except that," Birdbright said. "Names don't matter anyway."

"How can you be sure of the projections?"

"Bu-Tech's Stat Division provides us with mega-reams of data. I can tell you that the American Federation of Freeness controls its destiny very tightly. Technology has mastered everything imaginable!"

"Intriguing," Carla said. Recalling the pleasie-meckie in her closet, she thought, *Not quite everything . . . now that I've met you.*

"Freeness has been charted for the next thousand years," Birdbright said. "It can take only one path, the path chosen by Uncle Rosy."

As Birdbright spoke, Onesayer Edward stood in the dimly lit Central Chamber of the Black Box of Democracy. He gazed up at Uncle Rosy across the internally illuminated pages of an open book, saw a hulking shadow of a man in a hoodless robe seated upon the chamber's only chair. Onesayer had seen tuxedo meckies carrying the Master's laundry, so he knew the robe was white—but it was made to appear light yellow by a row of tiny soft yellow overhead bulbs which cast weak shadows around the room.

It was silent in the chamber, except for a soft, almost imperceptible humming sound which came from Uncle Rosy's lips. Onesayer recognized the melodic, lilting notes of the Hymn of Freeness. Uncle Rosy loved that tune. He had composed it himself.

Uncle Rosy's chair was immense, suitable for the size of its occupant, and rested upon a raised platform to one side of the room. Threesayer and Twosayer stood to each side of Onesayer, holding open volumes as well, dressed as he was in hooded dark brown friar robes without jewelry.

"There will be no further reading today, Uncle Rosy said in a kindly, resonant voice which echoed off the black glassite surrounding walls. "Onesayer, I will hear your report."

Onesayer closed his volume, slipped it into a robe pocket and moto-shoed forward. Looking at Uncle Rosy from this new position, he tried unsuccessfully to catch a glimpse of the Master's facial features. He had never seen the Master's face in person, remembered decades earlier when he used to imagine what a glorious countenance it must be. Lately Onesayer's thoughts had been altogether different. He had grown tired of waiting for the Master to step down and turn the holy duties over to him. It was cool and damp in the chamber. Onesayer shivered.

"Your report?" Uncle Rosy said, with the tiniest bit of impatience.

The corpulent Onesayer nodded, and with a graceful turn to one side extended an arm toward the center of the chamber. As he did this, a circular floor screen flickered on, revealing a view of galactic space. Uncle Rosy leaned forward, studied a fiery purple and yellow fireball which moved silently across the star-dusted expanse.

"The view from Drakus Ohm," Onesayer said, "one of AmFed's deep space observation stations."

"I know what Drakus Ohm is," Uncle Rosy said. This time Onesayer detected more than a hint of irritation in the tone. It surprised him. Never before had the Master displayed such an emotion.

Onesayer heard the whir of fast-approaching moto-shoes, watched a tuxedo meckie carry a tray of food up a ramp behind Uncle Rosy's chair. The meckie had six little blinking white lights down the front of a black headless metal body, with an oblong speaker box on each side. Its mechanical arms had a rim of white dress shirt at the wrists which appeared dirty yellow in the low light. The meckie placed the tray on a mini-table to one side of the great chair. It waited several seconds for further instructions. Not receiving any, it left the chamber.

"The comet continues to behave erratically, Learned One. It turns one way and then the other, always returning to a collision course with Earth."

"As if it had a life and brain of its own," Uncle Rosy said. He leaned to the right, resting an arm on one of three chrome handles beside the chair.

"Yes. It is strange indeed. Bu-Tech and Bu-Mil are combining in an effort to stop the comet, but..." Onesayer fell silent, clasped his hands behind his back and gazed up at the distant row of yellow bulbs along the ceiling.

"But?" Uncle Rosy prodded.

Onesayer dropped his gaze, looked at the Master. "I have been in the Bureau Monitoring Room since midday, reviewing all the lifelog and minicam tapes on Dr. Hudson and General Munoz."

"And?"

"I do not think much of their plan. No back-up provision or evacuation contingency. And now Munoz has some wild idea that an officeworker named Malloy—a man with absolutely no space experience—should pilot the ship. We have checked the lifelog tapes on Malloy, Master. The fellow is pathetic—a real loser."

"I see," Uncle Rosy said.

"They are sending along another man who has experience . . . he's been doing garbage shuttle duty the past couple of years. So far, they can't locate him."

Uncle Rosy said nothing, sat leaning to one side.

Onesayer noticed the chrome handle moving down slowly beneath the weight of Uncle Rosy's arm. "Master!" he yelled. "The Zero Handle! You are leaning on it!"

"Oh," Uncle Rosy said absent-mindedly, pulling his arm away from the handle. "Suppose I was." Uncle Rosy pushed the handle back into place.

Onesayer took a deep breath, resisted an urge to shake his head in dismay.

"Foolish of me," Uncle Rosy said cheerfully. "Another five seconds and Earth would have gone boom!"

"Yes, Master. That reminds me. . . . What would you think of using the second handle at this time?"

"The Orbital Handle?" Uncle Rosy said, placing his hand on the central chrome handle. "You hope Earth can elude the comet by modifying its orbit?"

"That is the obvious benefit, Master. But there is another."

"Which is?"

"The AmFeds have always been pretentious, thinking that their technology can deal with any situation."

"It has worked well for them in the past," Uncle Rosy said in his resonant voice.

"And the past is always a precursor of what is to come?"

"Ah, Onesayer Edward," the Master said, pleased. "You are learning!"

False encouragement, Onesayer thought bitterly. "On this pretentiousness, Master, the AmFeds do not know of the existence of our Orbital Handle."

"Nor of the other handles. It would cause them to stop and think, eh, Onesayer?"

"It would be healthy if they were forced to re-evaluate assumptions."

"Under normal circumstances, I would agree, Onesayer." Uncle Rosy removed his hand from the Orbital Handle. "But this is quite a different situation."

"Then why did you install the handles? I understand number one, the Zero Handle. As Master, you may find it necessary to detonate the planet. And number three . . . our army of ten thousand armadillo meckies that can fly, swim and break through walls. But number two, Master . . . I cannot think of a more opportune occasion to use it for the first time."

"Continue as I have instructed, Onesayer. Dr. Hudson and General Munoz are to be eliminated."

"At least hear me on one point, Master. Hudson could improve the odds of stopping the comet. We should not kill him yet."

Onesayer saw the shadowy head of Uncle Rosy shake slowly from side to side. There was no other response.

Onesayer shifted nervously on his feet. "He is a genius, Master. You have often said this."

"He is dangerous, Onesayer. We cannot tolerate someone who reads the thoughts of the citizenry and forces them to vote as he wishes!"

"I see that, Master. But . . ."

"There are no buts to be considered. When I thought of mentoing, I saw it as an aid to the economy . . . making consumption easier . . . more automatic. In my early lab work, I hoped thought transmission would make life more pleasurable for my people."

"Hudson IS evil, but we can get him later."

"No, Onesayer!" Uncle Rosy said angrily. "He has gone too far!"

"Learned One, you speak with anger. But the AmFeds can ill afford to lose him now . . . in the presence of suc. grave danger."

"No matter, Onesayer. I have given my orders."

"But Master—"

"You HAVE instructed our operatives to sabotage the products used by General Munoz and Dr. Hudson?"

"Uh, the contract is out on Munoz."

"And Hudson?"

"Uh, not yet, Master."

"I gave that order YESTERDAY, Onesayer. Why was it not completed yesterday?"

"I had hoped you might reconsider. . . ."

"Onesayer Edward!"

"Forgive me for arguing, Learned One, but the Thousand Year Plan . . . the glory of Freeness and the AmFed Way . . . all could be destroyed! Surely *this* matters!"

"Much remains for you to learn, Onesayer," the hulking shape said. "Some things can be controlled. Others cannot."

Onesayer did not reply. He glanced at the two sayermen standing silently nearby in the hope that one would speak up on his behalf. But they said nothing, making Onesayer feel very much alone.

"They will stop this comet themselves," Uncle Rosy said, "or it was not meant to be done."

"I have never heard you speak this way, Master."

"And you are disturbed?"

"I am concerned. We are responsible for the work of many lifetimes . . . for tradition and honor . . . for dreams brought to reality."

"Well put, Onesayer. But there are forces at work here even I do not understand. I have never admitted such a thing before, and it is not to go beyond this chamber."

"Yes, Learned One. I will follow your wishes."

"One more thing, Onesayer. Tomorrow morning you are to notify President Ogg of the electoral conspiracy against him. Show him that they thought-speak, and assure him that we are in control of the situation. But say no more."

As the conversation ended and Onesayer rolled out of the chamber, he felt centuries of suppressed anger coming to a head. *I must kill the Master, he thought bitterly. He will never step down . . . and besides, he has gone mad! If I can hide the body and take his place . . . no one will know the difference!*

For a fleeting moment, it occurred to Onesayer that there might be no body. Uncle Rosy might be a projecto-image. *No,* he thought. *The Master leaned on one of the handles. . . . Still, it could be a meckie. The Master might be somewhere else, watching. Or he may be dead already, and another sayerman has taken his place. . . .*

The range of possibilities nearly drove Onesayer mad.

It was late Saturday evening when Onesayer took the elevator to the top floor of the Black Box, rolled along a long hallway and entered his suite. As he rode the escalator to his prayer loft for the final daily prayer, Onesayer felt emotions different from any he had ever experienced before.

He reached the prayer loft landing and short-stepped off. *This has always been automatic for me,* he thought, *but I feel*...

Onesayer could not form the feelings into coherent thoughts. He stood for a moment staring at the bust of Uncle Rosy which rested in its usual position on the leading edge of the prayer rug. An overhead mini-spot illuminated the bust, and Onesayer recalled feeling that this gave it an inspirational appearance in the surrounding shadows of night. But the bust did not look inspirational to him now. There was something insidious about it.

I should be on that rug by now, he thought, *pledging myself anew to the Master....*

Onesayer rolled slowly to the sculptured bust, felt hot with anger as he reached it. *I have prayed to this idol for the last time!* he thought, glaring down at a "Keep the Faith" inscription on the pedestal. His foot darted forward swiftly, dealing a powerful blow to the bust. The little sculpture flew a meter and a half into the air, crashed and shattered as it fell to the hardwood floor.

Uncle Rosy's fate as well, he thought, staring bleakly at the broken pieces. A portion of the bust's pedestal remained intact, along with its "Keep the Faith" inscription. Words echoed in his brain: *Keep the Faith...Keep the Faith...Keep the Faith....*

Onesayer lifted the pedestal piece angrily and hurled it to the floor. *There!* he thought as the piece shattered. *I am free of it!*

A shudder ran through his body.

* * *

The youngsayermen were gathered in the high-ceilinged gallery of the Great Temple at Pleasant Reef. They stood around Sayer Superior Lin-Ti at a glass display case, watching intently as he unlocked the case.

"This is the actual cross worn by General Munoz," Lin-Ti said, lifting out a burnished gold cross and chain.

"Does it still work?" a youngsayerman asked.

"Oh yes," Lin-Ti said. "Of course, we are too far from Earth to change their weather or votes. This is a mechanical device, you know. It is not spiritual...."

FIVE

WHAT FREENESS MEANS TO THE AMFEDS: FOR FURTHER READING AND DISCUSSION

"Something for nothing is perfectly acceptable. The most important people get ahead by luck, you know. They are in the right place at the right time. Once a person understands Freeness, there is no limit to how far he can go!"

Remarks to a newsy reporter by Charley Chance, twelfth minister of Bu-Free

Sunday, August 27, 2605

Garbage Day minus five began in the Black Box of Democracy with Onesayer Edward rising at his usual time before dawn. This morning, for the first time in more than three centuries, he would not perform the prayer ritual. *I will never return to the prayer loft!* he thought as he pulled a clean robe over his head. *It is finished!*

New thoughts whirled through Onesayer's brain as he rode the elevator to the second level and moto-shoed the short distance to the Bureau Monitoring Room. *I will disfigure his face after killing him. Then if I can get one of my robes on him*... Doubt returned to his consciousness, and Onesayer wondered if Uncle Rosy really occupied the Master's chair. *Whoever it is,* he thought. *I'll get him.*

"Peace be upon you, Onesayer," a sayerman said as Onesayer entered the room. Onesayer nodded without noticing who had spoken. He rolled directly to the broadcasting alcove located along a side wall. It was shift-change time, and sayermen arrived and left, exchanging blessings and touching together their class rings.

Oblivious to this activity, Onesayer mentoed the minicam broadcaster as he entered the alcove: *One-five-six-three-oh-nine-four-one-Ogg*. He glanced at a computer sheet on President Ogg, then took a seat on a high stool and stared intently at a round telescreen as it flickered to life.

Onesayer watched the screen as an immense black man wearing a bright green leisure suit short-stepped onto the running board of Autocopter One, then turned to retrieve a briefcase from the expando-cart which lifted it to his level.

President Ogg heard his satin suit rustle as he moved. He placed the case behind the single copter seat, short-stepped into the cockpit and sat down. From the helipad on top of his penthouse, the President could see the morning sun beginning to do its dawn-peek over a dusty horizon. Its golden-orange rays across New City gave a reddish silhouette to mountains in the distance. He enjoyed taking a heli-spin at this time of day, had often commented on it by saying, "The morning is as new and bright as the best products in our American Federation!"

Onesayer spoke from the Bureau Monitoring Room: "Good morning, President Ogg."

Ogg jumped. The voice seemed to come from somewhere inside the cockpit. "Who said that?" Ogg demanded, sitting straight up and looking around nervously. He saw no one.

"My name is not important," the voice said.

Onesayer smiled as he watched President Ogg reach for his radiophone. Onesayer mentoed a force-field gun, and Ogg felt invisible restraint against his forearm, preventing him from lifting the receiver.

"There is no need for that," the voice said.

"Great Suffering Depression!" Ogg cursed angrily. He took a deep breath, released his fingers from the receiver and pulled his arm back.

"Not to be alarmed, Mr. President," Onesayer said. "The Black Box of Democracy would have a word with you."

"The Black Box? What sort of prank is this?"

Ogg noted that the voice did not sound male or female. It could be a syntho-voiced meckie. Or someone speaking through a voice scrambler. He pinched the thin skin on the back of one hand to be certain he was awake. It hurt.

"There is an evil electoral conspiracy, Mr. President. In violation of the American Federation of Freeness Constitution."

"Oh?"

"An interesting dinner party will take place this evening, at the home of General Munoz."

"Munoz? What's he up to?"

"He is the leader of the conspiracy."

"I will need evidence," the President said, "enough to appoint an investigating committee." His gaze darted around the cockpit.

"You will have the evidence, Mr. President, because you should always be kept informed. But there will be no investigating committee."

"We MUST have a thorough investigation," Ogg insisted, his voice fervent, "with reports, meetings and photographs." Ogg wiped perspiration from his brow. "We'll set up a crisis bureau, employing thousands of people!"

"No time for that! They plan to rig Tuesday's election! Munoz will take power the same day!"

"But we can't take action without reports," Ogg lamented as he shifted in his seat. His satin suit rustled. "It's not possible!"

"Leave it to us, Mr. President. And do not be alarmed at what you see happening."

"What will that be?"

"Do not be impatient. First, there is a bit of evidence for you to observe, as required in the by-laws of the Black Box of Democracy."

Ogg rubbed the thumb and forefinger of one hand together nervously.

"The Munoz dinner party," the voice said. "In the glovebox of your autocopter is a palm-held video receiver. Flip it on at six-thirty this evening."

President Ogg located the receiver, held it in one hand. It was blue plastic and chrome, had one red switch and a tiny darkened screen. "All right," he agreed. "I'll do that."

"They will say nothing incriminating at the table," the voice said. "But watch their gestures and expressions. Pay particular attention to their eyes."

"This doesn't sound like evidence to me!"

"They thought-speak, Mr. President, with the aid of brain-implanted transceivers."

"My Rosenbloom! I've never heard of such—"

"They also have a powerful subliminal transmitting device. At this moment, it is changing the voting preferences of a majority of the electorate."

"Munoz as a punch-in victor?"

"Right. We have been on full alert for some time now. But we could not take action until they committed the overt act of changing votes. Just planning to do it was no crime."

"I see. No I don't! Munoz isn't clever enough for this!"

"Dr. Hudson's doing. Remember last year in your office when he explained the subliminal receiving features of every consumer brain implant? They were to make Harmak and Home Video advertisements more effective, he said."

"I remember. But how did you . . ."

"They found another use for Hudson's discoveries. I must caution you not to tell anyone about our conversation, Mr. President." The voice fell silent.

Ogg listened to the quiet in the cockpit, and a feeling of urgency came over him. He watched the golden orange layers of dawn give way to pale blue daylight.

Whose voice was that? he thought. *God's?*

Dr. Hudson attended church services alone Sunday morning. Since the church building was overflowing, Hudson and hundreds of others sat in cars out in the parking lot, listening to the sermon through drive-in speakers.

"Uncle Rosy and God are side-by-side in the Happy Shopping Ground," the minister's metallic voice said.

Hudson turned a knob on the speaker to lower the volume, then glanced around nervously at the occupants of nearby cars. *Did anyone see me do that?* he thought.

Across town in Building B of the Bu-Tech Space Center, General Munoz and Colonel Peebles stood in a sixth-floor briefing room. They squinted at one another against the glare of the midmorning sun which flashed through a nearby window. Peebles mentoed a window shade, watched it roll halfway down until the sun's rays were covered.

"Hudson's people did a nice job, wouldn't you say?" General Munoz asked, looking through a clear glassplex barrier to admire a three-dimensional galactic model. .

"Adequate," Colonel Peebles said, fingering a strand of gold braid which encircled one shoulder epaulet and hung at the side of his Space Patrol uniform.

"Adequate? It's identical to our real model next door, except in this case the planets and other heavenly bodies don't follow the impulses of parent bodies. These little spheres move in accordance with our fabricated control room instructions."

"Very nice," Peebles agreed. He smiled as he looked at the model. Miniature comets and meteors made their way along varying courses in slow motion, trailing emerald green, blue or orange flames against a black, star-encrusted backdrop.

Munoz glanced at the briefing room's digital wallclock, noted the time: A.M. 10:26:33. Below that, another digital reader showed the Estimated Time of Arrival of the garbage comet:

DAYS	HOURS	MINS.	SECS.	D/SECS.
5	7	28	13	0.73

Looking back at the squeak of a door, they watched two dark blue-uniformed military policemen escort Tom Javik into the room. The MPs saluted, did a moto-boot about-face and left. Javik folded his arms across his chest, glanced around defiantly.

"Mr. Javik!" General Munoz exclaimed, caressing his orange mustache. "So nice that you could make it!" The voice was honey-sweet but carried with it a threatening undertone.

"Our brawler has a cut over his eye," Peebles observed. An

I-told-you-so smile touched his mouth as he added, "They had some difficulty restraining him last night at the Sky Ballroom."

General Munoz rubbed his chin thoughtfully as he studied Javik. He noted a torn and wrinkled tunic, fearless and defiant deeply-set blue eyes. "We'll order you more suitable clothing," Munoz said. "But then I'm getting ahead of myself. You know who I am?"

"Yes," Javik said, meeting the tiny General's gaze. "And I've . . . met . . . Major Peebles."

"It's *Colonel* now," Peebles said stiffly. Javik heard a familiar whine to the voice.

"Getting directly to the reason you are here," Munoz said, "I am prepared to reinstate your commission in the American Federation Space Patrol. As a First Lieutenant. An Akron class cruiser is being prepared for the mission right now."

"Fast ship," Javik said. "And long-range." He narrowed his eyes warily, asked, "What's the catch?"

"No catch," Munoz replied. "Your assignment is Project Romo."

"Who's heading up this mission?"

"Captain Sidney Malloy."

Javik's eyes opened wide. "Huh? . . . Not the same Sidney Malloy I know?"

"One and the same."

Javik laughed. "You've got to be kidding!"

"Your crippled little friend will be commander in name only. Operationally, you will be in charge." Munoz touched the burnished gold cross which hung from his neck.

Peebles stared at the ceiling.

"I like Sid," Javik said, "but what in the hell is going on? The cockpit of an Akron cruiser is no place for him!"

"There are reasons," Munoz said, staring at a trash can across the room. "Command reasons." He gestured toward the galactic model, adding, "You leave tomorrow. Malloy will meet—"

"I haven't accepted the assignment yet," Javik pointed out, smiling faintly.

"True enough," Munoz said. "If you don't accept, we'll find someone to replace you."

Javik twisted his face, trying to think.

"Malloy goes in any event," Munoz said. "He will go separately to Saint Elba, receiving therapy there before joining you . . . or someone else. There are no therapy facilities here."

"This is crazy," Javik said.

"As if you're in a position to be choosy," Peebles sneered, staring disdainfully at Javik.

Munoz glared at his adjutant, then motioned to the galactic model again and explained: "That is Earth," he said, pointing to a tiny sphere in the galactic model. The sphere began to pulsate with a white light at the General's mento-command. "And there, in orbit between the Earth and Moon at L_5, is the therapy habitat of Saint Elba." A pulsating blue light marked the orbiter's location.

"Saint Elba is the first recharging stop," Colonel Peebles explained. "It is there that Malloy will be picked up, along with two mass driver units and fire probes, all partially assembled."

"Partially assembled?" Javik said.

"Due to a shortage of time," Munoz said, "assembly crews will accompany you on the journey, doing their work along the way."

"How many people?"

"Two hundred. All cappies. They'll be released to rescue craft when the mass drivers are complete."

"I see. Fire probes, huh? What am I supposed to hook onto?"

Munoz activated a red blip adjacent to the Earth sphere. "This represents your ship, the Shamrock Five," he explained. The blip moved to Saint Elba, then continued off into space. "From Saint Elba you and Malloy will proceed in the direction of the Ikor Constellation, along a heading of thirty-two-point-five degrees from the Columbarian Plane. Three additional recharging stops will be necessary before rendezvous. Charging stations are now being established along the route." Javik noted three pulsating yellow lights, watched the red blip pause at each.

Javik furrowed his brow. "I don't see what . . . I mean, it's clear space beyond that for millions of kilometers."

"You'll be changing course twenty-six thousand kilometers beyond the last recharging station, along a new heading of ninety-two-point-one degrees C.P. This will conserve the E-Cells by taking advantage of strong space currents in the region."

"I'm familiar with the area," Javik said, watching the red blip change direction along its new course.

Javik glanced at the impact countdown wallboard, asked, "What day will it be at the time of the last course change?"

"Thursday," Colonel Peebles said, glancing at a palm-held note screen. "Eighteen hundred thirty-six hours to be precise."

"The object of rendezvous is THERE!" Munoz said, revealing excitement in his voice. The largest of several comets in the Columbarian Quadrant began to pulsate. "That celestial body is on a collision course with our mining base in the Romo asteroid group, threatening our principal source of Argonium One."

"E-Cell gas," Javik remarked.

"Argonium One's use is classified," Peebles said, officiously.

Javik narrowed his eyes and leaned closer to the galactic model. "That . . . celestial body, as you call it . . . looks like a comet to me."

Munoz hesitated, then said: "Correct."

"There are rumors of a comet headed toward Earth, General. Some say it's our own garbage."

"Nonsense," Munoz said firmly. "Utter nonsense." He mentoed a time-advance button to speed up the motions in the galactic model. "I'm eliminating your ship," he explained, "and doing a fast-forward on the celestial body. The blinking green light is our Romo mining base."

The comet sped across space in a blur and hit the Romo asteroids dead center. Javik shielded his eyes as a bright, silent explosion filled the model with tiny fragments of smoldering matter.

"Any questions?" Munoz asked. He stared sidelong at Javik, noted Javik was staring down the bridge of his nose at the model.

Javik mumbled something.

"What was that?" Munoz asked.

"Project Boomerang," Javik said. He smiled defiantly. "That's a better name for the project. After all, it is our own garbage coming back."

"Not true!" Munoz huffed.

Colonel Peebles glanced at Javik haughtily and said, "Bu-Tech studied photographic plates taken by deep space gamma ray cameras. The celestial body's—"

"You mean the *comet's?*" Javik asked, glaring ferociously.

"Very well. The comet's composition is quite standard...primordial noble gases and the like, with a fusion-hardened nucleus of—"

"Bull!" Javik said. The smile returned.

"Look," Peebles said, his voice trembling with anger. "Experts plotted its course with coordinate measurements of Right Ascension and Declination...obtained by angular offsets to the adjacent field stars. That is the course you see here." Peebles nodded toward the galactic model.

"Do you really understand any of that?" Javik asked.

"Certainly!" Peebles's pale blue eyes peered icily at Javik.

"Well, your galactic model is wrong. I think it's intentionally wrong. And your impact board refers to the comet's E.T.A. here, not at Romo."

"We don't have to listen to this!" Peebles huffed, glancing at Munoz for support. Peebles mentoed the window shade, and it snapped up, throwing a flash of sunlight in Javik's eyes.

Squinting, Javik flushed with anger and said to Peebles, "Listen, you wet-behind-the-ears armchair...."

"STOP THIS! BOTH OF YOU!" Munoz thundered. He glared at Peebles, then mentoed the window shade down, returning the coolness of shadow to Javik's face.

"I accept the assignment," Javik said, "with a couple of provisos."

Munoz took a deep breath, tried to exude calmness. "Which are?"

"Firstly, two cases of Chambertin Clos de Bez wine pellets are to be placed aboard.... Vintage twenty-five-seventy-two."

"Done," Munoz said.

"Rather expensive taste for a brawler," Peebles sniffed. "A jug of White Rippo sounds more suitable."

Javik disregarded the remark, said, "And I want Brent Stafford assigned to command his own ship...at least a destroyer."

"Who?" Munoz asked.

"Our brawler's co-pilot during his garbage detail," Peebles said.

"And during the Atheist Wars," Javik said. "He deserves his own command, General...somewhere in the galaxy."

"All right," Munoz agreed. "Take care of it, Allen." Munoz furrowed his brow, faced Javik. "Keep your cappy friend out of the way during the flight. Give him innocuous little tasks...."

"He's in command, General," Javik said, smiling.

"You know what I mean. Common sense must prevail."

"Right, General. Boy, this is the damndest mission I've ever seen!"

"We're depending on you, Lieutenant Javik. We can't use remote-control pilotry on a deep space mission of this importance. If we had an equipment malfunction, with a meteor storm in the way . . . why, remote repairs by signal from Earth would be impossible."

"I know," Javik said. "One more thing. . . . I'll need papers to get Malloy free on Saint Elba."

"You'll have them," Munoz said, glancing at his adjutant.

"I want them signed by you, General," Javik said. "Not by an *aide*." Javik smiled viciously in Peebles's direction and saw his comment hit home as Peebles's eyes flashed angrily.

Slipping into his unspoken conversation mode, Munoz mentoed to Peebles: *We must cooperate, don't you see? I have to send Malloy, and this Javik knows him best. . . . THE MISSION MUST GO SMOOTHLY!* Munoz sighed deeply. "Very well," he said. "Prepare the papers for my signature, Allen."

Peebles rolled to a corner desk and began to prepare the forms.

"And give me something to get into Therapy Detention right now," Javik said, throwing the words at Peebles as if they were a command. "I'm going over to see Sid. It's less than a block away."

Peebles's gaze met that of Munoz.

Munoz nodded. "Don't say anything to Malloy now about his captain's commission. Be discreet, Javik. We don't want word of this getting out." Munoz pressed a set of Lieutenant's bars into Javik's palm.

"Yes sir."

Presently, the forms were prepared and signed. As Javik took them, Munoz said: "Report to Conditioning by thirteen hundred hours, Lieutenant Javik. Room C five-thirty-four."

Javik saluted and rolled toward the door.

Looking at Peebles, General Munoz mentoed: *Is the Madame ready?*

Almost. Peebles smiled his characteristically cruel smile. *Hudson told them to sharpen her knives.*

Good. She will have two heads to sever!

*   *   *

"We must imagine now," Sayer Superior Lin-Ti said, "for we have no record of what happened in the Realm of Magic, except so far as they spoke to humans."

Lin-Ti closed his eyes. "Picture a realm far across the galaxy, with no land or water mass, populated by bodiless beings. They were at a party, and from all around came the sounds of laughter and merriment. For this was a comet party—a real event at which all the citizens of the realm watched while the fleshcarriers learned their lesson.

" *'Ha!'* one said. *'That fool Malloy is captain of their ship. He'll find a way to botch the mission. Mark my words!'*

" *'Right,'* another said. *'He'll take some 'heroic' action to blow their pitiful little plan. Ah, but we have chosen him well—a nobody with delusions of grandeur!'*

"Other beings spoke of similar matters," Lin-Ti said, "and all agreed they had selected a delightful way to have fun. These beings were not malicious: they just wanted to have a good time. . . ."

*   *   *

Lastsayer Steven paced the hallway nervously outside Onesayer's suite. *Almost eleven,* he thought. *Could Onesayer have forgotten my first audience with the Master?*

He mentoed Onesayer's doorbuzzer, watched the button go in and then return as the chime sounded. There was no answer.

Lastsayer turned dejectedly to leave, considered going to the audience alone. *Dare I?* he wondered. He rolled partway down the hall toward the elevator bank.

"Lastsayer!" a boisterous voice called out. "Do come back!"

"Lastsayer turned, saw Onesayer Edward peeking around the corner of the doorjamb with a silly leer on his face. He wore no hood, exposing the shaved head of the Sayerhood.

Lastsayer began rolling back. "Onesayer!" he said. "It is three minutes before the hour!"

"So it is. So it is." Onesayer motioned with one hand. "Come in for a moment. I must tidy up before we go."

Thinking that Onesayer's voice sounded odd, Lastsayer arrived at the doorway with an excited protest: "But we will be late!"

"Don't worry about it. The Master can't tell time."

"What?"

Onesayer smiled as he said, "I was just kidding. I'll explain our lateness to him. He won't blame you." Onesayer short-stepped to one side, motioned for the other man to enter.

Stunned, Lastsayer looked up at the taller Onesayer. "You used apostrophic words!" Lastsayer said.

"What? Oh yes. You're . . . uh . . . you are quite correct. Thank you for pointing that out to me."

Lastsayer touched his onyx ring to Onesayer's as he rolled into the suite. "Peace be upon you," Lastsayer said.

Onesayer returned the blessing, fumbled in his pocket for something.

"You look tired," Lastsayer said, noting faint lines around Onesayer's large olive eyes. "And you do not sound the same."

Onesayer laughed as he rolled through the foyer into the dining area. "I was doing my Uncle Rosy impressions before you arrived. Guess I lost track of my own voice."

"Is that permitted?" Lastsayer looked around the dining room module, noted Greek urns on a blue slate floor. A long marble dining table in the center of the room was bathed in sunlight from an overhead solar relay panel. Somewhere, in another room, a bird chirped.

"I found no specific rule prohibiting it in the Sayers' Manual," Onesayer said, using the full resonant tone of Uncle Rosy.

Frowning uneasily, Lastsayer said, "I feel out of place asking this, but are you well?"

"Of course I am well! A couple of Happy Pills, no more!"

"Forgive me for asking, Onesayer."

"All is forgiven! Now relax and listen to my impression. Fivesayer says it is very good."

"I do not believe we have time. The audience with . . ."

But Onesayer was not listening. He clasped both hands in front of his waist in a very dignified fashion and said in the tone of Uncle Rosy, "You have much to learn, Onesayer Edward. You understand it will be a while before I step down and allow you to become Master . . . all the details remaining to resolve. . . ." He paused and looked fully into the smooth face of the younger sayerman. Lastsayer stared back with a worried expression. "Pretty good, eh?" Onesayer asked, in his own voice.

"I have only heard tapes. I was hoping to meet the Master in person this morning."

Onesayer smiled. "A bit of sarcasm! I like the way you

think, youngsayer! I like the way you think!"

"Thank you, Onesayer. Now can we—"

"Is something else bothering you, Lastsayer? Other than being a few minutes late?"

"Since you ask, I'm disturbed...better to say concerned...at the way you mimic the Master."

Onesayer's tone became decidedly hostile. "Oh you are, are you?" He moto-shoed toward a side doorway, paused to glare back at Lastsayer.

"It occurs to me that Uncle Rosy should be informed of this, Onesayer. A strict interpretation of the Sayerman's Code of Ethics...."

"Hang the code!"

"This might be a test, Onesayer. A test of my loyalty. How am I to know?"

"Inform him, then!" Onesayer yelled. He rolled through the doorway to another room, calling back, "Inform away!"

Lastsayer followed and caught up with the elder sayerman in the living room module, a bright room with deep blue shag carpeting and throw pillow furniture. "Wait, Onesayer. I have not yet had my first audience with the Master! I will not say anything because I do not feel qualified to make judgments yet."

"You have much to learn, Lastsayer," Onesayer said in the voice of Uncle Rosy. He smiled wryly.

Lastsayer felt frightened, furrowed his brow. "You do appear tired, Onesayer," he said. "There are lines around your eyes. Possibly we could postpone the aud—"

"Lines you say?" Appearing startled, Onesayer rubbed a middle finger beneath his right eye and snapped: "I have no lines!"

"I would suggest rest, Onesayer. Things will appear better to you afterward."

"You SUGGEST rest, do you?" Onesayer's voice was high-pitched, near cracking. "A Lastsayer does not SUGGEST anything to a Onesayer!"

Lastsayer's jaw dropped. He rolled back half a meter. "Excuse me," he said. "I am very sorry."

"Wait here," Onesayer ordered angrily. He gathered his robe in a very dignified fashion and swept out of the room.

I said too much, Lastsayer thought dejectedly. Uneasily, he looked around the room, noting a brown-and-gold sayer's edition of *Quotations from Uncle Rosy* on a sidetable. He picked up the book and manually turned a sheet of rice paper to Uncle Rosy's picture.

Lastsayer nearly dropped the book in astonishment. The picture had been defaced! Someone had penned in lambchop sideburns and a short goatee on the Master's face! The sacrilege of such a thing! He closed the volume, returning it to its place on the table.

Best not to say anything about this, he thought, moving away from the table. *Such occurrences may be commonplace here.*

In the bathroom module, Onesayer peered into the grooming machine mirror. A terrified face looked back. *Lines,* he thought, rubbing the skin around his eyes. Shallow, barely discernible lines were to the sides and below each eye. They had not been there the day before. He was sure of it.

He recalled smashing the Uncle Rosy idol the evening before. *This was how it happened with Sixsayer Robert before he died,* Onesayer thought. *It started with a few lines....*

Onesayer slammed his fist down on the sink, felt pain shoot through his hand. *So soon,* he thought. *How could it happen so soon?*

As he turned away from the mirror, a thought raced through his mind. Uncle Rosy knew of his disloyalty and was trying to kill him! *But I'll get him first!* Onesayer thought.

Sleep voices, at the edge of Sidney's consciousness:

"Malloy doesn't know about the killer meckie yet."

"Ah, but he will learn of it soon enough... when the Montreal Slasher gives him a neck full of steel!"

"Ingenious, the way these fleshcarriers destroy one another....Imagine that... an entity which is programmed to kill! It has no other function!"

"Their ingenuity... as you call it... is moronic in comparison with our garbage comet!"

Sidney dreamed he and Javik were in the command cockpit of a space warship. Suddenly they turned and saw two long knives approaching through the hatchway. Swish...swish...swish-swish-swish! A faceless being controlled the weapons, and Sidney was terrified of the entity he could not see.

The dream-Javik drew his service revolver and fired. But

the knives kept coming. Closer and closer. Swishing and darting through the air.

Fwoosh! A blade severed Javik's head. It fell to the floor
with a dull, distant thud. With a twisted and unusable arm,
Sidney could do little to defend himself. It would be over in
seconds. Sidney sensed relief ahead...a nothingness beckoning to him across the cosmos....

"Wake up, Malloy! The morning's almost gone!"

Sidney felt a strong arm shaking his shoulder. He opened
one eye and turned his face up to see a ruddy-faced male
attendant looking down at him. The white-smocked attendant
was young and muscular, with tiny rat-like dark eyes.

"A lady's here to see you," the attendant said.

"What is this place?" Sidney asked. He used his good hand
to brush tousled curls of black hair off his forehead.

"You're in the Hotel Ritz-Broadway," the attendant sneered.
"And I'm your private manservant! WHERE DO YOU THINK
YOU ARE? THIS IS THERAPY DETENTION, PAL! YOU'RE
SCHEDULED TO LEAVE FOR THE ORBITER TOMOR-
ROW!" The attendant shook his head scornfully.

Sidney rolled over on the cot to turn his face away. He
curled his legs into a fetal position. Every muscle ached, especially those in direct contact with the unsympathetic cot. The
grand mal seizure of the previous evening had left him with
the fatigue of a thousand sleepless nights. The left side of his
face felt numb, and his left arm and left-hand fingers were
contorted horribly. He saw bones almost popping out, stretching their skin to the limit. Taut muscles appeared ready to snap.
He tried to straighten the fingers, could not.

"You guys that get special treatment really burn me," the
attendant said. "All the other applicants have been to Sunday
services this morning, but not you!"

"I don't know what you're talking about," Sidney mumbled.

"Somebody called in with a Presidential code...said you
were to await a visitor. What are you, Malloy? A bigwig of
some sort? Well it won't keep you off the orbiter, pal. Nothing
will!"

Leave me alone, Sidney thought. *Just leave me alone.*

"Come on, fella," the attendant said, again shaking Sidney's
shoulder.

"Go away. I don't want to see anybody." Sidney's deformed
arm twitched as he spoke, then jerked violently. He grabbed

it with his good hand, took a deep, determined breath.

"The lady's a looker," the attendant said, short-stepping around the cot to the side Sidney faced.

Sidney did not reply. He turned away from the attendant. *Carla*, he thought. *I can't let her see me like this*. Sidney recalled what Javik had done for him the night before, wondered if he was all right.

"Hey, maybe the lady CAN figure a way to keep you off the therapy orbiter," the attendant said. "You'd better smarten up and talk to her. Once they get you out there in space, you can forget about coming back."

I'd rather face that than Carla, Sidney thought. He turned away once more and closed his eyes.

"All right," the attendant said, weary of the argument. "Suit yourself."

Sidney heard the whir of departing moto-shoes. He opened his eyes and looked across rows of empty cots, then turned his head the other way to see additional rows. He was in the middle of a large sleeping room, and the surrounding sameness reminded him of his desk in Central Forms. Noticing a plasti-tag around his right wrist, he read it:

"Malloy, S./Client No. 165632029"

Maybe Carla can get me out of here, he thought. But he made no effort to get up or to cry out. A door slammed. Echoing quiet dominated the room.

After the meeting with General Munoz, Javik changed to casual Space Patrol togs. A high overhead sun cast distorted, short shadows of Javik's body as he rolled up the long ramp to Bu-Med's Detention Center Building shortly before noon.

Carla was leaving the building as Javik entered. She smiled attentively, and to Javik she seemed particularly receptive to him.

Attractive woman, Javik thought. *And vaguely familiar....*

Now there's the sort of man I should pursue, Carla thought as she rolled down the ramp. *Instead of wasting my time with Sidney. This one's really in the Space Patrol*.

After presenting his pass at five checkstations inside the building, Javik found himself facing the rat-eyed attendant in charge of Sidney's sleeping room. The attendant was seated at a small desk at the end of an eighteenth floor hallway.

"Another one to see Malloy?" the attendant said as he examined the pass. "Forget it, mister. He won't see anybody."

"I'll go in and see for myself," Javik said, retrieving the pass.

"Not permitted. You can only see him in a glassplexed visiting area."

"Do you see the signature on this pass?" Javik said forcefully, holding the pass only centimeters from the attendant's face. "General Arturo Munoz!"

"Uh, yes. I noticed that."

"And you know who he is, I presume?"

"Of course, but . . ."

"Show me the way," Javik said. "Unless you want to explain to the General why you wouldn't let me through."

"No, of course not." The attendant was flustered. He thought for a moment, then rose and said, "This way, please."

Designating a room several moto-paces away, the attendant opened the door to it. He started to enter with Javik, but Javik told him to wait outside.

The attendant followed the instruction, although it obviously made him uncomfortable to do so.

Javik mentoed the door shut behind him.

The sleeping room was large, and at first scan appeared empty. Smelling woodsy sweetness, Javik looked up to see the fine mist of air freshener as it dropped from ceiling nozzles. Presently he made out a solitary form huddled fetally on a cot near the room's center.

"Sid," Javik called out as he rolled along an aisle between cots. "Hey, Sid. That you, buddy?"

The form stirred. It rolled over to face Javik, exposing a twisted, unrecognizable face.

"Oh, I'm sorry. . . ." Javik caught himself as he recognized half the face. "Hey, Sid," Javik said as he reached the cot. "How ya doin'?"

"Tom! You shouldn't be . . ." Sidney felt self-conscious under Javik's stare and turned away. "Leave me, Tom. *Please.*"

"Good news, Sid. You're assigned to a space cruiser with me! I'm a First Louie now!" Javik sat on an adjacent cot, stared at Sidney's back.

"Don't humor me," Sidney whined. "I'm no kid."

"Honest, Sid. General Munoz signed an authorization. After you're treated on Elba, he says I can pick you up. You'll be on Elba tomorrow. We blast off from there Tuesday."

"Really?" Sidney said, not turning around.

"I can't give you any mission details now, and you're not to mention it to anyone. But take my word. It's legit. Look at this pass here. See that signature?"

Sidney took the slip of paper with his good hand and read. "Hey!" he said. "This is signed by General Munoz! Isn't he the Bu-Mil Min—"

"You got it, buddy." Javik retrieved the pass, then patted Sidney's back like an older brother. "You and me on a big mission, Sid! We used to dream this day would come!"

"What's the assignment?"

"Classified for now. Our ship's the Shamrock Five. It's a beauty, pal!"

"You asked for ME? Re-a-ll-y?"

"Yeah, sure. Listen, Sid, I gotta go. I'll see ya on Elba!"

"This is fantastic!" Sidney said, turning the good side of his face up to Javik, with the twisted part concealed beneath a forearm.

After Javik left, Sidney recalled the nightmare he had suffered that morning. The vision had prophesied correctly that he and Javik would be on the same ship. But those terrible knives . . . Sidney assured himself that this part of the vision would not happen.

A nice way to spend Sunday evening, General Munoz thought. *After dinner I'll call for a game of Knave Table. . . .*

Munoz sat on a pillow at the head of a walnut-grained plastic banquet table with his eyes closed. One tiny hand rested on the burnished gold cross that dangled from his neck. He smiled serenely and listened while his dinner guests took their seats in the candlelit dining room module. On the inside of his eyelids, a video weather transmission revealed Afrikari blanketed by dark AmFed-made clouds. It had been this way since just after Friday's meeting with the Alafin, thus rendering their telescope useless. The General was pleased.

He opened his eyes, spread a white lace napkin across his lap. Looking around the table, he smiled and nodded to each of the eight men and four women as they placed napkins on their own laps. These were the hand-picked members of his inner circle, a group whose loyalty was unquestioned. Munoz knew every thought they made in his presence. And they knew his, since each had been given the ultimate gift, an implanted mento transceiver.

Unknown to anyone at the table, President Ogg watched them intently at that moment from his study, using the palm-held video receiver given him by the Black Box of Democracy. *Thought-speak,* Ogg thought. *The voice said they thought-speak.*

"Good evening," Munoz said. He raised one hand, causing meckie-arms in front of each plate to pour red wine into crystal goblets. The General glanced for a moment toward a great fireplace along one wall, studied a large gold cross which stretched from the mantle to the ceiling. Along the mantletop were his favorite war trophies, gold and silver mementos inlaid with precious stones. Candlelight flickered and danced on the cross and on the trophies. He considered mentoing the fireplace but decided against it. The evening was warm.

General Munoz lifted his wine goblet, sloshed wine and peered through the crystal at the drip pattern made by the liquid as it ran down the inside of the goblet. He smelled the bouquet, tasted.

"Magnificent!" he said, watching the guests as they raised their goblets. He nodded to Dr. Hudson on his immediate right, mento-addressed the gathering: *Election programming has been initiated. I selected fifty-seven-point-three-six percent as my portion of the vote.*

Good choice, Hudson mentoed. He pushed his eyeglasses forward to scratch the bridge of his nose.

Allen and I are going to my country condo tomorrow, Munoz mentoed. *An early celebration, you might say!*

"Excellent wine," a dark-haired woman at the other end of the table said. "A LaTour, I believe?"

"You are quite correct, Miss Stevens," Munoz replied.

Congratulations, General, she mentoed while raising her glass in toast. *Soon you will be President of the American Federation of Freeness!* "A toast!" she said aloud. "I propose a toast to the General for his hospitality!"

"Thank you," Munoz said, raising his glass. *And a toast to each of you,* he mentoed happily, *the future ministers in MY council!*

They drank and laughed and spoke of harmless things for several minutes. Then the center of the table opened up, with its walnut-grained plastic panels sliding down into the surface.

An oblong-shaped conveyor track appeared, carrying a variety of dishes which moved slowly around the table. The conveyor stopped and started, following mento-commands given by the diners.

Colonel Peebles sat to the General's immediate left. He watched a meckie-arm as it piled honey-basted Peking Goose, Mandarin Pancakes and plum sauce on his plate. The meckie-arm spread plum sauce on Peebles' pancake with a scallion brush, then dropped bits of goose and scallion on the pancake and rolled it up.

That will be enough for now, the light-eating Peebles mentoed. The conveyor clicked into motion, stopping at the next diner.

General Munoz nibbled on a piece of gooseskin, tasting the pungent bite of spices. Suddenly he dropped his gooseskin and stared wide-eyed at a trash can near the fireplace. A piece of paper fluttered in the air over the can!

"Leave me alone!" Munoz yelled, putting his hands up and recoiling. "Leave me alone!"

"What's wrong, General?" Hudson asked.

"There!" Munoz said, pointing at the trash can. "There!"

But before Hudson and the others could turn their heads, the piece of paper had fallen back into the can. "Didn't anyone see it?" Munoz wailed. Realizing they had not, Munoz buried his face in his hands and felt his pulse thump wildly.

"What was it, General?" Colonel Peebles asked. He read General Munoz's thoughts, saw the vision of a piece of paper fluttering over a trash can.

Picking up the same thought, Hudson asked: "Another fireball?"

Munoz kept his face buried in his hands. "Get it out!" he yelled. "Get it out!"

Hudson barked a command, and a servant hurried over to the can, removing it to another room. "We'll have your disposa-tubes reconnected, Arturo," Hudson said.

Munoz nodded, rested his forehead on the back of one hand and sat there breathing hard. Little droplets of perspiration were visible on his forehead. *Don't any of you think it,* Munoz mentoed. *I am not mad!*

"Why did you send Javik along?" a distant, teasing voice said, speaking from inside General Munoz's skull.

There! Munoz mentoed to the gathering. *Did you hear that?*

Hear what, General? they mentoed. *We didn't hear any-thing.*

The voice returned: *"This is private conversation, General. We told you to send Malloy alone. But you got Javik involved."*

"I couldn't put a cappy on the ship by himself!" Munoz yelled. "We can't rely on a god-damned cappy!"

Munoz's guests sat at the table in shocked silence, afraid to do or think anything.

"You should have listened, General," the voice said. *"You should have listened!"*

"Blast you!" Munoz bellowed. "I'll do as I damn well please!"

The voice receded, and Munoz closed his eyes tightly, his face contorted in pain and fury.

What in the hell is going on? President Ogg thought as he watched these events. *The man is mad . . . stark, raving mad!*

Attempting to change the subject, Colonel Peebles mentoed the gathering: *I almost wish military action had been necessary, just to see if the Black Box is what it's cracked up to be!*

Surprised, Hudson looked away from General Munoz. *Huh?*

What do you suppose is inside those shiny black walls, Doctor? Peebles mentoed, looking with pale blue eyes across the table at Hudson. *A robot army? Or some terrible array of automatic weapons?*

Hudson made idle chatter, then mentoed: *Your guess is as good . . . or should I say as bad . . . as mine. We must be careful about undue curiosity, Allen. It could lead to our undoing!*

"I must have this recipe!" exclaimed a pudgy man seated halfway down the table. He wiped his chin with a napkin.

"Certainly, Brockman," Munoz replied, straightening as he regained his composure. "Have your chef give mine a call." *You'll make a fine Bu-Cops Minister,* the General mentoed.

"Thanks, General," Brockman said with a wink to make it clear he was responding at once to the spoken and to the un-spoken. *I'd like to investigate the possibility of giving thought-reading powers to my police detectives,* he mentoed. *Dr. Hud-son tells me the Council Ministers' transceivers can be tuned to a private wavelength . . . making our thoughts unreadable by subordinates.*

A simple modification, Hudson mentoed. He sipped his wine and sloshed it in his mouth before swallowing it.

Munoz nodded in affirmation, then mentoed angrily: *In two days that fool Ogg will be out of office! He doesn't know the first damned thing about technology, but loves to use it for his own purposes and take all the credit! Look at the beautiful weather he told Bu-Tech to create just before the election!*

"A toast!" Colonel Peebles exclaimed, lifting his wine goblet. "To President Ogg's re-election!"

"Yes!" everyone said, raising their glasses. "To President Ogg!"

"Good man," Munoz said, drinking his last bit of wine. He touched his cross with one hand and closed his eyes to watch simultaneous cloudbursts dump on Afrikari and on the Union of Atheist States.

"That lying bastard!" Euripides Ogg raged as he watched the tiny video screen. "The way their eyelids flicker during long silences . . . they're making conversational gestures without speaking aloud! The Black Box . . ."

A chill ran down the President's torso as it occurred to him that someone might be eavesdropping on him at that moment. He fell silent, turned off the video screen and stared at his bookcase.

I should do something, he thought. *But what?*

* * *

After collecting the homework assignments, Sayer Superior Lin-Ti stacked them neatly and slipped them into his briefcase.

"During the balance of the week," he announced to the class, "you will read Chapters Six through Eight on your own. I have been called away on urgent business. . . ."

SIX

HISTORICAL PERSPECTIVE, FOR
FURTHER READING AND DISCUSSION

August 6, 2326: The Last Holy War. "A great little war," in the words of colorful General William C. ("Bomber Bill") McKay, Bu-Mil's seventh minister. On that day, AmFed turbo bombers rained holy bombs on non-Christian enclaves around the world. The Treaty of Rabat followed, in which the planet was divided into three nations—the American Federation of Freeness (encompassing North and South America, India, the Middle East, Europe, Australia and S.E. Asia); Afrikari (all of Africa except Egypt); and the Union of Atheist States (Soviet Union, China and several minor nations).

Monday, August 28, 2605

It was the first morning coffee break, Garbage Day minus four. Carla mentoed the galactic pool cue, watched her white cue ball carom off an obstacle post and enter a side pocket. A wallscreen over the table lit up with bright yellow and purple gamma flashes as the cue ball's matter was consumed by one of the game's synthetic black holes.

"Damn!" Carla said. She looked at her opponent, Samantha Petrie. Petrie was plump, perhaps three years Carla's junior, with saucer-like round eyes and a toothy smile.

"Too bad," Petrie said with an I-got-you smile. "That'll cost you another hundred bucks."

Carla nodded with resignation. "That's enough for me," she announced, reaching into her belt purse. Carla wore a tangerine orange business suit dress, with a ruffled white blouse and a narrow striped tie. A tiny painted orange beauty mark graced her left cheek.

"Three straight!" Petrie said. "I've never beaten you like that!"

"I beat myself. Too many things on my mind." Carla passed three crisp new hundred dollar bills to Petrie, then closed her belt purse.

They moto-shoed across the crowded Presidential Bureau Gameroom to a wallscreen on which President Ogg could be seen delivering a campaign speech. "Do you want to talk about it?" Petrie asked.

Carla thought for a moment, then: "Might help."

They sat on a couch in front of the wallscreen, listening while Ogg harangued about Hoovervilles and unemployment lines in the "bad old days." People on nearby lounge chairs and couches watched the screen or chatted in low tones. The President concluded by requesting that everyone punch Tele-Charge voting button number one on Tuesday. "A vote for me is a vote for prosperity," he promised. The screen went dark.

"Sidney has a terrible handicap," Carla began sadly. "He's being sent to a therapy orbiter."

"Oh," Petrie said, her tone sincere. "That's unfortunate."

Carla picked nervously at her cuticles. "I tried to visit him yesterday at the detention center, but he refused to see me."

"What does he have?"

"A nerve disorder. I've known about it for years, but he was always able to control it...until Saturday night. He had an attack at the reunion."

"How sad."

"I just wanted to give him some code information—a few

numbers and names to drop in the right places. You know, to make life a little easier for him up there." Carla felt tears welling up in her eyes. "I also wanted to say goodbye."

"I wish there was something I could do."

"I know what you must be thinking," Carla said, glancing at Petrie. "He should have submitted himself for therapy long ago."

"I didn't think any such thing. I know how you feel about him."

"Do you? How?"

"It's been obvious to me for a long time that one of you had to have a problem . . . loving one another the way you do but never becoming permies."

"I suppose I do love Sidney, but I just never . . ." She cleared her throat, wiped tears from her cheeks. The orange beauty mark smeared. Petrie put an arm across Carla's shoulder.

Carla chewed at her upper lip. "It's been terribly difficult. And I hurt him by not going to the reunion."

"No one can blame you for that," Petrie said consolingly. "If that hunk Billie Birdbright had called ME at the last minute, I'd have found a way to go out with him too."

"I couldn't turn Billie down. All the girls want to go out with him. Just think of it, Samantha—He's Chief of Staff!"

"You shouldn't feel ashamed. This may sound cold, but you have every right to be happy. It's Sidney's problem, not yours."

"I suppose."

"How was the date with Billie?"

"Fine."

"You can tell me, Carla. Did you? . . ."

Carla laughed and pushed her friend away. "You're a Nosy Nellie!"

"I hear a lot of good stuff that way!"

Carla's face grew sad again and she stared at the darkened wallscreen. "I've seen the statistics," she said. "One institutionalized cappy supports seven-point-three-two-five government employees. But . . . well, I don't know." She sighed.

"Cappy sounds so impersonal, doesn't it?" Petrie said.

"He's much more than a statistic," Carla said. "Sidney is flesh and blood, a warm, loving human being!"

"Yes, but maybe this is better for him. You know, being with his own kind. Everything in the American Federation is so perfect. Their kind is better off in a separate area, where people won't laugh and call them names."

"I suppose you're right." Carla rubbed her temple with the fingers of one hand and thought back over the years she had known Sidney—all the good times and special occasions.

Will I ever see him again? she wondered.

From the fifth floor conditioning room in Building C, Javik could see New City Field perhaps a thousand meters to the East. A mid-morning sun seemed to drift in a clear blue sky, casting the profile shadows of rockets and support aircraft across the asphalt of the field.

Javik smelled the acridity of his own perspiration, looked down at rings of sweat on his grey workout suit. The lung pump to which he was connected throbbed and surged, strengthening and cleansing his body's breathing system. He removed the mouthpiece, watched a large group of people in the distance who were gathered around an older model passenger rocket. Small guard contingents could be seen posted at other ships on the field, and Javik knew the reason: people trying to escape the comet had already stolen a number of small and medium sized rockets.

Javik looked to one side as he felt the pressure in the room change, saw Colonel Peebles moto-shoe in carrying his military cap in one hand. "Greetings," Peebles said.

The tone was sinister to Javik's ears, and he did not return the salutation.

"Getting in shape?" Peebles asked. His nose wrinkled. "Smells like it."

Javik smiled as he noted the lack of muscle tone on Peebles's emasculated body. This was Peebles's second visit of the day, and Javik saw no point in feigning civility. They had nothing to discuss.

"The General would like me to brief you on certain ship's functions," Peebles said, "and on the method of approach you will use in getting close to that streaking ball of fire."

"Ha!" Javik said. He lifted a dexterity amplification cube, held it between both palms and went through a series of joint and muscle tone exercises. "That'll be the day, Peebles... when I take instructions from you!"

"This mission is no simple exercise," Peebles said, glancing around the room irritably.

"There are message box briefing systems onboard ship, I presume?"

"Of course."

"I'll study inflight. You didn't tape them yourself, did you?"

"No. Job-Sharing wouldn't permit such a thing."

"Good. I don't want to listen to your whining voice in space." Javik smiled as he twisted his torso.

Peebles took a deep, exasperated breath, turned to leave.

"I do have one question for you," Javik said as he continued exercising. "I was grabbing a cup of coffee from the vending machine outside the briefing room... right after I talked with you and Munoz."

"Oh?"

"The door was open, and I heard you say something about hoping for the best. What the hell kind of a comment was that?" Javik set the dexterity amplification cube on a bench. "All our technology, and you're hoping for the best?"

"I don't recall saying anything like that," Peebles said, lifting and dropping his eyebrows. "You must have misunderstood." He rolled out of the room hurriedly with this thought: *What I wouldn't give to watch the Madame do her slicing routine on that insolent bastard!*

Peebles just retreated, Javik thought. *Wonder how that weakling got to be an officer....*

Alone in his office, Dr. Hudson mulled over what he had to do. A half-eaten donut lay on a napkin at the right side of his green desk mat. He stared at the donut disconsolately.

Munoz has gone crazy, he thought. *I've got to get off a message to Nancy. She can keep that blasted cappy off our ship....*

Hudson formulated the wording of an electronic letter in his mind. *I'll send it myself after hours,* he thought. *Then I can destroy all record of it on this end.*

But Hudson understood too well the hardest part: in his presence, Munoz could read his thoughts. *I'll have to control every thought when he's around,* Hudson thought. *I'll clutter my head with other things. He'd kill me for this....*

* * *

A slushpile of humanity was assembled in the cool morning shade of the passenger rocket. Sidney Malloy stood in their midst, wearing a light green hospital gown. He shivered at a gust of wind, squeezed the gown collar shut around his neck with his good hand. Having lost track of the shots given him by attendants since his capture, Sidney felt numb and wobbly.

For a moment, he wondered if Javik had really visited him in the sleeping room, or if it had been a drug-fogged dream. *It happened*, Sidney told himself. *It happened!*

Blind and crippled babies cried incessantly in the arms of white-uniformed Bu-Med attendants, next to people who had met similar fates by accident or disease in their later years. They leaned on moto-crutches and sat in wheelchairs, drooling, chewing, grimacing, having convulsions and throwing up. Sidney breathed through his mouth because of the stench, looked from face to face at forlorn eyes and hopeless expressions on all sides. These were the traditional clients of Bu-Med.

Another group of clients waited to be taken aboard for the trip to Saint Elba. These pale-skinned men and women stood apart in handcuffs and chains, surrounded by black-uniformed Security Brigade guards. Moments earlier, Sidney had heard an attendant explain that they were "doomies," the dangerously insane who demonstrated against Freeness and the AmFed Way. The attendant said this type always searched for causes, and now their cause was a comet which allegedly would destroy the planet. The doomies spoke in angry tones, lunging and pulling at their chains in great clatters and surges of fury. Some had rebellious, angry eyes that glared at anyone daring to look upon them. Others were heavily sedated, and their eyes rolled up and around, not focusing upon anything.

A sea of white-uniformed attendants surrounded and far outnumbered these groups of clients. Sidney overheard two female attendants talking nearby:

"You *volunteered?*" said one. "I was assigned to this rotten duty by the Job Board."

"I don't think it's rotten," the other said. "We can help these poor creatures."

"You've got a strange attitude, sweetie," the first said. Sidney detected cruelty in her voice.

A small boy with straw-yellow hair screamed suddenly and fell to the pavement at Sidney's feet, writhing and kicking spastically. Sidney started to reach down to him, when a female attendant rushed over and administered an injection in the boy's arm. Sidney felt a sharp pain in his own twisted left arm, as if the needle had punctured his skin too. He rubbed the arm. Feeling a little dizzy, he shook his head to clear it.

When Sidney's head cleared, he watched the boy's jerking motions gradually slow and subside. The boy lay there unconscious on his side, with a twisted, pained expression on his thin face. Two attendants placed him on a moto-cot and rolled him to one side.

"Is this craft spaceworthy?" an attendant asked. Sidney did not hear another attendant's reply. Voices were drowned in the whir and clank of an approaching entry lift.

Hearing a mumble to his left, Sidney looked down at a hunchbacked old man whose lips were moving slowly. The man had sparse grey hair, deeply creased skin and dark age splotches across his face and on the backs of his hands. A single black hair grew out of a mole on the old man's chin.

Forgetting his own situation momentarily, Sidney was revulsed at the sight of such a decrepit human specimen. *He's not far from the Happy Shopping Ground,* Sidney thought, dismayed that anyone had to reach such a loathsome state. Then Sidney asked, "What did you say?"

The old man cleared his throat, hawked and swallowed. "This is a bunch of shit," he said in an angry, gravelly voice.

Sidney stared down at a broken front tooth as the man spoke, then asked, "What do you mean?"

"The good things in society are reserved for normal, youthful people." The voice was bitter. "They're throwing us away, like someone's garbage."

Sidney wanted to tell the man he was going to be in the Space Patrol with Tom Javik, but decided against it and said, "I'm sure they'll take good care of us." He watched the entry lift lock into place against the passenger rocket.

"My son hid me out for years," the old man said, rubbing the mole on his chin. "But finally his wife . . . the bitch . . . turned me in."

"You should be thankful for having such a wonderful son."

"Thankful? There's nothing to be thankful about! I couldn't go out in public! They don't want people like me around!" The old man started to lose his voice, coughed.

"There are a lot of good things about the American Federation," Sidney said.

The old man wiped saliva and phlegm from his chin with his gown collar, then glared up at Sidney and demanded, "Name just one."

"Freeness."

"Ha!"

"There were terrible depressions before Freeness," Sidney said, "with millions of people out of work. They stood in souplines and begged for survival."

"Employment for everyone isn't worth the price," the old man said, coughing and hawking again. "Now leave me be!"

Sidney stared at the old man in disbelief, for Sidney still believed in the AmFed Way. It was not a perfect society, he told himself, but it was the best ever devised. Then a distant, wafting voice in Sidney's brain said, *"The old man is right, fleshcarrier. The AmFeds don't give a damn about you! And they'll never let you near the cockpit of a Space Patrol ship!"*

"Tom promised me," Sidney said, aloud.

"Sure, but the AmFeds will find a way to keep you in your place. You're worth more to them as a cappy."

"You're wrong!"

"Each institutionalized cappy supports seven-point-three-two-five government employees."

"Who are you?" Sidney asked. "And why do you call me fleshcarrier?"

"We live in the Realm of Magic," the voice said, *"where there is no flesh. You live in the Realm of Flesh ... where there is no magic."*

"What do you mean?"

There was no further response from the voice, and Sidney noticed a paunchy male attendant looking at him strangely. "Mental case," the attendant said, glancing at a brunette female attendant next to him.

She nodded.

Sidney flushed red. He saw a white driverless limousine approach and pull to a stop near the passenger rocket. A tall, black-robed priest short-stepped out onto an expando-platform. As the platform rose straight up in the air, the priest stood with white-gloved hands clasped in front of his round belly. When the platform stopped just above the height of his limousine, he raised his arms and spoke in a tone that was at once powerful and soothing.

"Let us pray," the priest said.

Everyone except the doomies bowed their heads.

"We are gathered here to embark upon a great journey of mercy," the priest said. "May Uncle Rosy grant us the ability to heal these broken bodies, to calm these troubled spirits."

Then the priest said "Amen" and came down to moto-shoe through the group, laying gloved hands upon the clients' shoulders and heads.

"Oh thank you, father!" a leper woman cried out. "Thank you!"

Pausing in front of Sidney, the priest reached down with gloved hands to touch his shoulders and said, "May Uncle Rosy bless you and make you well, my son."

Sidney looked up into the holy man's clear brown eyes, saw sincerity and eyes that were close to tears. *I'm going to get on that ship*, Sidney thought. *The voice was wrong.*

Onesayer Edward grasped the edge of his Basin of Youth and peered down into the mirror-like surface of the holy water there. *Blast it to Hoover!* he thought, looking at the skin around both eyes. *The lines are deeper today!*

It was mid-morning Monday, and he stood at a greystone basin which had been designated with his name. The basin felt rough to his touch, was closest to an arched entrance to the central chamber, one of sixty-six basins along the same wall. Brown-robed sayermen stood silently at each basin with their hoods thrown back, revealing shaved heads. They splashed holy water on their faces and drank the sacred elixir from red plastic cups.

Onesayer dipped a hand into the warm water, rubbed liquid against the creases on his face. He waited for the water to grow calm, then again peered into the reflective surface. It was definite. The lines around his eyes had grown deeper. He shook his head sadly.

"What is it?" Twosayer William asked, looking over from the adjacent basin. A noticeably consumptive sayerman, his oval face was punctuated by a prominent hooked nose. Twosayer wiped holy water from his eyebrows with two fingers, awaited a reply.

"Nothing," Onesayer replied. He leaned over and threw holy water on his face.

Twosayer rolled closer, said, "You are certain?"

Onesayer flicked a quick glance up out of the corner of one eye, saw Twosayer standing erectly over him, looking down inquisitively with grey green eyes. Onesayer looked down quickly, closed his eyes and splashed holy water on his face. *Get away from me!* he thought.

Twosayer was the shorter of the two, by at least half a head, and to Onesayer seemed the sort who was always trying to gain advantage over the next sayerman. Twosayer looked for weaknesses in others or tried to position himself so that he appeared taller than he actually was . . . standing on the higher portions of sloping ground or floor whenever he had the opportunity.

Onesayer felt an open hand on his back. "You can confide in me," Twosayer said in a tone that seemed false to Onesayer's ears.

"I am fine," Onesayer said forcefully. Grasping the basin edge tightly, he stared angrily at the ripples of water. Onesayer was startled to see a tiny blotchy shadow on the back of one hand. He dipped the hand into the water quickly. *Did he see it?* Onesayer wondered. Then Onesayer spoke without looking up, "Please . . . I will talk with you later."

Onesayer felt the hand leave his back.

"All right," Twosayer said slowly. "But if I can . . ."

"Peace be upon you," Onesayer said irritably. He watched peripherally as Twosayer rolled back to his own basin after he returned the blessing. Twosayer drank holy water from a red cup and then threw the cup into a wall-mounted disposa-tube. Machinery inside the wall whirred.

Onesayer wiped his face dry with a towel, then straightened and turned away from Twosayer. Feeling warm under the presumed gaze of Twosayer, he rolled away hurriedly into the Central Chamber. The low light of the chamber felt refreshing to him. It protected him from enemies.

SEVEN

BASIC DISINTEGRATION THEORY,
FOR FURTHER READING AND DISCUSSION

1. Wherever possible, the product or a key component is constructed of a fragile material; 2. Ideally, the product should self-destruct, taking other products with it; 3. Never rely on one part to break down—systems should be designed so that several key components fall apart at once.

Monday, August 28, 2605

It took an hour for the priest to complete the blessings.

When Sidney rode an entry lift up the side of the HLLV passenger rocket with a group of clients and attendants, he thought about how old and dingy the rocket appeared. Dull silver flecks of EZ-plating hung from the great bird's skin, barely reflecting sunlight, and numerous dents gave the ship an anachronistic appearance. Some rivets were missing. Others hung loose, ready to fall at any moment.

"Why do you suppose this ship hasn't been replaced?" a man behind Sidney asked. Sidney turned his head to look at the speaker, a thin man in a green client's smock.

"I was just wondering the same thing," Sidney said, scratching one of his black, bushy eyebrows. "Something got bogged down in red tape, I guess."

The lift came to a stop, and the attendants escorted their clients through an oval doorway into the ship's worn interior. Like Sidney, some clients moto-shoed under their own power. Others had to be carried or pushed, and some rolled in shakily on moto-crutches.

As Sidney entered the rocket, an overwhelming stench burned his nostrils. The odors made him nauseous. They were an amplification of the unwashed crowd smells he had experienced since being taken into detention. Trying to breathe through his mouth, he glanced around the compartment while awaiting instructions.

All seats in the passenger module had been removed, and the grey creme painted walls had a wide, dark green stripe along the bottom. An attendant told Sidney to sit on the floor against one wall beneath a tiny porthole. Sidney brushed away rust flakes from the dirty metal floor, then sat down cross-legged. The floor was cool under his thin smock. His twisted left arm ached.

"Put her over there," a burly male attendant said. Sidney watched two white-uniformed attendants guide a saggingly heavy retardo client to her spot on the floor. Stringy brown hair almost covered her face. She sat facing Sidney with her knees hunched up, lolling her head from side to side and appearing to laugh uncontrollably without uttering a sound.

Sidney laughed too, then looked away to watch the attendants leave. Presently, he looked back at the woman. The smiling mouth changed now, almost imperceptibly, to a grimace. She seemed to be screaming out in silent pain, and it was no longer funny.

"Is there anything I can do?" Sidney asked her.

The woman did not reply. She continued to smile and grimace. Then she rocked forward and back, her hands clasped together about bruised and scabby shins.

All the clients were told to take seats on the floor, and

Sidney felt the suffocating press of humanity all around him. The doomies were pushed and dragged into the compartment. They sat in an area near the door, still chained together and accompanied by Security Brigade guards. Other clients were directed to an elevator for placement in upper and lower passenger compartments.

It took perhaps an hour and a half to load the ship. By the time the heavy metal door rang closed, Sidney was not feeling at all well. The air was close and hot. His deformed arm twitched spasmodically. Stinging sweat trickled down his brow and into his eyes.

As the rocket engines surged, Sidney detected the licorice odor of G-gas filtering into the compartment. The rocket rumbled into the blue, nearly cloudless morning sky, and Sidney watched the skyline of New City through a large porthole on the opposite side of the compartment.

"This ship is so slow!" someone said. "How could they be concerned about G-forces?" A tittering of laughter lasted several seconds, then subsided.

Sidney closed his eyes. He tried to calm himself by recalling his scrapbooks and dreams of space travel. Javik's words came back to him: *You and me on a big mission, Sid. We used to dream this day would come!*

As the ship settled into flight, some of the attendants tried to cheer their clients by organizing singing commercials, and Sidney participated in a mediocre round of the "Shiny New Song." It went:

> Our land is full of pretty things,
> Cars and homes and plastic rings;
> Shiny New! All Shiny New!
> Happy times for me and you!

The doomies refused to take part, and sat to one side talking in low, angry tones. Finally the attendants gave up their effort, and the clients slipped into silent thought, each to his own remorseful, self-pitying corner of consciousness.

Sidney had such feelings as well, but felt better when he realized his days of boredom as a G. W. seven-five-oh working five hundred floors underground were gone forever. *I'm going to a zero-gravity region!* he thought. Sidney's ill feelings and twitchings subsided now, and he told himself that a positive attitude would make him feel better.

The retardo woman facing Sidney dozed off and leaned her head against a large, ruddy-faced blind man who sat next to her. The sightless man wore dark wraparound sunglasses and had a tuft of unkempt dark brown hair that appeared not to have been combed for days. A small mouth and high cheekbones appeared oriental to Sidney, although he could not determine the shape of the man's eyes behind the sunglasses.

The blind man allowed the woman to slip her head onto his lap as she fell into a deeper sleep. Her grimace-smiles subsided in slumber, and soon she appeared more at peace. Sidney looked around to stare at the disjointed jerks and unusual mannerisms of crip-clients. And he listened to the haunting, guttural grunts of retardos. A tow-headed boy with only one arm sat to Sidney's left, staring straight ahead.

Sidney rose to his knees with a bit of difficulty. *Not so easy with only one good arm*, he thought. He peered through a tiny porthole on the wall. The HLLV was traveling through a region of sparse cirrus clouds, and Sidney saw a fleet of Atheist sky mining ships working the area. They looked like giant pot-bellied beetles, with scores of anteater-like vacuum snouts swishing the air on all sides.

Sidney had studied the ships as a boy. He knew the snouts collected recyclable minerals and chemicals which were in the atmosphere as pollutants. He had always wondered how such a resource retrieval system could be practical, considering the E-Cell fuel such ships must consume. *They must be spy ships*, he thought, *working busy AmFed shipping lanes*.

A great burst of noise and clatter came from the doomie area, and Sidney turned to see them jostling about, pulling and rattling their chains as they chanted rhythmically:

> Crazy are we, no. . . .
> The comet's in the sky!
> Fire will rain upon us. . . .
> And surely we will die!

"Get 'em!" a stocky Security Brigade sergeant yelled.

Black-uniformed guards and Bu-Med attendants rushed the doomies and overpowered them with numbers. Sedative injections were administered, and the doomies passed out in a heap on the floor.

Shortly afterward, the HLLV left Earth's atmosphere and Sidney felt a momentary weightless sensation. It excited him when he was lifted a few centimeters off the floor before dropping back gently as the ship's gravitational system began to whir.

His studies told him what would happen next. Soon they would reach the staging area for transfer to an Inter-Orbital Transport Vehicle. The HLLV would release its passenger module for pickup by the transport, a lighter craft that never touched planetary surfaces. It would take the group to the orbiting L_5 city and therapy habitat of Saint Elba.

That afternoon, Tom Javik stood alone in a gold and white Space Patrol uniform at the base of the Shamrock Five. He glanced up at the shimmering black-and-silver Akron class cruiser, thought how fortunate he was to be assigned to it.

He watched Colonel Peebles short-step out of a computer-operated limousine parked at the edge of the landing pad. A woman with hair cut boot-military length followed. The pair moto-shoed toward the waiting ship's captain.

"Jeez!" Javik said in a low tone out of the side of his mouth. "That woman is UG-LY!" He smiled, picked food out of his teeth from a just-completed afternoon meal.

"This is Madame Bernet," Colonel Peebles said as they arrived. "She will be Onboard Systems Coordinator for the mission." Javik detected a sneer in the colonel's expression.

"This wasn't mentioned previously," Javik said.

"Oh, wasn't it?" Peebles said, feigning innocence. "It's quite standard now. But then you wouldn't know that . . . having been out of touch for two years."

Disregarding the remark, Javik studied the Madame intently and saw a clear, lineless face with a sloping, weak chin and a bulbous nose. She was quite short, and seemed lost in a loose-fitting white-and-gold dress emblazoned with the Space Patrol crest. Her hands remained in pockets at each side, and her smile never touched her eyes.

Glad I didn't stumble into this Madame's pleasure dome, Javik thought, attempting humor to allay the inexplicable fear he felt.

Madame Bernet saluted crisply. "Request permission to board, Lieutenant Javik."

"Very military," Javik said. A gust of wind blew his amber

hair across his eyes. He pushed the hair back.

A look which Javik could only describe as murderous flashed across the Madame's face. "Request permission. . . ."

"Permission granted," Javik said, scowling at the Madame.

As Madame Bernet short-stepped onto a boarding elevator, Javik turned to Peebles and said, "She's a meckie. Nicely done, I might add."

Peebles lowered his eyelids and asked: "What makes you say that?"

"The eyes. They never lie. The eyes are not human."

"I see. And that is a professional opinion?" Peebles shifted uneasily on his feet as he watched the boarding elevator ascend.

"Yes. I assisted Bu-Industry several years ago in a meckie experiment where human-like meckies were given tasks onboard ship."

"Re-e-e-ally?" Peebles said, a strange grin on his face.

"No matter how they were programmed, there always seemed to be an emergency they could not handle. Your Madame Bernet is a meckie."

Peebles's grin faded. "All right," he said, irritably. "It is a meckie. But that really doesn't make any difference on this mission. It will be coordinating the cappy workcrews, tending to them so that you can operate the ship without distraction."

"Show me the program track," Javik said, looking up to watch Madame Bernet roll off the entry platform and enter the ship.

"There won't be time for that," Peebles said. "It's not accessible without special tools."

"How convenient," Javik said. He scowled as he motoshoed around chrome thrust deflector fins to a spot beneath the Shamrock Five. There he inspected a trailer release mechanism.

I don't like unknowns, Javik thought, touching the cool metal surface. *But God I want to fly this gorgeous ship . . . and I promised Sidney. . . .*

Something troubled Javik about the meckie. But he put all such thoughts out of his mind.

An hour later, a six-armed Union Maid meckie discovered the bodies of General Munoz and Colonel Peebles at Munoz's country condominium. Water covered the floor of the bedroom module, and the men were found in a lovers' embrace on top of the waterbed.

Finding no life signs, the meckie automatically went to Emergency Mode. "Rule one-one-nine," the meckie said in its halting tone while rolling into the hallway. "Report death of ministerial personnel directly to the President."

Nineteen minutes later, the meckie stood in President Ogg's sunny office giving its report. "Product failure," the meckie said, waving its six mechanical arms demonstrably. "Minister Munoz died of electrocution when his water-filled mattress ruptured, causing liquid to come in contact with an electrical heating coil."

"Who programmed you?" Ogg demanded, his blue green eyes flashing angrily. "Report the ministerial death only! A forensic team will determine the cause of death!"

The oval office fell into shadow momentarily as a small cloud passed in front of the sun.

"I was programmed by Bu-Tech," the meckie said as the sun returned, "with input from Bu-Med enabling me to substantiate human death."

"Well they went too far! It's bad enough that they've got you cleaning AND playing doctor. Now you're an entire police team too!"

The meckie did not respond. Its arms fell disconsolately to its sides.

"What else can you do?" Ogg asked angrily, rising out of his chair. His voice throbbed with emotion as he asked, "How many citizens are you putting out of work?"

"I am a complicated mechanism," the meckie replied.

"Meckies!" Ogg gruffed. He rolled to the meckie's side and mentoed to open the control box on its top. Scanning the switches inside he thought: *There it is*. He mentoed a combination of numbers to activate the meckie's selective memory erasure feature. *No memory of the Munoz incident*, the President thought, wishing he could destroy the mechanical servant. He kicked it, causing a dull thud.

Billie Birdbright entered as the meckie left.

"I want a full confidential investigation into the cause of death of General Arturo Munoz," Ogg said. "His body is at his country condominium . . . on Kingsgate Road near Lake Ovett."

Surprised, the dimple-chinned Birdbright said, "Yes, Mr. President."

"Send in an entire forensic team by autocopter fleet. I want a preliminary report before quitting time today!"

"Yes, Mr. President."

"Not a minute later, Birdbright! You know how I feel about working after five o'clock!"

The Shamrock Five cleared Earth's atmosphere minutes after takeoff. Javik checked the flight-clip and mentoed course co-ordinates to the ship's mother computer. The sleek space cruiser rolled gently to starboard and accelerated in the vacuum of space.

"What a beautiful bird!" Javik said.

"Handles sweet," Madame Bernet agreed. She sat in the co-pilot's seat, stared dispassionately at Javik.

"I'm at the controls of the finest ship ever built!" Javik exclaimed. "Had a couple of good ships before, but this baby tops 'em all!" But when Javik glanced to his right at Madame Bernet, his elation faded. *That damned meckie keeps staring at me*, he thought.

Madame Bernet grunted, did not take her eyes off Javik.

"Shamrock Five," the radio blared. "This is H.Q. What are your coordinates?"

Javik looked at the gleaming control panel and responded: "Twenty-nine degrees, sixteen minutes, fourteen-point-seven A.T. We've just set course for Saint Elba. Speed twenty-one thousand K.P.H. and accelerating."

"Very good, Shamrock Five. Over and out."

Javik snapped his gaze toward the meckie. It was not staring at him now, seemed interested in a red plastic ball attached to the instrument panel. The meckie's fingers darted forward to touch the ball. A red sign below the device proclaimed: "LEAVE NO SECRETS—SQUEEZE TO DETONATE."

"HEY!" Javik barked. "Get away from that!"

The meckie withdrew its hand, then stared at Javik insolently with cold and inhuman eyes.

Plasto-cyanide bomb, Javik thought, recalling his military days. *Could blow this ship to powder!* "You're no co-pilot," he said tersely. "I want you out of here immediately. Get in the passenger cabin."

"As you wish, Lieutenant," the meckie said, rising to its feet.

After Madame Bernet left, Javik lit a chromium tintette and blew a thoughtful puff of silvery yellow smoke through his nostrils. *That thing gives me the creeps,* he thought.

He shivered.

"Don't think about it," Javik murmured to himself as he flipped on the auto-pilot. "They're not going to send someone . . . or some*thing* . . . along to screw up the mission."

But Javik wondered if the perfume of the new ship had blocked the stench of the mission. Something did not seem right.

EIGHT

**UP CLOSE WITH THE MASTER,
FOR FURTHER READING AND DISCUSSION**

April 8, 2299 through April 21, 2299: Uncle Rosy's famous "Long
March," in which he led a moto-shoe procession from New City
to Philadelphia for the cause of newness, collecting old consumer
goods for disposal.

Monday, August 28, 2605

To President Ogg, quitting time was as sacred a moment as
starting time. Glancing irritably at his watch, he thought, *Seven
minutes past five. The preliminary forensic report on Munoz
should have been here twenty-two minutes ago!*

He rose angrily and rolled into the outer office. *Crisis or
no crisis,* he thought, *I'm not staying any longer!*

Two minutes later, he rolled out of the elevator at the rooftop
helipad. While crossing the pad to reach Autocopter One, Ogg

heard the elevator doors open behind him. He turned to see Billie Birdbright rush out, face flushed, carrying a sheet of paper.

"Mr. President!" Birdbright gasped, holding the sheet up. "The report! It just came in!"

"And?" Ogg said, raising a bushy eyebrow impatiently.

"I glanced at it in the elevator. Product failure, sir. Munoz was electrocuted when his waterbed sprung a leak. Apparently the water touched a hot wire."

"Just as the meckie said. . . ."

"What was that, sir?" Birdbright rubbed a fat cheek nervously with one finger.

"Nothing, nothing. Get the committees set up first thing tomorrow. I want a full investigation into—"

"Mr. President, Munoz was found in an embrace with Colonel Peebles."

"Dammit," President Ogg said, his enthusiasm deflated. "Can't afford a scandal. Not with the election tomorrow."

"What shall we do, Mr. President?"

"Keep the committees out of this one." Ogg scowled, hardly believing he had spoken these words. "We can't release this to the public. Don't mention it to anyone."

"It WAS a product failure, sir, and they are entitled to posthumous Purple Badges."

"I suppose that's true. Uncle Rosy wouldn't want them denied full honors."

"That's right, Mr. President."

"We'll set up a different scenario for their deaths," Ogg said, smiling as if a light had just gone on inside his head.

Birdbright's smile reflected that of his superior. "Another product failure, sir?"

Ogg nodded. "Have the bodies placed in Munoz's autolimo after dark tonight. The car is to be pushed off Saint Patrick's Bridge. That's on a little-used road near Lake Ovett."

"And the death certificates will be documented to show the story the way you want it told."

"Correct." Ogg turned toward the autocopter.

"Brilliant, Mr. President!"

"That's why I'm Head of State, Billie," Ogg said, beaming proudly. He short-stepped into Autocopter One. The machine's rotors whirred to life.

During the flight home, Ogg worried over the decision he

had just made. *The Black Box couldn't have arranged the waterbed failure,* he thought, nervously. *Surely they would have made the deaths more palatable . . . more readily acceptable to the public.*

But as the autocopter prepared to land at a private helipad on the landscaped roof of his condominium building, it occurred to Ogg that the Black Box of Democracy may have wished to discredit Bu-Mil, feeling too much power had gravitated to that arm of government.

Did I interfere? he thought. *Will I incur the wrath of the Black Box?*

Autocopter One made a crisp landing on top of the building.

It was late Monday afternoon when the Inter-Orbital Transport Vehicle picked up Sidney's passenger module.

"We're only a few hours from Saint Elba now," the blind man sitting across from Sidney said.

"That so?" The retardo woman seated next to the blind man smile-grimaced as she spoke.

"I remember not so awfully long ago," the blind man said, "when it took much longer . . . before G-gas allowed passengers to travel at high speeds."

Sidney leaned forward to touch the blind man on his bulky arm and asked: "Were you in the Space Patrol?"

"I sure was!" the blind man said, excitedly. His wraparound sunglasses slipped. He adjusted them. Then his voice slowed and the words slurred as he added, "Until we had an explosion. . . . I was checking an argonium gas leak in the E-Cell compartment of a turbo-bomber hangared at New City Field. . . ."

"You were in maintenance?"

"Uh huh. Left pilotry to the glamour boys."

"You were lucky to survive an explosion."

"Funny thing," the blind man said. "I remember seeing a brilliant flash of orange light. They found me fifty meters away. Didn't have a scratch on me, but the eyes were gone."

Sidney stared at the blind man for several minutes without thinking of anything to say. He did not want to sound patronizing and was afraid Javik would not want him to mention the important mission they were going to share. *This is a stranger,* Sidney thought. *He may be a spy.*

The blind man kept his face pointed in Sidney's direction for a couple of minutes, and Sidney saw the man's lips quiver twice, as if he had a thought but then decided against saying anything. Presently, the blind man turned his face away from Sidney, and his features grew rigid.

Most of the passengers slept during the IOTV flight. They leaned on one another or against walls. A few found places on the floor to curl up in tight balls. Sidney dozed off too, for short periods. Each time he woke up, he looked at the blind man.

The blind man continued to stare straight ahead, or Sidney assumed he was staring behind the dark wraparound sunglasses.

"No more bathroom privileges for clients!" a female attendant called out at one point. "All clients wait until Saint Elba!" Sidney recognized the voice. It was the same attendant he had heard earlier at the field . . . the one with the cruel voice.

"Our johns are on the fritz and the lousy bastards don't wanna touch the same toilet seats we do!" the blind man yelled.

"How much longer?" clients called out.

"Three hours more," an attendant replied. Presently Sidney heard "two hours," then "one hour." The quarters began to smell of ammonia and excrement to Sidney, and in the close hotness he felt he might throw up at any moment. He too had to use the bathroom, but tried to think of other things.

The side porthole over his seating area occupied his attention almost totally during the last hour of flight. Sidney pressed his face against the glass, trying to get a first glorious glimpse of the habitat. The porthole was prismatic, allowing him to see forward along the ship's course by adjusting a wall-mounted lever.

In the blackness of space ahead, Sidney knew one of the bright stars was not really a star. He watched until one began to grow dramatically in brightness.

The Saint Elba habitat! he thought, realizing it was reflecting sunlight from its position between the orbits of the Earth and the Moon. Gradually the habitat's brilliance far exceeded that of the stars beyond. Then it became a narrow band of reflected sunlight.

Within minutes, Sidney could make out identifying features. He recognized the burnished solar collector suspended above Saint Elba, and then the central hub, spokes and tubular outer rim. Saint Elba appeared to be graceful and serene, at once in harmony with itself and with the heavens.

For a time, Sidney was surprised at how small Saint Elba appeared, but as the IOTV matched the habitat's orbit and approached, he began to realize the immensity of the structure. A thick glassplex and titanium outer rim resembled a balloon bicycle tire. He saw twinkling lights and buildings through glassplex on one side of the outer rim, then lost sight of the interior as the IOTV dipped to the habitat's south side.

"Note that the spokes are rotating about the central hub," an attendant said. "This creates pseudo-gravity in the outer rim."

The attendant spoke while looking through another porthole two meters to Sidney's left. Sidney looked at him, saw folds of pink flesh popping out of the man's smock and hanging over his belt.

"I don't see any movement in the outer rim," Sidney said, raising his voice to be heard over the rustlings of people who were awakening.

"A thick cosmic shield is on this side," the attendant said, glancing at Sidney. "The habitat rotates inside it. That shield is made of millions of metric tons of compacted Moon slag and dust."

Sidney nodded appreciatively and peered out the porthole again. The IOTV moved to a position on the south side of the orbiter's sextagonal hub to wait with another ship that was about to dock.

Sidney barely made out the name of the other craft. *The Shamrock Five*, he read, recognizing it as an Akron class long-range space cruiser. *Hey! That's my ship!*

Being faster than standard transport craft, the Shamrock Five arrived at Saint Elba almost simultaneously with the IOTV carrying Sidney.

"You have priority, Shamrock Five," the radio on Javik's command console blared. "We'll bring you in."

Alone in the cockpit, Javik mentoed the Auto-Docking Mode, scanned the blinking lights and glowing dials of the instrument panel.

From the IOTV standing by several hundred meters away, Sidney watched Javik's ship enter the docking tunnel. *Just coax 'er in, Tom*, Sidney thought, seeing a tiny form in the cockpit of the sleek black and silver ship. *What a beauty!* Then Sidney recalled what Javik had done for him at the reunion and glanced down at his twisted arm.

It twitched.

Why would Tom want ME? Sidney wondered, feeling self-pity. *He said I'd be treated here first....* Sidney thought of Carla now, and of his former co-workers, neighbors and friends ... people he might never see again.

At the same instant, Javik thought of Sidney. Maybe Javik half-noticed a round-faced fellow with curly black hair peering out of a porthole on that IOTV, but surely it was too far away for recognition. Still, Javik too reflected upon the reunion, and looked forward to his rendezvous with Sidney on Saint Elba.

They'd better turn him over to me without a runaround, Javik thought, *or somebody's going to wish he didn't get in my way....*

The Shamrock Five was drawn by titanium magne-drive deep into Saint Elba's cavernous docking tunnel. Squinting under the glare of exterior docking spotlights, Javik said to himself, "So far so good."

He flipped on the console screen and checked four outside views of the docking operation. "No problems," he murmured.

"Docking five hundred meters," the onboard computer announced.

"Passenger cabin view," Javik instructed, leaning forward to speak into a speakercom.

The screen flickered and showed Madame Bernet seated alone in the ten-seat passenger cabin, eating a sandwich. *Nice feature,* he mused. *Wonder how the meckie processes the food.* As the meckie finished the sandwich, it licked its fingers.

Javik looked away for a moment to watch the dock come into view, a broad, dimly-lit platform with several ships tethered at the sides. *I'll take a trouble detector through the ship tomorrow before liftoff,* he thought. *I don't want to leave the cockpit with that sub-human wandering around.*

As his eyes darted back to the console screen, Javik saw Madame Bernet staring directly at the camera. *She seems to know I'm watching. How in the hell?* ... He flipped off the screen, and it went dark.

Maybe the damned thing IS human, he thought, reflecting on the way the meckie continually stared at him. *And it has the hots for me.* Javik realized this was a feeble attempt at levity, and he felt uncomfortable.

"Docking two hundred fifty meters," the computer reported.

Let's see, he thought, planning his activities of the following day. *I'll look at the ejection pods and other safety equipment. That would be through hatch seventeen. . . .*

Javik saw the docking platform clearly now. He watched dockworkers in white bubble suits as they scurried about on moto-boots.

Saint Elba's magne-drive turned the Shamrock Five to one side, and the ship began to approach the dock sideways. Presently the ship jerked, then rocked gently and settled into place in its padded docking slip.

As Javik and Madame Bernet rolled off the Shamrock Five onto Saint Elba's shadowy docking platform, Madame Bernet yawned. The meckie stretched, locked its fingers together and cracked the knuckles. "God, I'm drained," it said. "Took a couple of sleep-sub pills in flight, but now all I can think about is a nice soft bed."

For Christ's sake, Javik thought. *This meckie is overplaying its part!*

Low-wattage light standards dotted the platform, providing enough illumination to cast weak shadows of the two as they rolled side by side toward an arched doorway. As they rolled through the doorway into a more brightly lit area, a loudspeakered woman's voice announced: "Welcome, brave crewmen! I am Mayor Nancy Ogg."

Javik focused on an illuminated glassplex viewing area above them. "There," he said, nodding his head in the direction of the viewing area. "She's a looker, too!" Javik realized too late that this was the sort of sentiment he used to share with Brent Stafford. He missed Stafford.

"I see her," Madame Bernet said.

"Decontamination showers are directly ahead of you," Mayor Nancy Ogg said. "The inconvenience is necessary, since we must be concerned about the tiniest micro-organisms brought in from outside." She paused and added, "But you understand this."

"Yes, ma'am," Javik replied with a cordial grin. "I most certainly do." *They're worried about Zero-G Plague*, he thought. *No one dares speak of it because of space superstition*. He recalled that it had been almost three decades since the epidemic at Saint Michaels killed sixty-six thousand people. . . . Stringent decontamination procedures had been established after that.

Javik watched as Madame Bernet entered a women's shower room silently. *Wonder if she'll rust,* he thought.

After the showers, Javik and Madame Bernet dressed in fresh Space Patrol uniforms they found in the dressing areas.

A tweed-suited Mayor Nancy Ogg greeted them in the hallway, accompanied by Sergeant Rountree. Javik passed the release authorization to Mayor Nancy Ogg and asked her to locate Sidney immediately.

"A cappy?" she said. "What do you want with a miserable cappy?"

"He's to be captain of the ship," Javik said with a bit of irritation. He stared down the bridge of his nose at the Mayor.

"What?" she said. "A cappy?" Dr. Hudson's electronic letter was in the lapel pocket of her suit. *We'll lose Malloy for a couple of days,* she thought. *It won't be difficult.*

"You're to treat him quickly and release him to me."

Mayor Nancy Ogg studied the release form intently. "General Munoz signed this?" She handed it to the security sergeant, adding, "We'll have to do some checking, of course."

"You weren't notified?"

"No."

"Christ! All right. Check all you want, but make it fast. If Malloy's not treated and ready to go tomorrow, the comet intercept mission is off. And you probably know it isn't headed toward any mining base."

The Mayor's dark brown eyes flashed angrily as if to say that Javik was acting impertinently to one of her status. *So you know that comet's coming down our throat,* she thought. *Well you'll go alone at the last minute—out of patriotic duty.*

Mayor Nancy Ogg said nothing further about the Malloy matter, and turned her attention to Madame Bernet. "Who might you be?" she asked, sweetly.

The meckie identified itself, after which Javik explained, "Madame Bernet is a meckie, our Onboard Systems Coordinator for the mission."

So THIS is the killer meckie, Mayor Nancy Ogg thought. *It looks human, except for the eyes.*

"This way, please," the Mayor said, motioning toward a nearby conveyor transporter. A strip which moved slowly and noisily, the transporter carried pop-up metal chairs.

Javik started to roll toward the conveyor, but stopped as he saw Madame Bernet and Mayor Nancy Ogg hold back.

"After you," the Mayor said to Madame Bernet in a syrupy, overly gracious tone. *I'm not going to turn my back on this . . . monster!* she thought.

Madame Bernet's eyes flashed angry glances at the Mayor and at Sergeant Rountree. "Thank you," the meckie said, smiling warily. It rolled by Javik.

Do they sense what I do about Madame Bernet? Javik thought. *Or do they know something?*

"Step aboard," Mayor Nancy Ogg instructed as they all reached the transporter. "Disembark at Landing Platform One."

Mayor Nancy Ogg watched the meckie and Javik take seats. Then she and Sergeant Rountree sat behind them. Mayor Nancy Ogg recalled seeing a decommissioned Atheist killer meckie once in the War Museum. She felt fascination and fear.

After a short ride on the conveyor transporter, they transferred to a monorail car destined for the habitat's outer rim. They sat in triple-wide seats, with Mayor Nancy Ogg and her sergeant on one side, facing Javik and Madame Bernet.

"There aren't many people moving about at this time of night," the Mayor said, glancing around the car at four scattered attendants in other seats.

Javik smiled at her, caught her gaze.

She looked away.

She carries herself with an air of superiority, he thought, feeling captivated by the Mayor's almond-shaped brown eyes. *But I see a passionate woman beneath the facade.* Javik flicked a glance to his left, saw Madame Bernet staring bleakly out the window.

The monorail car jolted.

Sergeant Rountree looked across at Javik and said, "I'm sorry the ride is so rough. We're working on the tracks, you know."

Javik insisted it did not bother him. Then he looked at the Mayor and asked, "Forgive me for prying, Your Honor, but are you related to President Ogg?"

"My older brother," she said, pinning her gaze on Madame Bernet. The meckie stared out the window at the blackness of the tunnel's interior, apparently unaware of the Mayor's interest.

"Fine man," Javik said.

"Yes," Mayor Nancy Ogg thought. *But a bigot?* she thought.

"I'd vote for him tomorrow," Javik said with a flirtatious smile in the Mayor's direction, "but there are other more pressing matters requiring my attention."

"I'm certain my brother understands," she said stiffly.

Cool one. Javik thought. *Too bad I don't have time to soften her with my charms.*

When the monorail car exited the spoke tube, it began to decelerate. Javik saw the lights of an arch-glass terminal building ahead, and beyond that the twinkling lights of a resting city.

They disembarked at the terminal. Sergeant Rountree led them along shadowy motopaths past a fruit tree orchard and into an area of apartment buildings surrounded by illuminated Japanese gardens.

"We're just outside the habitat's principal shopping district," Mayor Nancy Ogg said as they negotiated an arched bridge.

"Very nice," Javik said, noting carefully manicured dwarf shrubs and trees along each side of an illuminated stream.

"I'm terribly sorry about the temperature," Sergeant Rountree said as they reached the end of the bridge and entered a narrow motopath. "We've had trouble with the solar heating system. It's been four degrees on the cool side for a week."

"There's no need to apologize for everything," Mayor Nancy Ogg said sternly, flashing an angry glance at her sergeant.

Sergeant Rountree did not meet the Mayor's gaze; he mumbled something in an apologetic tone.

"Hardly noticed the temperature," Javik said, amused at the confrontation.

They stopped at a fourplex building, where Mayor Nancy Ogg handed Javik and the meckie plastikeys. "Separate apartments have been prepared for each of you," she said. "The apartment numbers are on the keys."

Then she turned to leave and remarked, "I'll send for you in the morning. We'll breakfast together. Your ship will be recharged and ready to go by tomorrow afternoon."

"I'd like to see Malloy right after breakfast," Javik said with a tone of authority.

"We'll see," Mayor Nancy Ogg said.

After decontamination showers in the Hub, Sidney and the other clients were allowed to use the bathrooms and were provided with fresh clothing. As the fatigued group boarded a monorail car for the trip to the habitat's outer rim, an attendant said, "Saint Elba's night barrier is in place now, shielding the reflected rays of the sun. The barrier moves back and forth automatically, creating day and night in the habitat. We even have seasons!"

They disembarked at the arch-glass terminal building, and from there were herded unceremoniously into the back of an autotruck. The truck moved quickly through shopping and residential areas. Presently, Sidney saw the lights of a massive building which stretched laterally as far as he could see. In height the structure was perhaps one hundred stories, limited as it was by the thickness of the outer rim.

"Elba House," an attendant said.

A few minutes later, the clients were lined up in the lobby of Elba House, awaiting admittance. Toward the front of one line, Sidney watched six desk attendants as they matched clients with counselors. Loudspeakered voices rang around the room as the attendants called for counselors. When Sidney's turn came, he rolled to the desk.

"I'm supposed to get rush treatment," Sidney said, leaning forward and speaking in a low tone to a beefy, flat-nosed attendant. "I have a very important mission. . . ." Sidney caught himself as he noticed the attendant sneering at him.

"Everybody here is on an important mission," the attendant said. "Especially the mental cases!"

Two attendants seated nearby tittered.

The attendant grabbed Sidney's right wrist and read the plasti-tag. "Malloy, S.," he said. "Client number one-six-five-six-three-two-oh-two-nine." The attendant checked his log-book, then spoke into a voice-amp: "Counselor, Ruth Bremer. Is Ruth Bremer present?"

A woman called out with military precision: "Present."

Sidney turned to watch a slender woman with neatly trimmed dark brown hair moto-shoe to his side. She wore a plain white Bu-Med dress emblazoned with a triangular Bu-Med lapel crest. "I am Bremer," she announced curtly.

Sidney studied his counselor as she leaned over the desk and mentoed an auto-pen to sign the custody form. The pen moved across the page without being held. Of a bit less than middling height, the counselor had hard features, with a protruding chin and a tiny nose. Sidney became conscious of how tired he felt. The excitement had begun to wear off.

"Take Malloy to one-four-six-five-eight in R Wing," the attendant instructed.

Bremer nodded and grasped Sidney by his good arm. "A maximum security wing," she confided as they rolled toward a double-wide door marked "SUBWAY."

"Maximum security?" Sidney almost spat the words out. "I'm not dangerous!"

"They know that," she said with a hint of condescension in her tone. "Anyone can see you're not in chains."

"Then why?"

"Orders, fellow," she said stiffly. "I just do what I'm told."

Pausing at a subway loading platform, they watched as a four-passenger mini-car approached. "I'll complete the necessary forms to get you out of there as soon as possible," she promised.

"Thanks for that," Sidney said. "But I'm supposed to—"

"Don't thank me!" she scoffed. "That will cost you two work credits! I don't fill out forms for nothing!"

"A Lieutenant Javik of the Space Patrol is going to ask for me tomorrow," Sidney said. "I'll be going with him."

"Sure," the counselor said. "I'll put the whole staff on alert."

"Thanks," Sidney said. Then he caught her frigid gaze and realized she was insincere. Sidney fell into silent and troubled thought.

R Wing was a six-minute ride away. They took an elevator to the fourteenth floor and moto-shoed down a long, curving hall which was punctuated with signs. One sign appeared more frequently than others:

THANK ROSENBLOOM
FOR
FULL EMPLOYMENT

"This is it," Counselor Bremer finally announced, stopping at a maroon door. She read an attendance screen on the wall, added, "Your roommates are already in bed. Enter quietly and find a bunk. I'll set up your therapy schedule in the morning."

She mentoed the door. It slid open to one side, revealing a darkened room with bunkbeds along the opposite wall and a table with two straight-backed chairs near the entry. A tiny barred window was high on one wall.

"I'll hold the door open for two minutes to give you more light," she said.

Sidney hesitated, then rolled across the threshold. But he felt a sudden wave of fear and turned to re-enter the hall. An unseen barrier in the doorway halted him abruptly.

"Ow!" he said, rubbing a bruised eyebrow. "What was that?"

"Thought barrier," she replied stiffly. "Get to bed. *Now*."

"But why?..." Sidney remembered and said, "Oh. Maximum security."

Counselor Bremer did not respond, stared at him coolly.

Sidney looked down at his twisted left arm, noted sadly that the elbow, wrist and fingers were lock-bent. Every muscle and tendon ached and appeared taut to the point of bursting. Angrily, he tried with all his energy to straighten the arm and hand. But it was to no avail. He stood there for a moment afterward breathing hard and glaring across the thought barrier at Counselor Bremer.

"You have forty-five seconds," she said.

Sidney turned like a whipped meckie-pup and found an unoccupied upper bunk. He unsnapped his moto-shoes quickly, then laid his weary body upon an electric lift which had dropped silently from above. His body weight activated the lift, and it carried him to an upper bunk. Darkness fell across the room as Sidney rolled into bed, wearing a thin green Bu-Med smock like the one issued to him on Earth.

How long will my treatment take? he thought. *Will Tom find me here?*

"Bremer's a tough one," a husky voice whispered from below. "She'll chew ya up and spit ya out."

Sidney did not respond. He lay awake with his eyes open watching faint shadows cast upon the ceiling by the high wall window. Tired to the marrow, he tried to collect his thoughts. The room gradually filled with light snoring sounds. As Sidney's thoughts ran together in a blur, he too drifted off to sleep.

*   *   *

Sayer Superior Lin-Ti resumed his place at the podium. Weary from three days away, he thought of the burdens of his position. *So much responsibility*, he thought. *I should delegate more....*

He flipped to Chapter Nine.

NINE

THE CAPPY PROBLEM, FOR
FURTHER READING AND DISCUSSION

February 16, 2341: Mandate of Retardation passed unanimously
by the Council of Ten. The major tenets of this mandate held that
"cappies" ("crips" and "retardos") were to be sterilized, could not
own real property and were to be committed to therapy orbiters.

Tuesday, August 29, 2605

In the few minutes before Garbage Day minus three began on
Saint Elba with the opening of the habitat's night shield, Sidney's room remained in darkness. A nightmare captured his
mind with a sense of reality that drenched his bed in perspiration—Sidney was imprisoned on a planet which rotated freely
in a round cage. Spaceships entered and left through iron gates

which clanked noisily in airless space as they opened and closed. He knew this was impossible, but his dream permitted no questions.

It was an unhappy place. Desperate prisoners plotted escape. . . .

"Escape . . . dawn . . . take the Hub. . . ." Words echoed in Sidney's consciousness and vanished like fine sand through burlap. He squirmed in his slumber, pushing blankets away to cool his body. Half awake now, he began to realize that some of the dream voices were real.

"The snoring!" an urgent voice husked. "It's stopped!"

"Is he awake?" another asked.

Sidney froze. His heart pounded. He sensed someone very near, listening to his breathing. Sidney tried to feign sleep by taking loud, deep breaths.

Suddenly a strong hand grabbed his throat. "One squeal and you're dead!" a man rasped. He pulled Sidney to the floor and held Sidney's good right arm in a clamp grip.

"What did you hear?" another man asked. His voice was high-pitched, commanding.

"Nothing," Sidney gasped, flailing his deformed arm helplessly. "I heard nothing!" Sidney looked beyond a shadow which hulked over him and saw faces half-illuminated by low light entering the room through the barred high wall window.

"Let's tie and gag him," one suggested.

"Maybe he'd like to throw in with us," said another. It was the same husky voice that had spoken to Sidney in the darkness when he first arrived, warning him about Counselor Bremer. This was a potential friend.

"Don't chance it," the man with the high-pitched voice said.

"But he's no threat to us," the potential friend said. "This is so big no one can stop it." But Sidney felt the grip of the man who held him tighten around his neck.

"Stone's right," the man with the high-pitched voice said. "We have hundreds set to break! And thousands will follow!"

Sidney breathed an audible sigh of relief as the grip loosened. The man released him, pushing him to the floor. Sidney rose to lean on the elbow of his right arm and looked at the dark outline of the man they called Stone.

"You okay, fella?" Stone asked.

But before Sidney could answer, the man who had held him

said. "He's a crip. Look at his arm."

"I can't go with you," Sidney said, thinking of his rendez-vous with Javik. He counted five other men in the room, four kneeling around him and another standing near the door.

"Suit yourself," the man with the high-pitched voice said. Sidney noticed that the man's face seemed pale whenever he got a glimpse of a section of it, even in the low light. *These are doomies,* Sidney thought.

Before Sidney could gather the courage to phrase a question, a great clamor arose in the building. There was a loud thump in the room above, and from all around came the sounds of breaking glass and people shouting. The hall door slid open, casting bright light into the room. The noises grew closer now, and half-dressed men ran or moto-shoed by the door.

"It's started!" Stone shouted, jumping to his feet. "The thought barriers are open!"

It was every man for himself. All except Sidney crowded to the door without another word, and then were gone.

Through the open door, Sidney watched with amazement as hordes of clients surged and pushed in their frantic flights to freedom. Sidney heard gunfire in the distance, and the incessant wail of sirens. He rose to his feet.

A group of armed Security Brigade guards rolled by, followed by a cluster of Bu-Med attendants. "Halt!" the guards yelled. Gunfire rang through the hallway.

Then Sidney smelled smoke, and heard screams of panic from outside the door. "Fire!" someone called out. "Fire!" Sidney snapped on his moto-shoes, peeked into the hallway.

Mayor Nancy Ogg had not gone to bed after seeing Javik and Madame Bernet to their apartments for the night. Instead she returned to her own apartment and studied a checklist at the kitchen table. Gradually she fell asleep there, dropping her head to the tabletop.

When the night shield began to open at dawn, reflected sunlight filtered through the kitchen module's greenhouse roof. The Mayor stirred, knocking papers to the floor. She sat up, stretched and yawned.

Busy day ahead, she thought.

As the Mayor leaned over to retrieve her papers, she heard sirens whining in the distance.

• • •

As Sidney poked his head out of the doorway, he saw flames at both ends of the hall. Agonized screams filled the smoke-contaminated air. Several paces to his left on the floor, Sidney saw the bleeding bodies of two green-smocked clients. It was apparent that they had been shot.

Sidney coughed as he ventured a few meters into the hall. Common sense told him to go back in the room and close the door. At least that would delay the inevitable, and left open the possibility of rescue from a window.

"Into the flames, fleshcarrier!" a tenor voice inside his head commanded. *"Down the hallway to your right!"*

"To certain death?" Sidney asked, aloud.

"To POSSIBLE death," the voice said, laughing.

"Possible?"

"If you're lucky, you'll get out." Again, laughter.

"Don't be ridiculous!" Sidney said. He watched as many clients, attendants and guards gave up and sat in the middle of the floor to await death.

"I will tell you this, curious fleshcarrier. It's a matter of simple odds . . . as in a card game or at a roulette wheel."

"How thick are the flames?"

"I do not MEASURE flames," the voice said haughtily. *"How does one MEASURE flames?"*

Sidney shook his head negatively, but started to roll in the direction designated by the voice. Rolling slowly at first, he passed seated and standing people who cried out or prayed. Others were already dead, and lay in confused positions on the floor. Sidney picked up speed.

When he was only two meters from the dancing violet and orange flames, the heat had become almost unbearable. Suddenly the floor above the flames cracked and broke away. A great burst of cool white foam hit Sidney and the flames. He slipped and fell to the floor, his body and face covered in foam.

"This way!" a voice called from above.

Sidney wiped foam from his face and clothing. His eyes stung. He looked up to the floor above and saw a red-and-yellow-uniformed fireman drop a flexible metal ladder to him.

"Hurry!" the fireman urged.

Sidney struggled partway up the ladder, having difficulty

on the flexible metal links due to his bad arm and slippery
foam on his body. About halfway up, he stopped, breathing
hard. "My arm!" Sidney gasped. "I can't climb any farther!"

Through blurry, watery eyes, Sidney saw three firemen lift
the ladder. They helped him off at the top, then dropped the
ladder back for more people.

"You're a lucky one," a fireman said. "Over there," he
instructed, pointing toward a group of people who were gathered near a window, their shapes forming silhouettes against
dawn light. "Get in the escape chute!"

Luck? Sidney thought as he followed the fireman's instructions. *Was it only a matter of odds?*

When Sidney's turn came, he slid down a spiraling escape
chute to ground level.

Javik awoke to the piercing whine of sirens. From bed, he
could see through the skylights of the bedroom module to the
edge of the habitat's outer rim far above. Beyond that, the sun
reflected off the solar collector and peeked around the night
shield, bathing the room in yellow light.

He went to the balcony and looked across a terraced Japanese
hillside garden to a large building in the distance. Flames licked
from the windows of middle floors. Black smoke billowed in
the air. Emergency vehicles screamed, rolling at high speed
toward the conflagration.

"Remain in your homes!" a loudspeaker truck boomed. "Keep
all doors and windows shut! Emergency oxygen systems will
not function if doors and windows are open!"

Javik went into the living room module and scanned its
contents. The room had bright green plastic tables and sidechairs, with a green paisley short couch that matched the cur-
tains. He rolled to a wall-mounted telephone in a pool of sunlight
near the couch, mentoed a tele-cube. It rose from its cradle on
the phone, hovered in the air in front of his face.

"Number please," a pleasant female syntho-voice said.

"Get me Hub Control," Javik commanded. "Hurry!"

"Sorry, sir. Those circuits are busy. Please try back in—"

"Damn!" Javik cursed. "Then get me Elba House."

"Sorry, sir. Those circuits are busy too."

Javik mento-slammed the circuit shut. The tele-cube floated
back to its cradle. *Sidney will have to fend for himself*, he
thought. *Right now I've got to take care of my ship.*

Javik dressed quickly and met Madame Bernet in the hall. Fastening the top button of a white-and-gold uniform dress, Madame Bernet asked, "You saw the fire?"

"Yeah, and I can't reach Hub Control! We'd better get to the ship! This whole orbiter may go up!" Javik wiped a hand through an uncombed shock of amber hair. The sleep-tormented hair did not smooth out.

Reaching the street in seconds, Javik and the meckie rolled hurriedly along a motopath in the direction of the habitat's spoke tubes, hoping to catch a monorail for the Hub. He smelled smoke.

As they passed a small cluster of fruit trees, Javik stopped abruptly. "There!" he said excitedly, pointing toward the arch-glass monorail terminal building several hundred meters away. A mass of green-smocked clients, many of whom obviously had severe handicaps, streamed into the building. Some operated moto-crutches or rode in electric wheelchairs. Others ran or moto-shoed.

"A breakout!" Javik moaned. "How in the hell are we..."

Madame Bernet drew a long, gleaming knife from a concealed pocket in its dress, rasped: "We'll force our way through!"

"You're armed?" Javik short-stepped back several paces and pulled his own pistol.

"For *your* protection," the meckie replied, glueing its gaze on Javik's weapon.

"Sheathe that!" Javik barked, glancing at two clients who were picking pears on the opposite side of the grove. "I have a better idea!"

The meckie hesitated, then followed the command with obvious reluctance.

Javik holstered his pistol and grabbed the meckie by one arm. "Come with me," he said.

Madame Bernet did not reply, seemed to think for a moment before accompanying Javik. As they approached the clients, Javik saw that both were men, and he recognized the puffy facial features and vacuous expressions of mongolism. One of the clients, who was quite tall and fat, smiled as he extended a pear to Madame Bernet.

Perplexed, Madame Bernet glanced at Javik.

"Take it," Javik said. "And smile."

Madame Bernet obeyed, then looked confused as she stood there with the piece of fruit in her mechanical grasp.

Javik addressed the shorter client: "We need your smocks," he said. "Okay?"

Unresponsive, the client stared back with wide open, child-like eyes. He extended a pear, which Javik accepted.

"They don't understand," Madame Bernet said, reaching into a deep pocket with her free hand. "My way now, Captain?"

"Wait," Javik said. "I'm going to try one more thing first." He removed a shiny coin from his tunic pocket and offered it to the shorter client. The mongoloid smiled, reached for the object. Javik pulled it back gently, touched the man's smock and said, "Trade." Then Javik offered him the coin again and pulled at the smock. "Trade," he repeated.

On the fourth attempt, the client understood. He removed his smock and handed it to Javik in exchange for the coin. Madame Bernet followed the same procedure to obtain the other smock. Entirely naked now, the mongoloids stood smiling as they examined their shiny new treasures.

"I don't see any.guards yet," Javik said, "but you can bet they're around somewhere." They threw on the green smocks over their own uniforms.

"Hide in the crowd," Javik said. "We'll get the smocks off when the Shamrock Five's in sight."

But when they reached the monorail terminal, the meckie stopped abruptly. "Go no farther," it said tersely.

"What?" Javik said, turning to confront Madame Bernet.

"I sense . . . danger," Madame Bernet said.

"You have a short-circuit," Javik snapped. "This is the only way!"

But the meckie stood rigidly, with both hands thrust into the pockets of its smock.

"Do as you please," Javik said. "I'll go on without you!"

The meckie stared straight ahead at an indeterminate point in the distance. Its expression was resolute.

"Damned thing can't respond," Javik cursed as he rolled away. "Just like the Bu-Industry meckies. The minute an unusual situation arises . . ."

Javik reached the terminal building and pushed his way through a noisy crowd of clients. It smelled of human waste and perspiration inside, and Javik spent a long hour pressed against other bodies before he was able to board a railcar for a standing-room-only ride.

Minutes later, the car came to a stop in the Hub. To Javik's surprise, he saw hundreds of black-uniformed security men standing outside next to long, clear glassplex units. Javik did not see a single client in the bunch. As the car squeaked to a stop, he realized the reason for this. The security men manually connected glassplex hall-tubes to each door of the monorail car, thus forcing all clients to follow a controlled exit path.

"I'm trapped!" Javik yelled, hardly able to hear his own words in the din of humanity.

When the car doors opened, most of the clients realized they had been tricked. "Let us out!" they yelled, beating furiously on the glassplex windows of the monorail car.

Javik smelled tear gas in the car. He was forced into the hall-tube in a rush to escape the gas, and Javik saw some clients pushed back against the walls. He lost his own footing momentarily then, but eventually was able to regain control and began to move forward with the crowd.

I've got to get back to the ship! Javik thought, desperately.

He saw a large holding room ahead, filled with a mob of green-smocked, angry escapees. The surging crowd slowed and stopped before Javik reached the room. He stared at a clear glassplex side wall just an arm's length away, felt hot, perspiring bodies against his own.

Maybe I can shoot holes in the glassplex, he thought. *I could break off a piece and crawl through....*

Someone stuck an elbow in his ribs. It hurt. *No,* he thought. *There are armed guards everywhere out there! They'll kill me if they see my weapon!*

Javik ran through the options with military precision. Soon it became apparent to him that he could do but one thing. *I'll have to find someone to listen to me,* he thought.

The telephone rang during Hudson's Tuesday morning shower. Earlier than usual this day, he was anxious to watch the first election returns on home video. *It never fails,* he thought irritably, mentoing the water off. *The minute I step into the shower....*

Hudson stepped out onto a simulated marble tile floor and wrapped a towel around his waist as he counted the third ring of the phone. He heard a thump overhead. *That damned crazy woman upstairs,* he thought. *Doing unsanctioned exercises in her bathroom again. I'll make another complaint to the Anti-Cheapness League. They'll take her away this time!*

Hudson sat on the commode cover and mento-answered the call. A tele-cube flitted forth, pausing in front of his mouth.

A scramble code beeper went off as Mayor Nancy Ogg identified herself at the other end of the line. "Lieutenant Javik is missing!" she said, her voice faltering. "We're searching everywhere!"

"What do you mean? He arrived, didn't he?" Hudson scowled as he heard a loud thump upstairs.

"Yes. Last night. I saw him . . . and the meckie . . . to apartments for the night. Personally. But there's been a major breakout from Elba House since, and a terrible fire there!"

"Judas Priest!"

"Elba House is still burning! We've got mass confusion here, Dick!"

Hudson put his hand over the tele-cube as he heard another thump upstairs, yelled: "Keep quiet up there!"

"Are you there, Dick?" Mayor Nancy Ogg asked. "Are you there?"

"Yeah," Hudson snapped, releasing his hand from the tele-cube. "Listen, Nancy, can you control the fire?"

"We think so. I'm getting reports on it every half hour."

"Where is Madame Bernet?"

Detecting anger in Hudson's tone, she replied nervously: "The killer meckie? Why, my Security Brigade took it in. They're checking its memory circuits . . . to see if it might have disposed of Javik prematurely."

The telephone beeped.

"How the hell did this happen?" Hudson asked, unable to suppress his rage any longer.

"Well, it wasn't my fault!"

"Maybe if you'd been a little more dedicated to your job, instead of always trying to think of ways to get off Saint Elba . . ."

"I tried. Really I did. I even stayed up late last night, trying to make sure everything would go right today." She sobbed.

"Don't use tears on me!" Hudson said.

Mayor Nancy Ogg continued to cry.

"Look," Hudson said. "I shouldn't have been so quick to blame you. There's a lot of tension here over this comet thing."

Mayor Nancy Ogg wiped her eyes with a tissue. "Okay," she said. She blew her nose. "Dick, don't stay on Earth too long. If it looks like the comet can't be stopped . . ."

"Don't worry about that," Hudson said. "All the council ministers have escape rockets. . . ."

After the call, Hudson rang Munoz's country condominium. It rang thirty times without an answer.

Damn it, Hudson thought. He placed the call again. Still no answer.

Hudson cursed again, called President Ogg. A recorded voice answered: "Thank you for calling the White House Office Tower. Our hours are nine to five, Monday through Friday. At the tone, you may leave your name, number and a brief message."

Hudson heard a tone, said, "Emergency message for President Ogg." He gave his name, then changed his mind and hung up the telephone.

I'll call during office hours, he thought. *This is too important to leave on tape*.

Hudson flipped on the videodome at a little past seven A.M. The polls had just opened, and returns were beginning to stream in from electronic tabulating machines on the East Coast.

"This is unprecedented, ladies and gentlemen," an announcer said, with the soul-less smile of one having political aspirations of his own. "A punch-in candidate, General Arturo Munoz, holds forty-six-point-three percent of the vote. President Ogg has a narrow lead with forty-nine-point-one percent, and Benjamin T. Morgan . . ."

Hudson smiled. *Precisely according to plan*, he thought. *The General will trail in a close race, then will vault to the front on the strength of late returns*.

A team of network news analysts was having a round-table discussion as the tabulated returns came in on a studio wall. Suddenly this picture disappeared and the sound went off. A message appeared on the screen:

IMPORTANT BULLETIN
PLEASE STAND BY

Then the videodome blared: "We interrupt this broadcast for a special announcement. General Arturo Munoz, fourteenth minister of Bu-Mil, has been killed in an autocar accident. The mishap occurred sometime before dawn when the General's limousine plunged through a guardrail and went off the edge of a narrow bridge near Lake Ovett. Another body has been discovered in the wreckage, believed to be that of his adjutant, Colonel Allen Peebles. Preliminary investigation points to a malfunction of the car's electromagnetic circuitry. The state funeral celebration and posthumous Purple Badge ceremony will take place Thursday, beginning with..."

Dr. Hudson mentoed the set to silence. He sat staring at the darkened screen in disbelief. *How could this have happened?* he thought, frantically.

He left the videodome and moto-paced back and forth the length of the living room module. *What the hell should I do now?* he thought. *But Arturo was insane.... Maybe we're better off....*

Feeling hot and clammy, Hudson wiped perspiration from his brow with one hand. *Could he have left any evidence to incriminate the rest of us?*

Hudson paused, stared at his feet and thought: *Too risky to check Arturo's office...but maybe my own....* It occurred to Hudson that something might remain to be cleaned up. A bit of paper, some item previously overlooked.

Hudson's autocar deposited him at the edge of Technology Square, then disappeared into an underground parking tube. The square was empty, recently cleaned. He moto-shoed across it and up the ramp to the Bu-Tech Office Tower. At the entrance, he placed his hand on the black glass of a security monitor identity plate. The vacuum went on, sucking at his palm. Suddenly he pulled the hand back, as if it had been burned.

My God! he thought. *The vacuum...it's...it's a cell reading mechanism!*

Dr. Hudson realized in that instant that the monitor had been reading all his memories, contained in the tiniest cell of his body. He cursed himself for being so stupid. He had even thought of the concept, but it had never occurred to him that his predecessors were so advanced!

A cold wave of fear spread over him, and a torrent of stinging sweat rolled over his eyebrows and into his eyes. Hudson turned quickly, nearly stumbling as he did so, and moto-sped down the ramp. The shoes accelerated quickly, and halfway down the ramp Hudson mentoed instructions for them to slow down. But they continued to accelerate!

I'm going too fast! he thought, panicky. The shoes were out of control, and raced across the square at full speed. *I can't turn!* he thought, frozen in fear.

The shoes carried him past the skatewalk and through a planting area, then barrelled onto busy American Boulevard. He saw a streetcleaning truck heading directly toward him! *Oh no!* he thought. *It's going to hit me!* Hudson closed his eyes, put his hands over his face and prayed for mercy from a God he had never served.

"Eeeeyah!" Hudson screamed as the truck hit him, dragging him into the midst of its whirring brushes.

Moments later, Hudson's mangled body was thrust out of the back of the machine. The streetcleaner skidded to a stop, and its crew of orange-uniformed drivers and helpers got out.

A small crowd gathered around the crumpled, bleeding form. Billie Birdbright was one of the first to arrive. "What happened?" he asked.

"Product failure!" a man next to Birdbright said joyously. "He lost control of his moto-shoes!"

"Praise be to Uncle Rosy!" Birdbright exclaimed happily, not recognizing Hudson. "Another Purple Badge!"

"And another soul for the Happy Shopping Ground!" the man said.

Everyone in the crowd bowed their heads and murmured, "Truly we are blessed! All of us are employed!"

Birdbright heard the happy whine of approaching sirens, saw a white-and-red Product Failure van screech to a stop nearby. Six white-smocked teammembers rolled out, each with bold red lettering across his chest. The first man's chest read, "DOCTOR," and two other men and three women had signs reading, "INS. AGENT," "LAWYER," "MORTICIAN," "P.F. STAMPER" and "HELPER."

"He's dead!" the doctor announced, kneeling over the body and checking the pulse.

"Wonderful!" the mortician said, clapping her hands in joy.

The lawyer, doctor and insurance agent mentoed auto-pens to scribble on clip-pads as the helper and mortician rolled the body over. "Stamp his forehead!" the doctor called out cheerily, glancing over the top of his clip-pad.

"I can't!" the P. F. Stamper called back. She smiled winsomely. "It's too mangled!"

"Oh my," the man next to Birdbright said. "His head's too mangled for a P.F. stamp!"

"Stamp him anywhere, then," the doctor said. "Just be sure it's on the skin and plainly visible. We want this brave fellow admitted to the Happy Shopping Ground!"

Birdbright watched the P.F. Stamper tear open the victim's shirt and lift a large chrome-plated auto-stamper over the body.

"KWAK!" the stamper went.

"Oh!" the crowd murmured, noting a large black "P.F." on the victim's bare chest. Below that the date of occurrence appeared, in smaller letters.

"A product failure!" Birdbright said, turning to a woman on his left. "Isn't it wonderful?"

The woman nodded, smiled and murmured something.

"A bonus, ladies and gentlemen!" the insurance agent called out. "The streetcleaning machine is scratched and dented!"

The orange-uniformed streetcleaner crew auto-clapped and whistled at this news. "Scrap it!" they said in unison. "It's not fair to repair!"

The Product Failure team loaded Hudson's body into the van, then ceremoniously radioed for a tow truck.

Moments later, feeling warmth in his stomach, Birdbright watched the van speed away. *It's all so wonderful!* he thought. *Praise be to Uncle Rosy!*

*   *   *

Ordinance Room One, inside the Great Temple at Pleasant Reef:

"The beings from the Realm of Magic would have laughed their heads off at this point," Sayer Superior Lin-Ti said from the podium, recalling the previous day's lesson. "But you see, they had no heads."

The youngsayermen laughed politely.

"Just think of it, youngsayers!" Lin-Ti said, raising his hands to emphasize the point, "Malloy stumbling around in a cappy riot; Javik heading for who knows where: Munoz, Hudson and Peebles all dead...."

Lin-Ti opened a discussion period, and the group agreed that these bodiless beings must have been terribly amused at the self-destruct capabilities of the fleshcarriers.

A youngsayerman asked if Malloy might have been insane . . . and Munoz too . . . because of the voices they heard. "No normal person hears voices like that," he pointed out.

"But this was not a normal situation," Lin-Ti said.

"And our Master heard voices too!" another youngsayerman said, blurting out the words.

Lin-Ti looked at the speaker. It was the tall one who resembled Onesayer Edward. "And how do you know this?" Lin-Ti asked, tersely.

"Uh . . . er . . ."

"You read ahead?"

The youngsayerman lowered his head in shame. "Yes, Sayer Superior," he said. "I am very sorry. . . ."

TEN

THE CAPPY PROBLEM, FOR FURTHER READING AND DISCUSSION

Mid-September, 2311: Bloody "Cappy Power" revolts on the therapy orbiters of Saint Joseph and Saint Michaels, in which cappies briefly took control. New security measures were established to prevent recurrence.

Tuesday, August 29, 2605

Sidney needed to catch his breath. He sat hunched forward on a piasti-marbo bench in the smoky morning shade of Elba House's rhododendron garden, a few meters off the motopath where hordes of clients rushed by heading toward the Hub. Sidney watched red and yellow helipumpers hovering over the burning R Wing as they sprayed long streams of white foam on the fire. It was warm in the garden, and the thin green smock clung to moisure on his body. He coughed sporadically in the contaminated air.

Sidney cupped his face in his hands, stared through his fingers at the ground. *I faced certain death up there*, he thought. *And yet . . . I got out! Was it merely luck, as the voice told me? Or . . .*

He took a deep breath, desperately attempting to collect his thoughts. He heard the throb and hum of oxygen pumps, felt a hot breeze across his hands. His nostrils burned.

"You!" a man called out from the motopath nearby.

Sidney looked up, saw a short, white-uniformed man standing at the edge of the motopath, staring back at him hostilely. The man held a clip-pad, had straight silver hair. A triangular Bu-Med crest adorned his left lapel. It read: "G.W. 500."

"Procedures Checker," the little man announced officiously. He rolled to Sidney and touched a button on his pad to auto-flip through several sheets of paper. "Name please," he said crisply.

After Sidney replied, "Sidney Malloy," the man scribbled something on his form and commented, "Odd first name."

"Sidney isn't so unusual. It was very popular when I was born."

The man scowled ferociously. "Last name first!" he snapped. "Always give your last name first!" Angrily, he tore out the partially completed form, crumpled it and tossed it to the ground. "Malloy, Sidney," the man said as his mentoed auto-pen danced across the page without being held. "Your client number?" he asked, not looking up.

Sidney glanced at his plastic wrist tag and provided the numbers, then watched the auto-pen move over the form.

"Now let me see your pass."

"My pass!" Sidney said. "What pass?" Sidney looked beyond the Procedures Checker to Elba House's burning section. He heard screams and felt empty in the pit of his stomach. The hot breeze carried smoke into Sidney's face. He coughed.

"Tut-tut, you must have a pass," the little man insisted, still not looking up. He wrote furiously with the auto-pen, shaking his head from side to side in disapproval the way Malcolm Penny used to do in Central Forms.

"What's this all about?" Sidney asked, growing alarmed.

"Clients who are out of the building must be escorted by

an attendant or must have in their possession a valid and countersigned pass. Rule twenty-four, section nine hundred six-point-three."

"But the building's on fire!" Sidney snapped. "A fireman told me to take the escape chute!" Sidney watched a woman slide to safety out the end of a chute as he spoke, tried to point her out to the Procedures Checker.

"Tut-tut, no excuses," the Procedures Checker said. He entered something on a form, then touched a button to flip to another sheet.

"I'm not trying to run away," Sidney said angrily, hearing his voice grow loud. "I'm waiting here for someone to give me instructions."

Sidney heard terrible, agonized screams from Elba House, saw an elderly man and woman jump to their deaths. Sidney felt the emptiness in his stomach again, saw his deformed arm quiver. His face was hot, and stinging drops of perspiration drenched his eyes.

The little man coughed, then peered over the top of his clip-pad at Sidney, narrowed his eyes and chirped, "Procedures are for a purpose. You must ask permission, don't you see? Forms must be completed, then reviewed by higher authority and referred to a pass committee for evaluation. . . ."

"A pass committee? I'd have died up there waiting!"

"I'll need your signature on this form," the Procedures Checker said, growing visibly nervous. Timidly, he extended the pad to Sidney, designating a signatory line on the form with his auto-pen.

Sidney grabbed the clip-pad violently, thundered, "PEOPLE ARE DYING UP THERE, AND YOU'RE TALKING ABOUT FORMS AND PROCEDURES?" Wedging the clip-pad between his chest and bad left arm, he tore off the completed forms, ripped them in half and scattered them in the hot breeze.

The Procedures Checker looked on in stunned terror, as if Sidney had committed a terrible sacrilege.

"GET AWAY FROM ME!" Sidney roared, lifting the clip-pad menacingly. "AWAY!"

The little man rolled backward over a bench. Mumbling something Sidney could not hear, he picked himself up and fled down the motopath.

Sidney hurled the clip-pad after the fleeing bureaucrat, then stood for several moments holding his quivering left arm against his chest in an effort to stop its shaking. His heart pounded so hard he felt it might break through bones and flesh. *I've got to find Tom,* he thought.

Sidney wiped perspiration from his eyelids with both forefingers, then rolled into smoke-filtered sunlight on the motopath. *I've never been that angry before,* he thought. *That was a very bad energy leak.* He thought again of people dying in the fire, felt helpless and confused.

Thoughts went by in a blur as he rolled forward. Barely aware that he was coughing intermittently, it astounded Sidney that he did not really care about the energy leak, was not even concerned about rules. These were frightening new feelings, but they gave him a strangely euphoric sensation, and a new feeling of freeness. These emotions mingled with the deeply felt sense of loss in his soul over the Elba House tragedy.

Never before had he openly questioned the AmFed Way, but things appeared so wrong to him now . . . paperwork and procedures having become more important than human lives.

Suddenly he realized that something was trying to enter his consciousness and crowd away his thoughts . . . an immense force clawing and pounding at his brain. Screams of agony continued from the fire above. Peculiar, repulsive odors touched his nostrils. A fit of coughing took over his body, then subsided.

"Burning flesh!" a tenor voice inside his skull said.

"Billions more fleshcarriers will burn when our garbage comet hits Earth!" another, deeper voice said.

Cackling laughter echoed in Sidney's brain. *"Die, flesh-carriers, die!"* the voices said.

Sidney swooned dizzily and fell to his knees in the middle of the motopath. Above the top of Elba House, the reflected morning sun was almost fully visible on the burnished solar collector. Sidney looked up at Elba House, squinting in the glare. A puff of black smoke covered the sun, then dissipated.

Sidney raised his good arm toward the smoky holocaust, opening the hand as if to place it against another in prayer. Slowly, jerkily, his twisted left arm rose, its quivering fingers groping heavenward. In a great final burst of energy, Sidney brought the deformed hand up, and it grew straight with true, beautiful fingers that pressed reassuringly against the other hand.

"Oh please," Sidney murmured, closing his eyes tightly. "Please. . . ." He fell silent and wished with all his being that the terrible conflagration would end. Believing he was making the greatest wish of all, the wish for someone else, his body trembled for a moment. When he opened his eyes, he saw no more flames, heard no more screams.

Soon he saw dozens of people sliding to safety through escape chutes. "It was miraculous," a Bu-Med attendant said as he reached the ground. "The flames were almost upon me. . . . I had given up hope." He wiped his face on the sleeve of a singed and dirty white uniform.

"They were spraying something on the fire," a woman said.

Sidney looked down at his left arm and hand. They had been healed! *A miracle!* he thought with rampant joy. *I've found God!* He extended his hand, flexing fingers which only minutes before had been twisted.

Have I been chosen for something more? Sidney wondered, watching puffs of grey smoke disappear through a hole in the habitat's glassplex skin. He thought of the doomies and what the voice had said about a garbage comet. *That's it!* he thought. *The mission I'm going on with Tom! My destiny!*

The voices in his brain returned, cackling with laughter. *"This one breaks me up!"* a tenor voice said. *"He thinks he's been chosen to save his world!"*

"Isn't it hilarious?" said the other.

"What the Hooverville?" Sidney said.

"You WERE chosen, fool," the second, deeper voice said, *"but not to save anyone. We selected you because you're such a magnificent sap! It increases our fun, don't you see?"* The voices laughed uproariously. Sidney heard more laughter in the background—unmistakable party sounds.

"A sap? That's what you think I am? Someone to laugh at?"

"Yes! And you're doing marvelously!"

"I HAVE found God!" Sidney yelled. He waved his healed arm and hand in the air. "This didn't heal through *luck!*"

"Your mind made the flesh sick," the first said. *"Then your mind healed it. . . . Flesh is like that, you know."*

Sidney shook his head in disbelief. "Oh come now. . . ."

"It's quite simple, fleshcarrier. Really, it is."

"Who are you?" Sidney demanded. "God? The Devil? And what do you mean by a garbage comet?"

The voices laughed in disturbing unison. Then the first said, in a tenor, lilting tone: *"As we told you, we occupy the Realm of Magic, and are unburdened with smelly, bulky bodies*

. . . with all their chronic pains, quirks, inefficiencies and frailties."

"You are more advanced than we?" Sidney asked.

"Fleshcarriers are next to lowest in the Great Order," the deeper voice replied. *"Magicians are second highest."*

"Only the Realm of the Unknown is higher," the other said.

"What are you, then?" Sidney asked, staring at a pebble on the motopath. "Concentrated energy?"

The voices laughed again. *"It is nearly impossible to explain in your terms, fleshcarrier,"* the deeper voice said. *"Energy is part of it, to be certain. But there is more, much more. Our existence is . . . essential . . . primordial, yet exalted. Words are inadequate."*

"But you are not God?"

"No," the tenor voice said. *"Like you, we have no proof of God's existence."*

"Or non-existence," said the other.

"We are what we are not," the tenor voice said.

"That is a good way to put it," the other agreed. *"We are what we are not. But come now—we can dispense with such serious talk. We're having a party!"* A wave of raucous laughter bounced around the inside of Sidney's skull.

Sidney stared at the pebble, wondering where it stood in the Great Order. "This is all very confusing," he said.

"Don't look for profundities," the deeper voice said. *"Philosophy is no fun . . . philosophy is no fun . . . philosophy is no fun. . . ."*

Other voices picked up the chant: *"Philosophy is no fun . . . philosophy is no fun . . . philosophy is no fun. . . ."*

"Shuttup, for Christ's sake!" Sidney screeched. "Shuttup!" He cupped his hands over his ears, felt a migraine headache at each side of his temple. The smoke over Elba House was white and wispy now. Sidney saw helipumpers hovering over the smoldering structure, searching for flare-ups.

"Listen to me!" Sidney yelled. "Listen to me!"

"Yes, fleshcarrier?" a sophisticated voice unfamiliar to Sidney said. Then others piped in with irritating whines: *"Yes, fleshcarrier? What do you want?"*

"I asked about the garbage comet. You didn't answer."

"You fleshcarriers didn't want all that garbage around," the sophisticated voice said. *"So you catapulted it . . . along with decaying, stinking bodies . . . all of it in flimsy, leaking*

*containers. Well we're sending this muck back to you now—
in a massive garbage ball!"*

"My God!"

"It will hit Earth Friday!"

"My Rosenbloom! That's only three days away! No! It can't
be!"

*"We couldn't send back the garbage without telling a few
fleshcarriers what was going on! That would take all the fun
out of it, don't you see?"*

"What'll I do, what'll I do, what'll I do?" Sidney lamented.
"Carla will be killed, and these monsters are enjoying it!"

The tenor voice returned: *"We always have fun! The most
complicated minds have the greatest need for play."*

"And you tried to spoil our fun, don't you see?" the deep
voice said, *"by hurling all that nasty, smelly crud at us."*

"What a rotten, terrible thing to do!" exclaimed the other.

They cackled uproariously, then faded off into a cavern of
Sidney's skull.

"Tom!" Sidney called out. "Where in the hell are you,
Tom?"

"Is everything all right?"

Sidney looked up from his kneeling position, saw a white-
uniformed little oriental woman staring down at him with her
hands on her hips. She smiled softly, kept one eye closed
against the sunlight on that side. "You were talking to yourself,"
she said. "Who is Tom?"

"Tom Javik. I'm supposed to operate a space cruiser with
him. There's a terrible emergency...."

"I will help you."

"You will? How?"

"Say," she said, studying Sidney's soft-featured face. "You
look like a fellow I saw yesterday, except half his face was
distorted, and one arm..."

"I've experienced a rather miraculous recovery," Sidney
said. He heard oxygen pumps throb, noted the air around him
no longer looked or smelled smoky. "Now how can you?..."

"How nice! I sat across from you on..." She interrupted
herself, laughing as she tossed a long ponytail of dark brown
hair over one shoulder. "But then you wouldn't remember!"

"I believe I would," Sidney said, rising to his feet. Although
the woman did not look at all like Carla, something about her

reminded him of Carla. He looked away, watched distant patching ships at work outside the habitat as they repaired holes made by the fire in the habitat's glassplex skin.

"I mean, you couldn't possibly! You see, I'm a chameloperson, bred in the laboratories of Bu-Tech."

As Sidney was trying to comprehend that statement, he looked back at the little woman and saw her body become very large and masculine, clothed in a green client's smock. Clear facial features disappeared, being replaced by puffy-ruddiness. The dark brown hair changed to a matted tuft. Dark wraparound sunglasses appeared over the eyes.

"You're . . ." Sidney said, pointing with a shaky forefinger, ". . . You're the blind man on the ship!"

"Quite so," a familiar masculine voice said. The chameloperson changed once more now, and presently it again was the oriental woman. "Very convenient for undercover work," she said.

"You must lead an extraordinarily interesting life," Sidney observed.

"Oh I do, I most certainly do! But now I'm concerned about you . . . out here on the motopath, talking to yourself."

"I must find Tom Javik," Sidney said. He motioned toward Elba House. "So many things are happening to me."

"You escaped from the fire?"

"Yes," he said. Then, with sudden excitement: "I prayed just moments ago, and the fire went out!"

Their work completed, some of the helipumpers began to leave, whirring high over Sidney's head.

"I see," she said, shielding the reflected sun with one hand. Her light brown, almond-shaped eyes narrowed suspiciously.

He looked at her with sudden hostility. "You don't believe me?"

"Sure. I believe you. But you may have received some assistance from the fire brigades." The wind blew her hair forward. She pushed it back.

"Didn't you notice? The fire went out suddenly . . . as I knelt!"

"I'm sorry. I didn't see that."

"Who are you anyway?" Sidney demanded, noting a Bu-Med G.W. 500 badge on her lapel. "A Procedures Checker?"

"No," she replied calmly, again tossing her ponytail over one shoulder. She noted Sidney's black, scowling eyebrows and said, "I CAN help you, if you'll just—"

"How many forms will be required?"

"Why, none. I'd like to—"

"No forms?" Sidney gasped with mock incredulity. His voice whined sarcasm as he added, "But you can't do anything without forms!"

"Interesting, the way you put that," she observed, studying him intently. "Were you ever in mental therapy?"

"Why do you ask?" Sidney replied, glaring.

"The anti-establishment diatribe. We hear a lot of it from . . ." She paused, looked away uneasily.

"I see." Sidney turned abruptly, intending to leave. *Maybe I am going wacko,* he thought.

"Wait," she urged, taking him gently by the arm. A hypodermic ring on one of her fingers injected Sidney's arm with a concealed needle. He did not feel the pinprick. "I will take you to your friend."

"You know him?"

"No, but I have powerful friends of my own." Her voice was soothing.

"It's important, you know." The drug had begun to take effect. Quickly, Sidney was losing the ability to doubt anything this woman said.

"I understand," she said.

"A terrible comet . . ."

"Try to relax. We can speak of this later. . . ."

"Yes, later. Of course." It did not seem so urgent to Sidney now. His large round hazel eyes stared back as innocently as a sheep about to be butchered.

"Just come with me," she said sweetly. "My name is Cherry Blossom." *Another doomie mental case,* she thought. *There is no doubt.*

Sidney looked into her eyes, saw deep compassion and thought of Carla again. Maybe it was the way the woman tossed her hair over one shoulder as Carla did when she wore falls. Or maybe it was the way she looked at him. Carla had cared, too.

"Okay," he said. "I'll go with you."

Beyond the rhododendron garden, a small one-story moonbrick building stood in the shade of two elm trees. Cherry Blossom led Sidney through a revolving door in the building to a small lobby containing striped yellow-and-green lounge chairs, some of which were covered by glassplex smoking bubbles. A bank of elevators dominated one wall beneath a picture of Uncle Rosy. They took an elevator to the sub-eighty-one level.

"I noticed several missing floor numbers on the carscreen," Sidney commented as they rolled off the elevator. "Seventy-one through eighty."

"Off-limits areas," Cherry Blossom said matter-of-factly. "Management personnel reach those floors on private elevators," she explained, leading Sidney along a wide yellow corridor which was painted with a broad green stripe along the bottom of each wall. The brightly lit hallway was crowded with orange-and-green-uniformed employees and yellow-smocked clients.

"What is this place?" Sidney asked as they slowed to roll around a cluster of lethargically rolling people in orange smocks. "Something seems unusual here." He noted a silver-and-black scroll sign on one wall which read, "JOBS ARE SACRED."

"Bu-Prog," she replied flatly.

"Bu-Prog? I've never heard of that bureau."

"I will explain it to you presently," she said with a smile in his direction.

A door to Sidney's left was marked, "ARTHRITIS DIVISION—JOINT LUBRICATION BOOTHS." Beyond that, a series of doors had signs describing services for the aged, including sight recovery and aging reversal.

"Is this part of Bu-Med?" Sidney asked. Then he yelled, "Look out!" suddenly and pushed Cherry Blossom to one side. A blue-and-grey star-shaped creature hovered half a meter over her head. Perhaps the circumference of a human head, the creature had an eye at the tip of each scaly and pointed tentacle.

To Sidney's surprise, she looked up calmly and extended a hand to the creature. "Don't worry," she said, undulating her fingers in a graceful, welcoming gesture. "This is Henry, my Jupiter Airfish." Cherry Blossom's light brown eyes danced happily.

"A pet?"

She nodded. "He's entirely harmless. Did you miss me, Henry?"

The airfish lit on her hand, made a cooing sound as she

petted its scaly back. "Found him dazed in Hub Warehouse Three one day," she said. "He'd come in as a hitchhiker on a cargo ship."

Sidney breathed an audible sigh of relief. "I've never seen anything like it," he said.

She tossed the airfish into the air, resumed moto-shoeing.

"We're in the moonslag radiation shield now, aren't we?" Sidney asked, glancing back to watch the Jupiter Airfish as it followed a few meters overhead. "I noticed that the elevator seemed to jump across a short gap. I assume that gap was the space between the habitat's rotating outer rim and the stationary radiation shield."

"Very observant," she said. *But not observant enough,* she thought. *Only three more applicants and I win the trip to . . .*

Sidney interrupted her thoughts. "This looks like quite a large facility," he said, glancing through an open double-doorway as he spoke. He saw endless rows of desk employees processing mounds of paperwork, heard the rhythmic tapping of rotatypers and the purr of Harmak.

"Yes," she replied, noting his interest in the room. "They are re-documenting identification papers for the cappies we process."

"This *is* part of Bu-Med then?"

"Oh no," she said. "Bu-Prog is a full-fledged bureau in its own right, voting by proxy in all votes taken by the Council of Ten." Cherry Blossom paused at a large imitation walnut door marked "ADMITTING" in bright gold letters. After touching a red wall button, she faced Sidney and folded open one of her lapels to reveal a green-and-yellow circular badge bearing the designation "G.W. 631."

Sidney furrowed his brow. "Bu-Prog?"

"Bureau of Progress. Wc have our own rehabilitation facilities. Our rehabilitation is not like Bu-Med's, however. Ours is very real, and includes relocation of the client in mainstream society."

"That sounds very nice." Sidney thought for a moment as he looked at the lettering on the door. He heard the Jupiter Airfish coo. "You're not planning to admit ME here, are you?"

She smiled as the Admitting Room door slid open. Two stocky attendants in green-and-yellow smocks rolled to Sidney's sides. "Hi, Cherry Blossom," one said as they took Sidney by each arm.

"Hey!" Sidney said, trying to pull away from their powerful grasps. "I can't go in there! You said you'd help me!" He glared at Cherry Blossom, his eyes wild with rage.

"This WILL help you," she said, smiling sweetly. "We'll cure your mental problems and then release you back to society. You'll be a contributing consumer again."

"I don't have time for that! A terrible comet—"

"Of course," Cherry Blossom said with a smile, "Bu-Med trackers may find you eventually. But we'll probably rescue you from them again. . . . The cycle goes on and on!"

The attendants dragged Sidney into the room. He pulled and kicked helplessly. "You lied to me!" Sidney yelled. "You lied!"

"This one said he stopped a fire through prayer," Cherry Blossom said as she followed them into the room. "And he keeps babbling about a comet."

"Another doomie!" one of the attendants exclaimed. "We get so many of them these days!"

The Admitting Room was long and narrow, with glassplex application booths along each wall. Perhaps half the booths were occupied when Sidney was dragged into the room, and outside each booth sat a Bu-Prog employee monitoring a C.R.T. control panel.

"Brain scanners will take your application automatically," Cherry Blossom said, designating an application booth for Sidney. She lifted his right wrist as the attendants held him, read the plastic nametag. "After the app," she said, "you'll be issued a yellow smock and will receive a rehab itinerary."

Sidney was strapped to a white plastic chair in the booth. "Just sit there and relax," Cherry Blossom said. "This won't take long."

Sidney watched her mento-close the sliding door, made an unsuccessful attempt to calm himself as he felt his heart beating too rapidly. His skin was warm and clammy, making the Bu-Med smock he still wore cling to his body. Closing his eyes to relax, Sidney leaned forward and touched his temple with the hand of one strapped arm, feeling beads of browsweat there with his fingertips.

Cherry Blossom was at the control panel now, and as Sidney closed his eyes, he felt the vacuum surge of powerful electronic equipment probing his brain, attempting to tear away his thoughts, delving into private areas of consciousness and re-membrance.

"Don't let them do it, fleshcarrier!" a voice said. It was the deeper of the two voices with whom he had grown familiar.

"The machine is too powerful," Sidney said. "I can't stop it!" He felt something tugging and tearing at the membranes holding his brain intact, and he wanted to scream out but knew that would do no good.

"Does it anger you?" the voice asked.

"Yes. Very much."

"Then concentrate upon resisting it, fleshcarrier! Don't let it rape your brain!"

Sidney concentrated, then became cognizant of a growing internal strength...and somewhere, beyond that, a vast and all-consuming nothingness. Words came back, dancing as thoughts upon an elusive consciousness: *We are what we are not.* From somewhere far away, he heard the metallic voice of Cherry Blossom screeching, "You're blocking, Malloy! You're blocking! Try to relax, damn you!"

Sidney felt his mind fighting, surging, dominating, pushing away the thought-probes of the brain scanner. A new serenity filled him. He saw his past and present self. All the motivations, hopes and desires of his lifetime were laid out in front of him. He was a child again, longing to join the Space Patrol, to explore uncharted and glamorous corners of the galaxy. Sidney felt pain returning as he re-experienced his first seizure at the age of nine. Years fled through his memory in seconds while Sidney relived the years of wishing as he worked in Central Forms...wasted time spent working and longing. Could it have been different? The fear of discovery returned. Again, Sidney kept his dreams alive in the pages of a scrapbook and in ego pleasure dreams.

"I've never seen such determined resistance," a man's voice said through the speaker.

"What does the manual prescribe, Dr. Arroyo?" Cherry Blossom asked.

Now Sidney was in pain, as he relived the grand mal seizure of that terrible evening in the Sky Ballroom. In his mind's eye, he writhed in the sidechair again, then slipped to the ballroom floor, screaming, twitching and drooling as a horrified crowd looked down at him, their faces contorted in revulsion.

"Rule sixty-three, section twelve-point-six-two, paragraph

three," Dr. Arroyo replied. "All clients must complete an application."

"He's refusing, then?"

"I would, say so, yes."

"What should we do?"

"All clients must complete an application."

"That's all it says?"

"I'm afraid so."

"Call in the advisers."

In a hushed conference held minutes later, the advisers determined that something might be faulty with the application equipment. So Sidney was placed in another application booth. But the same thing happened again. They tried yet another booth, and then another. All to no avail.

By this time, Mayor Nancy Ogg was made aware of the unusual situation, and she immediately recognized who Sidney was. She issued orders that he was to be sent to a holding room for the time being. The whole situation resulted in a very confused and upset group of Bu-Prog employees. They had never seen anything like it before, and were anxious not to displease the Mayor.

In a semi-conscious state in the holding room, Sidney wondered, *Why did the voices help me again? The fire, and now....* His own thoughts floated across his consciousness as if thought by someone else, and he almost felt able to answer them himself. The answers seemed on the very tip of his tongue, there but not there at the same instant.

It was warm that noonhour in the Spartan Cafeteria. Lastsayer Steven stood with his tray of bread and holy water, scanning the tables for a place to sit. The cafeteria was a glassplexed greenhouse at one side of the Black Box of Democracy's roof. He saw an autocopter landing on the rooftop helipad outside, heard the whine and thump of the engine and rotors. The cafeteria was beginning to fill, and sayermen spoke to one another in low, polite tones.

Seeing Twosayer William seated alone at a corner table, he rolled over and asked if he might join him.

"Why, certainly," Twosayer replied somberly. "Go right ahead." Twosayer thought of the comet, wondered if the intercept mission was proceeding smoothly.

Lastsayer noticed that all the sayermen threw their hoods

back as they sat down. He did the same, and loosened a draw-
string at his neck. "Frightfully hot," Lastsayer said. He smiled
nervously, lifted a red cup of holy water to his lips and sipped.

"That it is," Twosayer said, shifting in his seat so that he
sat higher than Lastsayer. "Sometimes it is a supreme test of
our faith to keep the robes on."

Lastsayer laughed uneasily, then said in a low tone, "I have
a problem, Twosayer. I need to confide in someone."

"Oh?" the elder sayerman said, touching one side of his
hooked nose. Smiling compassionately, he asked, "How could
someone with us only a few days have such an ominous problem?"

Lastsayer took a deep breath.

Twosayer tore a piece of white bread off the portion on his
plate, added, "Surely it is not as earthshaking as all that!"

Lastsayer looked around as Twosayer ate the bread, watched
sayermen at nearby tables to be certain they were not listening.
"Could we speak somewhere privately, Twosayer? It is a most
delicate matter."

"THERE ARE NO SECRETS IN THE SAYERHOOD,
YOUNGSAYER! Speak up! I will listen!" Twosayer nibbled
at another piece of bread, stared across the table with grey
green eyes.

Lastsayer rubbed a finger nervously against his red paper
cup of holy water. "I had my first audience with Uncle Rosy
Sunday," he said.

"So I understand. A bit late too, I hear."

"Onesayer was not prepared at the appointed time. I awaited
him, but—"

"A sayerman does not cast aspersions upon one of his brothers!" Twosayer snapped. Lastsayer noted the voice was angry
but the eyes seemed bright and alert, almost pleased.

"I was taught properly on Pleasant Reef," the younger de-
votee said. "Normally, I would not have said anything about
it."

"Normally, I would not listen to such talk," Twosayer huffed.
"Tell me why I should."

Lastsayer shook his head sadly. "Onesayer was in his suite,
apparently high on Happy Pills."

"You are qualified to make such a judgment?"

"He told me had taken a couple."

"Continue."

"When I came upon him, he was behaving strangely."

"Be specific." Twosayer's eyes narrowed to intense slits as he stared across the table.

Lastsayer glanced around, met Twosayer's gaze and said, "He did . . . well . . . um . . . he did impressions of Uncle Rosy."

Lastsayer saw a smile glimmer at the corners of Twosayer's mouth, but it faded quickly. "Come now," Twosayer said. "I can hardly believe such a thing!" He took a drink of holy water, sloshed it casually in his mouth.

"It is true. I swear it! Could it have been a test, Twosayer William?"

"What do you mean?"

"To see if I am loyal to Uncle Rosy?"

"We do not use . . . tests . . . of that sort."

Twosayer finished his bread, took a gulp of water. "There are no secrets in the Sayerhood," he said.

"Does that mean I should inform the Master?"

Twosayer's eyes flared, and Lastsayer detected hostility in them. "That is all I wish to say on the matter," Twosayer said.

"As you wish." Lastsayer finished his bread and holy water hurriedly, then excused himself from the table.

At the same moment, Onesayer Edward stood alone in his kitchen module, looking around. According to Uncle Rosy's rules, he was permitted to eat in his own kitchen every other day, and the fare there was not limited to bread and holy water. That was for the gathering places of the Sayerhood, where ceremony was essential. The vibrating sound of a circulating air fan touched Onesayer's consciousness, then receded. He felt dull. Something seemed to be blocking out a portion of his mind.

He rubbed a fat cheek thoughtfully with one hand, said, "What will I have for lunch today?" *I must be discreet*, he thought. *It would be too obvious to ask anyone for a weapon. Sayermen have no use for such things.* He stared at a built-in microwave oven, looked at the plastichrome food door above a countertop conveyor strip. *Shouldn't tear anything apart. . . .*

Atheists in Hell! he thought, placing his hands on his hips. *Everything is automatic or built-in! I see no heavy objects which could be concealed beneath my robe. . . .*

Onesayer mentoed a dispenser next to the food conveyor, watched a cellophane-wrapped package of eating utensils pop out. Removing the white plastic knife from the package, he fingered it. The blade was blunt, serrated. It chafed the tip of his finger a little bit. *This would not even penetrate Uncle Rosy's skin,* he thought.

Onesayer placed the knife on the counter, next examining the plastic fork. He pushed one of the tongs with his forefinger to test its strength, broke the tong. With a furious grimace, he slammed the fork to the counter, shattering the utensil into many pieces.

"Plastic is fantastic," he intoned. "Every break is a new task."

Whirling angrily, he left the penthouse suite and moto-shoed toward the elevator bank. Onesayer considered sneaking into the Master's suite to sabotage one of the consumer products there, but discarded the idea. *What if he has an armadillo meckie in there?*

Seeing Twosayer William approaching, Onesayer placed a hand over his eyes to make it appear he was scratching his forehead.

"Peace be upon you," Twosayer said cheerily, stopping as he neared Onesayer.

"Yes, yes," Onesayer replied hurriedly, rolling past the other sayerman with his hand still over his eyes. "Peace be upon you. Excuse me, please. I am very busy."

He does act strangely, Twosayer thought. *Hiding in the shadows . . . covering his face.*

Onesayer reached the elevator bank, mentoed for an elevator. *I have never seen an armadillo meckie near the Master,* he thought. *Maybe I can rush him in the Central Chamber. There should be something lying around that I can use as a weapon . . . something I did not notice before.* He decided to search every floor of the Black Box of Democracy.

A bell rang, signifying the elevator's arrival. *I will strangle him if necessary,* Onesayer thought.

When the elevator doors opened, one of Uncle Rosy's green-and-white delivery meckies rolled off, carrying a bundle wrapped in white cloth. "Master sent this for you," the meckie said, extending its mechanical arms with the bundle. "You are to open it when alone." A frosted white dome on top of the headless little mechanical servant pulsated with a dim light.

Onesayer felt his pulse quicken as he accepted the bundle. It was not heavy. Two flat cloth strips were wrapped around the girth. "Did he say what it is?" Onesayer asked.

"I know nothing about it." The meckie moto-whirled, returned to the elevator.

A bomb, Onesayer thought nervously as he rolled back to his suite. *Uncle Rosy plans to kill me first!*

He set the bundle on the kitchen table, stood back and stared at it. *What if I do not open it?* he thought. *But surely the Master will ask me about it....*

Onesayer touched the bundle, thought: *He could order me killed at any moment anyway. If the Master knows my intentions, I might as well die this way as another.* Onesayer wiped perspiration from his brow, took a deep breath.

He removed the cloth straps slowly, pulled at an edge of the bundle. Expecting it to explode, he twisted his face as he unravelled. *Something hard inside,* he thought, feeling the remaining unwrapped portion. *It is long and thin....*

An object clattered to the table, ringing metallically. "A knife!" the startled Onesayer whispered, hardly able to believe what he saw. "And it is steel!"

Onesayer rubbed one finger across a flat side of the gleaming blade, watched moisture from his finger fog the surface and then disappear. The handle was black pearl, topped with delicate scroll work. He studied the scroll work, saw this: "For my good friend, Willard... from Alafin Inaya."

'Willard' expects me to kill myself, Onesayer thought angrily. *Well, I won't do it!* Onesayer lifted the knife, rubbed a thumb against the lettering on the handle.

I will get HIM with this. He knows I am desperate ... will be prepared. It might be suicidal for me....

Onesayer looked at the reflection of his face in the gleaming blade. The image was distorted, but he saw deep lines framing his eyes and beginning to crease his cheeks. *I must hurry,* he thought. *There is not much time.*

At five minutes before two that afternoon, Mayor Nancy Ogg stood at the Hub Control Room viewing window, watching as two grey cylindrical mass driver shells were pulled by space tug to the waiting Shamrock Five. She held a lime tintette nervously in one hand, stared intently as the four-hundred-twenty-meter-long mass driver shells were connected behind the space cruiser like railroad cars behind an engine. She knew the fin-like chrome thrust deflectors at the rear of the Shamrock

Five would keep rocket exhaust away from the trailers.

A computer printout slip lay on the counter to her left. It was the memory slip on Madame Bernet. *The last day and a half is blank*, she thought, taking a deep puff on the tintette. *What a time for an equipment breakdown!* She wondered if the meckie had killed Javik, and blew a thick cloud of red smoke through her mouth. *Where in the Hooverville is he?* she thought.

Her security personnel had been searching for Javik since midmorning. Now the ship was nearly ready to leave, exactly on schedule, and it had no captain! It occurred to her that Sidney Malloy was the titular captain. *He's an enigma*, she thought. *A milktoast weakling, I've been told . . . but we can't get an application out of him!*

These problems aren't my fault. I can't be blamed for them! But the Mayor had been associated with the government long enough to know how easily the blame could be pointed at her. After all, Javik had been on Saint Elba when he disappeared. And never before had a cappy defied an application machine.

She picked a bit of tobacco from the tip of her tongue with quivering fingers, glared down across the loading dock to the Shamrock Five. Madame Bernet stood inside the dock's glassplex waiting area, talking with two black-uniformed security men.

Mayor Nancy Ogg turned at the hum of approaching motoboots, watched the muscular Sergeant Rountree roll to a stop and deliver the rotating wrist salute of the Security Brigade.

"You've found Javik?" she asked nervously.

"No, Honorable Mayor," the sergeant replied. "I am here to report that the fire is under control. Patching ships are repairing holes in the radiation shield."

"And the escaped clients?"

"We believe all have been recaptured. They've been routed into the cargo holds of two surplus freight rockets, as you instructed."

"Good."

"Do you have transfer authorizations on them?"

"Yes," the Mayor said. "Saint Michaels will take all our overflow."

"I hate to see a reduction in your client count, Honorable Mayor. But we'll get more cappies when the burned-out wings have been rebuilt."

I don't give a Hoover's dam about client counts! she thought, raging inside. *I just want to get off this dismal orbiter!*

"Shall we run an identity scan on the escapees before shipping them out?" Rountree asked.

Mayor Nancy Ogg was deep in thought. "Eh? Oh . . . I don't think that will be necessary. We have more important matters to consider." She lifted a shaking tintette to her lips, inhaled deeply. Cool nicotine entered her lungs, then surged out of her nostrils in a red puff. "Get the I.D. data from Saint Michaels," she said.

"Yes, Honorable Mayor."

"Put out the word, Sergeant Rountree. . . . Fifty thousand dollars to the man who finds Javik! I want him located . . . NOW!"

The sergeant saluted brusquely, spun on his moto-boots and sped away.

Mayor Nancy Ogg glanced at a red console-mounted security phone, mentoed the receiver. "Get me Dr. Hudson," she said into a tele-cube which floated in front of her mouth. "Priority One."

By radio telephone from the Hub Control Room seconds later, Mayor Nancy Ogg reached Dr. Hudson's office.

"I'm terribly sorry," a receptionist at the other end of the line said. "Dr. Hudson is no longer with us."

"NO LONGER WITH YOU? WHAT DO YOU MEAN?"

"That is all I know," the receptionist said. "Shall I connect you with personnel?"

Seeing the conversation going nowhere, Mayor Nancy Ogg ended the call and rang President Ogg instead. Her brother took the call in his office.

"Sorry about Hudson," President Ogg said.

"He's been fired?"

"He's dead, Nancy. Product failure."

"Huh?" The Mayor leaned forward on her stool, felt numbness in her brain.

The line beeped. It was on scramble code.

"Moto-shoe fatality. Happened this morning, near Tech Square."

"Oh my God!" She coughed. Mayor Nancy Ogg knew she should be happy at the news of a product failure. There could be no finer way to die. But tears welled up in her eyes, overflowed her lower lids and poured down her cheeks.

"Nancy . . . are you all right?"

She cleared her throat, asked, "Have you ordered an investigation?"

"Not necessary, Sis. A Product Failure team has already stamped his body. It's all approved."

"Did they analyze his moto-shoes?"

"What on Earth for? No one wants to jeopardize Hudson's admission to the Happy Shopping Ground!"

"I WANT TO KNOW IF THE SHOES WERE SABOTAGED!" she blurted, unable to keep her composure.

"No one would want to harm Hudson," President Ogg said, trying not to betray uncertainty in his voice. *The Black Box did this one*, he thought, *and I'm not going to tamper with it!*

Mayor Nancy Ogg wiped tears from her face angrily, asked: "What about the comet intercept mission?"

"I'm not directly involved in that," President Ogg said. "But it's in competent hands."

"Didn't Dick discuss it with you this morning?"

"No. There was a recorded message that he called quite early. He started to say something, then said he'd call back."

"Lieutenant Javik is missing! That's what Dick wanted to tell you!"

"What? You mean the pilot?"

"I have the ship ready, Mr. President," she said in a sarcastic tone, "and there's no one here to operate it! Do you have any bright ideas?"

"Certainly," he said, presidentially. "I'll appoint a committee to look into it." He sat back in his chair, pleased with himself at seeing an opportunity for additional employment through committeeship.

"We're talking about a very large garbage comet, dear brother. This is Tuesday. It's due to hit Earth late Friday afternoon!"

"I know . . . I know. . . ."

"Why don't you just send a substitute fly boy?"

"Without going through channels? I couldn't do that! Uncle Rosy would never have approved such a thing!" *The Black Box will stop the comet anyway*, he thought. *I can make myself look good on this one!*

Knowing her brother and seeing it was hopeless to argue the point, Mayor Nancy Ogg said, "I suppose you're right."

"Jobs are sacred, you know," he intoned.

I'd better find Javik soon, the Mayor thought as she hung up the telephone receiver. *Or we'll never stop that comet!* Mento-activating the speakercom on the Hub Control Room console, she said, "Sergeant Rountree, stake out all nightclubs and taverns on the habitat."

"Yes, Honorable Mayor," the speakercom blared.

"And round up everyone we have who might be able to operate the Shamrock Five." *I'm not waiting for instructions on this baby,* she thought.

"Yes, Honorable Mayor," the Sergeant's speakercom voice said. "Does that include clients?"

"Yes, I suppose it does. . . ."

"They may be our best hope. We have a couple of ex-pursuit craft pilots in the psycho ward."

"I recall. They went mad several weeks back and became doomies."

"Right, Honorable Mayor. They have Comet Fever."

"We'll use them if we have to, with mind control drugs. But that's the bottom of the barrel."

"I'll get right on it," Rountree said. "Maybe we can find someone else."

Mayor Nancy Ogg heard the line click shut.

Minutes after President Ogg completed his call with Saint Elba, Billie Birdbright rolled into the office ebulliently. "You've won, Mr. President! All the networks are projecting you a big winner!"

"That's wonderful," Ogg said, unenthusiastically because of the important duty on his mind.

"News of Munoz's death broke before a lot of people voted. You really opened up a margin after that!"

"Get me the Manual on Committees," Ogg said. "We have something important to do, and I want it done correctly."

Later that afternoon, President Ogg stood near the head of a long simulated walnut table in Conference Room fifty-seven. Interim ministers Nigel Larsen of Bu-Tech and Meg Corrigon of Bu-Mil stood nearby in newly-donned white and gold ministerial robes. Standing off to one side, Chief of Staff Birdbright awaited instructions from the President.

The conference room occupied one-fourth of an entire floor of the White House Office Tower, along an exterior building wall which permitted illumination of the room by natural daylight. The windows were large, and the room radiated cheerfulness. President Ogg peered at chairs on the far end of the table. He envisioned all the chairs occupied, papers strewn across the table. This pleased him, and he smiled.

Ogg tapped a bulky forefinger on the table-mounted microphone in front of one chair, said, "I want to see this room full tomorrow morning, gentlemen!"

"Ahem!"

Ogg turned to see Lieutenant Colonel Meg Corrigon looking at him with a bemused expression. Corrigon was fiftyish, a career military woman whose neatly trimmed black hair came to a sharp widow's peak at the center of her forehead.

"I mean ladies . . . er, ah . . . lady and . . . well, you know what I mean!" Ogg smiled sheepishly.

Corrigon broke into a squeaky laugh.

"This committee will explore every angle of Lieutenant Javik's disappearance," Ogg continued. "It is an exciting opportunity for committeeship!"

"Excuse me, Mr. President," Nigel Larsen said, clearing his throat nervously.

"Yes?" Ogg turned a bit on his moto-shoes to get a better view of Larsen, looked upon a man with a very heavy face and an immense, pendulous triple chin. Curiously, Larsen's body was rather slender.

"Forgive me for asking," Larsen said, "but couldn't we simply send another ship's pilot now?" Noticing a scowl forming on Ogg's face, he added quickly: "Just this once, sir?"

"No!" Ogg said, glaring ferociously. "If we make an exception now, where will it stop?"

"But I don't think there are any other options, sir. And a pilot is needed up there quite desperately."

"WHO ARE WE TO DETERMINE OPTIONS?" Ogg thundered. "COMMITTEES DETERMINE OPTIONS!"

"Uh, sir. . . ." Larsen's triple chin quivered.

"There are always options, Larsen! Options are the soul of committeeship!"

"Yes, Mr. President."

"It takes only one tiny break in the system, Larsen . . . and then everything falls apart."

"Like a house of dominoes," Corrigon piped in.

"Well put, Corrigon!" the President said.

"Thank you, Mr. President." She placed both hands on the back of a chair, beamed proudly.

This woman's not at all like her predecessor, Ogg thought, comparing her with General Munoz. *I can work with her!* Ogg extended his large hands to each side, palms up. "Can you imagine the destruction of everything we've built, Larsen?"

"No, Mr. President. I didn't think. . . ."

"You didn't think!" Ogg said, pouncing on the miscue. "Well, snap out of it, man!" Ogg mentoed a microphone on the table, snapped his fingers against it. The sound echoed around the room. "Wake up!"

"Yes, Mr. President," Larsen said, afraid to meet Ogg's powerful gaze. "I see your point."

"By the book, ministers!" Ogg said. "Strictly by the book!"

"Yes, Mr. President," the interim ministers said in unison.

The President wouldn't approve of me working late, Chief of Staff Birdbright thought, glancing wearily at a digital cuckoo clock on the wall. A tiny cuckoo bird above the digital reader popped out upon Birdbright's mento command, chirped: "Tuesday P.M., nine-fourteen and twelve seconds." The mechanical bird retracted with a crisp snap.

Birdbright stood at the telephone message board outside the oval office in a pool of white fluorescent light. The rest of the floor lay in night shadows. He mentoed for a transcript of the evening's messages, and a phone printer beneath the message board began to type, spewing out words and paper into a plastic tray. Birdbright sifted through the sheets, sorting them into two retained piles while tossing away a third category of junk messages.

Here's something, Birdbright thought, holding a sheet up. *From Larsen at Bu-Tech . . . sent about an hour ago*. Birdbright read aloud: "Comp six-oh-two reports it is too late to divert comet to nitrogen-rich atmosphere of Kinshoto for burnout. Shamrock Five must take off before six P.M. tomorrow for Thursday rendezvous with comet. Still possible to divert fireball away from Earth."

Birdbright looked away, shook his head. *Larsen won't last long when the President sees this*, he thought. *Imagine that . . . attempting to rush the work of a committee with a computer report!*

He looked down at the sheet again, squinted and pulled his

head back to keep from throwing a shadow across the page. Birdbright blinked his eyes, read on: "If substitute crew cannot arrive before deadline, Comp six-oh-two recommends strategic placement of orbiting missile launchers around Earth for atomic assault on comet. . . ."

Birdbright took this and several other messages into the oval office, mentoed on an overhead light and set them in the center of the President's desk. *I can see President Ogg's position,* he thought. *But Larsen may have a point too.* . . . He grimaced, noting that Larsen had sent a copy of the report to Saint Elba's Mayor Nancy Ogg.

Sparks are going to fly tomorrow! he thought.

Birdbright noted two white plastic sacks bearing bureau ministerial crests on the desktop. He recalled receiving them from a courier just before quitting time that afternoon. President Ogg had left without examining them.

Birdbright knew these were the personal effects of Munoz and Hudson. As President, it would be Ogg's sacred duty to review their contents and decide which items would go on display in the White House Tower Museum.

Birdbright poured out two neat piles on the desktop. He picked through Munoz's effects first . . . a gold wrist digital, gold and silver coins, a gold cross and chain. . . .

I recall him wearing this cross, Birdbright thought, lifting the cross and dangling its chain across one hand. The metal was cool to his touch.

Wearily, he mentoed off the overhead light and sat in the President's chair, spinning it to gaze out the window. New City sparkled below like a freshly honed jewel, and above that a lazy quarter moon stood vigil. He held the cross up, rotating it to pick up glints of reflected light upon the cross surface.

Strange what I'm feeling now, he thought. *Can't quite put my finger on it.* . . .

Birdbright held the cross against his chest, scanned the heavens. Somewhere between the orbits of the Earth and the Moon was Saint Elba, and beyond that a great comet which threatened to destroy everything man's technology had built. He strained to see the tiniest speck of unusual activity in space, but nothing seemed out of the ordinary. Had he not been privy to information about the impending disaster and the uncoordinated efforts to stop it, Birdbright might have thought it was just another lovely summer night in God's chosen land.

*   *   *

As Sayer Superior Lin-Ti rounded the top of the hill approaching the Great Temple, he thought of the day's lesson. *There is history and then again there is HISTORY*, he thought. *I fear the history writers may have included too much unsavory detail in this text. These are impressionable youngsayermen....*

The fog on the valley floor below was lifting early this morning, and he could see the upper half of the temple. Reaching a fork in the motopath, the Sayer Superior rolled over an arched bridge to the left.

Ah well, he thought. *There is always Selective Memory Erasure. I have ordered its application many times....*

ELEVEN

THE ECONOMICS OF FREENESS, FOR
FURTHER READING AND DISCUSSION

October 20, 2415: Council of Ten declare Tic-Tac-Toe, Hangman,
Battleship and dot-to-dot games to be against the public interest
unless played on manufactured sets.

Wednesday, August 30, 2605

Garbage Day Countdown (Earth impact): Two days, eleven
hours, fifty-four minutes. . . .

Dawn formed reddish outlines across New City's skyline
and around hills partially visible in the distance. Onesayer
Edward was only dimly conscious of the view as he sat by the
one-way window in his kitchen module. He had important
matters on his mind this day.

Feeling tired, he swallowed a sleep-sub pill and followed

that with a water capsule. It had been a fitful night of sleep, punctuated by periods in which he lay awake in darkness worrying about the distasteful task he would perform the following day. When the new day broke, he had no cohesive plan of action . . . only the conviction that he would kill Uncle Rosy that day or would perish in the attempt.

I'll cut up his face to erase the features, Onesayer thought, staring disconsolately at an untouched plate of presto-eggs. *Then I can report that Onesayer died while attempting to kill the Master*.

Onesayer left the breakfast table without eating anything, took an elevator down to the Bureau Monitoring Room. *Act normally*, he told himself as he entered the room, touching a small bulge at his waist where the knife was concealed. The weapon was there, reassuringly, concealed beneath the folds of his robe and secured against his body by an extra robe belt.

Sayermen were busy at their posts, operating mento-activated keyboards and scanning video screens on the walls. The barely discernible hum of pink sound absorbed harsher machine noises, giving the room an air of smooth efficiency. Through a distant one-way window, morning sunlight filtered into the room, glinting off chrome trim on the machines.

"Great Suffering Souplines!" he heard Twosayer William exclaim. The hook-nosed Twosayer stood at a minicam screen near the entry, shaking his head from side to side in dismay.

Onesayer rolled to the station, asked: "What is it?"

"You are feeling better?" Twosayer asked, studying Onesayer closely. *He is aging!* Twosayer thought, elated at what he saw. But then Twosayer felt fear, as he saw Onesayer glare back at him disdainfully with crease-framed eyes.

Onesayer touched the bulge at his waist. His expression became menacing.

"Uh, take a look," Twosayer said, nodding nervously toward a cluster of six wallscreens.

Onesayer narrowed his eyes, glanced from screen to screen without comprehending what was happening.

"Javik . . . the Shamrock Five pilot . . . is on Saint Michaels!" Twosayer said disgustedly. "Instead of on Saint Elba!" He sneaked a glance at lines on Onesayer's cheeks as Onesayer concentrated upon a minicam screen. Twosayer suppressed a smile.

Onesayer saw Tom Javik at the head of a line of clients.

Javik glared across a countertop at a Junior Therapist on the other side. . . .

"You *must* complete these forms," the Junior Therapist insisted. He extended a packet of legal-sized forms and an auto-pen across the countertop. Fair-haired and with a light complexion, the Junior Therapist was vacuous-faced, with a slack jaw and unintelligent eyes. It was the same bureaucratic personality Javik had encountered so many times previously, and he felt rage building up inside.

"There's no form for what I'm trying to communicate to you," Javik said. "I was sent here in error, and it's imperative that I return to Saint Elba."

"Fill out the forms. I must have the forms!"

Onesayer shook his head in disbelief. The screen flickered off, went back on. . . .

"Fill out the forms, please," the Junior Therapist said firmly.

Javik scowled ferociously across the counter, said in a threatening tone: "I'll give you thirty seconds to say something sensible. Then I'm coming after you!"

"You're forgetting your place!" the Junior Therapist huffed.

"Twenty-three seconds," Javik said, glancing at his wrist digital.

"I don't believe this is happening!" Onesayer said, gazing at the ceiling. He looked back at the screen. . . .

"Guards!" the Junior Therapist screeched. "Guards!"

Javik reached for his concealed pistol, but had a second thought and relaxed his hand. "All right," he said. "Give me the damned forms."

The Junior Therapist took a deep breath and pushed the forms across the counter.

Javik glanced at two black-uniformed Security Brigade guards who had approached and were standing three meters away, watching intently. Javik looked down at the forms, took the auto-pen. "Where do I write 'help?'" he asked, without humor.

Onesayer looked away from the screen as it went dark, asked angrily: "Has a substitute pilot been dispatched to Saint Elba?"

"No," Twosayer said. He turned his oval face away, afraid to meet Onesayer's burning gaze. "There is still that cappy Malloy that Munoz picked in a vision. . . ."

"Aaay! Captain Cappy!"

"Now President Ogg has turned the whole matter over to

an investigating committee. Ogg wants the committee to provide him with options."

"This is no time for committees!" Onesayer yelled.

"I know that, but. . . ." Twosayer stared at the darkened screen.

"And you're just sitting here watching? That's all you're doing?" Onesayer was hurling apostrophes with reckless abandon.

"There is nothing we can do." Twosayer threw up his hands helplessly. "The Master has given us specific instructions not to—"

"We'll see about that!" Onesayer said. He stormed out of the room, intending to take a moto-stroll until his head cleared..

Forty-five minutes later, Onesayer Edward stood in the great central chamber, glaring up at the shadowy form of Uncle Rosy. Uncle Rosy cleared his throat, shifted in his chair. Onesayer heard the iron door to the chamber slide shut behind him, and a rush of fear washed through him.

Calmness, Onesayer thought, attempting to mento-command himself. *Utter calmness. Then he dies.*

"I grow weary of all the monitoring and controls," Uncle Rosy said in a resonant, soothing tone which echoed softly off the black glassite walls of the chamber. "So much is required to support the AmFed system."

We'll get to the point soon, Onesayer thought, oblivious to his unspoken pun. He placed a hand against his robe over the knife.

Uncle Rosy cleared his throat again, and Onesayer heard the low strains of humming that came from the Master's lips. The notes were soft and lilting, unmistakably the Hymn of Freeness.

Feeling tears building up in his eyes, Onesayer blinked. "With the deaths of Munoz and Hudson," he said slowly, trying to exude strength with each word, "all has fallen into bumbling disarray."

"It went bad before that," Uncle Rosy said. "General Munoz chose the cappy last week."

"But Hudson might have taken corrective action after Munoz's death—once he was free of the General's dominance."

"This is an I-told-you-so speech?"

Onesayer forced a smile, kept his hand over the knife as he asked: "Why did you send a knife to me yesterday, Master?"

"You wanted it, did you not?"

"I did, but not to take my own life." With these words, Onesayer took a deep breath and drew the knife. Locking his moto-shoes, he bounded up six steps to the level on which Uncle Rosy sat. He pointed the blade at Uncle Rosy, and it glinted in the low yellow light of overhead globes. Onesayer could see Uncle Rosy's features now less than a meter away, a cherubic face smiling back at him without the tiniest hint of fear.

"You hesitate, Onesayer. He who hesitates to take a thing is not yet ready for it."

"You *want* to die?"

"I feel . . . there are more perfect states than the sustenance of flesh." Uncle Rosy rubbed his chin thoughtfully, added, "I sense . . . serenity."

Onesayer switched the black pearl handled knife to the other hand. "You refer to the Happy Shopping Ground?"

Uncle Rosy laughed with a hint of derision. "I made that place up! I made everything up!" Noting a look of surprise on Onesayer's face, Uncle Rosy said: "The place to which I refer has no shopping centers, no products, no people, no machines. . . ."

"You have found God, Master? Truly?"

"No, Onesayer Edward. Though I have tried. Voices have spoken to me recently . . . since this garbage comet matter came up. . . ."

"Voices, Master?"

"They speak of a Realm of the Unknown, say it is the highest state of existence. There are other . . ." His voice trailed off.

"I hope you find serenity, Master."

Uncle Rosy smiled benignly, said, "Perhaps I have attempted to control too much, Onesayer. If not you at my throat now, eventually it would be someone else."

"You gave me the weapon, Master. Is that not controlling?"

Uncle Rosy raised one hand to support his chin. Nodding slowly, he said, "I merely sped the inevitable. Forces were already in motion." He laughed. "You argue with me to the end, eh, Onesayer?"

Onesayer smiled lovingly, said, "I feel . . . closer to you than ever before."

"We are one," Uncle Rosy said. "You will find a clean robe on the ledge behind my chair. The wearer commands my meck-ies."

Onesayer felt the blade quiver in his grasp, asked, "How do I stop aging?"

"Look within yourself, Onesayer Edward. It is your second test."

"And the first . . . is killing you?"

"That is correct."

"There will be other tests?"

"Always, Onesayer. There will be no end to them."

Onesayer closed his eyes and lunged forward, plunging the knife deep into Uncle Rosy's chest. Onesayer felt ribs cracking and flesh tearing away. He released his grip on the knife and pulled back in revulsion at what he had done.

Uncle Rosy's face was contorted in pain—holding both hands against his chest, he gasped: "Finish it!"

Onesayer bit his upper lip hard, pulled the knife out. He held it with two hands now, samurai style, and plunged the blade again and again into Uncle Rosy's face and torso. Uncle Rosy gurgled as he swallowed his own blood, gasped and slumped dead over the Zero Handle.

"No!" Onesayer yelled, only half-conscious that he was speaking to a corpse. "Do not touch it!"

The Zero Handle began to move down toward contact under Uncle Rosy's enormous weight. Onesayer dropped the bloody knife and lunged for the handle. With both hands and all the power of his legs and back, he tried to stop the handle from proceeding farther. It slowed, but continued to drop. Releasing one hand from the Zero Handle, Onesayer tried to push the corpse away. But the weight was too great.

"I can't . . . hold . . . this . . . much longer!" he gasped, seeing the point drawing dangerously near. "Earth is going to blow!"

In a desperation move, Onesayer released the handle entirely and knelt under the corpse's shoulder. With blood dripping on him, Onesayer mustered all his remaining strength and pushed the corpse up and off the Zero Handle.

THUD! Uncle Rosy's lifeless form slumped to the floor.

Then, afraid to breathe or make a move, Onesayer stared wide-eyed at the Zero Handle. It had stopped less than a cen-timeter above contact! He lifted the handle carefully, and this required all the strength he had left. Panting, he felt great gears in the mechanism move with painstaking slowness, like megalithic tumblers. Finally the Zero Handle was back in place, and he breathed a deep sigh.

An unexpected test, Onesayer thought. *And the Master's body is not yet cold.*

He glanced at the Orbital Handle, then back to Uncle Rosy's crumpled form, which lay in a pool of blood. Blood ran down the steps. *First things first,* he thought. *I must get him into my robe.*

Onesayer removed Uncle Rosy's torn and bloodsoaked robe, tossed it into a disposa-tube next to the chair. Then he pulled a black jade ring off Uncle Rosy's finger, replacing it with his own brown-and-black-striped onyx ring. Inside Uncle Rosy's ring, Onesayer read the gold scroll inscription: "For my good friend, Willard . . . from Alafin Inaya."

Identical to the knife inscription, he thought. Onesayer tried the ring on several fingers, settled on the forefinger of his right hand.

Wonder who Alafin Inaya was, he thought, pulling off his own robe. He stood in his shorts now, still wearing about his belly the second sash he had used to secure the knife to himself. The ends of the sash dangled against one leg. Onesayer stared down at Uncle Rosy's body, then took a deep, agitated breath and set about performing the remaining distasteful task.

With great effort, he dressed Uncle Rosy's body in the brown sayerman's robe. When the garment was on, Onesayer slashed the front of it to make it appear the victim had been killed while wearing it. He considered throwing the black pearl handled knife into the disposa-tube, but instead wiped the blade on the sayerman's robe and slipped it into the sash about his waist.

By this time, Onesayer was hot and breathing heavily. After wiping his hands on a clean portion of the sayerman's robe worn by Uncle Rosy, Onesayer used both hands to wipe perspiration from his own forehead and eyebrows.

It is done, he thought, not feeling particularly proud of himself. *Now where is that Master's clean robe?*

He rolled around behind the chair, located the ledge Uncle Rosy had spoken of before he died. He selected one of three neatly stacked white robes, slipped it on.

Onesayer smoothed a wrinkle out of the robe and sat in the

great chair. Continuing to perspire, he settled down into the chair's leather cushioning. Presently he began to cool down and to feel better. A sense of supreme satisfaction came over him.

I am Master! he thought, suddenly exhilarated. *Lord of all....*

He recalled the terrible peril of the comet now, stared down to his right at the middle chrome handle. *All things can be controlled,* he thought. *Even this.*

Onesayer pressed the handle all the way forward and down to its contact point, read a chart next to the handle and mentoed: *Orbital coordinates, B-six-seven-seven, normal...planetary speed one-point-one-two-five...rotation one-point-oh-oh, normal.*

Sitting back in the chair, he thought, *No one will feel that extra bit of speed. Just enough to get Earth out of the comet's path.*

Onesayer mentoed for a meckie, recalling that the wearer of the Master's robe commanded Uncle Rosy's mechanical servants. Shortly, a black tuxedo meckie appeared at the base of the steps. Six tiny white lights down the front of its body blinked as it awaited instructions.

"Yes, Master?" the meckie queried.

It calls me Master! Onesayer thought. Speaking in the resonant voice of Uncle Rosy, Onesayer said, "Onesayer Edward tried to assassinate me. I killed him instead. Send the body to Astro Disposal and have it launched in an unmarked cylinder."

"Yes, Master."

"Tell no one of this disgraceful act."

The meckie wrapped the body in plastic and dragged it down the ramp and out of the chamber. Moments later, it returned to clean the blood that had spilled.

At the moment of Uncle Rosy's death, Sidney was seated in Admitting Room Two at an autopill dispensing application machine. An admitting clerk stood nearby, watching intently.

A woman approaching forty, the admitting clerk had frost blue hair and a matching, icicle-cool personality. Sidney glanced out of the corner of one eye at the scowling woman, then quickly looked back into the mechanical face of the application machine.

"Take two more capsules, dosage AA-nine," the machine instructed, pushing forth a tiny tray containing two yellow pills and a water tablet.

Sidney obeyed, felt a cool surge of water as the water tablet opened and expanded inside his stomach. Now Sidney felt the machine probing his thoughts again, heard it report in a hesitating, impersonal voice: "Con-reading* ninety-four-point three."

"May Hoover take you!" the admitting clerk cursed. "Wait here," she instructed tersely. Then she spun and rolled through a double swinging door to the outer hallway. Fully conscious, Sidney watched her leave.

Moments later, Sidney heard low, anxious voices outside the door. He smiled to himself, pleased that he had been able to resist all attempts thus far to break down his will. Sidney closed his eyes, tried to connect with the voices in his brain. *You must help me find Tom,* he thought. *Please....* Getting no response, he thought: *They come and go as they please.*

"He'll fill out that blasted app!" a woman's voice boomed.

Sidney opened his eyes as the doors squeaked open, saw a black woman in a yellow tweed suit. The woman rolled toward him at a fast pace with an angry expression on her face.

The admitting room clerk was close behind. "Wait, Mayor Ogg," she urged. "Maybe we should try something else."

"*I'll* try something else," Mayor Nancy Ogg snapped, grabbing Sidney forcefully by the collar. Sidney felt sharp surges of pain as she backhanded him across the face four times.

"Wait, Mayor Ogg," the admitting clerk pleaded. "I'm not sure we should—"

"Silence!" the Mayor rasped.

Sidney tried to grab Mayor Nancy Ogg's hand before she could strike again, but she was too strong for him. "You'll fill out the app, won't you, you weakling little creep," she demanded, slapping Sidney hard across both cheeks.

Sidney pulled his head back, tried to protect his stinging face with his hands. A crushing blow struck him on the temple, knocking him out of the chair and tearing his smock where the Mayor had been grasping it. As Sidney tumbled to the floor, he saw a hazy impression of the Mayor's and clerk's feet.

*Consciousness reading.

"Uhhh," Sidney groaned, half-conscious. He saw Mayor Nancy Ogg's foot lash out at him, but could not move out of the way. An excruciating pain cut through his rib cage. "Aaaagh. ...."

"I'm rather enjoying this," a tenor voice in Sidney's brain said.

"Malloy doesn't seem like such a clown anymore," the other, deeper voice said. *"Maybe we should give him half a chance...."*

Grimacing in pain, Sidney heard the voices argue heatedly. Then Sidney thought-said: *Help me out of here! We're running out of time!* But there was no response. He felt himself slipping off, into deep sleep.

"I think he's unconscious," a distant woman's voice said. It was the admitting clerk.

"Get a con-reading! Quickly!" a man yelled.

Sidney envisioned himself as the hero of a military-political movement, leading the twisted and pitiful slushpile of human garbage that Earth did not want. He controlled an immense army of cappies which threatened to attack Earth. The people of Earth begged for mercy, sent two emissaries from the Council of Ten to see Sidney.

"I hate the way he plays hero," the tenor voice said.

"It is a bit irritating," agreed the other. *"Still, I've grown rather attached to him."*

Sidney heard the voices argue again inside his skull, but they faded quickly. *Come back!* Sidney thought, futilely. *Come back!*

"Over a hundred! He buried the needle!"

"What the Hooverville? No one could have a con-reading that high! Check the equipment!"

Hearing these words in an awakening haze, Sidney knew they were not the voices he wanted to hear. Suddenly his awareness surged, and he almost felt able to stand up and moto-shoe around the admitting room. But the surge was short-lived, and soon he felt himself sinking once more. The evil thought-probing machine was at it again now, trying to tear away his innermost secrets.

"Don't give in, fleshcarrier!" the deeper voice in his brain said. *"This is making you stronger!"*

Sidney experienced another vision, imagined he was being

given a private audience with Uncle Rosy. In a darkened chamber, Uncle Rosy sat upon a great chair, looking down at him with kindly, concerned eyes. . . .

"You are the only one who can do it," Uncle Rosy said in the vision. "A holy mission lies ahead!"

"I'll do it!" Sidney said in the vision. "Thank you, Master! Thank you! . . ."

"There he goes again," the tenor voice said, irritably. *"The Chosen One, the hero. Why, this fleshcarrier doesn't even understand his own motivations!"*

"Give him a break," the deeper voice said. *"He's only a fleshcarrier. You're using OUR standards."*

"True," the tenor voice said. *"But when will he realize he wants these things for himself, not for the good of others?"*

"In time," the other voice said. *"In time. . . ."*

Sidney heard the voices fade, saw himself as President of a bright AmFed nation, populated by contented, consumptive citizens. He felt the joys of Freeness, Job-Sharing and Leisure Time. It was a brilliant society, showered with all the wonders of advanced technology.

"He has a nasty looking gash," a far off voice said. "We'd better get him into Emergency."

"But he hasn't been admitted to Bu-Prog yet! How can he be treated?"

"The equipment checks out."

"Put him on an autocart," Mayor Nancy Ogg instructed angrily, "and get him out of my sight!"

Sidney felt strong arms lifting him from the floor, heard a cacophony of voices. He struggled to open his eyelids, but they seemed weighted.

The cart was rolling now, and someone said, "What's the difference, anyway? He's only a cappy."

Managing to lift one eyelid, Sidney squinted angrily in the glare of bright hall lights. He tried to sit up, wanting to tell that person that cappies would get even someday. But a terrible pain in his ribcage kept him from rising. His head throbbed, and he cried out in agony before falling back on the cart.

"The client is awake," a woman said, her tone condescending.

"Who cares? By all rights, Mayor Ogg should have killed him."

I'll get them! Sidney thought. He felt something warm and wet on the side of his head, touched a throbbing temple with one hand. Then he looked at the hand. It was bloody! He felt weak, closed his eyes.

"Put him in detention," one of the enemies said. "We'll hold him until he fills out the app. No medical treatment until he cooperates!"

"Each cappy supports seven-point-three-two-five government workers," another said, "and this doomie creep won't fill out the form!"

"It's positively un-AmFed!"

"I have a better idea," a female voice said. "A call just came in from Hub Assembly. They need a disposable cappy for an in-flight job."

"What's the job?"

"Who knows, but I hear they've been having problems keeping their cappies in line. Now they need a replacement."

"Sounds like a good chance to eliminate our little problem. I'll check with the Mayor."

Disposable? Sidney thought, his head throbbing. *What do they mean disposable?*

It was a busy morning.

Mayor Nancy Ogg moto-shoed wearily down the wide central area of Mass Driver One, craning her neck to watch green-and-yellow-smocked client workcrews on scaffolds. To Mayor Ogg, the clients looked like bees in a honeycomb, working two to a scaffold filling individual compartments of the massive E-Cell with Argonium gas and then setting exterior valves. Voices echoed around the walls, as did the metal-on-metal ring of tools.

Odd, isn't it? Mayor Nancy Ogg thought, *that most of an E-Cell has to be constructed by hand....*

She paused to watch a Bu-Tech foreman go over a set of computer-printed plans with two yellow-smocked client workmen. "Be sure to set the gas diffraction valve on each cell," she heard the foreman say.

Then the Mayor recognized one client as Sidney Malloy and thought angrily: *That weakling cappy! Now I'll get rid of him once and for all!*

The foreman smiled when he noticed the Mayor, said to her

in a derisive tone, "Replacements." He flicked a sidelong glance at Sidney and the other client. Sidney heard contempt in the foreman's tone.

"It's looking good, foreman," Mayor Nancy Ogg said, glancing hostilely at Sidney. She resumed moto-shoeing, thought, *Jesus! I hate these stinkin' cappies! I hate everything about this place!*

Her thoughts were interrupted when a yellow-smocked girl rolled frantically toward the Mayor from a forward area. "We're not coming back!" the girl screamed. "They're going to eject us in space when the E-Cell is finished!"

Disposable, Sidney thought, recalling the words he had heard while lying on the autocart. *So that's what they meant. . . .* He glanced around nervously, saw the foreman glaring at him.

"Pay attention!" the foreman snapped.

"Yes, sir," Sidney said.

Mayor Nancy Ogg short-stepped to one side as the girl rolled past, watched a Security Brigade officer capture the girl a short distance away and wrestle her to the ground.

"Another loony," the security officer gruffed, looking up at the Mayor as he knelt and handcuffed the girl.

Mayor Nancy Ogg nodded, said tersely: "Find out where the rumor started."

"Yes, Honorable Mayor," the officer said. "I know how to handle it."

Turning at the whir of fast-approaching moto-boots, the Mayor watched Sergeant Rountree roll to a crisp stop as he reached her. He snapped a rotating wrist salute, stood at attention.

"The ex-pursuit craft pilots are our best bet," Sergeant Rountree said. "That's not saying much, but with drug therapy we can alter their doomie mentalities."

"The killer meckie will keep them in line, too," she said.

As Mayor Nancy Ogg said this, Sidney and the other replacement were being led past her to a forward area of the mass driver. *Killer meckie?* Sidney thought, overhearing the remark. *What the hell are they talking about?*

"There are refresher tapes on mass driver mechanics aboard the Shamrock Five," Sergeant Rountree said, out of Sidney's hearing range. "They are rather technical, and we can only hope the pilots will understand them. . . ."

"Have them start on the tapes now," Mayor Nancy Ogg said, pursing her lips thoughtfully. "But we'll wait until the last minute before committing ourselves."

"Right. I saw the letter from interim Minister Larsen. The Shamrock Five can leave as late as six o'clock tonight."

"It's *ex*-interim Minister Larsen now. My dear brother the President led a council recall move this morning. It just came in on my porta-receiver. Something about Larsen advocating anti-job measures."

"He was too pro-computer," Sergeant Rountree said.

"Now that Munoz and Hudson are out of the picture, my brother can run the operation as he pleases." She bit at her upper lip, tried not to display emotion at the thought of Dr. Hudson. She glanced at the Sergeant's broad shoulders. Her gaze dropped, moving down along the center of his chest to his silver and black belt.

"I'm sure that's true, Honorable Mayor." Rountree caught her gaze, snapped his eyes back to attention. A little smile touched his mouth.

That was a lightning stroke on Euripides's part! she thought, looking away and rubbing her eyes. *No committees involved . . . he had to justify it as a Job-Support measure.*

The central area Mayor Nancy Ogg stood upon was in the process of narrowing slowly as work progressed. After Sergeant Rountree left, she overheard another foreman say, "In the final construction stage, the mass driver core itself will be filled with gas compartments, leaving only a tiny corridor beneath."

Looking up at the silver-metallic curved ceiling, she thought: *The final construction stage will also involve ejection of the worker clients to their deaths in space, followed by automatic connection of the E-Cells to their mass driver engines.* It occurred to her that every "stinkin'" cappy should be ejected in space. She scratched the small of her back.

Mayor Nancy Ogg could see grey tubes and valves through an open forward firewall hatch, knew from a previous inspection that this was the base of a powerful mass driver engine that towered more than one-hundred meters above her.

Closing her tired eyes, she held the thumb and forefinger of one hand against her forehead. *Just a minute!* she thought, popping open her eyes. *The escapees that were shipped to Saint Michaels . . . could Javik be among them?*

Mayor Nancy Ogg started to roll at high speed toward the

exit Sergeant Rountree had just taken, but had a second thought and slowed. *No,* she thought, answering her own question, *It's not possible.*

* * *

"Was Onesayer Edward an evil man?" Sayer Superior Lin-Ti asked, gazing across the ordinance room at his group of youngsayermen.

"He became power-mad, Sayer Superior," a voice in the back of the room said. "And he murdered our beloved Master."

"Yes," Lin-Ti said, "but Uncle Rosy gave him the knife. And remember, Onesayer Edward waited patiently for nearly three centuries."

The youngsayerman did not respond. Lin-Ti saw troubled expressions on the faces of the group. Then Lin-Ti asked: "Would Uncle Rosy have entrusted the Sayerhood helm with an evil man? These are disturbing questions, youngsayers, many of which we cannot answer. . . ."

TWELVE

UP CLOSE WITH PRESIDENT EURIPIDES OGG, FOR FURTHER READING AND DISCUSSION

"There is no more certain way to reach the Happy Shopping Ground than to lose your life in the face of a disintegrating product."
Remarks made by President Ogg at Astro-Burial Inc.'s No. 14 Launcher, November 18, 2603

Wednesday, August 30, 2605

Master Edward sat on Uncle Rosy's chair for several hours after setting the Orbital Handle. He lost track of time, and just sat there reviewing three centuries of memories. It was late morning when he finally moto-shoed to the ramp at the rear of the platform and rolled down to a passageway he knew had to lead to the Master's private suite.

Master Edward heard only the whine of his own moto-shoes

as he negotiated a sharp right turn in the arch-ceilinged black brick passageway. It was cool and damp in there, illuminated dimly by widely spaced yellow globes.

I feel like an intruder, he thought, shivering. *No one has....* He interrupted his thought at the sight of a tuxedo meckie a short distance ahead, standing off to one side of an ornate oak door. The meckie's button lights blinked rhythmically.

"Greetings, Master," the meckie said in a sophisticated but mechanical voice. The door slid open as the meckie spoke, and Master Edward saw Uncle Rosy's suite beyond, shimmering warmly.

I am Master! he thought happily. *Everything is at my command!*

His elation faded quickly, for as Master Edward entered the suite, he recalled his personal aging crisis. *Maybe there is something here to explain it,* he thought, recalling the terrible spectacle of Sixsayer Robert before he died...those deep, terrible wrinkles framing desperate, screaming eyes.

He paused to look around the suite, found himself in a large light wood paneled living area, with bookshelves on three walls. Reflective solar panels on the walls and ceiling provided the room with cheerful semi-natural light. The furnishings were beige fabrics and light wood, the carpeting soft driftwood grey.

Nice, Master Edward thought, fingering the smooth linen fabric of his Master's robe, *but simpler than I would have expected.*

An agatestone fireplace dominated one wall, and above the mantel hung a three-dimensional painting of a woman working in an old-style kitchen. Another tuxedo meckie stood near a raised panel door to one side of the fireplace, and the meckie began to blink its button lights when Master Edward looked at it.

"Greetings, Master," the meckie said in a voice identical to that of the first tuxedo meckie.

"And who are you?" Master Edward demanded, taking care to mimic the voice of Uncle Rosy.

"I have no name, Master."

"How do I tell you and the other meckie apart?"

"There are three of us, Master. You have never felt a need to tell us apart before."

Master Edward pursed his lips thoughtfully, said, "Hmmm."

He rolled past a striped beige-and-grey couch at the center of the room, noted a blond wood coffee table in front of it with the words "Keep the Faith" inlaid on the tabletop in dark letters. The memory of Uncle Rosy's words danced across his consciousness, then flitted away: *Look within yourself. . . . There are things even I do not understand. . . .*

Master Edward took a deep, exasperated breath, tilted his head back and stared at the ceiling. The ceiling consisted of yellow and black mosaic tiles arranged in a stylized brain design. He chased an elusive thought through the alcoves of his mind, looked away.

Rolling to a bookcase, he scanned titles: *Journal of Holistic Medicine . . . the Einsteinian Phenomenon. . . .* Another section contained religious books. Other sections were devoted to political, economic and historic readings. He ran inquisitive fingers over the volume covers, glanced briefly through a volume entitled *Chairman Mao: His Life and Times*.

After replacing this volume, Master Edward was about to remove another book when his concentration was shattered by a piercing woman's scream: "Willard!" The voice seemed to come from somewhere near the fireplace, behind Master Edward and to the left. But he saw no one.

"What the hell?" Master Edward cursed.

"Willard!" the voice screeched, a little louder this time.

"Who is that?" Master Edward asked, looking at the tuxedo meckie.

"Your wife, of course, Master," the mechanical servant responded, pointing at the picture over the fireplace. "On a simu-life projector."

Master Edward's eyes opened wide as he focused on the painting, because the three-dimensional woman in the picture was glaring directly at him with her hands on her hips. "Willard!" she howled, revealing a very large mouth. "Answer me!"

"What do I do now?" Master Edward inquired of the meckie.

"Answer her, Master. You always say, 'Coming dear.'"

"Oh yes. It slipped my mind." Master Edward looked at the scowling woman. She seemed ready to leap out of the picture. "Coming dear!" he yelled. Lowering his voice, he looked at the meckie and asked, "Now what?"

"Nothing, Master. The simu-life projector yells at you during the day to keep your spirits up."

"Oh."

The miniature woman seemed placated now, as she turned her attention to a steaming pot of food on the range. As Master Edward continued to stare at the picture, the moving, lifelike portions stiffened subtly, and once again it appeared to be an ordinary three-dimensional painting.

"I do not know how that slipped my mind," Master Edward said, wondering why he needed to explain to a meckie. "Too much going on, I suppose." Delving into his knowledge of Uncle Rosy's past, he added: "Jennifer was killed in a roller-coaster accident more than three centuries ago . . . along with my children. . . ."

"Yes, Master. At Glitterland. They are in the Happy Shopping Ground now."

Uncle Rosy must have been terribly lonely, Master Edward thought. *No one with whom to share his troubles.* . . . Resuming his interest in the books, Master Edward reached for a weathered brown volume entitled *Laboratory Experiments of W. R. Rosenbloom, 2261–2266.* He blew dust from the top of the volume, opened it slowly. The book smelled of must. Its pages were yellow-edged and cracking.

Turning the pages carefully, he noticed each sheet was ruled in light green lines, with headings along the top and spaces below where Uncle Rosy had entered dates, techniques and comments concerning each experiment. He scanned the opening pages. All concerned a technique referred to as "S.M.E."

I recall those initials, Master Edward thought. *Selective Memory Erasure. Uncle Rosy used it on anyone who helped build or design the Black Box of Democracy.*

He read on, saw human subjects listed by consumer identification number on the pages, with a medical malady designated next to each. He located a guide in the back of the volume which connected names and numbers. *Where did he get all the volunteers?* Master Edward wondered.

Then he saw a pencilled notation next to one name which read, "Returned to t-orbiter. Uncooperative." Several other names had notes which said, "Dec. Brain in jar 506" or "Dec. Brain in jar 712." Master Edward shuddered as he realized that "t-orbiter" referred to "therapy orbiter," and "Dec." meant "deceased."

These were NOT volunteers! he thought.

The middle section of the volume outlined a series of "placebo effect" experiments. Master Edward read that subjects given sugar pills were told these were "new cures" for their maladies. Locating a page outlining the results, he read aloud: "The higher the suggestive force used by the controller, the more likely it was that a placebo would work. Subjects having the greatest faith in the placebo responded most favorably to treatment. . . ."

Faith, Master Edward thought. *Keep the Faith. . . .*

Flipping through a number of experiments describing mentation for the purpose of operating consumer products, he found an entry near the end of the volume dated December 2, 2266: "I embarked upon these brain experiments with the intent of improving economic conditions through control of each consumer's buying impulses. This remains a valid concept, and I intend to leave copies of key experimental data where it can be utilized by future generations. I feel there is much more to discover concerning the brain, but I am somewhat fearful of proceeding."

Master Edward looked away from the book, gazed across the room at the painting over the fireplace. The three-dimensional woman was in motion again, and four children sat at the kitchen table eating cookies and drinking milk. *Faith,* Master Edward thought again, unsure of the reason for the returning thought. *Keep the Faith. . . .*

He replaced the book on the shelf, turned forcefully to face the tuxedo meckie. "Tell me the secret of eternal youth," Master Edward demanded.

"Look to the holy water, Master. Then look within yourself. You have always said this."

"Elaborate."

"I cannot, Master," the meckie replied, raising its arms in helplessness. "That is all you have told me." The meckie's white button lights blinked. Curiously, it seemed nervous.

As Master Edward glared at the faceless mechanical servant, he felt a strong impulse to knock it over. "What is the source of our holy water?" he snapped.

The tuxedo meckie turned toward the raised panel door. The door slid open. "There is the source," the meckie replied. "Beyond the one-way glassite."

Master Edward moto-shoed to the open doorway, peered through it into a darkened room. He mentoed for light. Overhead fluorescent panels flickered on, flooding the room with harsh white light. A paper-littered desk stood to one side next to an electronic mail terminal. The opposite wall was clear one-way glassite, looking out upon a freestanding wall which contained instrument dials.

He rolled quickly to the glassite window, peered through it at the dials. There were six dials in all, each connected to an upside-down U-shaped black pipe which rose from and re-entered the floor on the other side of the glassite.

Master Edward saw something written on each dial, squinted to make out the words. He mouthed them slowly as they became clear: "New City . . . Water District . . . Number one-oh-four."

He pulled his head back in surprise, said, "What the Hooverville? New City Water District? THAT is the source of our holy elixir? Ordinary tap water?"

Feeling shaky, Master Edward rolled the short distance to the desk and picked up a piece of electronic mail. Printed on blue-bordered computer paper, he saw:

NEW CITY WATER DISTRICT NO. 104
PAST DUE ACCOUNT—NOTICE OF SERVICE TERMINATION
BLACK BOX OF DEMOCRACY   ACCT. # 18DR-17654499Q
BALANCE DUE: $26,312.15

DEAR CUSTOMER:
    THIS ACCOUNT IS SERIOUSLY PAST DUE, AND IT IS APPARENT THAT YOU HAVE CHOSEN TO IGNORE OUR CORDIAL RE-MINDERS. IF THE BALANCE IS NOT PAID BY AUGUST 31, 2605, YOUR WATER SERVICE WILL BE DISCONNECTED.
                                    SINCERELY,

                                    J.D. LAIRD
                                    COLLECTION DEPARTMENT

Master Edward rolled out of the room in a state of shock, letting the slip of paper fall from his grasp as he passed beyond the doorway. *The secret was within my mind all the time!* he thought. *But now that I know . . .*

"Shall I pay this bill now, Master?" the tuxedo meckie asked, retrieving the paper. "Tomorrow is the thirty-first."

"What? Oh, yes. Go ahead and pay it."

The meckie rolled into the room with the slip of paper in its grasp. Moments later, Master Edward heard the whir and throb of the electronic mail terminal.

Master Edward glanced down at the inlaid coffee table with its familiar "Keep the Faith" message. *There can be no doubt,* he thought.

Stopping at the fireplace, he leaned both forearms on the mantel and stared down into the brick-lined pit where two wood logs rested on a grating. Master Edward mentoed the fireplace, watched orange and blue flames spring up instantly around the logs.

And in what did Uncle Rosy believe? he thought.

"Willard!" the woman's voice screeched. "Willard!"

"Yes, dear," Master Edward called back. "Coming, dear." *I should check to see if we are eluding the comet,* he thought. *But does it matter?*

It was early afternoon of Garbage Day minus two when President Ogg and Billie Birdbright looked into Conference Room fifty-seven through one-way glassplex. The two-hundred-twenty-meter-long room was full to bursting with committee-members, messengers, auditors and an assortment of support personnel. Lieutenant Colonel Meg Corrigon stood at the head of the table, addressing the throng. To President Ogg's ears, her lips moved silently, for he had turned off the sound in the viewing room.

"Look at them!" President Ogg said, elated. "By tomorrow, they'll branch off into subcommittees, and the next day there will be sub-subcommittees!"

"It IS exciting, sir," Birdbright said.

"You're seeing government organization in its embryonic form," Ogg said, barely able to contain his excitement. "Why, who knows, Billie?... This could be the beginning of a new sub-bureau!"

"Marvelous, Mr. President," Birdbright said, trying to sound enthusiastic. "That would keep people occupied for years!"

"I can see it now," Ogg said, lowering his eyelids and gazing at an indeterminate, far-off point, "a new building, hundreds of construction workers... required forms by the million!"

"Uncle Rosy would have been proud, Mr. President!" Birdbright turned to look at the President, saw tears forming in his eyes.

President Ogg cleared his throat, then glanced quickly at his Chief of Staff to see if Birdbright had noticed his moment of emotional weakness. Birdbright had already turned away and was watching the committee meeting.

Ogg looked through the glassplex again, saw people streaming out the doors into adjacent conference rooms. "They're breaking off into splinter groups already!" he said. "My Rosenbloom, but this is exciting!"

"May I ask a rather pointed question, sir?" Birdbright queried, looking sideways at the President.

President Ogg lifted an eyebrow in surprise, replied, "Why, yes, feel free. . . . Always feel free to be direct with me."

"Sir, the crux of this comet matter is that Earth is going to be turned to garbage in fifty-one hours."

"And the necessary committeework will take much longer than that," Ogg said. "That concerns you, doesn't it, Billie?"

Noticing a twinkle in the President's eyes, Birdbright said, "Yes, Mr. President. To be quite honest, I don't see how you can possibly remain so calm."

"Consider the AmFed system, Billie!" Ogg said in a deep, presidential tone. "Upon what is it based?"

"Why . . . upon the teachings of our Beloved Master, Uncle Rosy."

"That includes Job-Support, does it not?" Ogg's blue green eyes took on the omniscient expression of a Freeness Studies Instructor.

"It does," Birdbright said cautiously.

"And where is Uncle Rosy now?"

"He is presumed to have died . . . nearly three hundred years ago."

"But he lives on, Billie! . . . In our hearts and dreams . . . and, not unimportantly . . . in the Black Box of Democracy!"

Birdbright scowled, said: "I don't see what you're getting at."

"Do you think the Black Box would allow Earth to be destroyed?" Ogg removed a red-bordered priority letter from his pocket, unfolded it and passed it to his Chief of Staff.

"Uh, no," Birdbright said, accepting the sheet. "I suppose not."

"Read it, Billie. Came in on the mail terminal a few minutes ago."

"From Bu-Tech," Birdbright said, scanning the message. "Orbital speed of Earth up twelve-point-five percent . . . possibly due to pumping effect on the planet from rhythmic garbage shots . . . checking planet's reduction in mass from garbage shots. . . ." He looked up. "Sounds pretty serious, Mr. President."

Ogg smiled. "The Black Box changed the orbital speed . . . to get us away from the comet!"

"How could they? . . ."

"Who knows, Billie. But I'm sure of it. We don't need to lift a finger! The Black Box is doing it for us!"

"Brilliant, Mr. President! Absolutely brilliant!" Birdbright wondered if his manner betrayed the doubts he felt. He handed the letter back to Ogg.

Ogg looked at his Chief of Staff askance while pocketing the message, said, "Don't repeat this to anyone, but I was contacted by the Black Box."

"Personally? When?"

"Sunday morning. I believe they arranged for the deaths of Munoz and Hudson as punishment for a plot they had to take over our holy government by illegal means."

Birdbright's jaw dropped. "How were they planning to—"

"I'll explain later, Billie. Rest assured the Black Box won't permit any harm to come to the AmFed system. I'm convinced of it."

"That makes me feel a little better, Mr. President," Birdbright said, still not feeling entirely at ease.

"All we need to do is what we've always done. That is to uphold the principles taught by Uncle Rosy. Without exception, Billie. Without exception."

Birdbright nodded in affirmation.

"Come along now, Billie," Ogg said, rolling toward the door. "I need to discuss the eulogy with you. Hudson and Munoz are to be astro-disposed tomorrow."

On their second Wednesday afternoon coffee break in the Cave Coffee Shop, Birdbright and Carla sat at a window table overlooking the underground waterfall.

"Oh Billie, don't be silly!" Carla said with a soft smile. "We've only been out on one date . . . and to coffee together a few times."

"I'm serious," Birdbright said, reaching into the vest pocket of his sportcoat to remove a pink and blue card. Smiling serenely, he reached across the tabletop to press the card into her palm.

Carla gazed into his smoke grey eyes adoringly, did not have to look at the card to know what it was. Her soft smile broadened as she looked down and read the card aloud: "Mr. William Birdbright requests the pleasure of your company for a Pre-Permie Counseling Session." She looked up to meet his gaze, beamed. "Oh, Billie!"

"Well?"

Their hands met at the center of the tabletop, and Carla felt the warmth and strength of Birdbright's grasp as he held her hands between his own. This was a table Carla had often occupied with Sidney. But Sidney seemed remote to her now, even though it had been only a few days since she had seen him.

Carla barely heard or saw the clamoring breaktime crowd at nearby tables. It was a private moment in an unprivate world, and even Harmak seemed to be playing her tune. She gazed deep into Birdbright's eyes, then looked away to watch the underground waterfall cascade over a stalagmite precipice. The water seemed to dance and sparkle with a magical quality. There could be but one answer.

"Yes!" she said, hearing her voice crack with excitement. "The answer is yes!"

Birdbright released her hands and jumped to his feet in an untypical burst of expended energy. "Did you hear that?" he yelled, looking from table to table. "She said yes!"

Several people laughed good-naturedly. "Congratulations!" said a blonde woman from the Sixteenth Request Department. "How wonderful!" exclaimed another. "When's the session?"

Birdbright beamed, reached down to pull Carla to her feet. "Right now!" he said, hugging Carla while the crowd auto-clapped and wished them well.

"Now?" Carla said, surprised.

"Why yes, of course. Our union contract says we can take off work for matters of permeage."

"I know!" she snapped. "But why did you make an appointment before receiving my answer?"

Birdbright winked. "I knew what you'd say," he said.

Carla's lavender eyes flared. She pulled away, said: "Why you egotistical, arrogant, self. . . ." Her words trailed off as she detected a worried expression on Birdbright's face. "I love you," she said softly, kissing him on the cheek.

* * *

Stork's Baby Bazaar was on the west side of the Bu-Permie Shopping Center, adjacent to a large bulletin board which proclaimed: LITTERING IS LAWFUL. Birdbright's bright blue autosport stopped several hundred meters away, and he and Carla short-stepped out onto a heart-shaped red platform. The platform was crowded and paper-littered, and they waited while other happy, laughing couples took turns rolling down to an eight-laned skatewalk. Carla turned to watch the autosport disappear into a parking tube.

Birdbright went first, followed by Carla. They rolled around an overpass and spiraled down to expressway level, taking the slow right-hand lane of the northbound side. They moved quickly from one lane to the other until they were in the fast lane, then zipped up an exit marked "STORK'S" onto another heart-shaped platform.

Holding Birdbright's hand tightly on the crowded platform, Carla looked up along the face of a three-hundred-story clear glassplex elevator structure which connected the platform with all floors of the building. The elevator cars were in the shape of babies wrapped in brightly colored swaddling blankets, seemed suspended from a massive ochre-colored stork's beak on top of the building. Carla could not see the entire stork now, but had seen it many times during helitours of New City. It was breathtaking.

The Stork Building looked like a baby shower gift, was covered with red, blue, green and yellow animal designs on a silver-white background. A broad pink ribbon encircled the building and flapped in a gentle breeze above a flashing neon STORK'S sign. An elevator car arrived, and a concealed door in a blanket fold whooshed open.

They disembarked at the seventy-fourth floor, short-stepping into a wonderland of baby products. The store had been decorated gaily, had pink and blue ribbons, bright product signs and dozens of eager salesmen ready to smother their customers in attention.

An exceedingly round salesman in a light blue bunting outfit moto-rushed over as Carla and Birdbright entered. He was propelled by white moto-baby shoes with bells across the top that jingled merrily when he moved. A teething ring necklace dangled from his neck, resting on top of a very firm and protruding tummy. His cheeks were bright pink, and a script nametag on his chest read "Jimmy."

"Oh goo!" Jimmy said, in the best jargon of the store. "We're so glad you're here! Do you have anything in mind?" He sucked on the teething ring, awaited a reply.

"We're looking for room seventy-four thirty-one," Birdbright replied.

"Ah!" the salesman said, oozing happiness. "Another Pre-Permie counseling session!" He waved an arm gracefully toward the rear of the store, flipping his palm to designate one of the side walls. "Right down that way, folks. Near the Ultra-Nu Combination Baby Set displays."

Birdbright and Carla moto-shoed in the direction designated, passed little bedroom sets, playpens, strollers, stuffed tigers and elephants, mobiles and a whole host of other items. Colorful banners hung over the various displays to announce: "AS ADVERTISED ON NATIONAL HOME VIDEO."

Pausing to examine a lifetime photography contract, they overheard a salesgirl in a pink bunting outfit tell a couple that Stork's prices were competitive. "The Stork's label on a product will tell your friends that you paid the very highest price," the salesgirl said. The couple was visibly impressed, and the salesgirl added, "All our products carry the Goodie Homemaker's Seal of Approval!"

Room seventy-four thirty-one was two aisles away and had a bright yellow door encrusted with tiny red hearts. Birdbright mentoed a heart-shaped wall button, watched it go in as a buzzer rang. The door swung open, revealing a small office which had been made to look larger with mirrors on the floor, walls and ceiling. A rotund woman sat at a heart-shaped plastic desk in the center of the office. She smiled. "Come in, come in," she said in a friendly but hurried tone.

Carla glanced lovingly at Birdbright, smiled. They entered and took seats on a glassplex loveseat which had heart-shaped red throw pillows. Carla noted a sign on the front of the desk which read, "A HAPPY PERMEAGE IS A CONSUMPTIVE PERMEAGE." A pink-and-blue broach on the lapel of the woman's white dress identified her as a G.W. two-hundred.

"I am Wanda Sutter," the woman said, "your Pre-Permie Counselor." Glancing at an appointment telescreen to her left, she said, "You are William Birdbright and Carla Weaver?"

"Yes," Birdbright replied nervously.

Counselor Sutter reached into an automatically stocked desk

drawer and removed a pink box which had a cameo baby picture on the cover. Opening the box, she took out several pamphlets and placed them reverently on her desktop. "This is a starter kit," she announced. "It contains government pamphlets on every conceivable subject, including that very popular publication, 'Consumption—How To Go On Full Automatic.'"

"Great!" Birdbright exclaimed.

"Wonderful!" Carla agreed, glancing up at the mirrored ceiling to watch the counselor from above.

"The kit also contains an instruction manual for conservation of energy during sexual intercourse," Counselor Sutter said, opening one of the pamphlets. "It's all arranged in a simple-to-understand step-by-step format."

Carla and Birdbright leaned forward to examine the pamphlet, nodded.

"Let me see now," the counselor said, reaching across her desk to pick up a computer sheet. "Mister Birdbright, you have a Consumption Quotient of eighty-three. Miss Weaver, you register eighty-seven. Now I would like each of you to hold hands and use your free hands to grasp the metal handles at your respective sides of the couch."

The lovers obeyed, and as they did so, the counselor mentoed a desk-mounted console. She studied the console screen for a moment, then exclaimed happily, "Marvelous! Your projected Combined Consumption Quotient is ninety-eight-point-three-seven! That's very high!"

"Oh!" Carla squealed, knowing the importance of this.

"A permeage made in the Happy Shopping Ground!" Counselor Sutter said, bubbling with delight. "Perfectly matched personalities! You will reinforce one another to buy, buy, buy!"

"Isn't it marvelous, honey?" Birdbright said, glancing at Carla.

"Oh yes!" she gushed.

Counselor Sutter stamped a duplicate form set, then placed the forms in a folder and handed it to Carla. "Now you must visit six more agencies to get their approval," she said, "after which you can obtain a permeage license at the courthouse. The addresses are listed on the inside cover."

Carla was so nervous that she dropped the folder. As she reached down to retrieve it, the counselor said, "Come back after the permeage and one of our salesmen will assist you in the selection of your first baby."

"We will," Carla said.

"Based upon the characteristics you want in the child," Counselor Sutter said, "each of you will be given specific birth pills which are guaranteed to produce a beautiful child from your union."

"Thank you," Carla said happily.

"Eye and hair color charts are on the wall outside my office," Counselor Sutter said, rising to her feet. "You may examine them as you leave. Now, if you folks will excuse me, I do have another appointment."

"I want a boy," Carla said as she and Birdbright rolled to the door, "with sandy brown hair with a touch of curl . . . and pastel blue eyes like the baby Becky got." ·

"Excellent selections," the counselor said. "And be sure to ask the salesman about baby's own cuteness machine. It will sleep-teach him to do the darndest things!"

"Oh!" Carla said. "I can't wait!"

Uncle Rosy's suite contained four large modular rooms: living area, kitchen, bath and bedroom. Additionally, there were a number of smaller adjoining rooms used for storage and offices. The suite was perhaps twice as spacious as a sayerman's quarters, and Master Edward had searched it rather completely by mid-afternoon, only a few short hours after the murder of Uncle Rosy.

He found nothing further of note, save for a large quantity of books. When the digital cuckoo clock on one wall struck four, Master Edward found himself seated on the carpet in a wash of reflected sunlight next to a bookcase, scanning volumes quickly. The sunlight warmed his head and shoulders but made it difficult to read the brightened pages.

Religious books in this section, he thought, closing a black leatherbound volume. *Buddhaic-Brahmanism, Judaism, Islamic-Taoism . . . all religions destroyed in the Holy War of twenty-three-twenty-six*.

He replaced the volume on the shelf, moved to another section and reached for a slender paperbound book, entitled *Franklin Roosevelt and the W.P.A.* As he opened it, a slip of white paper fell out upon his lap. Master Edward retrieved the paper and read these notes penned neatly in Uncle Rosy's handwriting:

The Great Order of Existence
1. Realm of the Unknown. God?
2. Realm of Magic.
3. Realm of Inertia and Gas.
4. Realm of Flesh.
5. Realm of Plants and Lower Life Forms.

At the bottom of the slip of paper, scrawled hastily, he read: "From voices in my brain, August 26, 2605. The voices returned two days later to say, 'The answer is not to be found within books. Important truths flow from the soul, like a primordial river.'"

He wrote this only days ago! Master Edward thought. *Voices? Munoz and Malloy heard voices too—insanity! But all of them? Even Uncle Rosy?* He wadded the paper and hurled it, followed by the book, at a tuxedo meckie which stood motionless nearby.

"Yes, Master?" the meckie responded as the book thudded off its metal front. The meckie's lights blinked. "You desire something, Master?" To Master Edward's ears at that moment, the meckie's synthetically sophisticated voice sounded particularly irritating and inane.

Master Edward grunted something angry and guttural which was not intended to be discernible, then moto-shoed into the bathroom module. There, for the third time that afternoon, he glared dejectedly at the reflection of his face in the grooming machine mirror.

The aging had accelerated today, and now a grotesque mask looked back at him, its expression more sad than angry. Frustration and guilt were etched into the features, and he saw deep lines around the eyes, with shallower lines on the cheeks, on the forehead and around the neck. The backs of his hands had dark brown age splotches. The skin looked taut, drawn.

He smashed both hands against the mirror, watched spokes from a break in the glass spread across the mirror. A trickle of blood ran down the side of one hand, and he wiped it on his white robe.

I feel so damned guilty! he thought. *To have destroyed a great man, and now* . . . Tears streamed down Master Edward's cheeks, running over his upper lip and into his mouth. He tasted salt.

Master Edward wiped his eyes and mouth with a handtowel, thought, *How can I step into the Master's moto-shoes? I am not as wise or as strong as he....*

Master Edward let the towel slip out of his grasp. It fell into the sink as he thought, *If only I could erase all memory of losing my faith, of killing Unce Rosy and of the holy water source...the meckies could pay the water bill without my knowledge....*

This thought started as a fantasy to him, but then something hit him with no less force than a Bu-Tech thunderbolt. *S.M.E.!* he thought, recalling the Selective Memory Erasure procedure.

Master Edward was yelling before he reached the living room module: "WHERE IS THE S.M.E. TERMINAL? WHERE IS THE S.M.E. TERMINAL?"

A tuxedo meckie blinked on its button lights as Master Edward roared into the room. "S.M.E. terminal, Master?" it said. "What is that?"

"Don't hold back on me, you little pile of gears!"

"Master, I know not of what you speak."

"Get the others, then!"

"The others, Master?"

"The other tuxedo meckies, you programmed fool! Get them!"

The meckie rolled out through the suite's main entrance, returned presently with two of its mechanical look-alikes. They formed a row on one side of the living room module, blinking busily. "Yes, Master?" they said in unison in their sophisticated, synthetic voices.

"Which of you took Onesayer's body?" Master Edward asked.

"I, Master," the centrally positioned meckie replied.

"And where is it now?"

"It, Master?"

Master Edward clenched his teeth, made fists. "The body, damn you! The body!"

"Onesayer's body, Master?"

"Yes, yes. Yes-yes-yes!"

"Onesayer's body was launched an hour ago, Master."

"Good." Master Edward unclenched his fists, relaxed his hands at his sides. "Now each of you pay close attention. I am looking for the S.M.E. terminal...the Selective Memory Erasure terminal."

"I do not know where the S.M.E. terminal is," they replied in unison.

"Why is the terminal not here?"

The meckies spoke at once, creating a jibberished sentence: "I do I not ordered know the terminal, Master."

"What?" Master Edward said.

The meckies repeated their jibberish.

"One at a time," Master Edward said, pointing to the centrally positioned tuxedo meckie. "You first."

"I do not know, Master," this meckie said.

"Now you." Master Edward pointed to the meckie on his left.

"I ordered the terminal, Master."

"Aha! Now we are getting somewhere!" Master Edward rolled very close to this meckie and demanded: "Where is it . . . uh, the terminal?"

"The terminal is on order, Master."

"Yes, but where is . . . Let me rephrase that. When did you order the terminal?"

"Thirty-one months ago."

"And why has the terminal not arrived?"

"This is a special order item, Master. One of a kind."

"Yes, but is it not important enough to rush through?"

"You have never said this in the past, Master. We have only made eleven requests so far. The Twelfth through Twentieth Request Departments have not been involved yet."

Master Edward took a deep, furious breath, put his hands on his hips and shot words at the meckie as if the words were bullets: "Send a request to all of the departments at once! Did that ever occur to you?"

"That has never been done before," the meckie said calmly. "Therefore it does not seem possible, Master."

Master Edward threw his arms up in exasperation and thundered: "LEAVE ME! LEAVE ME IMMEDIATELY. ALL OF YOU!"

The tuxedo meckies turned and scurried to the main doorway, but tried to exit simultaneously. The one in the center scraped through, but the other two bounced off the doorjambs on each side. This knocked something loose in their mechanisms, and the damaged meckies began to roll in circles, emitting high-pitched, whining sounds.

"Quiet!" Master Edward screeched, looking for something to throw.

The damaged meckies collided with one another head-on, tipped and fell to their sides. For several moments the whining continued, along with the whir and clank of gears. Finally the death knell ceased, and Master Edward stared at their fallen metal bodies. A moto-wheel on one meckie continued to roll silently for several seconds, but under his intense gaze this too came to a stop.

Master Edward looked around the room . . . at the simu-life painting, at the books, at the digital cuckoo, then back to the motionless tin can servants. All were silent. He felt alone, very much alone.

A half hour later, Master Edward looked up with one sleepy eye from the living room couch where he lay, saw the surviving tuxedo meckie standing in the doorway. In a voice devoid of emotion, the meckie said, "Master, it is time for the afternoon audience."

Master Edward scratched the back of one hand, said, "Cancel it!"

"But they ask of Onesayer, Master. What shall I tell them?"

"Tell them nothing."

"They wish to know when you will announce Onesayer's replacement."

Master Edward rose to rest on one elbow, glared. "You told them he is dead?"

"No, Master. They assumed it."

"How dare they demand this information? I will notify them when . . . and IF . . . there are to be promotions!"

"Yes, Master. They also say Earth's orbital speed is up twelve-point-five percent, and that—"

"I know that," Master Edward said angrily. "Who do they think did it?"

Continuing where its sentence had been interrupted, the meckie said, "—the comet changed course to match our adjustment."

Master Edward sat up, startled. "It remains on a collision course with Earth?"

"It does, Master."

"I feared as much! Go out and set the Orbital Handle at a one-point-five-three-seven factor." *The maximum,* he thought.

Any more and our solar system falls apart....

"I will, Master."

"Then tell Twosayer and Threesayer I will see them promptly at nine A.M. tomorrow."

"I will, Master."

Master Edward recalled his training in the physics of orbital modification as he watched the tuxedo meckie roll away. He thought back to a more pleasant time many years before when he had stood at the tutelage console with Sayer Superior Lin-Ti....

Youngsayer Edward: "But what of the laws of physics, Sayer Superior? Will not the Orbital Handle cause havoc with the Moon and with the AmFed orbiters?"

Sayer Superior Lin-Ti: "No, youngsayer. The Orbital Handle's force field extends to the Moon and to the orbital positions at L_4 and at L_5. The system will make adjustments as a unit."

Youngsayer Edward: "Are there limits? Surely we cannot make radical adjustments without affecting other planetary systems!"

Sayer Superior Lin-Ti (laughing): "Be patient, youngsayer! You will learn such things in time...."

Working at deck level Wednesday afternoon in the forward E-Cell area of Mass Driver One, Sidney gave the Argonium gas handle a final spin. Workmen were busy all around. Their voices and the clanging ring of tools echoed off the walls.

"Now hand me the stitch-welder," another client workman instructed.

Sidney looked at the workman as he spoke, saw a young fleshy-faced man without apparent debility, his goggles pushed up out of the way over his forehead.

Sidney lifted the tubular brass stitch-welder, passed it to the other man. As Sidney bent over, a bolt of pain shot through his ribcage and his temple throbbed. These were the places Mayor Nancy Ogg had kicked him.

The man smiled slowly and guardedly, seeming to stare at the white bandage on Sidney's left temple. "You're learning fast," the man said.

"I've always had an interest in space mechanics," Sidney said. "It's been a hobby with me since I was a kid."

Sidney had helped the man build two compartments since noon, but still did not know his name. Sidney recalled introducing himself earlier, but the man had simply grunted something in return.

Sidney flipped protective goggles over his own eyes, lifted a feather-light compartment assembly from the deck. He held it in place abutting the forward firewall next to the compartment they had just completed.

The man flipped his goggles down and began to stitch-weld the assemblies together. Sidney watched as the zig-zag weld took shape, then glanced back at the center of the mass driver shell, where Mayor Nancy Ogg and her security sergeant stood speaking with a strange-looking short-haired woman.

I suppose it's a woman, Sidney thought, noting a faint breast line. The woman was short, had a weak chin and a bulbous nose. Her hands were thrust deeply into the pockets of a loose-fitting white-and-silver dress. The expression was chilly, unsmiling.

"Okay," the man with the stitch-welder said. "It'll hold now."

Sidney let go, glanced through a hatch in the forward firewall where two men in green-and-gold space mechanic's coveralls were rolling aft. They passed a maze of grey tubes at the base of the mass driver engine, rolled by Sidney. "Did you lock the Shamrock Five entry hatch?" the taller of the men asked.

"Huh?" the other man said. "Yeah, I guess." To Sidney, the tone seemed disinterested.

The Shamrock Five! Sidney thought. *That's my ship!*

Sidney watched them roll aft down the center of the mass driver shell and recalled his arrival on Saint Elba less than two nights earlier. It seemed like a month before when he had peered through a porthole in the IOTV to watch the Shamrock Five dock.

Sidney pictured the sleek black and silver cruiser in his mind's eye. *It's nearby . . . and the hatch may be unlocked!* he thought, feeling his pulse quicken.

Impulsively, Sidney flipped off his goggles and moto-darted through the firewall hatch. He pressed himself against the firewall on the other side, breathing hard. *Don't stop now,* he thought, touching the bandaged bump at his temple. *You're disposable anyway. . . .*

He looked up. The mass driver engine towered like a government office building, except it had tubes, valves and ramps.

Sidney's heart skipped a beat: a Security Brigade guard on a lower ramp had just spotted him!

"You!" the guard bellowed. "What are you doing in here?"

Sidney took off before the guard finished his question, sped around the base of the engine. He saw the Shamrock Five now through two glassplex portholes in the mass driver's forward-most wall. *There!* he thought, seeing a hatch between the portholes. *The hatch!*

He heard guards yelling from above and behind. "WHERE DID HE GO?" one asked.

"FORWARD!"

"THERE HE IS!"

"GET HIM!"

Sidney was at the hatch, expecting to feel the searing pain of bullets at any moment. *Will it open?* he thought. He mentoed the door, held his breath as he listened to tumblers rolling inside the door. He looked back, saw three guards speeding toward him.

"Pttting!" A bullet ricocheted off the wall near his head.

The door slid open!

Sidney rolled through quickly, mentoed the door shut. A red handle inside on the wall at one side had a sign below it which read: "DOUBLE LOCK—No Access From Rear."

He threw the handle down, looked forward.

Sidney stood on a short glassplex-sealed gangway, could barely see in the low light from one underfoot light panel. He heard distant, angry voices and pounding on the other side of the hatch. Another hatch was forward, and he rolled to it quickly.

Sidney mentoed this hatch. It opened. Just inside was another red double lock handle. He threw it on.

Sidney fell to his knees, still grasping the handle and breathing hard. He caught his breath, yelled: "Tom! You here, Tom?"

There was no response.

Sidney wondered why two trailers full of cappies were connected to the Shamrock Five. *Disposables,* he thought. *Did Tom know about that?*

Sidney rolled through the passenger compartment and peeked into the cockpit, still calling for Tom Javik. Then he searched two aft magnetic container storage rooms.

He's not aboard, Sidney thought, rolling back to the cockpit. *Where is he?*

Inside the cockpit, Sidney touched one of the white molded plastic command chairs. He looked around the dimly lit area, saw the faint twinklings of stars far out at the end of the docking tunnel. He slid into the seat.

An array of dials, levers and handles confronted Sidney, and he studied them intently. He focused upon a brass plate marked "SHAMROCK FIVE—SP-1607," and next to that recognized a red ball plasto-cyanide bomb detonator from photographs he had once seen.

Let's see here, he thought, moving his fingers across a row of blue handles. *Direct Command Mode, Takeoff Mode, Docking Mode, Attack Mode. . . .*

"Attack Mode!" Sidney whispered excitedly to himself, resting his hand on that handle. "My Rosenbloom! I can't believe it!" For a moment, he imagined being under Uncle Rosy's direct orders to save Earth. . . . Atheist fighter ships were attacking the Shamrock Five from all sides! . . .

Returning to reality, Sidney retracted his hand. There was a slight throbbing at his bandaged temple where Mayor Nancy Ogg had kicked him. He touched the bandage, felt the bump.

I've got to be realistic, he thought. *I'll radio for Tom.* Sidney scanned the instruments, located the speakercom. He mentoed a switch to open the circuit, heard the crackle of static electricity. *We'll get the ship out to where we can see the garbage comet: . . . I'll pray for it to go away. That's how I stopped the fire. . . . Garbage comet? Can it really be?*

Just then, laughter cackled distantly in Sidney's brain. It drew closer. *"Ha!"* a familiar tenor voice said. *"He's at it again—thinks he's a miracle worker!"*

"It is pathetic," a second, deeper voice said. *"Now listen, fleshcarrier. You can't pray to God. God didn't send that comet! We did!"*

The voices cackled with laughter again. To Sidney, it sounded orchestrated.

"You listen to me!" Sidney said angrily. "I'm trying to help people! Millions will die if I don't try!" Sidney thought of Carla, felt tears coming on. He fought them back.

The voices receded, laughing merrily.

"Who's there?" a speakercom voice asked. "Who said that?"

"Get me Lieutenant Tom Javik," Sidney said, addressing the speakercom. "Tell him Sidney Malloy is aboard the Shamrock Five, ready for takeoff."

Presently a rasping voice came on the frequency. "Who?" the voice asked. "Who is this?"

"Sidney Malloy. I'm in command of the Shamrock Five until Lieutenant Javik takes over." Sidney was not aware of his appointment as titular captain by General Munoz. "Get Javik for me!" Sidney rasped. "Now!" He rested his hand on the Takeoff Mode handle.

"Javik is missing, fella. You're that cappy he asked for, aren't you? Just open the hatches and give yourself up."

"No! What do you mean he's missing? You're lying!" But Sidney read a voice pitch meter on the dashboard. The meter dial was in the green zone.

It's true, Sidney thought, his spirits sinking. *Tom isn't here!* Static crackled across the frequency.

"You're just making it hard on yourself," the voice said. "Be reasonable. No one's going to hurt..."

Sidney mentoed the frequency shut. *I'll have to fly this baby myself,* he thought, studying the instrument panel. *Now how do I cut the trailers loose? Maybe Direct Command Mode....*

He threw on the appropriate handle, saw the words "Direct Command Mode" illuminated in blue over the handle, and beneath the handle, in blinking red lights, the words "Standing By." The entire instrument panel blinked on with luminescent green, red and blue dials and blinking lights.

Release trailers, Sidney mentoed.

There was no response.

"Release trailers!" he yelled.

Still no response.

Sidney stared at the words "Standing By," drummed a finger on the instrument panel.

"Ship's computer," he said, speaking into a console-mounted microphone. "How do I release the trailers?"

"That is not in my program," the computer replied.

"Where would such a thing be programmed?"

"That is not in my program, either."

"Can't you even suggest where I might look?" Sidney asked, pleading.

"No."

Frustrated, Sidney shook his head. *A bureaucratic computer,* he thought.

* * *

At the forwardmost hatch of Mass Driver One, Madame Bernet confronted five black-uniformed security guards, one of whom was Sergeant Rountree.

"Roll aside!" Madame Bernet commanded. "I'm going through!" The meckie stood with both hands thrust into its pockets, glared menacingly.

"This hatch is double-locked," Sergeant Rountree said angrily, holding one hand on the handle of his holstered pistol. "Stay the hell out of our way now, Madame!"

Without another word, Madame Bernet drew two long knives out of her pockets. The meckie crossed them in front ceremoniously, then swished them through the air, their steel blades glimmering brightly.

Sergeant Rountree and the other guards drew their pistols, commenced firing at the meckie.

"Pttting! Pttting! Thud!" Bullets ricocheted off walls and off Madame Bernet's plastic and metal body.

The killer meckie smiled, a death's head smile. Then, with five precise strokes, it decapitated the guards. Sergeant Rountree was first to die. The guards fell in blood-squirting heaps, their bodies separated from their heads.

Madame Bernet crossed the knives, then slid them into pocket-concealed sheaths while mentoing a code to break the hatch's double lock.

The hatch slid open.

The meckie passed through the door, double-locked it again.

Seconds later, Madame Bernet stood at the rear hatch of the Shamrock Five. The hatch slid open at a mento-command. As the killer meckie rolled in, the Shamrock Five shifted on its tether, causing a raised surface to appear underfoot. Madame Bernet's moto-shoes struck this bump, and the meckie fell violently to the floor, butting its forehead against a bulkhead.

The meckie jumped to its feet with knives drawn, rolled in a confused pattern. Something had been damaged in the fall, and a programmed track commanded: *Mission complete! It is time to kill!*

Madame Bernet rolled forward through the passenger compartment, paused uncertainly when she saw the seat upon which she had ridden from Earth to Saint Elba. *Mission complete!* the program repeated. *It is time to kill!*

The meckie restarted, rolled to the cockpit hatch.

Sidney turned at the sound of steel hitting the hatchjamb.

"Who the hell are you?" he asked, recognizing the short-haired woman he had seen on the mass driver.

Madame Bernet did not respond, appeared disoriented to Sidney. With a gaze that rolled all over the cockpit, not focusing upon anything, the meckie began to swing its knives while rolling into the cockpit. The knives moved slowly at first, then faster and faster.

"Swish! . . . Swish! . . . Swish-swish-swish!"

The meckie closed in on Sidney, flailing wildly like a blind man fighting a burglar. Sidney fell against the instrument panel, accidentally tripping the "Takeoff Mode" handle. He ducked, climbed around the command chairs and rolled into the passenger compartment.

The ship's four Rolls Royce engines rumbled on, then smoothed out. Sidney lunged to the floor behind a double chair to hide, peered across the top of an armrest at the cockpit. The meckie was still in there, thrashing around and cutting everything to pieces. Sidney heard breaking glassite, thuds and crashes.

Sidney recalled the dream he had experienced in the detention center sleeping room on Earth . . . the knives that approached inexorably . . . Tom's head being severed horribly. . . .

He's dead, Sidney thought, grimacing at the thought. *That monster killed him!*

The engines whined, and Sidney felt a surge of power. *Tethers are holding it back,* he thought. *This thing's trying to take off!*

The tethers snapped, and the ship lurched violently, throwing Sidney against the seat behind him.

Mayor Nancy Ogg stared impatiently in the direction of the forward firewall hatch Sergeant Rountree had gone through minutes before. Just as she started to roll forward, the mass driver shell lurched, and she rolled hard against a quarter bulkhead. Grabbing the bulkhead to stay on her feet, the Mayor read a Patterman Gravitonic Indicator dial mounted there. The reading: "1.027."

She saw other people sprawling upon the floor, heard confused yells and the clanging of unsecured metal tools. A scaffold fell to the deck just a meter away, sending its occupants flying and screaming in pain.

"Get medical attention for the injured!" Mayor Nancy Ogg

yelled. *For cappies?* she thought. *Who cares about them?*

Acknowledging the command, a melon-shaped security corporal snapped a first aid kit off the bulkhead. But the mass driver lurched again, and the corporal went sliding across the floor.

"We're taking off!" someone yelled. "The tethers just broke!"

The Shamrock Five surged unhesitatingly through Saint Elba's main docking tunnel, probing the darkness ahead with its collision sensors. Still in the passenger compartment, Sidney lifted his head and peered out a porthole. Outside spotlights flashed on.

Presently, Sidney no longer heard Madame Bernet slashing about in the cockpit. Instead, he heard the radio blaring from that direction. *They've found an override frequency,* he thought, recalling when he had shut off communication.

"Shamrock Five!" a voice said over the radio speakercom. "You do not have takeoff clearance!"

Sidney rolled cautiously to the cockpit hatchway.

"Shamrock Five!" the radio blared. "Acknowledge!"

Sidney looked around the doorway with one eye, saw the meckie crouching in a corner, knives crossed in front of its body. A piece of plastic skin on the back of one of the meckie's hands had been peeled off, and Sidney saw metal gears and nylon tendons inside.

A meckie! he thought. *Is it out of power?* He recalled the comment he had overheard concerning a killer meckie, shivered with fear.

Sidney lifted a manual from the floor, hurled it at Madame Bernet. The meckie did not move.

"Shut down your engines!" the radio commanded, "or we will blast you away!"

Sidney lunged for the instrument panel, replied: "Accidental takeoff. Do not fire upon us! Your mayor is a passenger in one of the trailers!"

The line clicked on, then went off.

They're checking, Sidney thought. *She probably didn't have time to get off.*

Sidney cleared debris off the command chair and slid into the seat.

The Shamrock Five and its mass driver trailers cleared Saint Elba's docking tunnel and darted into open space. Sidney saw twinkling vastness ahead, flipped on the semi-automatic Direct Command Mode. A red "Standing By" light went on under the mode's handle.

Presently the voice returned to the radio, and it demanded, "Shut down your engines! Hit the master switch!"

"Request refused," Sidney said. "This ship is not turning back!"

"Why not, for Rosenbloom's sake?"

"Call it a holy mission."

There was a pause, followed by: "You're crazy!"

I don't think so, Sidney thought.

After another pause, the voice said, "Release the trailers."

The Mayor IS aboard, Sidney thought. "I'd be happy to," he said. "How is that accomplished?"

"We'll find out. Stand by, Shamrock Five."

"Standing by for course coordinates," the ship's computer said.

Sidney flipped through a console-mounted clip-file which miraculously had survived the meckie's onslought. *Ah,* he thought. *Here it is!*

"Course eighty-four degrees, seventeen minutes, C.P.," Sidney said. "Fifty-eight. . . ." He paused, adding, "Wait a minute, computer. This says takeoff was supposed to be yesterday! Won't that change the coordinates?"

"Give me the original figures," the computer said. "We are tracking the comet, and will correct."

The comet? Sidney thought. *If I'm nuts, so is this computer!* Sidney completed the entry of coordinates.

"Course received," the computer said. "Over and out."

Sidney felt acceleration in the gravitonically normal cockpit, was pushed back against his seat. *They'd better tell me how to release those. . . .*

"Shamrock Five, this is Saint Elba. Locate a green panel box on the cockpit bulkhead, just behind the co-pilot's chair."

Sidney turned around, reported back: "I see it."

"Open the box. Push two green buttons inside. Hit them simultaneously."

"All right," Sidney said. "But no funny ideas about firing on me afterward. I'll have the rear guns trained on those trailers."

"No tricks," the radio voice agreed.

Within seconds, Sidney had cut the trailers loose. On the console screen, he watched two ships close in on the trailers.

Sidney gave the command for maximum speed, and the Shamrock Five hyper-accelerated. The images on the screen became pinpricks, then disappeared entirely.

He glanced at the killer meckie out of the corner of one eye, thought he saw an eye open. Sidney did a double-take, but he saw nothing unusual the second time. He looked away, took a deep breath.

I must have been seeing things, he thought.

* * *

On a page margin of the history primer, the tall, fat youngsayerman penned this note: "If there be a nerd Heaven, Sidney Malloy is there."

Wait a minute, the youngsayerman thought. *Did the cappy die?*

He flipped ahead to find out. . . .

THIRTEEN

THE ECONOMICS OF FREENESS,
FOR FURTHER READING AND DISCUSSION

Patent Law 78 was an unwritten law mandated by the Council of Ten in 2366. It stipulated that the government would buy out and shelve any patent which threatened national economic security, and further that future patents were to be denied upon any such items.

Thursday, August 31, 2605

Master Edward sat alone in the Central Chamber, staring down from his perch at the round illuminated floor screen in the center of the room. Only half conscious that it was nearly two o'clock in the morning, he studied a video schematic of the Great Comet's trajectory.

"Blast!" he said in an angry undertone, noting that the future paths of Earth and the garbage comet continued to meet. A digital readout at the bottom of the screen described the comet's Estimated Time of Arrival:

DAYS HOURS MINS. SECS. D/SECS.

Impact Countdown: 1   16   5   46   .38

He watched desperately as the deciseconds and seconds flipped away, then mentoed for a videograph report.

There, he thought as the graph appeared on the screen, pointing in the low yellow light of the room. *That is where I altered Earth's orbital speed yesterday. And then the comet changed its own trajectory to remain on a collision course....*

His gaze moved to the point where the tuxedo meckie had increased the orbital speed again the prior evening. Master Edward shook his head sadly as he saw the comet had altered its own course to match that change.

At Master Edward's mento-command, the screen changed once more, and he watched the Great Comet as it flashed across space. The comet emitted bright blue and amber tones, illuminating the ceiling of the room. He felt fascination, fear and awe.

He considered fleeing in an escape rocket but discarded the thought almost at the moment it came to him. *If I have any hope of reversing the aging process,* he thought, *I must remain here.*

Master Edward longed for a simpler time. His life had grown unbearably complex in a few short days. He touched the handle of the knife at his waist, thought, *I could end my misery in an instant.*

He gazed at the screen with unfocused eyes, reminding himself as he had several times since killing Uncle Rosy that he could never be as great a leader as the Master had been. *Uncle Rosy must have sensed I could not handle the job,* he thought. *That is why he delayed....*

An overwhelming feeling of loneliness came over him.

"Master!" a voice called from across the chamber. "Might I have a word with you?"

Master Edward saw a hood-robed figure standing in the doorway which led to the antechamber containing the Basins

of Youth. Surprised, Master Edward called back: "Who is
there?" He realized as the words came out that he had forgotten
to speak in the tone of Uncle Rosy. *Did he notice?* Master
Edward wondered.

"Lastsayer Steven."

"Enter," Master Edward said, remembering to use the resonant tone of Uncle Rosy.

The robed figure rolled forward to one side of the floor-
screen, and Master Edward saw Lastsayer's smooth face in the
illumination of the comet. *Too much light in here,* Master
Edward thought nervously, pulling his robe over the lower part
of his face and nose.

"Peace be upon you, Master," Lastsayer said.

"What is this about?" Master Edward asked without returning the blessing. He peered over the edge of his robe, heard
his own words muffle in the robe and pulled it several centimeters out from his mouth.

"I heard of Onesayer's disappearance," Lastsayer said.

"And you are here about a promotion?" These words dripped
with acidity. Master Edward looked for the tiniest indication
that Lastsayer had noticed the earlier vocal faux pas, saw only
fear and curiosity in Lastsayer's expression. *One of the others
would have noticed immediately,* Master Edward thought, re-
lieved. *This sayerman has not been here long enough.*

"No, Master. It is something far more important."

"And what is so important that you could not sleep?"

"Undoubtedly you already know of what I am about to tell
you. . . ."

"I have no time for dilly-dallying, Lastsayer! Get straight
to the point or get straight out of here!"

"I should have come to you sooner," Lastsayer said hurriedly. "Sunday morning, I saw Onesayer high on Happy
Pills . . . and he performed disrespectful imitations of you."

"I can hardly believe that!" Master Edward exclaimed,
showing false emotion.

"It is true, Master. Although I risk my position in the Sayerhood by speaking against him."

Master Edward smiled grimly to himself, and said in Uncle
Rosy's voice, "Tell me more."

"Onesayer seemed bitter about you remaining as Master. I
received the distinct impression he wanted to take your place."

"By force?"

"It did not seem so to me at first, but as I thought about it more . . ."

"You saw this nearly four days ago, and waited until now to inform me?"

"I was not certain if I had been here long enough to recognize improper behavior."

"You think disrespect for me is commonplace?" Master Edward snapped. He studied Lastsayer's smooth face in the comet's reflection, saw trembling fear. The lower lip quivered. *No hatred there*, Master Edward thought. *Not yet.*

"N-no," Lastsayer stammered, shifting uneasily on his feet.

"You WERE disciplined at Pleasant Reef, were you not?"

"Yes, Master. There is no excuse."

Master Edward pulled the robe tightly about his face, thought, *Maybe I should bring an armadillo meckie in here to guard me. One of the sayermen could kill me easily if my plan occurred to him. . . .*

Master Edward stopped at the thought, felt himself welcoming the serenity of death. *Twosayer would kill me for sure*, he thought with a macabre sense of humor. *I could force it by promoting Steven to Onesayer. . . .*

Noting Lastsayer Steven awaiting further instructions, Master Edward pulled the robe out from his mouth and said, "Go now, Lastsayer. And say nothing of this matter. I will deal with it."

During the early morning hours according to New City time, Sidney remained attentive in the cockpit, scanning the sky for a first sign of the Great Comet. Presently, he grew weary of the unchanging scenery and began nodding off.

As he slipped into slumber, the command chair on which he sat began to straighten, forming a sleeping platform. A soft pillow popped out beneath his head, and Sidney rolled over on one side to get comfortable.

Nervously, he opened one sleepy eye to peer at the meckie. Something seemed different. The meckie remained rigid, knives crossed in front.

It's turned a little! he thought with a sinking feeling. *Toward me!*

Sidney sat straight up. *No*, he thought. *I imagined it. Or the motion of the ship did it. . . .*

Sidney searched the cockpit for a weapon, opening compartments quietly and looking under chairs and behind instrument panels as he stayed out of range of the killer meckie. Nothing was found. Then he rolled into the passenger compartment, thinking, *I can't sleep in that cockpit!* The hatch shut behind him upon his mento-command.

The ship's flying smoothly, Sidney thought, staring at an oxygen cart which was secured to the forward bulkhead. *And with gravitonics near Earth normal . . .*

Sidney released the oxy-cart, rolled it in front of the cockpit hatchway. *There,* he thought, mento-locking the cart's wheels. *At least I'll hear the damned thing coming.*

He found a passenger seat, and it folded flat invitingly as he lay upon it, accepting the weary frame of the inexperienced space traveler. Soon Sidney was fast asleep, dreaming of magical things and wondrous places.

Sidney pictured himself in full dress Space Patrol uniform, riding in an open limousine down American Boulevard. Cheering throngs of people lined the street, and they waved national banners while calling out to him: "Captain Malloy! Captain Malloy!"

In the dream, a pretty girl threw flowers to him and blew kisses. It was Carla, his darling Carla! He reached out to her. She smiled, and her image faded into a crowd of smiling faces.

Suddenly, his pleasant dream became a terrible nightmare. Where Carla had been, he saw Madame Bernet, slashing spectators with both knives. Then the killer meckie leaped into Sidney's limousine, swinging its knives viciously.

"You did it for yourself, didn't you, fleshcarrier?" the meckie screeched in a familiar tenor voice as it cut Sidney's face and chest. "You don't care about other people!"

Sidney sat bolt upright on the sleeping platform, found himself drenched in perspiration. Wide-eyed, he stared across the shadowy passenger compartment at the cockpit hatch. The hatch remained closed as he had left it, with the oxy-cart in front of it.

Gradually, fitfully, Sidney fell asleep again.

The morning of the state funeral celebration was grey and cloudy. President Euripides Ogg stood regally on a red-and-yellow gazebo trailer parked at the base of Astro-Burial Inc.'s number three launcher. He shivered as a cool gust of wind blew in from the east.

"Tell Bu-Tech to warm this weather up," Ogg snapped to Billie Birdbright, who rolled up a ramp onto the trailer. "This is supposed to be a celebration!"

"They need clouds for the special effects," Birdbright said as he rolled to a stop. "The sun will pop out when—"

"I know, I know. But they could have made it a little warmer. . . ." Ogg brushed a lock of hair away from his eyes and surveyed the crowd which stood silently below, waiting for the eulogy to begin. An ocean of faces looked back at him, and for the first time in many years, Ogg was struck by the sameness of their features and dress.

Birdbright leaned close to President Ogg and whispered in his ear: "It's all set, Mr. President. We're locked in on the comet's trajectory. These caskets are going right down the maw of the comet!"

"Very good, Billie," Ogg said, unsmiling.

As Birdbright left, the President shifted his gaze, looking to his right at two astro-disposal casket capsules which rested side-by-side on the launch track. The capsules were draped with white-and-gold ministerial cloths, weighted at the ends and emblazoned with large star-shaped purple badges signifying that the men inside had been killed by malfunctioning products. Ogg suppressed a smile at the thought of Munoz actually being killed by a faulty waterbed during a homosexual encounter instead of in the auto accident the government said had occurred.

President Ogg cleared his throat and mentoed his auto-speech implant. He began to speak at the direction of the programmed track. "This is both a sad occasion and a happy occasion," he began in a hesitating, remorseful tone. "We are saddened at the passing of General Munoz and Dr. Hudson . . . two great leaders who guided their respective bureaus through the challenges of our age." Ogg smiled on cue, adding, "But heartened we are at the thought of these men buying eternally in the Happy Shopping Ground!"

"May Rosenbloom bless them!" the crowd thundered in a tremendous outpouring of emotion.

Ogg reached into one of two urns which rested on a ledge at his side, removing a handful of white confetti, then dipped into the second urn with his other hand and brought forth strands of multi-colored plastic streamers. He opened both hands, casting their contents out upon the casket capsules with these words:

> Paper to paper,
> Plastic to plastic;
> Take them, Uncle Rosy,
> On a journey fantastic!

A gust of Bu-Tech-made wind picked up the confetti and streamers, carrying them up into the air and away over the heads of the crowd. As this occurred, the sun broke through a cloud layer, casting warm golden rays upon the casket capsules. The crowd oohed and aahed at this, for indeed it had to be a message from Uncle Rosy.

Ebullient now, President Ogg said happily, "To your bosom, Uncle Rosy, take them today!" Then he mentoed the magne-launcher, catapulting the capsules out along the length of the nine-thousand-five-hundred-meter-long launch track into a patch of blue sky. The crowd turned their heads in unison to watch the path of the capsules, cheered moments later when they heard a sonic thump.

President Ogg thought of the garbage comet traveling toward Earth along the same trajectory. "There, you bastards," he cursed bitterly under his breath. "Stop the comet yourselves!"

* * *

"In this chapter," Sayer Superior Lin-Ti said, "you will see why our modern social hierarchy was developed. Uncle Rosy set up a wondrous AmFed society . . . but ultimately it relied upon the control of the Sayerhood . . . and the Sayerhood relied upon Uncle Rosy. Everything hinged upon one man, you see, and when he died, chaos reigned.

"But this should not be interpreted as a failure of the Master. For he advanced humankind, hoping it ultimately could stand on its own. Today we are closer to that goal, much closer indeed. . . ."

FOURTEEN

**UP CLOSE WITH THE MASTER,
FOR FURTHER READING AND DISCUSSION**

"Do not shoot at something until you know what it is. It may shoot back."

> Admonition from Alafin Inaya to Uncle Rosy during a hunting trip they took together in the Kenyatta Highlands, September, 2312. (As related in Emmanuel Dade's unpublished notes.)

**SHIPLOG OF THE AMFED
SPACE CRUISER SHAMROCK FIVE,
SP-1607
Date:** *Thursday, August 31, 2605—early
afternoon*
Garbage Day Countdown: *1 day, 5 hours,
17 minutes*

When Sidney awoke, he felt a dull pain in his ribcage where Mayor Nancy Ogg had kicked him. He touched the bandage at his temple and was pleased to find that the swelling had subsided. Sidney sat up, stretched and looked across the shadowy room at the cockpit hatch. The hatch door remained closed, and in front of that stood the oxy-cart precisely where he had left it.

His chairback rose automatically seconds later, and as it did the passenger compartment lights brightened. Sidney looked up upon hearing a whir of gears, and watched a tray of food drop slowly from a ceiling-mounted levitator onto his lap. *I AM hungry,* he thought, studying a synthetic egg on bagel sandwich with interest. He stuck his finger in a bowl of reconstituted tomato soup. It was tepid. Sidney wolfed down the sandwich, gulped the soup. As he set the empty bowl back on the tray, the tray returned to its ceiling compartment.

Sidney considered ordering more food, but decided instead to roll across the room. After re-securing the oxy-cart to the bulkhead, he mentoed the cockpit door. As it slid open, he heard the sexless voice of the ship's computer. "Re-charging stop, twenty-three minutes," the computer reported.

Re-charging stop! Sidney thought. *If it's not completely automated, and there are people there, I could be in trouble....*

Sidney flicked a nervous glance at the still motionless Madame Bernet. *Don't see any further movement,* he thought, rolling to the instrument panel. Without sitting down, he spoke into the command speakercom, asking, "Can re-charging stop be avoided?"

"Remaining charge two-point-seven-four times greater than anticipated," the computer reported. "Unexpected beneficial space currents account for increased efficiency, and . . ."

"Answer the question," Sidney said, slipping into the command chair.

"Answer depends upon variables."

"What variables?" Sidney drummed a finger impatiently on the instrument panel.

"Comet behaving erratically. It has accelerated and changed course in the past twenty-nine hours."

"Explain."

"Orbital speed of Earth has increased twice, to its present factor of one-point-five-three-seven normal. Cause unknown.

Comet matched each change, is in apparent pursuit of Earth."

"So we need less E-Cell charge to rendezvous with the comet?"

"Assuming comet continues at present speed . . . and assuming a rendezvous in deep space is required . . . that is correct."

"Returning to my original question, do we have adequate charge onboard?"

"Answer depends upon variables."

"We've already been over that!"

"There are other variables."

Sidney sighed. "Be specific," he said.

"Comet's speed and course may change. Space currents are subject to variation. Earth—"

"Assuming an average condition for all such variables, do we have an adequate E-Cell charge to reach the comet?"

"This computer does not deal in probabilities. It deals in facts."

Sidney slammed the butt of his hand on the instrument panel. "Do not stop for recharging," he said tersely.

An hour later, Sidney felt bored. He glanced around the cockpit at the white plastic walls and at the still rigid Madame Bernet. *This isn't what I imagined*, he thought sadly. *The ship is flying itself!*

He touched the Manual Mode handle, felt a rush of excitement as he considered taking the ship off its semi-automatic Direct Command Mode. *Should I do it?* he thought.

He threw the handle down in answer to the question and grasped a gleaming tita-steel-plated control stick at his right side. The stick was cool to his touch. Sidney moved the stick halfway to starboard, and the Shamrock Five banked gracefully to the right.

This is more like it! he thought, suddenly exhilarated.

Sidney pressed a black button on the stick, causing the ship's twin Rolls Royce engines to blast. *It's so simple,* he thought, feeling acceleration in the gravitonically normal cabin. *Just as I imagined. . . .*

Sidney pushed the stick to port, giving another blast to the rockets. The Shamrock Five responded quickly, and Sidney leaned into the turn, just as he had done so many times in dreams.

It seemed too good to be true. . . . Sidney at the command

of a Space Patrol cruiser, flashing commands to powerful rockets! *I'm the only one who can do it!* he thought, *the only person who can save Earth!*

He reached to his uniform tunic with his left hand to feel the medals he had been awarded for past missions, patted his chest where they should have been. "What the?. . ." he grunted.

Sidney looked down at his chest, saw only a thin green smock that had been issued to him on Saint Elba. "Oh," he sighed. "For a moment. . . ."

"Ha-ha-ha!" Distant laughter echoed through his brain, grew louder quickly. *"Ha-ha-ha!"*

"Enjoying yourself, fleshcarrier?" a familiar deep voice asked.

Sidney felt warm now, embarrassed at the daydream. *You're alone out here!* he thought. *Get ahold of yourself!*

The cockpit was silent. He looked across the starboard bow at a distant shooting star streaking to his left. The shooting star angled off into the starcloth beyond, then flashed brilliantly, followed by a wisp of white light as it turned toward Sidney.

Wait a minute! Sidney thought. *That's no shooting star!*

Inadvertently, Sidney pulled the stick back sharply, and the ship's nose tilted up. He pushed the stick forward to compensate, and the Shamrock Five dropped its nose.

It's the Great Comet! he thought. A wave of euphoria passed through his body.

The comet veered heavenward for an instant, and this time its color and configuration changed so that it was a pale blue iceball trailing six silvery jet-ray tails from its nuclear region. The tails were magnificent plumes of gas which swept across millions of kilometers of space, as delicate and translucent as spun glass against sunlight. The midnight blue backcloth of space gave definition to the comet's icy nucleus, and it occurred to Sidney that he was witnessing the most beautiful spectacle in all of creation.

Now the comet swooped back, much as his ship had done moments before, returning to its original course. As the comet swooped, its silvery plumes turned to fiery yellow, while the pale blue nucleus became soft lavender. As Sidney thought about the comet's complexity, another thought hit him: *Did it mimic my ship's motion?*

Thinking the comet might follow him away from Earth, Sidney mentoed a directional computer button. The ship turned around one hundred twenty degrees. Nudging the speed toggle to decelerate, he watched the Great Comet on a video console screen.

But the comet remained on course, not flinching an eyelash. Sidney brought the ship around again and resumed acceleration. Then he moved the control stick. First one way, then the other. The comet refused to follow.

Now Sidney closed his eyes and clasped his hands together in prayer. *Please*, he thought, recalling his prayer when the Elba House fire was raging, *swerve and go in another direction. Please don't hit Earth!*

He opened his eyes. The comet had not changed course. Sidney repeated the prayer four more times, but nothing happened.

Elba House was on fire, he thought, trying to sort out events that had become a blur in his mind. *And the comet is fire....*

He tugged at his upper lip pensively, then moved his head from side to side. *Maybe the comet's too big,* he thought. *Too free....* Sidney hit a red super accelerator toggle on the console, felt G-forces push him against the chair back.

The comet grew visibly larger as the distance between it and Sidney narrowed. He saw its nucleus flare bright red. Then the misty tail plumes changed to emerald and gold. It was a spectacular display of raw primordial power, at once terrifying and delicately beautiful.

I feel...strangely compelled...to continue this journey, Sidney thought, *as if some immense presence is beckoning to me across the heavens....*

Sidney heard faint laughter in a distant cavern of his skull. He rubbed his temples with the thumb and two fingers of one hand. Gradually his head cleared, leaving him with a mixture of intense and conflicting emotions.

The black pearl handled knife lay on Master Edward's dining module table, and he leaned over the table with both hands on its cool marble edge, staring at the weapon despondently. He felt tired and dispirited. Although it was long past lunchtime of Garbage Day minus one, he had not looked in the mirror at all that day.

No use looking at my face, he thought, noting deep creases and brown age blotches on his hands. *I know what it looks like.* He sighed. *I am so weary!*

Master Edward straightened, lifted the knife. He pricked the tip of one finger intentionally, watched blood squirt out and drip to the table. The blood seemed impersonal, somehow not his own.

"Willard!" the simu-life picture screamed from another room. "Willard!"

"Yes, dear," Master Edward called back. "Coming, dear."

I am going to join her . . . and the Master, he thought. *In death.*

He glanced to the doorway at the sound of rolling machinery, saw the remaining tuxedo meckie enter. "You did not call for lunch, Master," the meckie said. "You are not hungry today?"

Master Edward did not respond.

"Can I get you anything, Master?"

Master Edward stared at the knife, replied: "Serenity."

"What did you say, Master?"

"I want you to kill me."

"But no one can kill you, Master. You are the most perfect creation."

"I am re-programming you," Master Edward said, extending the knife to the meckie. "What was said before is not true. I *can* die. I *want* to die."

"As you wish, Master," the meckie said in its sophisticated, emotionless voice. Its button lights blinked uncertainly.

"Take the knife," Master Edward instructed.

The tuxedo meckie complied, stood motionless with the knife blade in its mechanical grasp.

"Kill me," Master Edward said, extending his arms to each side as he recalled Uncle Rosy's similar words the day before.

The meckie rolled forward quickly and slammed the knife handle into Master Edward's midsection.

Master Edward grunted and grabbed his stomach. But the injury was limited: his wind had been knocked out. "You tin can fool!" Master Edward gasped. "Turn the knife around!"

"This way, Master?" the tuxedo meckie asked, grasping the black pearl handle.

"Yes," Master Edward said impatiently. "Now hurry, blast you! Hurry!"

It was Thursday afternoon. Mayor Nancy Ogg had been brought back to Saint Elba three hours earlier.

She passed a stack of telebeam memos across her desktop

to Sergeant Keefer. This was Rountree's replacement, a man whose appearance very much resembled that of his predecessor: tall and muscular, just the sort of man with whom she would like to share a bed. Dr. Hudson had been a brain, and that had attracted her to him physically. It certainly had not been Hudson's appearance. She thought of her longings to be held by Sergeant Rountree. Now he too was gone....

The Mayor sighed, recalling the crisis she faced. She lit a lemon tintette and sat back in her chair with an intense expression. She heard the chair squeak, studied the black-uniformed man who stood in front of her desk. "Beams have been arriving all night," she said.

Sergeant Keefer flipped through the memos, appeared to be ill at ease.

"Sit," Mayor Nancy Ogg commanded.

Sergeant Keefer took a seat in a lattice glass suspensor chair, continued to flip through the slips of paper. "News travels fast," he said. "I see the psychotherapeutic community wants videofilm and brain scan reports on Mister Malloy. Requests from San Dimitrio, Mariana City...every quadrant of the galaxy...." He paused upon seeing Mayor Nancy Ogg shake her head from side to side, an unspoken comment that she was not interested in such information.

"This Malloy; I've never seen anything like him," Mayor Nancy Ogg said, taking a puff on her tintette. She blew bright yellow smoke through her nostrils, peered through the smoke at Sergeant Keefer.

"Most unusual, Honorable Mayor. Most unusual."

"Where did Malloy learn to operate an Akron class cruiser?"

"We're checking his dossier file now, Honorable Mayor. We show him as a G.W. seven-five-oh, Presidential Bureau, Central Forms."

The Mayor scowled, flipped ashes into an ashtray. "Munoz chose him to command the ship. Why?"

Sergeant Keefer leaned forward to return the telebeam slips to Mayor Nancy Ogg's desk, remained on the forward edge of his chair and said, "I don't know."

"Come now, Sergeant. Surely you can think more clearly than that. General Munoz was drugged—or hypnotized!"

Sergeant Keefer remained leaning forward, looked confused.

Mayor Nancy Ogg snuffed out her tintette in the ashtray, stared at the wall. "Another problem," she muttered.

"What did you say, Honorable Mayor?"

"Nothing, nothing," she replied irritably, still staring at the wall. Then, turning to glare at Keefer with angry, smoldering eyes, she announced: "I'm putting the orbiter on immediate Evacuation Alert. Malloy duped Javik and then killed him. Malloy is a saboteur!"

"He c-couldn't have p-planted bombs," Sergeant Keefer stammered. "He looked so harmless. . . ."

"And that would make him the perfect saboteur!" Mayor Nancy Ogg boomed. "Surely, even you can see that, Sergeant."

"Yes, of course." Sergeant Keefer hung his head.

"Speed up your background investigation," the Mayor commanded. "I want a full report on this man in one hour!"

From the couch of her living room module, Carla heard the chimes of a neighbor's digital cuckoo, counted six chirps. *Supper time*, she thought, infuriated.

She wiped tears from her face, took a deep breath and mentoed her telephone to call Samantha Petrie. A tele-cube rose from the phone's cradle. The cube floated through the air, paused in front of Carla's mouth.

"Billie hasn't called all day," Carla said, trying to regain her composure.

"You were going to get some of your permeage license forms filled out today, weren't you?" Petrie asked. "Why didn't you call me earlier?"

"I took the whole day off," Carla said, oblivious to the question. "He should have been here this morning." She sobbed, put her hand over the tele-cube, then released it. "That dirty . . ."

"Maybe something came up," Petrie said, trying to reassure her friend.

"Yeah. About five-ten, blue eyes, a good—"

"No, I mean at work. Did you try there?"

"Several times. I tried his home too."

"That IS strange."

"I don't know whether to be angry or worried."

"Get some sleep, Carla. I'll see you at work tomorrow. If he's not there, we'll call Bu-Cops."

Carla hung up the telephone, watched disconsolately as the

tele-cube flitted back to its place. She curled up on the couch, and presently great sobs came upon her, reverberating through her body.

"Damn him!" she cursed as her anger and suspicion took control. "I thought he would change. . . ." At long last she fell into a troubled slumber, resolving never to speak with Birdbright again.

Twosayer William stood on the lowest step of the platform which supported Uncle Rosy's great chair, looking across the chamber at a full assemblage of hooded sayermen. They looked back in the low light with sorrowful eyes, their mouths partly open in shock and turned down at the corners. It was nearly time to retire for the night, but no one thought of sleep. Rumors of murder and intrigue had been in the air since mid-afternoon.

"The memory circuits of Uncle Rosy's tuxedo meckie have been checked," Twosayer said, raising his voice so that all could hear. "Onesayer died yesterday in an attempt to take our Master's life."

The sayermen gasped.

Twosayer continued: "This morning, for reasons unknown, Uncle Rosy instructed the meckie to take his own sacred life as well."

A whispering and moaning swept over the group. Some sayermen fell to their knees, crying and wailing. Twosayer heard their swellings of despondency: "It cannot be true!" they said. "What are we to do now?" "All is lost!"

"Peace be upon you, brothers!" Twosayer called out. "Calm yourselves!"

"Did you see the Master's body?" Threesayer asked from the front of the assemblage.

"I saw His Holiness," Twosayer replied sadly. "But his features had so aged I could not recognize him."

"We wish to see him," another sayerman called out, "To pay our final respects."

"I thought it best to send him directly to Astro-Disposal," Twosayer said, narrowing his eyes and glancing around the chamber. "I expect he is being catapulted now."

"That is best," Foursayer said.

Then others agreed. "Yes," they said. "That is best."

"Our Master would not have wanted the sayermen to see

him like that," Twosayer said. "Let us remember him as he was."

"Yes," most of the assemblage agreed. "Let us remember him as he was."

"After a suitable period," Twosayer said, pushing out his chest a bit in pride, "I shall assume the duties of Master."

"Do we have time to wait?" a sayerman asked, his voice reflecting panic, "with the garbage comet due to hit tomorrow?"

"There is no stopping it!" someone said. "A cappy has stolen the space cruiser . . . the comet follows each change in Earth's orbit!"

Twosayer did not reply, considered the crisis.

"Take the holy duty now," a sayerman in the back urged.

"We need you now!" another said. "The AmFed people need you now!"

A murmuring rolled across the chamber, and generally it was agreed that Twosayer should not delay in donning the Master's robes.

But then Lastsayer rolled to the front, holding a copy of the Sayer's Guide high over his head. "It is not so easy!" he announced, yelling to be heard over the multitude.

"Who is that?" someone asked.

"What did he say?"

"Who is he?"

"It is Lastsayer Steven! He holds a Sayer's Guide!"

"What is it, Lastsayer?" Twosayer asked nervously.

Lastsayer opened the volume, auto-flipped to a page near the back and read aloud from an internally-illuminated page: "If the Beloved Master dies or falls so gravely ill that he cannot conduct the responsibilities of his holy chair, that person holding the position of Onesayer will assume the holy chair." Lastsayer looked up from the book and gazed around the room. "We have no Onesayer," he said somberly.

"I am the senior sayerman!" Twosayer exclaimed, wrinkling his hooked nose angrily. "I am first in line to assume the holy chair!"

"But it does not say so in the guide," Lastsayer said. "A strict interpretation . . ."

"But surely we can discern Uncle Rosy's intent," Eightsayer said, rolling forward.

"Yes," agreed another.

Threesayer rolled to the front, short-stepped to the stair level on which Twosayer stood. He was taller than Twosayer, and Twosayer moved to the next higher step. "Our newest sayerman is correct," Threesayer said. "Who are we to speculate upon Uncle Rosy's intentions? He often skipped one sayerman over another. For all we know, he intended to advance any one of us to the position vacated by Onesayer Edward."

Now the assemblage swung another way. "That is right," they said. "Threesayer is right."

"Uncle Rosy always had a special liking for me," remarked one.

"I disagree. He favored me!"

"He called me exceptionally bright."

"I was skipped twice."

"Maybe *I* am the Chosen One."

"It could just as easily be *me!*"

Twosayer became increasingly angry as the sayermen continued to argue, and he pushed Threesayer off the step. "You and Lastsayer plotted this to take away what is rightfully mine!" Twosayer screamed.

Threesayer fell to one knee, then recovered his footing and shot back: "Not true!" Turning to the assemblage, he said in a loud, clear tone: "Uncle Rosy would never have made such a sayerman our Master! A sayerman does not push his brother!"

"That is right!" the assemblage called out. "That is right!"

A murmuring rolled across the group, and this gradually increased in intensity. The consensus was that Twosayer should not have done what he did.

After that, a wave of sentiment went in favor of Threesayer becoming the new Master. But this succumbed when Foursayer and Ninesayer rolled forward to cite a host of apparently logical reasons why Threesayer should not assume the chair.

So it went into the wee hours of the morning, with all the sayermen arguing heatedly over the matter. Everyone had a favorite, be it himself or another, and there was a good deal of shouting back and forth. Finally, they grew tired of battling, and the sayermen retired for the evening without having decided upon a leader. They would pray for divine intervention to stop the comet.

* * *

In Ordinance Room Six, the youngsayermen were seated on the floor in a half circle around Sayer Superior Lin-Ti:

"What sort of force was the comet?" Lin-Ti asked. "Was it a godlike thing?"

"In a sense, yes," a youngsayerman to Lin-Ti's right said. "For all things contain an element of God. But it was not sent by God . . . not directly, anyway. God gave all the life forces in the universe free will, and those from the Realm of Magic. . . ."

"What do you mean by God?"

"It is a convenient term, Sayer Superior . . . for the being which resides in the Realm of the Unknown."

"Think on this, youngsayers: ask yourselves if each layer of existence might not have another layer beyond it . . . supervising . . . or perhaps just watching . . . the layer below. We know that there is a Realm of Inertia and Gas which is higher than the Realm of Flesh . . . and beyond Inertia and Gas is the Realm of Magic."

"And beyond that . . . the Realm of the Unknown!" a youngsayer said.

Lin-Ti lifted one hand, pointing his forefinger upward. "But what if this 'unknown' is really many realms . . . a succession of realms going ever higher?"

The youngsayerman thought for a moment, then said: "And what if the realms are not hierarchical? What if they are all at the same level?"

Lin-Ti smiled as he watched the youngsayerman think.

Excitedly, the youngsayerman said: "What if we are at the same level with God?"

"You mean we are God?" Lin-Ti asked.

"Yes. And no. We are magical, too . . . all these things could be part of the truth . . . of one existence. . . ."

"It is a circle, is it not?" Lin-Ti said. "We are what we are not . . . ever-changing but ever the same. . . ."

FIFTEEN

Labor Intensity Code (L.I. Code): Established by the Council of
Ten in 2518, in honor of the two-hundredth anniversary of Uncle
Rosy's disappearance. The key tenet of the code held as follows:
"If two people can perform a given task, that is better than one."

Friday, September 1, 2605

A digital reader on the Shamrock Five instrument panel indicated it was nearly four A.M. by New City time, and Sidney
gave this a fleeting thought as he unclasped his hands.

Prayer isn't working, he thought. His eyes and bones ached.
His brain was unsupportive. *How many times did I pray during
the night?* he wondered, wearily. *I called out to God AND to*

Uncle Rosy. . . . For a moment, Sidney attempted a count, but quickly gave up the effort.

Sidney stretched and yawned as he stared across the dashboard at the Great Comet. It loomed so large now that he imagined reaching out of the cockpit to touch it. An immense sweeping fountain of luminous lavender and green dust flowed from the comet's flaming orange nucleus, forming a single tail. Only moments before, there had been six distinct yellow tails and an icy blue nucleus, but the comet had changed as it was wont to do.

Sidney smiled and spoke in a tone reserved for the endeared: "You're a vain one, aren't you? Like a fine lady, you are . . . changing outfits all the time. . . ."

The comet veered off against the midnight blue starcloth of space, then returned to its original course. It drew closer, ever closer.

"You heard me, didn't you? We're friends now, Great Comet—but why don't you do as I ask?"

The comet was unresponsive, and Sidney thought, *Friends, hell. I love that mass of fire and gas . . . as much as . . . no, more than . . . I love Carla.*

Sidney turned his head to the right at a metallic clang, saw Madame Bernet stirring to life. The meckie rattled its knives against a wall as it struggled to get up, its eyes open wide and flashing crazily.

Sidney half surprised himself by remaining calm. *I had hoped the comet would get me instead,* he thought.

But now he entertained no thoughts of fleeing. Instead, he watched the killer meckie rise to its feet with its razor-sharp knives slashing at the air.

"Die, fleshcarrier!" the meckie screeched as it rolled toward him slowly, smiling evilly.

Sidney's brain went numb. *Fleshcarrier?* he thought. *Am I having another nightmare? Things are getting mixed up!*

The killer meckie continued to close in on him, repeating the epithet: "Die, fleshcarrier, die!"

Sidney's gaze fixed on the blades. He saw glimmering red and orange reflections from the comet on the shiny steel surfaces. *Any second now,* he thought. *The first cut . . .*

He closed his eyes and grimaced from the expected pain. But it did not arrive, and at the sound of gears grinding, Sidney opened his eyes slit-wide. The blades were poised there, only centimeters from his face!

Then the blades receded, and as Sidney opened his eyes all the way, he saw the meckie tip backward and fall to its back. Within seconds, the cockpit was silent, and all Sidney sensed was the pounding of his own pulse.

"Was it luck again, fleshcarrier?" a tenor voice in his brain asked.

"Don't tease him anymore," the other, deeper voice said. *"We've had our fun."* The voice paused, then said: *"We activated the meckie, fleshcarrier . . . through magic."*

"Just wanted to have a little fun with you," the tenor voice said. *"But you're a fuddy-duddy of the first order!"*

"I have to agree," said the other. *"At the very least he could have tried to get away!"*

"I imagined the whole thing," Sidney said, staring at the comet. "The meckie, the comet, voices in my brain . . . this whole adventure." He smiled, threw both hands up in the air. "Actually, I'm in a Bu-Med psycho ward somewhere having part of my brain cut out."

A staccato peppering of laughter riddled his brain. *"Heh-heh-heh-heh-heh-heh. . . ."*

"Emergency!" the ship computer reported. "Ship's E-Cell charge almost consumed! Begin throwing loose articles into the emergency fuel hopper!"

Before Sidney could react, the speakercom blared: "We have you in sight, Shamrock Five! Heave-to and prepare for boarding!"

Sidney's heart jumped. In the video console he saw two long-range gunships approaching from the rear and closing fast.

"Don't listen to them, fleshcarrier!" the voices in Sidney's brain said. *"Try to get away! You must get away!"*

"More of your blasted party games?" Sidney asked.

There was no response.

"Heave-to, Shamrock Five!" the speakercom repeated.

"Aw, what the hell!" Sidney said. He tore a biomedical support pack off the wall and tossed it into the emergency fuel hopper. Flipping to manual mode, he grabbed the control stick. His palm was warm and moist against the cool tita-steel plated surface.

Now the Shamrock Five seemed only minutes from a collision with the comet. *I've got to get away from these guys,*

Sidney thought. *Maybe I can still....* He grimaced.

"Okay, Captain Malloy," Sidney whispered. "Here we go!"

He hit the red super-accelerator toggle, watched his console as the gunships disappeared in the distance. *They'll punch-out too,* he thought, his gaze glued upon the screen. *And that was my last bit of energy.*

The two gunships were back now, and Sidney saw brilliant lances of weapons fire cutting toward him. "Damn!" he cursed. "Just give me a little more time!" He felt there was no use trying to escape, but leaned on the control stick anyway. The Shamrock Five responded quickly, darting ahead, still closer to the comet.

"Veer away!" Sidney yelled, glaring at the comet's flaming orange nucleus. "Veer away, damn you! Don't hit Earth!"

But the comet continued to bear down on him.

The console screen showed the gunships changing course, then went black. *What a time for my equipment to go gunny-sack!* he thought. The screen flickered back on, and he saw lances of weapons fire again. The Shamrock Five cut to star-board.

When Sidney next looked in the console screen, he saw only one pursuer. The other gunship had either fallen back or was taking a different attack course. Sidney mentoed for an-other view, but the screen went dark again. He hit the butt of his hand against the set. The screen remained black.

"Charge zero," the computer reported.

A silent explosion tore through the cockpit, throwing glass-plex and plastic in every direction. Sidney felt the screaming pain of torn flesh and broken bones. *My right leg!* He thought. *So hot! It's burning!*

"Emergency!...Emergency!..." the computer blared.

Sidney felt faint, then something cool bathed his leg. He looked down to see it immersed in blue foam. None of the instruments were working now. The ship was not moving.

He took a deep breath, waited for the next hit. *Either that or the comet,* he thought. *It's almost over now.*

But as Sidney looked in his console, he saw the pursuing gunships veer off and speed away in the other direction. They became pinpricks, then disappeared.

Sidney bit his lower lip hard, braced for more pain. *I'm ready,* he thought. *Ready to die.* This was the way Captain Malloy would have gone...risking his life for mankind.

A tear ran down his cheek. More followed. *Who will know?* he thought. *No parade, no words spoken in praise . . . no thought whatsoever of Sidney Malloy.*

"It doesn't matter!" he yelled. "It doesn't matter!" But then he grimaced and thought: *It matters. I can't lie to myself.*

The Great Comet was icy blue and flaming red now, from its head to its misty toe. Eccentrically placed within the burning nucleus, Sidney saw the first appearance of a miniature comet having a head and tail of its own. This tiny comet flared white hot and expanded quickly until it consumed the entire mother comet, then faded into a nebulous haze and disappeared into the womb of the mother. Sidney thought of the comet's complexity, wished that he could become a part of it, to roam forever through the heavens.

Oh, what an exalted existence that would be!

As Sidney thought this, the comet flared white hot again, but this time the tail was pulled into the nucleus and the comet appeared as a star. Although it was exceedingly bright, Sidney did not shield his eyes. This comet was not garbage to him . . . it was the most beautiful primordial state in the universe, a delicate but powerful combination of all elements.

"That trash IS rather pretty now, isn't it?" one of the voices said.

"This fleshcarrier appreciates beauty, I'll say that for him," remarked another.

"Rather an appealing fellow, but slothlike. . . ."

"Turn the comet away!" Sidney screamed. "Turn it away!"

"We won't," a tenor voice said. *"But you can."*

"Flesh be gone!" a deep voice exclaimed.

Now the comet was a glowing, jagged ball of red fire, growing larger as it bore down on Sidney's motionless ship. He felt it reaching across the icy darkness to him with an awesome, unstoppable power. For the first time in his life, Sidney felt very special. He shivered, then felt wonderfully warm and calm as the Great Comet consumed him in a cosmic whirlwind. As this happened, Sidney had a vision of a magical land in which suffering and pain were nonexistent.

"An idealist," the tenor voice said, scornfully.

"He'll learn," said the other. *"Give him time."*

"Had a lot of fun with this one, didn't we?" the tenor voice said.

"Oh my, yes! Maybe we should keep the fleshcarriers around

for a while. There seems no end to their foolish predicaments!"

I'll give the fleshcarriers your message, Sidney thought. *You can trust me....*

The jagged fireball turned to gold, and a hundred violet plumes surged across the heavens to form a new tail. Men on the deep space observation station Drakus Ohm reported that the comet hung in the sky for several seconds like a giant scimitar. Then it began to move, slowly at first, like a pony trying out its legs for the first time. Soon the comet was frisky and lively, streaking one way and then the other across the great expanse of space.

Carla opened one eye, peered drowsily across the top of a tiny package wrapped in silver paper which sat on her coffee table. She was in the living room module of her condominium, and as she rose to rest on one elbow, a shooting pain from having slept on the couch all night shot through her lower back. Golden streaks of artificial dawn light washed across the room from a sun-lite panel along one wall, glinting off the shiny wrapping paper of the package.

Friday morning, she thought. *I should call Samantha.*

She shook her head briskly, swung both stockinged feet onto the carpet and stared at the neatly wrapped parcel. Leaning forward, she looked down to examine a tiny white scroll card which read, "For Carla." That was all it said.

"From Billie," she murmured angrily, grasping the parcel and lifting it to hurl it across the room. "If he thinks he can sweeten me..."

But something told her it was not from Billie, and she lowered her arm to hold the object in one open palm. Then Carla rolled it over and over, searching for a place to tear away the wrapping. But there was no edge to the paper, making it appear that it had been molded onto a box beneath.

Perplexed, she set the package back on the coffee table. As Carla pulled her hand away, the paper folded open along invisible seams, revealing a black velvet box. A hinged lid swung open automatically, and Carla's astonished eyes beheld a star-shaped mother of pearl and burnished gold brooch inside.

"Oh!" she squealed, reached for the treasure. "It's beauti..."

She caught herself, withdrew the hand. But she reached back quickly and lifted out the brooch. Seeing a hinge along one edge, she used her fingernail to open the brooch along the opposite side. Inside, a shimmering black surface filled the right side of the brooch as it lay open. On the left interior surface, a scroll inscription read: "Dearest Carla—This star will keep you safe."

Carla flipped the brooch over several times, tried to find something more, a clue as to who might have given it to her. She examined the velvet box and the paper wrapping as well, but there was nothing whatsoever to indicate its source. She held the brooch open in both palms, stared into the black glass star inside.

Presently, Carla saw tiny twinkling silver stars in the blackness, as if she was looking into a window upon the universe. Away off in the distance, she saw a bright star approaching rapidly, blocking out the blackness around as it grew in size. Soon the star became too bright to behold, and Carla dropped the brooch to shield her eyes.

When she peeked through her fingers to look at the brooch where it rested open upon the carpet, she saw the brightness fade away to a white mist. Then the mist cleared and she saw an image taking form. It showed a man and a woman asleep on their sides in a round bed.

Why, Carla thought. *It's Samantha Petrie. . . . Who's she with? . . .* The man had covers over all but his forehead and hair. He stirred and rolled to his back, causing the covers to slip a little.

Carla recoiled in shock. *My Rosenbloom!* she thought. *It's Billie!* She reached down to pick up the brooch, watched Birdbright shift again, throwing one arm over Petrie's shoulder.

Tears streamed down Carla's cheeks and fell on the brooch, giving the image in the black glass a distorted appearance. She wiped her face with the back of one hand, snapped the brooch shut angrily.

I knew he was this way, she thought, forcing the tears to stop. *I shouldn't take it so hard. But I had so hoped . . .*

The tears came anew now, and much harder than before. She sobbed and fell back on the couch in a fetal position with the brooch clutched tightly between her hands.

*   *   *

"I do not understand something," a youngsayerman in the first row said.

Lin-Ti gazed down at him from the podium. It was the youngsayerman with the long body and fat features . . . the one who looked so much like Onesayer Edward.

"How did the history writers obtain details on the lives of the sayermen and of Sidney Malloy?" the youngsayerman asked. "The sayers never touch identity plates . . . and Malloy did not come in contact with one after losing his position in Central Forms."

Lin-Ti smiled. "As we so often discover," he said, "the words of Uncle Rosy hold true today, as they did centuries ago: 'Much remains for you to learn, youngsayer. Much remains for you to learn. . . .'"

SIXTEEN

UP CLOSE WITH THE MASTER,
FOR FURTHER READING AND DISCUSSION

"The facts with which we operate are not all the facts, but are merely all the facts available to us at a particular time."

Spoken by Uncle Rosy (excerpt from E. Dade's unpublished notes)

Friday, September 1, 2605

President Ogg used an automatic thumb to flip through a pile of papers on his desk, pausing to scan a bureau employment summary sheet. The report pleased him. Ogg glanced at his wrist digital and mentoed the desk intercom to call for his first afternoon coffee.

In the outer office, Carla Weaver looked up from her rota-typer screen to watch a pamphlet meckie roll toward her with its purple "TAKE SEVERAL" signs flashing. She thought of the brooch she had found on her coffee table that morning, smiled. *Someone really cares about me,* she thought, still feeling the effects of a Happy Pill she had taken half an hour earlier. *Wonder who it is.* Assuming the powers of the brooch to be technological in nature, she surmised that her benefactor might work in Bu-Tech.

"Hi, Wordie," Carla said cheerily as the pamphlet meckie arrived and waited patiently. She short-stepped down from the rotatyper platform, took five pamphlets and placed them in her purse.

"Ringgg!" A bell sounded across the office. It was time for the first afternoon coffee break.

Billie Birdbright rolled by in a big hurry, dodging the workers who had begun to fill the aisles. "Excuse me! Excuse me, please!" Birdbright said nervously as he pushed his way through. He caught Carla's pill-glossed gaze for a moment. She watched him disappear into the President's office.

"Mr. President!" Birdbright exclaimed breathlessly as he rolled into the oval office. "Have you seen?"

President Ogg looked up calmly and replied, "This is my coffee break, Billie. Can't it wait?"

"No, Mr. President! Look out your window!" Birdbright pointed.

Ogg spun his chair, saw a distant streaking emerald-green-and-red comet moving across the southeastern horizon. His jaw dropped. "Is that IT? I thought Drakus Ohm reported it was going off in another direction!"

"It changed, Mr. President . . . and came out of nowhere!"

Ogg moto-paced around his desk, then stopped and shot a terse command to his Chief of Staff: "Get me a trajectory report on it!"

"Just got it minutes ago, sir. Bu-Tech says the comet came in on us fast, then veered off. It's in a holding pattern now."

"A holding pattern? How can a comet be in a holding pattern?"

"That's what the report said, sir."

Ogg glared at the comet, saw it flash brilliantly, followed by a wisp of white light. Birdbright moved to the President's side, and together they watched in astonishment as the comet began a most unusual series of maneuvers. It moved up and around, then back down and in zig-zags, trailing white smoke as it went.

"It's writing something, Mister President!" Birdbright said.

Ogg did not reply, leaned close to the window to peer at the horizon. "WE...ARE...NOT..." he said, reading the skywriting, "...YOUR...GARBAGE...DUMP!" A muscle on the President's cheek twitched.

Birdbright furrowed his brow. "What the hell does that mean, Mr. President?"

"How the hell do I know?" Ogg thought for a moment, then said, "Tell Bu-Tech to lay out a thick blanket of clouds until we can find out what's going on. We can't have consumers getting upset!"

"Yes, Mr. President," Birdbright said, rolling quickly to the door.

Euripides Ogg shook his head sadly, muttered: "And I told everyone there was nothing to worry about."

"What was that, sir?" Birdbright asked, pausing at the door.

"Nothing, Billie," Ogg said, glaring at his Chief of Staff. "Now get it in gear, man! Get it in gear!"

Birdbright scurried out of the office.

President Ogg watched Birdbright go, then fixed his gaze on the "Faith, Consumption, Freeness" sign over the door. *I have a feeling things aren't going to be the same around here after this*, he thought.